RELENTLESS

"Fast-paced. . . . Delivers a healthy dose of action, sensuality, and romance."

—*Publishers Weekly*

"Think Indiana Jones with lots of lust."

—*All About Romance*

AFTERGLOW

"A dangerous, exciting adventure . . . infused with humor and surprising revelations."

—*USA Today*

"Sexual tension that is set to explode at any given moment. . . . One of the best romantic suspense authors out there!"

—*Night Owl Reviews* (Top Pick)

HUSH

"Addictively readable. . . . Testosterone-rich, adrenaline-driven suspense. . . . Packed with plenty of unexpected plot twists and lots of sexy passion."

—*Chicago Tribune*

"Adair is a master of pulling together exciting adventure and burning passion to make a spine-tingling read!"

—*RT Book Reviews*

Blush

Cherry Adair

Gallery Books

New York   London   Toronto   Sydney   New Delhi

G

Gallery Books
An Imprint of Simon & Schuster, Inc.
1230 Avenue of the Americas
New York, NY 10020

First Gallery Books trade paperback edition April 2015

GALLERY BOOKS and colophon are registered trademarks of
Simon & Schuster, Inc.

For information about special discounts for bulk purchases,
please contact Simon & Schuster Special Sales at 1-866-506-1949 or
business@simonandschuster.com.

The Simon & Schuster Speakers Bureau can bring authors to your
live event. For more information or to book an event, contact the
Simon & Schuster Speakers Bureau at 1-866-248-3049 or visit our
website at www.simonspeakers.com.

Manufactured in the United States of America

10 9 8 7 6 5 4 3 2 1

Library of Congress Cataloging-in-Publication Data

Adair, Cherry, 1951–
    Blush / Cherry Adair. — First Gallery Books trade paperback edition.
        pages ; cm
    I. Title.
    PS3601.D348B58 2015
    813'.6—dc23
                                            2014041177

ISBN 978-1-4516-8434-6
ISBN 978-1-4516-8435-3 (ebook)

To Lauren McKenna, editor extraordinaire.
Thank you for your honesty, humor, and eagle eye.

Chapter One

No gun. Cruz Barcelona didn't require a weapon. Death by natural causes was his trademark. His specialty. Speculation had his target currently somewhere in Europe "on vacation." Read plastic surgery.

Amelia Wellington-Wentworth, aka Mia Hayward, was neither in Europe nor having surgery. Currently his target resided in Bayou Cheniere, Louisiana. His for the taking.

Her death tonight would be clean. Uncomplicated. A tragic, unfortunate accident. He was being paid a king's ransom to ensure that it appeared that way. The balance of his kill fee—7.5 mil—wired to his offshore account on proof of death. He didn't give a shit about the money. Cruz considered what he did a public service.

He didn't need the shelter of night to do his job. But he enjoyed the thick darkness of the Louisiana night, and the unfamiliar sounds and smells surrounding him. The chirp of crickets, the hollow bark of a dog, the intermittent splash of water in the nearby bayou, were the subtle musical score for the evening. The air smelled a little like overripe strawberries and a lot like stagnant swamp water with a touch of ozone.

The bug-laden air was thick enough to eat with a spoon. It was going to rain long before he started the three-mile return trek back to town.

Without benefit of a flashlight he edged down the side of the house. Ducking under a thick, curved branch, he shoved his way between dense, dripping vegetation. All the windows on this side of the overgrown walkway were dark, and he couldn't get near enough to look inside the house without a fucking machete to slash his way through the foliage.

Oh, how the mighty had fallen. From a thirty-million-dollar Pacific Heights mansion in San Francisco to a run-down plantation house that hadn't seen a renovation, from what Cruz could tell, since the Civil War. And next door to a graveyard, of all places.

The odds against anyone other than himself finding her here were astronomical. No one would imagine or believe that the powerful Amelia Wentworth would detour through this small town, let alone live there.

No security lights to illuminate a skulking killer. How convenient. Of course, out here in the heart of rural bayou country, no one expected a skulking killer. Here people left their doors unlocked and let their children play outside until well past dark.

The hundred-plus-year-old house was crumbling around her diamond-studded ears, from what he could see by the iffy moonlight playing tag with heavy rain clouds. *Fixer-upper* was an understatement. Two stories of broken siding, peeling paint, and encroaching unidentifiable flora. The house was too big for a woman by herself. No hot and cold running servants. Not presently, anyway. Was she expecting a large group of houseguests or just so used to living in a mansion, she forgot it needed people to maintain it?

The chatty gas station attendant—while repairing the "broken" manifold on Cruz's truck—had told him about the new woman who'd bought the old Broussard plantation house three weeks ago. Killer legs. Pretty. Single, he thought. The heavy-set, middle-aged owner at the diner told him Mrs. Broussard's place had been "empty these last ten years, a money pit; mark my words that uppity Yankee woman will live to regret it," as she poured lukewarm coffee and lingered to chat. And the friendly woman at the B and B said Miss Mia kept to herself but had nice manners.

Cruz had an unshakable code. He accepted jobs to off only people who deserved to die. He was judge, jury, and executioner. The dossier he had on Amelia Wentworth filled in details that would disturb the people of Bayou Cheniere. Deeply disturb.

Driven. Obsessive. Manipulative. Power hungry. Considered herself above the law. None of which were grounds for her death. However, keeping underage kids in horrific working conditions in her factories in China was a different story.

The woman was directly responsible for numerous deaths in her factory in Guangzhou, Guangdong Province, China. Not that she gave a fuck that hiring kids under the age of sixteen was illegal, even in China. Her factories were staffed by minors working under subhuman working conditions, in cramped living quarters, with too little food, forced to work killer hours with few breaks. All in the name of bigger profit margins and bigger dividends for herself and her shareholders.

Yeah. Deciding to accept this job—whether she *deserved* to die—had been easy. The transgressions were so heinous, they could've paid him less. It had been a bitch to find her due to her wily and convoluted disappearing act, and the number of underworld creeps she'd paid to keep changing her ID across first Europe and then back into the US. Cruz had finally caught up with her in Atlanta, then followed her to Louisiana.

He was eager to kill her. Move on.

Tucked under a freestanding carport was the truck she'd purchased in Atlanta last month. A shiny, new black F-150 pickup with all the bells and whistles. She'd had her own chauffeur since the age of six. He doubted she'd bothered with a driver's license.

Driver, bodyguards, and little kids dying were the norm for her just to maintain her multibillion-dollar world. His fee was half her annual income of thirty mil minus the perks—fifteen million dollars. Half up front. Balance on completion.

Cruz understood money. Had plenty of it. Only the world he used to obtain it rotated on a completely different axis than Amelia Wentworth, aka Mia Hayward. He disposed of evil individuals who deserved to die. She killed and exploited innocent children.

He turned the corner onto a large, open area sloping down to the water. A pale gold square, shining from a cracked window, illuminated scraggily grass and the twisted wheel of an ancient bicycle as Cruz emerged like Bambi through the goddamned undergrowth onto a wide expanse of mud, dirt, and weedy grass passing for a back lawn.

The moonlight glinted off the water of the bayou, which was filled with alligators, water moccasins, and assorted other useful creatures as backup should he need to make the scene look more convincingly accidental. He wasn't fond of snakes and kept an eye open as he walked.

He was dealing with the situation in China himself. The kill, the cash, all of it had been set up on a fast track. Just the way he liked it. Anonymity all the way. Cruz was the best. He didn't give a fuck who hired him. As long as the target met his strict criteria, his unique skill set could be bought.

The bayou side of the house was littered with the body parts of toys, garden implements, and assorted debris scattered among tall weeds. A pirogue and what appeared to be a gator lay on a sliver of dirt near the water, both barely visible for the thick grass and deep shadows.

A scattershot of fat raindrops struck his bare head and shoulders with the portent of a deluge. The impending rain would effectively wash away any sign of an intruder. As far as the town knew, his truck was still at Bucky's Repair Shop, and he was in his room at the back of Miss Gracie's B and B drinking beer and watching the game.

He'd be done and gone in less than fifteen minutes, and in time to get back to the B and B to catch the end of Stanley Cup Finals with his team, the Chicago Blackhawks. Which was ironic, since he hasn't lived in Chicago in more than twenty years.

Keeping his steps nimble and light despite his height, Cruz made his way toward the deep, shadowy wraparound porch. The sagging steps needed replacing; the rickety handrails were dangerously useless. A bullfrog croaked as he quietly crossed the porch to peer through an uncurtained window.

The living room, illuminated by light coming from the hallway, revealed scant furnishings, a swaybacked red velvet sofa, a stepladder, paint cans, and drop cloths that looked like rippled beach sand on a scarred, worn wood floor. With her money, she could easily afford to have an army of workmen and decorators flown here from San Francisco to restore the old house to something special. Why hadn't she done so?

For a nanosecond, Cruz had an insane desire to get his hands dirty in another way, and could almost feel the vibration of the sander, smell the sawdust and tung oil. A throwback to his youth working at his father's construction sites.

Then that life-altering moment that had changed everything. He checked his memories. Water under that bridge. All he wanted these days was to breathe in salt air and the perfume of an uncomplicated, naked woman. Hot, sunny, uncomplicated. This time tomorrow, he'd be basking on a beach on Fernando de Noronha, Brazil.

New name, new look, new life. This was Cruz Barcelona's last job. Retirement was in reach.

As he quietly made his way to the next window, the brightly lit kitchen, he paused as music suddenly blared through the open window. No one in the kitchen, a throwback to the fifties, with harvest-gold appliances and crap piled on every flat surface. The smell wafting through the heavy night air changed to that of hot, baking cookies.

Then he saw her.

Amelia Wentworth, one of *Forbes* magazine's top ten richest women in the world, danced into the kitchen wearing a skimpy silky burgundy robe and high animal-print shoes with gold heels. Creamy legs, long and toned, kept the beat as she danced to the radio, twirling around the room with an imaginary partner.

Chin-length dark hair, shaggy and sexy as hell, arced around her head, catching the light as she spun. He knew her eyes were blue, stood five six, and she was left-handed. What Cruz hadn't known was that her mouth was lush and a little too big, and just looking at that mouth made his dick twitch to life as he imagined what she could do with it.

Right now she didn't look anything like the president and CEO of Blush Cosmetics, with more money than anyone could spend in a lifetime, and hundreds of thousands of employees under her thumb. She looked sexy, innocent, and drop-dead gorgeous.

Cruz swiped his palm over the prickle on the back of his rain-damp neck. A warning. Even more alert now, he stopped in his tracks, looking beyond the dark night reflected in the window to see if he'd been followed. He knew he hadn't. He was no amateur. Yet that warning itch persisted.

Something was . . . off.

Not her behavior. She was just a chick who thought she

was dancing unobserved. No—his gut was sending him signals he couldn't interpret. A first.

Remaining motionless in the rain-drenched darkness, he gave his instincts a moment to analyze as he sifted through what he knew. Compared it to what he was watching. Sorted. Catalogued. Evaluated.

As he dispassionately observed his target, she suddenly broke into song, loudly and off-key, punching the air with her fists to the chorus as she twirled around the kitchen. ". . . hap-ppyy. Like a room without a roof . . ."

He winced. She sang with gusto, and god-awfully flat.

He was misinterpreting the warning itch. Last job. Wanted to do it right. Nothing more than that. No one had followed him. She was the correct target. He earned what he earned because he never made mistakes. Ever.

He did one more circuit of the house, noted the boarded-up front door, with a sign directing deliveries to the back door. He returned to the side facing the black waters of the bayou, this time not muffling his footsteps as he crossed the porch. The doorbell didn't work, so he knocked. Three hard raps to indicate a friendly neighbor. He liked to see the whites of their eyes as he told them why, just before he killed them.

The sky opened, and it began to pour. The singing abruptly stopped, leaving the night filled with the sound of rain pelting the tin roof overhead and the lone bullfrog croaking somewhere nearby. A large plop of water across his cheek indicated that the porch roof leaked.

Despite the downpour, Cruz heard the sharp staccato of her heels on the wood floor as she approached the front door. The door swung open with the ominous creak of a haunted house.

For a moment they stared at each other. She was prettier, softer up close and personal. The thigh-length, deep-wine-colored silk robe clung to her sleek body, leaving no doubt that she was naked beneath it. The slope of her unfettered breasts showcased her nipple's response to the cooler air outside. Glossy dark, layered hair was tucked behind one ear. Holding onto the door with white-knuckled anticipation, she smiled.

Elegant bone structure, dark wings of eyebrows, piercing blue eyes, a soft, plump mouth. For a cosmetic heiress, she was surprisingly free of cosmetics. She didn't need them. Her skin was flawless. He wanted her. Wanted all that elegance mussed up as he fucked her. Wanted to feel that creamy skin flush against his as she cried out. Wanted to be on top, thrusting inside her when he told her she was about to die.

But fantasies like that would distract him from his main goal.

Sharp blue eyes tracked him from head to boots and back again, coolly sizing him up. Her gaze was intelligent, unafraid, and seemed to see directly into his skull. "You're early. Don't say anything," she instructed. Her voice, low and naturally husky, went straight to his groin, bypassing his brain completely. Jesus. His heart quickened and his dick stirred.

Get a fucking grip. He was here to work. Not play. His dick had no say in this.

Pulling the door open, she stepped back, giving him a better view of her long, taut legs and arched instep, sexy as sin in nosebleed-high leopard-spot heels. Wrapped like a second skin in silk, she showed a velvety valley of pale cleavage and miles of sleek leg. His lungs stopped working, but he managed to raise a brow at her commanding tone.

The lady was used to people scurrying to do her bidding. Since she couldn't possibly know who he was, or why the fuck he was there, he wordlessly stepped inside and followed her down the brightly lit hallway with its peeling red flocked wallpaper and water stains and Home Depot "crystal" chandelier. The place smelled of hot, fresh cookies, of damp, and, faintly, of roses. Uncarpeted stairs rose off to one side of the wide hall. At the other end he noted the boarded-up front door and more paint cans.

"You're remodeling?" Judging from the amount of paint cans, drop cloths, and boxes of wallpaper, she planned to be around a long time. Too bad he was about to cut her decorating project tragically short. Nice of her to supply the ladder.

"I like three minutes of nipple stimulation," she told him crisply without responding to the rhetorical question. The staccato tap of her heels on the scuffed wood floor matched her words. "No less, no more. Then penetration until climax. Your money is in the kitchen—I'll show you where—and you can come down and get it when we're done. No lingering afterward, no cuddling, no kissing. The back door will lock automatically behind you when you leave."

She liked her sex exactly as he did. His dick was very excited by that. No! Cruz didn't bother responding to her instructions as they passed the room to the left, kitchen to the right. The house smelled strongly of baked cookies, but this close to her, his senses were filled with the lush, creamy fragrance of tuberose and clean woman as she walked ahead of him, the taut curve of her almost naked heart-shaped ass swaying tantalizingly beneath the thin burgundy silk.

His heartbeat kicked up a few more notches, and his cock responded.

"Through here," she said, a flush creeping up the back of her neck. Cruz realized, for all her sangfroid, Miss CEO was nervous. "I'm not sure of your company's policy. Do I pay you half now and half afterward or all up front?" Her voice told him she considered this half risky. Still, she led him into the brightly lit kitchen without waiting for his response, then backed against the counter to face him.

He glanced around. Not at the crap décor, but to ascertain exits and hiding places. But the decoration was hard to miss. He was in a fucking time warp, circa 1950. Yellowing cabinets, beige Formica countertops, a peeling beige linoleum floor. None of which was enhanced by the giant butterflies in unnatural colors flying on every wall. The curtains sported surreal-looking sliced fruit. Three buckets, strategically placed to catch the rain, played musical notes as water dripped from the ceiling.

A round glass-topped table by the window was the only thing in the room from the current decade. A center island took up a good portion of floor space. A lead crystal vase filled with spiky purple flowers looked incongruous standing in the middle of the chipped countertop. Beside it several trays of cookies cooled. Very homey.

Stepping forward when he turned to face her, her pupils dilated as she realized how close he was. "I want to get the business end of this established befo—"

Bathed, perfumed, opening the door to a stranger—business. It didn't take a genius to figure out who or what she thought he was. This was an interesting development. It seemed there'd be a bonus before the job.

Cruz had never had sex with a mark. Impersonal was a given in his line of work. But he had no qualms about fucking Miss CEO before he killed her tonight.

In one, quick, fluid motion, he wrapped his hands around her waist, lifted her, and planted her naked ass on the cold Formica countertop. She gasped, her expression indicating that the sound wasn't due to the change of temperature on her ass but from the change of control.

Without giving her time to protest, he nudged her knees apart with his hips, then stood in the juncture of her thighs, pulling her forward so that she was unbalanced and had to grab his shoulders to maintain her precarious perch. Her lips parted as her lashes fluttered up and she stared at his mouth.

"Put your hands on the counter."

She gave him a slightly dazed, questioning look.

"Now," he snapped out like a lash, and waited, stone-faced, as she cautiously let go of him to place her hands beside her hips. The angle canted her shoulders forward. An awkward tilt of her body with a cabinet directly behind her head. Good. He wanted her off balance physically as well as emotionally.

He knew how to detach mentally. But it had never been this hard to do so. If he had the time or inclination, he'd tell her not to be fooled by any illusions that he was safe in any way.

He didn't act like a badass. He *was* one.

The fingers of one hand curled, white-knuckled, over the metal edge of the countertop, the other she slapped against his chest as she said with authority, "Just a min—"

The pulse at the base of her throat fluttered, then started beating faster beneath her pale skin as he slowly untied the sash at her waist. "You're the one who made the no-talking rule." Cruz slowly slid the sash free from the loops, fascinated by how her nipples hardened beneath the thin layer of fabric as silk slid against silk. He wanted to put his mouth there, suck those peaks through the material. She'd said three minutes of nipple stimulation—he could probably make her come in less time with his mouth.

"Actually, I was telling *you* not to talk." Sounding stiff and formal, she looked a little shell-shocked by the turn of events. "Before we get started, I'd like to establish those ground rules—"

Yeah, he bet she would. He gave her a thin smile. "I'll let you know what those are when I'm done here," he told her dryly, plucking her hand off his shirt and firmly placing it at her side. Gripping her hips, he tugged her even closer to the edge.

Spread open to him like a juicy feast, she offered him an up-close-and-personal view of her delicate pink folds as she listed forward. Cruz maintained eye contact as he let her ass teeter on the edge. "Stay still and you won't fall."

He stood between her legs; she wasn't going to fall. Not anywhere except onto his dick.

When he was ready.

His cock hardened. Pretty fucking ready right now.

Down, boy.

"Good girl." Without touching, he let his heated gaze meander over her body. Her skin flushed a soft shell-pink. His dick pressed painfully hard against his jeans. Jesus, he'd never seen skin like hers. Creamy pale, flawless. He checked for the three small identifying freckles near her left clavicle. There.

Slipping his hands beneath the thin satin lapels of the burgundy robe, he skimmed his fingertips over the cluster of freckles, holding her somewhat dazed gaze. She opened her mouth to protest.

Giving her a hard look, Cruz shook his head in warning. In response she shut her gorgeous mouth, but dangerously narrowed her eyes. She'd be hell to deal with in the boardroom. Cruz imagined her saying, with icy calm, "Off with his dick," blue eyes glacial and unsympathetic.

Lips tight, she watched him a little like a mongoose watching a snake. So far, so good. She was used to being in charge. Had any man mastered her? Cruz doubted it. The lady was a ball-buster, but even at the close proximity, she didn't kick him in the nuts, inches from her knee, and she didn't jump off the counter.

The heady scent of tuberoses blended with the musky

scent of her arousal was permission enough. He inhaled the complex mix of fragrances, fascinated by the way her intense blue eyes held his in challenge.

The material of her robe felt like warm wine against the back of his hands as Cruz slid the skimpy garment off her shoulders, leaving the rich burgundy-colored fabric to pool on the bend of her elbows.

A sheen of perspiration made her skin luminescent. "There's a bed upstairs," she suggested, voice thick and husky, the muscles in her slender arms taut as she gripped the edge of the counter with fingers turned white from the pressure.

The kitchen lights were bright and unforgiving. He didn't need a soft bed or mood lighting to do the trick. "I don't need a bed to fuck you."

Eyes gleaming she murmured, "I do."

"Then you should've gotten me upstairs a hell of a lot faster." Her pale skin was the texture of warm satin, her body long and lean, breasts small, plump, and high, her nipples a deep puckered rose. Cruz's mouth watered as he trailed just his fingertips along the upper curve of one breast, watching her pupils dilate as she arched her back unconsciously to get closer. Her fingers flexed on the counter's edge.

"Keep your hands right where they are," he ordered as she shifted restlessly. When he brushed one tight nipple with his thumb, she clutched the countertop on either side of her hips with a death grip.

Her body was flawless except for the fairly fresh six-inch red scar on her upper right arm, and the trio of beauty marks on her collarbone. The scar hadn't been part of her file. But it wasn't relevant. Not now, and not later. Cruz let his gaze travel leisurely over her body, feeling her muscles tense as he drew out the anticipation. For both of them.

Now completely open to him, her pulses throbbed at her throat, at her wrists, and in the plump pink folds not quite hidden by silky dark hair gleaming with moisture. His dick, already hard, jerked in response to the open invitation.

The taut muscles of her inner thighs flexed on the sides of his hips so that he felt the heat of her open body against his belly. Her baby blues went huge as he rubbed himself against her wet heat.

"Pleasure before business," he murmured, covering her mouth with his before she had a chance to respond. So close he saw his own need mirrored there, her eyes went wider, and her body tensed for a second, then her lashes fluttered down and she gave him her tongue, accompanied by a throaty hum of desire as she pressed her breasts to his chest. The hard points of her nipples activated such a powerful lust response in him that Cruz jerked back mentally in surprise. Whoa. Sex was sex. It was scratching an itch. A biological function.

Usually a cockstand was handled in minutes. He didn't do much foreplay, and, like her, he didn't enjoy kissing. Cruz never allowed himself to be overcome with hunger. This ravenous beast inside him had appeared out of left field.

By now, if *he* were the customer, he would've fucked her, paid her, and been on his way. Lingering was killing him, but the anticipation was, in itself, an aphrodisiac.

He forced his heartbeat to slow. Mentally told his dick to chill. Reminded himself who and what she was. This was all about Miss CEO.

Control. Domination.

Creamy flesh, wet with desire, breasts pressed against his chest to plump perfection, mouth avid and juicy, pulse pounding in response to the lightest touch.

Cruz ran his fingers through her thick, silky hair, then cupped her head and angled her mouth the way he wanted it and kissed her. Hot and deep.

One sharp twist and he'd break her neck. Then, strategically positioning her near the ladder—

Fuckit. She tasted minty. Toothpaste. He slid his tongue over her teeth, felt hers come out to play in a heated glide that had his blood roaring through his veins like a supernova. All caution evaporated, replaced with a buzz of euphoria.

She made a low sound of need, leaning into him as she slid her hands around his neck in response to the kiss, her fingers fisting in his hair. Her mouth was made to fit his like two pieces of a jigsaw puzzle.

Gripping her hair in his fist, he sank into the kiss, although kissing wasn't his thing either. He liked to fuck. He didn't like to cuddle or kiss. But kissing her felt . . . good. Which was bullshit. Kissing her felt like the prelude to fucking her. That was all.

She drew back slightly, opening her mouth to say something, and he quickly laid a hand on her cheek, positioning his thumb so it fit perfectly into her mouth. Her lips closed around it delicately; then, holding his gaze, she sucked on it with deliberate implication.

After several moments of pulsating energy buildup, when his cock pulsed with every pull of her mouth, she delicately spat out his digit. Cheeks pink, mouth set, she said tightly, "Either fuck me now, or leave."

"What's your hurry? I'm not on a time clock, are you?"

The elegant arches of her dark eyebrows lifted while displeasure tightened lips lush and damp. "I'm ready, and clearly so are you. Just do it and get it over with. There's a bonus if you can make me come more than twice."

Cruz's own brows lifted at the queen-to-serf tone. "Here's the thing, lady. I didn't give you permission to speak, and I didn't give you permission to move. And I'm not giving you permission to come." Cruz had no idea why he was toying with her like a panther batting a hummingbird from the air. Maybe because he knew he was going to kill her, and fucking her now, in some twisted way, seemed wrong.

Maybe to test himself? To see if he—what? What the fuck?

He was reaching the outer edge of his self-control, which was not aided by the rush of sex-induced adrenaline the smell and sight of her evoked.

Easy solution.

Kill her.

Now.

Chapter Two

*B*ody rigid, Mia Hayward gave the man tormenting her a cold look warning him to do his damn job or suffer the consequences. Unfortunately, mixed with her annoyance, she also felt a fluttery surge of excitement. "Then I have absolutely no use for you—"

In response he used both hands to shove her knees farther apart. Her thigh muscles flexed as she attempted to close her legs, but his hips were already wedged between them. The hard bulge behind his jeans zipper, and the coiled tension in his muscular body, indicated he was as ready as she was.

He knew exactly what his tone and actions were doing to her, and he was enjoying his mastery. His dark eyes were hot but also impersonal. And why wouldn't he be? He was doing his job.

"Wider," he murmured, looking between her legs as he clasped her hips to propel her forward the few inches separating them. Straight black lashes lifted, and he gave her a look so provocative, she expected to go up in flames any minute. "I want to see all of you—every wet pink inch."

God. God. God. When the hell had she lost control? This wasn't how she liked things done. Her body was acting independently of her mind and her usual common sense. A first. She was learning how powerful and primitive pure lust could be, and how quickly scruples and conscience went out the window.

"It's good to want things, but wanting isn't getting, and since I'm not getting, you might as well take that impressive erection out of here and leave me to finish the job my—"

The brightly lit kitchen swirled in a dizzying arc as he lifted her with both powerful hands under her bare ass and swung her around. Her back hit the center island with a thud. Vaguely she heard the crystal vase crash to the floor and the clatter of the cookie sheets as they bounced. He'd swept everything off the counter.

Mia found herself flat on her back, squinting up at the underside of the hideous light fixture hanging from the ceiling.

Face burning, she struggled to sit up. The counter was cold. The lights too bright. She felt exposed and dangerously vulnerable spread-eagled on the counter with a strange, albeit gorgeous man, fully clothed, between her dangling legs. He wore jeans, a T-shirt stretched over an impressive, wide-shouldered, narrow-hipped, rock-hard physique that she'd only been allowed to touch briefly.

Black eyes looked like obsidian glass as he leaned over her to stretch her arms over her head, clamping both wrists in the manacle of one large hand. The soft fabric of his black T-shirt brushed her breasts, and the zipper of his jeans, and his impressive erection behind it, pressed exactly where she wanted his naked, rampant damn penis inserted.

She shifted her butt, trying to leverage herself upright. Again he anticipated the movement, canting his hips so that all of him ground against all of her. When she gasped and froze, he swiveled his hips. Grinding, rocking. Pushing. All the while watching her with those dark fathomless eyes. Pleasure so intense it was close to pain sizzled through her, from her toes to her already tight nipples.

Toes curled, thigh muscles quivering, Mia was so turned on she could barely drag a real breath into her constricted lungs. She fought to get her hands free. Her shackles tightened. Her skin was on fire as her blood rushed to the surface. It was a shock when he moved his hips away from hers. Automatically Mia lifted her hips to regain that contact.

Face inches from hers, he murmured silkily, "You want to be fucked?"

"I might have mentioned it—" Horrified that her voice wobbled, she clamped her mouth shut, shuddering with the power of her need. Shit. He was a piece of work. Who the hell did he think he was? A paid "escort," that's who. Mia had no idea why, with all his tightly leashed menace, she wasn't terrified out of her mind. Intellectually, she knew she should be. But her body urged her to ignore any rational caution and just go for it.

She was so primed, so freaking ready, that if he touched her between her legs, she'd go off like a rocket. And so far, he'd done not much more than give her orders and look at her.

She should've specified the rules before—oh, yeah. She'd tried that.

His face was inches from hers, taut with the same tension that suffused her entire body. He needed a shave. "Would you like me to suck on your pretty tits?" he whispered, shifting so his hard chest massaged her breasts. It was too much and not nearly damn well enough.

Even the suggestion of him having his mouth, and that rough beard, anywhere near her breasts made all her girl parts clench. Mia gritted her teeth, wanting desperately for him to touch her for real. Only inches separated their mouths. Unbearable tension coiled deep inside her. Tighter and tighter, the tension torqued and spiraled, causing her head to thrash and her hips to jerk to try to get closer.

Anticipation was one thing, but this was torture. Another matter entirely.

She was starting to hate the son of a bitch. The frigid look she gave him had zero effect. His dark gaze was hot. Smoldering, in fact.

"That window of opportunity," she said hoarsely, "is closed."

His smile was feral. "Is that a fact?"

Hard as hell to do haughty when she was naked under the unflattering glare of the bright light, only his shadow covering her. He was still fully dressed.

He shook his dark hair out of his eyes. It was too long. Longer than hers, for God's sake, and tickled her cheeks, a curtain of shiny dark silk as he leaned over her supine body.

The heat, her helplessness, his deliberate withholding of something so damned easy to give her—something she was *paying* for, damn it—made Mia crazy. This was all a matter of control, she knew.

Except the wrong person was exerting the control and he was taunting her.

"You don't like being the one taking orders, do you?" He sounded mildly amused. "You like to be boss. But here's a revelation. Your skin's flushed. Your eyes are shining, and your pussy's swollen and wet. For me. You're angry because you're enjoying this. Which pisses you off even more."

The fact that he was amused when she was about to go nova, and the fact that he'd read her mind, infuriated her. "If I didn't want to be here, you'd be on the floor clutching your package." Mia rarely lost her temper. The more pissed she was, the icier she got. But she was teetering on losing her temper now. She was a sexual pressure cooker ready to blow.

His coffee-scented breath was hot on her face; she'd tasted it earlier. "So that makes me in charge, doesn't it?"

Mia snarled. "Let me up. I didn't hire you for your charming conversational skills or your pretty hair. I've got better things to do with my evening. Besides, I'm cold." The very opposite of true. Sweat beaded at her hairline, and her skin felt prickly hot.

No foreplay, no penetration, no damn anything, and her skin was on fire, and so sensitive to the touch that the mere brush of his shirt made her nipples painfully hard. She felt her juices hot and wet on her inner thighs.

A moan, so low it trembled—a mere vibration between them—came from her throat. The pleasure was so fierce that she almost came with the anticipation. Her body screamed for her to beg for him to do her. She might be pretending to be someone else, but even as deep as she was into the pretense, she was still Amelia to the core, and Amelia never begged for anything.

She struggled to leverage herself up on her elbows, but he merely pressed his hand between her breasts and gently pushed her back down. "Let me up," she said, hating him because her voice sounded desperate. She had BOB upstairs. In two minutes or less, with her eyes closed and imagining what this man must have been, she'd have relief. "I'll pay you, and you can be on your way."

She didn't even notice that he'd freed his impressive length from his jeans with his free hand until he rammed himself to the hilt deep inside her, filling her, impossibly thick and deep.

Mia climaxed instantly.

She woke at six the next morning—bare-ass naked on the kitchen island. Throwing an arm over her eyes, she groaned. "Oh. My. God."

Unfortunately, she didn't have amnesia. Last night played in Technicolor in her brain, and her body ached deliciously. Casually she lifted her elbow to look around to confirm that she was alone and the man of her well-lived fantasy was not there.

Amazingly, she'd fallen asleep exactly as he'd left her. Legs dangling over the edge of the counter, a buffet for his dining pleasure. And holy God, had he dined!

Dined and dashed apparently. There was no sign of him. And it wasn't as though she could yell his name. Mia had no frigging idea what it was.

Her only nod to being dressed was having an arm in one sleeve of her silk robe. One hundred percent vanilla all the way, in her whole life she'd never had sex anywhere but in her bed, lights off. Never done anything more adventurous sexually than receive oral. Once. She was a missionary position woman. As for oral—she preferred being the giver than the receiver. She liked to be the one in control. And a woman was never more in control than when she had a guy's penis in her mouth.

She liked sex. Sex was good. Hence hiring someone to take care of the needs a BOB just couldn't meet. She'd wanted heat. The friction of skin.

She'd gotten that. In spades.

Last night had been . . . incredible, shocking, incendiary. But last night she'd been on the receiving end, and she'd been so aroused, so turned on by him, there hadn't been time to be embarrassed or have second thoughts about her loss of control.

It took one split second with him inside her for her to get over the anger he had inspired. Once she was over it she'd been receptive to anything and everything he did. Dear Lord, the man knew how to give, and obtain, pleasure.

She'd never felt more vulnerable in her life. Exposed, wanting. Needing. Her, all but naked, and him, merely unzipping his jeans before taking her. She'd somehow just given him all the power, and God! It had been liberating, and a powerful release of all her inhibitions.

Now, as she rolled off the center island in the brightly lit kitchen, Mia felt both embarrassed and shocked at how uninhibited she'd been. Now she had third and fourth thoughts about hiring him.

She was supposed to call the shots. She *always* called the shots. With him in power, she felt more alive, more aware of her body, than she'd ever felt in her life. The guy knew his way around a woman's body. He was a professional, after all.

As she ran lightly up the stairs, she debated calling him back. He could teach her things she didn't know she wanted to learn.

"Of course," Mia mused as she turned on the leaky shower in the master bedroom, postponing the cleanup downstairs for after she'd showered and had at least two cups of coffee, "when would I have the opportunity to use what I learn?" Showers right now were fast. The house needed a new hot-water tank, and the water came out in a lukewarm drizzle, necessitating speed.

"But why wait for an opportunity? Why not enjoy the experience for what it is?" She smiled as she dressed, a first. Usually not a lot of smiles in her mornings. Most days she got ready listening to the stock reports, or to one of her assistants somewhere in Blush's worldwide offices giving her the day's agenda, or . . . business. Always business first thing in the morning and last thing at night.

Now that she was away, she had to trust that her business

26

was in capable hands, because she had only one contact right now, her right-hand man, Todd. So, with no business to consume her every waking hour, she had other things on her mind.

A very, very long to-do list to work on, for one, and he had just helped her accomplish a very important item.

Number seventeen. SWAS. Sex with a stranger. A dangerous stranger at that. Cross that off her list. Several times.

After putting on a large pot of coffee, Mia clasped her hair back in a stubby tail with a giant shocking-pink plastic clip purchased at Walmart. That trip had been number fourteen on her list. An eye-opening experience, too much fun to have missed. There was a whole other world out here that she'd never been exposed to. Walmart. Driving. Filling her new truck with gas, number five. Simple things that everybody took for granted.

She'd call Bon Temps later and have a do-over. She hadn't given them her number. Only one person had that, and that was Todd. "A do-me-over." She smiled, wiping her hands as she looked out of the window toward the broad, majestic Spanish moss–draped oaks bordering the swampy wet edges of the bayou. From there the water glistened between patches of water hyacinths and the trunks of the cypresses.

The grass was overgrown and gone to seed, heavy heads sparkling as the sun broke through the rain clouds that had come in last night. That lazy old alligator was still there, sunning himself, which made her loath to go to the bayou side of the house to start clearing ten years of crap off the lawn. Fortunately, Marcel Latour, recommended by the clerk at the local hardware store, was a gardener, and he would be over later to start the massive cleanup necessary on the property. There were things Mia was willing to give a shot, but yanking out a snake-infested jungle single-handedly was not one of them. She'd hired him to do the things she wasn't interested in learning.

The burner phone rang as she swept up the dead cookies littered around the island. Todd. They'd been raised from toddler age on all things Blush. They were more like brother and sister than cousins, and he was her best friend and trusted confidant.

Mia grabbed the receiver out of the sugar canister. "Hi."

"You sound very chirpy for a woman afraid for her life who's hiding out somewhere beachy and sunny and looking hot in a bikini—unless it's a nudist beach, in which case, go you." Todd didn't waste time taking a breath when he talked. Even when talking, he was always go, go, go.

Mia didn't correct him. Fat drops of rain played a musical score as it plopped into the buckets and on the tin roof, and the only beach around was the muddy strip of sand her gator friend slept on. Tucking the phone between ear and shoulder, she picked up the large chunks of broken crystal and used her toe to open the trash can so she could dispose of the evidence of last night's passion. Her skin felt hot.

"No one knows where I am." She poured a large mug of steaming coffee, and doctored it standing by the sink. "Not even you."

"Good. Let's keep it that way until we figure this out, 'k?"

Suddenly chilled, Mia dropped down onto a ladder-back chair beside the glass table in front of the window, bare feet crunching on broken cookies and flower stems still scattered on the floor. Someone had attempted to kill her. Several times. Blush's security had yet to nail down any solid suspects.

"Clearly an incompetent killer, since he didn't pull it off," she muttered, righting a bar stool she'd kicked over as she climaxed the second time. The time she straddled and rode him, at his urging, as though there were no tomorrow. The irony had been lost upon her as she spent long, long moments clenching her thighs and relishing the slide of him in and out of her, but now, in the daylight, the meaning of *no tomorrow* brought reality back with a bang.

Someone wanted her dead. The first clue was a drive-by shooting six months earlier, which had scared the crap out of her. The scar on her upper arm was from the second shooting, late at night, in her San Francisco office.

A month later the brake line on the Mercedes was cut. Hardly original. And she hadn't even been in the car when Carlos, her driver, crashed. He and her assistant who'd been with him in the car had both had minor scrapes and bruises, and the car was totaled. She'd wanted it in red anyway.

The elevator "accident," at least, was somewhat creative. But only Beverly in Accounting had broken her arm. Amelia had just been shaken and annoyed.

The sniper shot through her office window had been the last straw.

Todd Wentworth, her trusted cousin/best friend/VP of

marketing, was sure she had an angel on her shoulder. Which would be kind of creepy. No, the would-be assassin was an idiot, or she just had exceptionally good luck.

Probably both.

But as Todd pointed out—repeatedly—even an idiot could get lucky. It would only take once. Not that she planned on being dead anytime in the next, say, fifty years. But both Todd and Blush's head of security, Miles Basson, had, in no uncertain terms, encouraged her to disappear under deep cover until they could figure out who wanted her dead. A woman with her wealth, connections, and power made enemies. That was the nature of owning an international multibillion-dollar cosmetics company like Blush.

"There's news?" She placed her ankle on her knee to brush crumbs off her bare foot. "Who—"

"No, sorry. No new developments. Miles is working on it. He's good, you know he is. He'll figure this out and we'll bring you home soon. All you'll have to show for this experience is a great tan and a few extra pounds."

Todd and Miles were bending over backward to figure out the who and why. In the meantime she was to keep a low profile and pretend she was on the vacation the rest of the world had been told she was on.

With cash, and strong motivation, Amelia had taken a circuitous route from San Francisco to Switzerland, where she'd procured a new identity. The papers weren't that good, but the guy she found in Prague did a better job, and the woman in London an even better one. She returned to the States and changed her identity once again. Now she was Mia Hayward. Apropos of nothing and nowhere. Nothing to connect her to Amelia Wentworth.

Really, all that running from pillar to post, all the name changes, all the freaking skulking, had become exhausting. She'd found the house in this small town in Louisiana online, bought it sight unseen, and was quite prepared to make it charming and livable for the foreseeable future. Or until her cousin told her it was safe to return to San Francisco.

It was difficult being Mia Hayward. No goals, no purpose, no action. Hence the long list. What did people who were married to their jobs do all day if not their jobs? She was finding out. This had been the longest freaking month of her life. There was a reason why she rarely took vacations. She was a workaholic, always had been. The thought of spending days lazing on a beach made her antsy. She needed projects. Deadlines. Challenges.

"How are Stephanie and her team doing on final tests?" she asked, switching feet to brush away yesterday's cookies. She now had to add *Sweep* to the list. The kitchen floor was a shambles. Considering what he'd done to her right here, Mia was surprised her brain hadn't been swept just as clean as the island.

"Pretty much on target."

Pretty much on target was Todd's shorthand for *Something's fucked-up*. "Crap, what's the delay?"

Their first foray into the lower-end market. The ingenious 3-D printer would give Blush customers the ability to produce their own makeup, at minimal cost, from their home computers. It was going to revolutionize drugstore makeup purchases for the public, making the choice of colors unlimited and inexpensive. It might be gimmicky, but she knew it would bring in a fortune and, more important, bring those same drugstore customers up to the lux lines as they got older. Blush planned to offer the 3-D printers to its customers for home use by Christmas.

"How are the lifeguards?" Todd asked innocently.

She knew he had it handled. She had to stop the long-distance micromanaging. "Will we be able to go into production in less than the ninety days scheduled?"

"Looks like," Todd said. "Shipped the first of the sponge compacts out yesterday," he added, switching gears. He knew her well.

Mia didn't like to be bogged down with details. She had competent people in key positions because she trusted them to do their jobs. Todd was her right-hand man, and everything was funneled through him before getting to her.

"Department stores have all exceeded their initial projections. Offering a one-stop SPF of fifty, plus BB coverage—gold. Shiseido is going to pee their pants when they get wind of these new products." Mia cut to the chase. "We'll need gold to pull off this buyout. As good as it is, a twelve point three uptick in sales isn't going to solve that problem."

"Yeah, well, the printer and this innovative compact are going to pull in half the gold. We'll come up with something for the other half."

"We'll have another fresh infusion with the twenty-eight-day antiaging kits," Mia pointed out, even though they both knew she needed millions of dollars more to achieve the buyout. "They start rolling out tomorrow, two weeks early. Yay us. So we can add another eleven point six percent to our stash. Still not enough to fund the LBO without Davis and Kent backing me."

The investment firm was still deciding whether they were prepared to do the leverage buyout so that Mia/Amelia could go through with her plan to take the company private and buy out the rest of Blush's shareholders. It was all hush-hush right now. The waiting was the hard part. She hated waiting for anything, but Mia's strength was her ability to hold her cards close to her chest, and her infinite patience.

"Maybe. But they haven't said no, and these numbers will make you, and Blush, look a lot more attractive. I'm not worried."

Mia got to her feet and started picking up the broken plates and other items swept off the island in the heat of passion last night. Piling the shattered cookies on the broken plates, she carried the mess to dump in the trash under the chipped enamel sink, holding the phone under her chin. "Still not e—"

"I know. We're working on it. Are you okay? You sound out of breath."

"I had wild monkey sex last night." She'd always had lists, but none like this. Those were all business related. This list was personal. As Mia Hayward, Amelia now had the opportunity, and unprecedented time, to indulge her every fantasy. None of which had anything to do with Blush.

So, for the moment, she had complete anonymity to work

her way up and down her list in any damn order she felt like. Not systematically or in logical order, as she usually did things, but in a wildly exciting, out-of-order, spontaneous, fun way, as things came to her.

Spontaneity was number one on the list. Check. Check. And check.

She'd jumped from number eight, *Bake cookies*, to number seventeen, *Sex with a stranger*. Fast and furious sex in the bright light of her kitchen. And the stranger had earned every damned penny of his fee.

Which was still in the envelope shoved to the back of the counter by their energetic exertions. *Insertions*. She smiled. God. She couldn't believe what she'd done the night before. Couldn't believe she'd let herself be swept away without her usual inhibitions or caution. Dear Lord. It had been liberating. Exciting. Mind-blowing. There was a lot to be said for anonymous, uncomplicated sex. A hell of a lot.

"Holy shit, woman," Todd said. "Don't stop in the middle of a sentence like that! Spill!"

She smiled. "Number seventeen on the list. *Sex with a stranger*. Done, done, and oh my God—done again."

There was a pause, before he said, with rude incredulity, "Say what? I thought you just said you had sex last night."

"Multiple times, and multiple *O*'s." The breathy quality of her voice gave way to a long pause as her cousin thought about that.

"Jesus. Are you having sex right now?"

34

Mia laughed as she dropped back into the chair and swung her bare feet up on the table. Another first. "I wish. No. Just cleaning up all the crap he swept to the floor when he did me on the kitchen counter last night."

"Please tell me you aren't kidding."

A blush she thought herself incapable of bloomed as her face heated. "Apparently this place employs very qualified staff. Very qualified."

"He was a rent-a-fuck? Who are you, and what have you done with my favorite cousin?"

"I'm fully embracing Mi—my new persona."

Todd breathed out a whistle. "I love this chick."

She grinned, then swung her feet to the floor. "I'm starting to, too. It was"—she closed her eyes—"amazing."

"What did he look like? Hot and sexy, or homely, diligent, and excellent at his job?"

"About six three, dark, shoulder-length hair, five-o'clock shadow, superdark brown eyes. Not an ounce of body fat. Broad shoulders, rock-hard . . . abs, strong hands. And big . . . feet."

"Are you making him up? This is a real guy, right? You aren't anthropomorphizing BOB, are you? Quite understandable, of course; we all do it."

Mia plucked a crumb from between her toes. Her new pinkie toe ring glinted as she rotated her foot to admire it. Maybe she'd get a tattoo. . . . "A real, heart-pounding, flesh-and-blood man of gigantic proportions."

"Judas! Be still, my jealous heart. Not to be prurient, but what size condom did he wear? Tell me it was a Highway to Heaven?"

"Oh, shit!" She suddenly remembered the enormous box of condoms in the drawer in her bedside table. Condoms had been the last thing on her mind because he'd driven her mindless in the damned kitchen, and the first time he'd finally used his penis, he hadn't given her warning. She made a mental note to keep a handful in every room of the house from now on. "You just made that up."

"No, actually, I— Holy crap, Louise! You rode this stud bareback?"

Mia shook her head with a combo of amazement and appreciation, and felt a rush of residual heat. She ached in places she'd never ached before, her breasts felt tight, her nipples hard with arousal just thinking about the hot, wet suckle of his mouth on her sensitized body. "He didn't give me time to think of anything other than what he . . . gave me."

"And that would be . . . ?"

"My first screaming orgasm. One of many."

"Jesus!"

"That name came up several times," Mia told him, voice dry. "Yesterday, I must admit, was a red-letter day. I baked cookies last night. Number four on my list. And while the fruits of my labor were a casualty of kitchen counter sex, I consider them a win. Today, number five: *Following a recipe with more than six ingredients*. Hear me roar."

Todd didn't comment on her change of subject. "All the

way here in San Francisco, babe. I'm proud of you. You'll bring all these news skills home with you soon."

"By the time this is all over, I'll weigh three times what I weighed before I left."

"You can afford a few extra pounds. What's on your schedule today?"

The sun had vanished in the last few minutes, and rain pounded the windows, making musical notes on the tin roof, and not-so-musical notes as it filled the strategically placed buckets throughout the house. "Remodeling the kitchen is top priority. I'll hire someone to tackle that. I have a company coming to replace the roof in a couple of weeks. And I need to figure out if I want to tackle the porch myself or hire out—"

"Or find a lovely rental—furnished condo with a view of the ocean so you can relax— Oh, wait, I forgot who I was talking to. 'Relax' isn't in Amelia Wellington-Wentworth's vocabulary."

No, it wasn't. But she was trying to shoehorn it into Mia Hayward's.

There was a loud knock at the back door. She had a discreet parade of deliveries every day, but it hadn't been that long ago that a bullet shattered the window in her office, and unexpected loud noises still made her start and caused her heart to race. Especially after she'd first moved into the two-hundred-year-old house tucked away on a cul-de-sac next door to the graveyard. Alone. No bodyguards. No secure building. For what either of those had been worth in San Francisco.

And she'd *still* been shot at.

The house was only ninety minutes outside New Orleans and she hadn't been there once since she arrived almost a month ago, but it seemed half of NOLA arrived at her doorstep on a regular basis with deliveries.

"Someone's at the door. Either my new gardener or UPS. I'll call you in a couple of days."

"Check before you open the door!"

"Yes, Mother. Love you, kiddo." Mia disconnected, then turned the ringer off and replaced the phone back in the metal sugar canister. "Coming!"

Chapter Three

*W*iping her hands on the dishcloth flung over her shoulder, Mia walked down the long corridor, past the stairs, to the back door. The gardener couldn't work outside in this deluge. She'd ask him if he knew how to install wallpaper and, if not, point him to the steamer to remove the red flocked paper in the entryway until the weather cleared. She really needed a whole army of tradesmen to put the house to rights, but she didn't relish people in her space when she was there all day herself. She wouldn't be here long enough to worry about it. . . .

"Hi—" she said as she flung open the front door. The dark-haired man dripping in the doorway topped her five foot six by almost a foot and made her heartbeat stutter, then race into overdrive. Long black hair clung wetly to his strong throat and brushed the rain-speckled dark T-shirt stretched over his broad shoulders. Dark stubble gave him a dangerous, sexy look, and his deep brown eyes said *Been there, done her.*

He was shockingly, mesmerizingly familiar.

Diamond droplets of water clung to his black lashes. Mia wanted to lick them off. He looked hard and dangerous, and not the sort of man who would take money for something he probably gave away for free on a daily basis. He must have women lining up around the block for his services.

He could've charged her double. Hell, triple.

She stared up at him, riveted. It wasn't anything as simple as physical good looks, although he had those in abundance. His nose was straight, his lips chiseled and sexy as sin. He needed a haircut and a shave, yet his unshaven jaw and his intense dark brown eyes made his personal grooming habits immaterial.

He wore jeans and a clinging wet dark blue T-shirt that showed his muscle definition. Abs, pecs, biceps . . . Mia's mouth went dry. The fabric clung to every rippling, solid muscle on his chest and belly, and the damp denim of his jeans cupped his sex. Sex appeal oozed from his very pores.

Every cell in Mia's body remembered the night before in pulsing Technicolor, as if he'd imprinted himself on her body in some way.

She had to consciously avert her gaze from the bulge behind his fly, back to his face. *Say something, for God's sake!* "You came for your money. Hang on a sec, I'll go get it for y—"

He put his hand on her bare arm. A hot electrical current zinged through Mia's veins at the contact, and her gaze jerked up to meet his dark eyes, making her completely forget what she'd been about to say. She felt as though her skin was magnetized to his. The energy pulsing between them was almost visible, it was so strong.

Disconcerting.

Intriguing.

"I think you have me confused with someone else." A trace of amusement tinged his voice, although he wasn't smiling.

Dragging her gaze away from a drop of water making its slow way down his temple to the dark, sexy scruff on his cheeks and jaw, Mia pursed her lips, then shook her head. "No. I don't believe so. We—" She, who ran a multibillion-dollar company with an iron hand, who'd dined with the president of the United States—several times—and had tea with Britain's queen, was at a loss for words.

"Fucked?" he offered politely.

"Not my favorite word, but applicable." Since she hadn't given Bon Temps her phone number, had his employer anticipated her wanting a repeat performance? Knowing how amazing he was, had they just sent him back because, honest to God, what woman *wouldn't* want a repeat of last night's performance?

He didn't look like anyone she would know in her other life. He looked real. The real that Blush's male models strived to emulate for their ads. That rugged, raw sensuality that was hard to duplicate. He looked— Hell, sexy wasn't a job description. "I'll get your mon—"

Thunder reverberated, and something large, hairy, and wet shot around her legs, causing her to stagger. The situation was already fraught with tension and she let out a small scream of surprise as she reached out for something to hold on to for balance.

He grabbed her upper arm to prevent her from falling. His hand was large, his skin considerably darker than hers.

Just seeing his fingers circling her upper arm made Mia's brain go blank for several beats. She blinked her brain back into action. "What on earth—" Glancing back, she didn't see anything other than splotches of wet mud in a meandering line from the door into the house.

"Sorry 'bout that. Oso is afraid of thunder. Okay if I go get him?"

She had no idea what an Oso was; she presumed a dog. "Wait here. I'll find him." Yes, he'd been inside the house before—hell, inside *her*—but that didn't mean he was welcome whenever he felt like dropping by.

She needed to establish some rules before she—they . . . before—

She started to close the door, and felt a twinge of alarm to realize he had his foot wedged against it, preventing it from closing.

He pushed it farther open with one large hand. His arm barring the opening now. "Oso won't come to a stranger. He'll hide until I find him. Let's start again." Dropping his arm, he stuck out his hand, which she automatically took. "Cruz Barcelona."

"Mia Hayward." Her much smaller hand was engulfed by his. Muscle memory felt the electricity of his touch as those fingers cupped her breast, his thumb strumming her nipple. *Get a grip!*

A person could judge a man on his firm, no-nonsense handshake. And if they were in a boardroom, Mia would've let go almost immediately. But they weren't in a business situation, and the way his fingers closed around hers was more intimate than a mere handshake. She withdrew hers as quickly as though she'd been burned.

A long dent, not quite a dimple, appeared in his cheek when he almost smiled. Mia's heart did calisthenics as her gaze slid to the chiseled curve of his mouth. Dear God, the guy had the mouth of a fallen angel, and the deep, dark eyes of a sinner. His effect on her was disconcertingly profound. Even more so because she'd never been this aware of a man before in her life.

"Dan Hicky at the general store told me you're looking for some help," he said easily, his deep voice curling through her veins like hot smoke. "Electrical? Some plumbing? I'm a jack-of-all-trades; he thought we'd be a good fit."

Mia knew the ways they fit, and felt her cheeks heat. She'd blushed more in the last few hours than she'd done in her entire life. "And you're employed by . . . ?" She was starting to suspect it wasn't the Bon Temps Escort Service.

"Currently unemployed. Unless you have work for me?"

It occurred to Mia that she could hire him to keep her sexually satisfied until she was able to go home. She pushed the door wider—something she wouldn't do in San Francisco, even if her bodyguards were with her. But then again, she'd left herself totally vulnerable last night and it had ended up being the best thing she'd ever done. "Your dog's probably in the kitchen. Come in."

Said the spider to the fly. Clearly she was under the misapprehension that he was trustworthy because he'd fucked her the night before. He gave her a slow, lazy smile, with just enough heat to help reinforce her misconception and keep her guard down.

Dressed in conservative pale blue shorts, a white T-shirt, and not a scrap of makeup that he could see, she looked like the girl next door. If the girl next door was gorgeous and sexy, and had creamy long legs and a livid six-inch scar on her upper arm.

He was disappointed to note she was wearing a bra. Her bare feet were oddly endearing, and sported bright red polish and a small silver toe ring he'd barely noticed the night before.

Her pale feet made her look vulnerable, defenseless. Why the hell did he give a flying fuck how she looked, or how vulnerable her goddamned feet looked? Coiled tension told Cruz to stay away from her magnetic sensual pull. No matter how unprecedented this attraction was, she was a job. Just a job.

"Not a smart move, inviting a strange man into your house when you're here alone," he said, carefully keeping his voice neutral as they followed the dark hallway, his mind filled with methods to take her life. "This place is isolated as hell, and you don't know me from Adam." A bright pink plastic clip held her hair off her pale nape. Cruz had an insane urge to put his mouth there.

She stopped at the foot of the stairs, turning to size him up. "You weren't concerned for my safety last night."

"You told me not to say anything. You don't give the appearance of being a woman who does anything unless she wants to do it."

"Well, clearly I wanted to—" A flush rose from her throat to her cheeks, but her gaze didn't waver. She was surprisingly tough; but then, she had the clout of her wealth and privilege to mask who she really was. "If you were a psychopathic serial killer, we wouldn't be having this conversation right now, would we?"

"Maybe I'm on my meds and haven't snapped and started my killing spree yet." The only reason she was alive now was because Cruz had a persistent itch that told him he didn't have all the facts necessary to complete the job. The itch was strong enough that he'd canceled his trip to Brazil this morning until he had more data.

The color left her face, and she shuddered, then briskly rubbed her arms despite the muggy heat. "Well, please don't start your spree with me. It would destroy my faith in the goodness of my fellow man."

"There's not a whole hell of a lot of good in man one way or the other," he pointed out cynically. *Jesus, I almost believe she's this naive.* It was an impressive act. "And you should've at least asked for my ID." Cruz had absolutely no fucking idea why her trust—even if it was feigned—annoyed the living bejesus out of him. But it did.

"Sure." She held out a slender hand. A hand that had never done anything other than lift a cup to her lips or sign a check. "Hand over your driver's license."

Cruz dug a wallet out of his back pocket, withdrew a license, and handed it to her.

A buzzy electrical current passed between their fingers. Odd, conducting electricity on a day like today.

"IDs can be faked," she pointed out, scanning the license before handing it back. And she would know. She had an excellent one herself. "You live in Idaho?"

Never been there, but it was as good a place as any for Cruz Barcelona to have gotten a driver's license. If she didn't like this one, he had two dozen others. "That's my home base," he told her easily. "I like to move around." The moving-around part was true. His work took him all over the world. But most of his free time was spent at his three-hundred-year-old farmhouse in the South of France or his penthouse in New York.

"Do you have any references?"

Cruz shrugged. "Yeah. How many would you like?"

Her eyes were steady on his face. "Three."

He could produce three dozen if that was what was required. He had plenty of aliases. *Irrelevant. You'll be dead by tomorrow, next day at the latest.* "No problem."

"Kitchen's this way," she told him briskly, foolishly turning her back. "Let's find your dog."

Cruz shook his head as he followed his exotic, sexy-as-hell prey down the dimly lit hallway, which held neatly stacked boxes, wallpaper rolls, folded drop cloths, and various gardening tools. In the four minutes it had taken to walk from the back door, down the hall, and into the kitchen, he could've staged her accidental death at least three times.

The kitchen was brightly lit and still somewhat chaotic. Oso was happily eating cookies off the littered floor. The purple flowers, stems shortened, were now in an orange milk pitcher on the center island.

She grabbed an envelope off the counter where he'd screwed her the night before, then turned back to face him. The flush on her cheeks was surprising, and made her blue eyes glow like the waters off his favorite Brazilian beach. A fathomless blue with a touch of clear turquoise. Dark lashes, long and spiky, shadowed her eyes as she held out the envelope.

Cruz kept his fingers tucked in the front pockets of his jeans. "I told you I wasn't who you thought I was."

Her gaze, frank and disconcertingly direct, came up to meet his. "Well, you did the job. You might as well get paid for it."

From the way her nipple peaked beneath the cotton of her T-shirt, he wasn't the only one thinking about what they'd done on the center island countertop. His dick lengthened on seeing that just the memory turned her on. "That was pleasure." Concentrate, damn it. She's the mark, nothing else. Her very naiveté was going to aid him in killing her. When the time came.

"But I'll accept work." He needed a few more days. Hell, he could afford the time, and the benefits to delaying killing her were worth the wait. He'd earn his money. But not quite yet.

"You left before I could—" she said coolly, tapping the edge of the envelope on her palm absently. What was she thinking about?

"Thank me," he finished, keeping his smile to himself. "You were too exhausted to wake up for the next round."

He'd intentionally left her right there on the table, legs open, and cookies, pans, bar stools, and papers scattered on the floor where he'd swept them before playing with her.

Her eyes flashed with heat. "Yes, well, um . . ."

Cruz watched her search for the right words. He leaned his hip against the counter and spread his arms to rest his palms on the cool Formica countertop on either side of him. "I gather you hired out?"

"That's none of your business."

"You made it my business last night."

She pushed the envelope against his chest. "Well, then, take this, and we'll be square."

Cruz didn't move to take it. And after a few seconds she dropped her hand and took a step back. Because she retreated, he advanced, stepping close enough for the sharp tips of her nipples to brush his chest, which set off a whole series of alarms through his nervous system. The smell of her skin, lush tuberose and a faint hint of something spicy, rose in a warm invisible cloud to twine around him. He saw the rapid rise of her pulse at the base of her throat and wanted to put his open mouth there to taste her again.

Standing so close, he could see the changing swirls of variegated blues in her widening eyes. He wanted to fill his hands with her again, feel the tight wet heat of her closing around him. Without volition, he bent his head, his lips hovering over hers, tasting her coffee-scented breath on the moist air between them. Her lashes fluttered as she angled her head to offer her mouth.

Cruz reached out to take the dish towel she'd slung over her shoulder before coming to open the front door. Her breathing stopped as he slowly slid it from her. Holding her gaze, he ran the dish towel over his wet hair. "I'd rather have steady work."

"Um . . ." Her eyes were a little unfocused, but she recovered her equilibrium quickly. "Okay. What kind of work can you do?"

Bring you to multiple orgasms and have you beg for more. "Pretty much anything this house needs." He'd worked enough construction jobs over the years; there was nothing she could throw at him that he couldn't handle. And besides, it didn't matter if he could or couldn't do whatever she asked. She'd be dead by morning. "Just finished a major three-month remodel in Los Angeles."

"For . . . ?"

"Aiden Cross. I'll give you his number." Which would be answered by voice mail.

"What kind of work did you do for him?"

"Remodeled his kitchen: custom cabinets, cement countertops, the whole nine yards. Converted a downstairs bedroom into an English-style pub, painted the whole place inside and out—" Cruz had recently done the remodel in his own French country farmhouse. He looked at the stack of wallpaper boxes piled in the corner. "I can handle anything you throw at me. What needs wallpapering?"

"Hallway, downstairs bath, and dining room. Do you have any experience installing—"

Keeping her under his watchful eye, having access to the house and any personal papers or shit he could find on her computer, might make this odd hesitancy he felt go away. He'd do the job he'd accepted a down payment on, then head off to Brazil, where he had a small house right on the beach. "Take me a week or so—"

An incredibly loud clap of thunder cut him off, causing Mia to flinch, and sent the dog skittering from beneath the table. In a blur of golden fur, Oso shot out of the kitchen and tore up the uncarpeted stairs. Frantically clicking nails indicated his terrified trajectory overhead.

"Stay put," Cruz ordered. "I'll get him." And take a quick tour of the upstairs. And when she opened her mouth—he presumed to tell him it was her house—Cruz finished: "He won't go to a stranger." And jogged upstairs, leaving her in the kitchen.

The dog, of course, would go to anyone. He'd chosen him without much thought from a pound an hour away. He'd just said "That one" to the first dog who'd come up to the fence looking friendly early that morning.

"Yo, Oso. Come on, boy." Slapping his jeaned thigh, Cruz whistled as he opened a closed door. Not looking for the dog, just . . . looking. Empty bedroom sporting peeling pink and gold wallpaper and a large, almost full blue plastic bucket off to one side to catch the drips from the water-marked ceiling. Pushed the next door farther open to see a mint-green and black bathroom, clearly not in use.

Another empty bedroom. And a third, set up as an artist's

studio, with gessoed stretched canvases stacked neatly against the wall. Cruz stepped inside, only imagining the smell of oil paint on the dusty air. An easel held a blank canvas, and beside it a tall table covered with a dish towel and a pretty blue glass vase held an assortment of high-pigment Lukas paint tubes and dozens of Kolinsky sable brushes in various sizes. None of them used. All of them, as he well knew, top-of-the-line. Interesting.

In the corner stood a pottery wheel, with an optimistically large pile of plastic-wrapped clay bricks. If she planned on throwing all that clay, she intended to be here for a while.

A clap of thunder apparently ensured that the dog would remain hidden until the weather cooperated. Cruz walked into the last room, pleased with himself. He'd picked the perfect prop in the nervous pound dog. Oso had chosen the master bedroom, the only upstairs room furnished. Cruz was instantly assailed with the opulent, creamy, carnal fragrance of tuberose.

Her bed wasn't anything like the feminine notes of her perfume. It was stark, almost masculine, with a sleek, modern black wrought-iron headboard, and was neatly made with crisp white sheets and a comforter. Cruz instantly saw himself fucking her on that pristine comforter, his dark skin against her fairness, her silky hair whipping his chest as her head thrashed.

How much time was he willing to indulge himself here to satisfy the odd sense that something wasn't right? How long to confirm what his research had already told him, which was why he'd accepted the job in the first place? She fit his benchmark for hits—only the worst of the worst. He had a team of researchers all over the world who verified the crimes. There was no mistake about Amelia Wellington-Wentworth, aka Mia Hayward. None. And yet . . .

Twenty-four hours should do it, he decided in that moment. In the meantime he'd satiate himself with her delectable body and see what it was like to have a pet. He'd fix some shit around here, because he enjoyed working with his hands.

"Oso, here, boy."

A black nose emerged from beneath the bed as the dog crawled out on his belly, black eyes watching Cruz's face. He recognized that look. Dropping to his haunches, Cruz slowly held out his hand for the dog to sniff. "Nobody's gonna hurt you, buddy. Not even that fierce thunder. Come downstairs, let's see if the pretty lady will offer us breakfast."

Oso's tail wagged slowly, his eyes never leaving Cruz's face.

Cruz stood. "Wanna eat?"

The tail picked up speed, and Oso got to his feet, then leaned his entire body against Cruz's legs. "Shit." Cruz reached down to fondle the dog's soft, floppy ear. "I'm the last guy you want to get attached to," he told the mutt as they went back into the hallway. "Fair warning: I walk away before anyone gets attached."

"What's that you're burning?"

"Yeah," she admitted, not looking up. "It *is* burned, isn't it?" With a shake of her head, she shot him a quick smile. It was sweet, open. Fucking stupid of her to be so goddamned *friendly*. Strange man in her house, in *her*. She should be barricade in a safe room, not attempting to fix him the most important meal of the day, dressed, with deceptive innocence.

"It was supposed to be breakfast." She eyed the pan, then looked back at him, blue eyes sparkling with humor. "But it's a steep learning curve. I like to eat, so I hope I master the first meal of the day *soon*. I see you found your friend."

The dog darted under the table as Cruz crossed the kitchen, checking out his hostess's prime ass, cupped by the blue shorts, and her long pale legs as he went to open a window a crack to let out the smell. The rain was coming down in sheets and turning the backyard to mud.

"Take it off the burner," he advised when the pan started to smoke. He breathed deep of the heavy wet air fluttering the fruit-patterned curtains before turning back to watch her.

She grimaced as she removed the pan from the stove top and carried it, arms extended, over to the sink. "I should get a smoke alarm; at least that way I'll be warned before I burn down the house."

Clearly a runner, her legs were sleek and muscled. Strong, as he knew from last night, when she'd clasp them around his waist as he pumped into her. "I'd suggest letting it burn and collecting the insurance money."

Her lips twitched. "The eggs aren't insured. But at the rate I'm going, that might be an idea."

"The house."

She made a rude noise. "She's going to be beautiful when I'm done with her."

Cruz braced his hands on the chair back to observe her. "*Her?*"

"A venerable old lady with good bone structure. She just needs makeup and a new hairdo."

"A gut job."

"Shhh. Don't let her hear you. I've promised to make her beautiful again."

Cruz shook his head, charmed in spite of himself. The dichotomy between who she was and what she looked like was throwing him off. He knew better.

He'd learned a lot about the misdirection of evil people in his line of work. It was the main reason he took what he did seriously. He wasn't playing God. But frequently the face these people showed the world was pretty, when their actions were evil. He got to stop those who lied, cheated, manipulated, killed, and stayed out of the reach of the law.

The most evil of men and women were like fucking chameleons, changing their colors to do their worst to innocent and unsuspecting victims in the world without anyone being the wiser. He wasn't an idiot. Cruz knew men did unspeakable things to one another and believed themselves to be in the right.

Which was why he did his due diligence and researched and checked all the facts *before* he did a hit. His jaw clenched as he remembered the most sanctimonious of the evildoers he'd taken out: A fucking pastor who walked through his stadium-size church like a damn saint while he collected dead redheads across five states. Young, sweet, troubled women who came to the prick seeking his counsel, his help. Only to end up fucked over and sliced into a garbage bag he tossed in the woods like yesterday's trash.

He'd had the face and demeanor of a saint and killed fourteen young women in five states over a span of three years. Authorities had never been able to prove beyond a reasonable doubt that he'd done the killings. Paid by one of the victim's families, Cruz had proven to himself, beyond any shadow of a doubt, that Pastor Smiley was guilty as sin.

The man had drowned while out fishing alone in a remote location of Alaska. A confession note had been found tucked in his fishing tackle box admitting to the eleven he was being investigated for and three others whom no one knew he had anything to do with.

Cruz had given those victims' families closure.

"I'm going to start this process again. Brave enough to join me for breakfast? Nothing complicated." Mia glanced over her shoulder to give him a half smile—which, for some fucking annoying reason, pierced Cruz's chest like a sharp arrow. Fucking evil chameleons didn't ever shoot arrows into his chest.

"I'm determined to master the humble egg," she told him cheerfully, cracking one on the side of a new frying pan. "You, if you choose this assignment, can be my taste tester." She dropped the egg into the dry pan and cracked another. "Eggs any way you want them—as long as you want them scrambled and are willing to risk however they turn out. Harder than I thought to cook a good egg. Bacon's done."

Bacon was burned. "Scrambled works." He opened a couple of drawers, made a mental note to get some screws and wood glue, and took out forks. After opening three cabinets, he found gold-rimmed white china plates. He raised a brow as he put everything on the glass-topped table under the window. "Your version of paper?" He shut the window as raindrops dotted the glass table.

"Absolutely," her lips twitched, and her eyes twinkled. The arrow in his chest vibrated. "I'm practically camping." The doorbell rang as she was beating the living shit out of the eggs. "That must be Marcel."

Cruz rubbed his sternum as he observed her killing any hope of fluffy eggs by stirring the hell out of them on high heat. "Boyfriend?"

"Gardener-slash-handyman."

Considering the jungle out there, the gardener was either incompetent or had yet to start the job. Cruz motioned to the whisk in her hand. "Go ahead. I'll get it."

Before she could respond, Cruz headed down the hall to the front door, Oso at his heels, nails clicking on the wood floor. Place was as dark as a cave. Needed lights. The dark-red flocked wallpaper didn't help. He flung open the back door.

The guy was almost his height, shave off a couple of inches. Wiry. Late forties, with long unwashed, colorless hair, and, despite the driving rain, he stunk of old sweat and booze.

The dog's hackles rose, and he growled low in his throat.

"*Mais*, who you are?" the man demanded, shooting Oso a nervous look. Then glaring at Cruz. His Cajun accent or a shitload of cheap whiskey slurred his speech.

"The man standing on the inside of this door," Cruz told him coldly. "Come back tomorrow when you're sober."

The guy put his foot in the door. "The lady hired m—"

Even the de minimis intrusion pissed him off. Cruz slammed his palm up into his nose and had the satisfaction of hearing a crunch. The guy was drunk at eight in the morning. Drunk and belligerent. The combo spelled wild card and was sure to fuck with Cruz's plans for Mia/Amelia.

This time next week, what the garden looked like would be immaterial.

Oso continued the low growl, but didn't make any move to attack. Not that Cruz gave a fuck. Marcel clutched his nose. Blood dribbled through his fingers. "*Merde!*"

"Don't bother coming back. Tomorrow or any other time. Consider this all the notice you're going to get."

"You can't do that—" Marcel started banging on the door when Cruz shut it in his face.

Pissed off, Cruz headed back to the kitchen and the unappetizing smell as the pounding stopped. How could she be so goddamned stupid as to invite a lowlife like that into her home? Either she was supremely confident that her slippery tactics and flunkies would keep her safe, or she was below average in the street-smarts department.

Disproportionately annoyed, because she had, after all,

fucked his brains out and invited him in for a second go at her, Cruz strode down the hall and into the kitchen, the dog, tail wagging, at his heels.

Mia glanced up as she ladled eggs—burned again, to judge by the smell—and charred bacon onto the plates. "Was that Marcel? I'll just go and tell him—"

Cruz motioned the dog under the table. "Jehovah's Witness."

"All the way out here?" she asked, clearly surprised as she sat down at the table under the window, unfolding a cloth napkin on her lap. She gave her plate a dubious look.

Cruz shoved the chair out with his foot, then dropped into the hard seat opposite her. The food looked as unappetizing as hell. Rubbery, singed eggs and bacon that crumbled to dusty charcoal before he managed to get it to his mouth. He tossed it down to Oso, who sniffed it, then dropped his head back onto his paws, keeping his eyes on Cruz as if asking where the hell that breakfast was that he'd been promised.

Cruz ignored the dog. He didn't do dependents. It would eat when he did.

Mia wrinkled her nose. Cruz didn't want to be captivated by her, but he was. "Not edible," she admitted, taking up his plate without apology. "I'll make toast—"

He got to his feet, too. He was hungry, and toast wasn't going to satisfy him. With no time to waste after he had fucked her, he'd picked up his truck, driven to NOLA, found the dog, and come straight back. Only a small part of him had hoped she'd be exactly where he'd left her. Now that he'd been offered breakfast, he was starving. She carried their plates to the garbage can, where she scraped off the food. She didn't think it was fit for the dog either.

Opening the Sub-Zero—which looked incongruous in the old-fashioned (and not in a good way) kitchen—he took out the carton of eggs and the milk.

She turned to him, eyebrow arched.

"I'm starving. I need protein. I'll make the eggs. If you really want to learn, stick around. I'll show you."

"Now, why does that sound like an order?" she asked, tone dry. "I'm all for learning new things, but if you're looking for a sycophant, I'm not your girl."

No subtext there. The lady was used to being in charge. "Sometimes," he told her smoothly, "it's more interesting to be on the receiving end of things." While she'd come multiple times, the intervening hours had given her plenty of time to have second thoughts about just who was in control. She was in for one hell of an eye-opener.

He held out his palm. "Hand me the butter."

Chapter Four

*H*e'd brazenly parked his yellow pickup truck, with a rusted, old-fashioned camper hauled behind it, right near the back porch steps that needed fixing. Without asking permission. She hardly knew him—he was a stranger in all ways except one—but it hadn't taken her long to figure out that the man wanted to do what he wanted to do . . . and did it. No permission requested.

As a CEO, she certainly appreciated that quality in a person, but it didn't compute that a man who demanded power and control would be doing odd jobs as a handyman. Mia was surprised that he hadn't reached a higher standing in life. She looked at the heap of rusty and dented metal behind his truck. He couldn't live in that thing, could he? The camper looked barely high enough for him to stand up in. If he lived in that pile of tin, he must really need this job. Mia wondered what his story was.

"Frequently things seem simple and turn out . . . not," Mia told him as, after handing him the stick of butter, she started rinsing off the plates, then scraped out the burned offering from the pan.

She was a little tongue-tied around him, she realized, surprised. She, who mixed and mingled on a daily basis with people at every social level, with ease. She was as comfortable making small talk with the president of the United States as she was chatting with the maintenance staff at Blush's headquarters in San Francisco.

She was intelligent and articulate, and enjoyed social interactions. But he made her feel—God, she had no idea why this man made having a conversation so difficult. He didn't scare her—well, maybe a little. What he did do was turn her on. Maybe it was because with him she felt vulnerable. Bare. Maybe. Or maybe it was her imagination. Low blood sugar was giving her head a rush and she needed to have breakfast.

"That's life for you."

He was right behind her—she hadn't realized just how close until she felt the heat of his body all the way down her back. Her skin instantly tightened in anticipation of his touch.

"Things are seldom as they appear." His deep voice dropped several octaves until his words were more vibration than sound. The hair on the back of her neck lifted in response. "It's what makes life interesting, right?"

"Sometimes." Mia braced her hands on the edge of the sink and looked through the Spanish moss–covered cypresses to the green, murky water of the bayou. The rain was letting up, just random drops plopping into the muddy puddles between sad patches of scrubby grass, turning the lawn into a marsh.

Goosies rose on her arms. Everything looked alien, unfamiliar. Dangerous in a beautiful wild way. If that wasn't a metaphor for what her life was right now, she didn't know what was. "It would be nice if the world were a simpler place," she whispered, her own voice low in the quiet. "If we could take things at face value and not have to read subtext or subversion into everything."

"You'd have to find a deserted, uninhabited island for that." His arm brushed hers. Bare skin to bare skin. She sucked in a breath. Anticipation surged through her veins—but he was merely reaching for the dish towel on the edge of the counter.

Still, she was trapped, caged by his proximity. "If you move, I'll get out more bacon."

Looking faintly amused, he stepped aside, then started hand-drying the plates, watching her out of dark, fathomless eyes.

Mia turned her back to open the refrigerator and get out the eggs he already had out, and a frozen package of bacon, since she'd used the last of the open package earlier. The diversion gave her a few seconds to collect her thoughts. She must look a mess. Tempted to excuse herself, to run upstairs and fiddle with her hair and put on some makeup. She felt exposed the way she was.

Before coming to Bayou Cheniere, she'd never been seen in public not fully made-up, hair expertly styled, and wearing discreet, exquisite, top-end fashion from international designers.

From the time she was twelve she'd never been out in public not fully made-up or beautifully dressed. When she was twelve years old, the PR team at Blush had made her into a walking billboard for the company's products. All of those ingrained habits had been left behind—by necessity—in San Francisco months ago. Now the simple act of being without makeup as this man stared at her was foreign but also liberating.

No mask. No pretense. Nothing to hide behind. He was one of the few people who'd ever seen her for who she was. Almost. There was the whole change of name and identity thing, but still, who he saw was who she really was. Her name was immaterial.

Yeah, go ahead and tell yourself that, Mia mocked. That name was on *Forbes*'s list of the richest women in the world. It might have some bearing on how he perceived her if he knew.

But Mia Hayward owned a run-down, two-hundred-year-old, weed-infested property in the wilds of Louisiana. Here, her net worth wasn't relevant, to him or anyone else.

Now she wore clothes bought at a store that also sold produce and cat food, and she'd had her waist-length hair chopped off at a walk-in chain salon. They'd done a crappy job. One side was longer than the other. Not in an avant-garde way, just a bad haircut. She kinda liked the way the messy, piecy style framed her face. It was different for her, not perfect, but fun.

If anyone had told her three months ago that she'd be clean-faced, wearing inexpensive, off-the-rack shorts, and loving the freedom it gave her to do these things, she wouldn't have believed them. It was just starting to sink in that she wasn't living her real life.

She didn't have to wake up at five, work out for an hour in her home gym with her trainer, and get her hair and makeup done while her staff prepped her for her day via teleconferences from around the world. She didn't have to hurry downstairs where her personal chef had a hot breakfast waiting for her. In her real life, she'd have to catch up with the news, make telephone calls, tackle urgent emails in the car, and be at her desk at Blush headquarters by eight thirty sharp.

She had never woken to find herself spread-eagled and naked on the kitchen table.

Mia Hayward's life was starting to get interesting.

"The bacon's frozen. Should I defrost it, or pass?" She should pass. As much as she loved bacon, at home she only allowed herself two strips once a month.

"Defrost in the microwave."

The microwave was in the cabinet beside the stove, necessitating her walking up right beside him. She popped the door to the microwave and shoved the package in. "High?"

"Defrost. You really don't know your way around a kitchen, do you?"

"I eat out a lot." Banquet-style meals, dinner meetings at upscale restaurants, or home with her personal chef.

"Come and watch."

Leaning her hip against a nearby counter, eager to watch. Him, not him cooking. Mia put her hands behind her, then realized it was the gesture of a three-year-old and stuck her fingertips in her front pockets of her shorts instead. She was almost as fascinated by her response to Cruz as she was by Cruz himself.

"Closer."

"I can see just fine from here."

"Hands-on cooking can be a very sensual experience. What's the matter? Scared?"

Heart pounding a little too fast for a cooking lesson, Mia raised a mocking brow. "Of an egg?" She didn't move, but he wrapped an arm around her waist and pulled her flush against his body, his hard front pressed to her back. She stood trapped between his heat and the stove. She stiffened. "I'll get burned." In more ways than one.

"I won't let anything hurt you. Turn the burner to low. We're going to do this nice and slow. French-style scrambled eggs must be seduced slowly."

Her legs felt as insubstantial as jelly as she felt the hard length of his penis in the crack of her ass through the thin cotton of her shorts. Hot all over, all her nerve endings feeling exposed, Mia turned the knob on the stove as if hypnotized.

Why did he smell so damn good? As far as she was aware, he wore no cologne. Just sexy, soapy-clean male skin. Her brain darted to an image of him standing in the shower, a slow trail of foamy white soapsuds drizzling down his slick, wet body as slowly as a glacier, then pausing, like the yummy frosting on a cake, on the hard ridge of his—

Mia blinked the stove back into focus. Holy crap! Get a grip!

He reached around her, his arm brushing her breast, to adjust the knob on the stove.

Mia put a palm over the warm burner. "That low?" she asked dubiously. It was barely on. They'd be there all day waiting for breakfast at this rate, and she'd melt into a drooling puddle of lust before an egg was cracked.

His voice, husky and low, was right beside her ear. "As low as it can go."

"Won't it take forever to cook the . . . the . . ." What the hell were they cooking? "Eggs?"

"What's your hurry?" His arms came around to cage her against him, one large hand flat on her belly. The heat of his fingers seared right through her cotton T-shirt, making Mia hot, then cold, then hot again. "Stand on your toes." He waited until she did so before pressing her against his erection with the flat of his large hand low on her belly. "Put the pan on so it heats up slowly."

Slightly off balance and all thumbs, Mia fumbled to get a grip on the skillet while he held her immobile, deft fingers opening the top button of her shorts. Surely he wasn't . . . She wrestled the pan two-handed onto the burner with a loud clatter, so distracted she could barely see, let alone get a grip on the heavy pan.

Nuzzling her neck, he grazed his teeth along her nape. "Grab the bowl." When he sank his teeth into her earlobe, sparks zinged directly between her legs. His hot breath made her shiver, and moisture pooled where those hot sparks sizzled. She bit back a moan. She should be galvanized into action. One of them had to be sensible. She stood inches from a hot stovetop. She'd get burned—just because she was captivated by the man seducing her. The kitchen was no place for sex. That's what her bed was for.

Six eggs clattered inside the glass bowl as she dragged it closer to the stove. Her movement rubbed her butt enticingly against his erection.

"Maybe we should take this upstai—"

He bit her nape hard enough for her to yelp, more with surprise than pain. Although, damn him, it stung.

"Take them out," he murmured, as if he hadn't just assaulted her. "Careful so they don't roll off the counter." He licked the sting, which made her shiver, and forget what point she'd been trying to make. "Okay. Now break them— No. Not like that. Here, let me show you." He demonstrated with one hand, deftly breaking the shell in two, then dropping golden yolk and glistening egg white into the bottom of the bowl. "Now you try. Use both hands. Crack it on the side of the bowl—gently! That's it. Now the rest. That'll work. Here, use the shell to get out the broken bits."

He slid the towel off his shoulder to wipe his hands in front of her, then tossed it on the counter and slid his fingers under her shirt to rest over her belly again. Oh, God. Bare skin to bare skin. His fingers felt rough and cool on the smooth skin of her belly. Her skin was on fire.

Her hands weren't exactly steady, so there were a lot of broken shells in the mixture. It took awhile.

"That's good." He wiped her fingers on a dishcloth. "Drop those cubes of butter into the pan so they can melt while we deal with the eggs." His other hand skimmed under her shirt, then unfastened the front clasp of her bra.

"Damn it, you studied for this test," she said on a half laugh, half sob, as his fingers curled around to cup her breast. His lips feathered down the back of her neck. "With Misty Rosetree as incentive, I practiced on my pillow for weeks when I was in eighth grade."

The damp warmth of his tongue teased her skin as he squeezed her nipple until it became a hard, tight bud. The sensation shot directly between her legs, where she was already wet and pulsing. "It"—Mia blinked her fuzzy vision clear—"paid off."

"By the time I was proficient . . ." he murmured, as if in casual conversation—as if his fingers weren't skimming under her skimpy bikini panties so that her entire body buzzed— "she'd started dating the quarterback."

"Her . . ." He combed his fingers through her pubic hair. Mia's face flushed. She hadn't had a Brazilian in months. He must think her prehistoric—"loss."

"Christ, your damp silk is a turn-on."

Mia blinked, instinctively canting her hips so his finger would get more serious. Instead he stroked and petted until her back teeth hurt. "This is like finding diamonds when I expected silver. Grab those two forks and hold them like . . . this." He removed the fingers toying with her nipple to demonstrate how to grip them in a hand with no motor functions because all her attention was focused on the sensation of the fingers of his right hand down her shorts.

"Now whisk."

He tilted the glass bowl, letting the eggs slide slowly into the sizzling butter in the warm pan. "Add salt and pepper. A bit more."

A finger glided in the wetness and Mia bit back a small moan as he inserted just his fingertip into the seam. Everything inside her coiled. Tighter and tighter.

He kissed her throat, inserting two fingers all the way, as he whispered, "Don't come," right in her ear.

"Don't—" As she started spasming around his fingers, he withdrew his hand, so his touch was on the swollen folds of her sex, butterfly-light. Mia thrust her hips forward but, off balance, she teetered and grabbed for his wrist.

"Pick up the spatula and fold. Don't stop, just keep them moving around slowly. That's it." Three fingers curved deep inside her, not changing rhythm as her muscles clenched unbearably. His fingers withdrew, leaving her teetering on the very edge of a climax.

Mia tried to think of something else as her body screamed and begged for release. Scrambling eggs wasn't complicated, she thought desperately, tightening her thighs to trap his hand. But then, she'd only ever eaten them, never watched their preparation. And never with a man finger-fucking her.

Dear God. Breakfast would never be about food again, not with this memory hitting her whenever anyone mentioned eggs.

Every time she was just about to crash over the edge, he

withdrew his fingers to give her another instruction on whatever the hell was in front of her. Commanding her to focus, commanding her not to come.

"You know," she snapped when he withdrew his fingers yet again, "I don't do instructions well. I can leave you to your devil eggs and run upstairs and . . . and . . . Oh, God—" She squeezed her eyes shut as he twirled his fingers deep inside of her, the exquisite sensation of release hovering like a dewdrop shivering on the edge of a leaf.

"Don't." He bit lightly at the tendon standing out in her neck, and she shuddered so damn hard that she dropped the spatula onto the stovetop with a clatter.

"Pick it up. Then bacon in the oven." Cruz gave her maddeningly detailed instructions on how to lay it out, and what freaking temperature to set the oven.

She. Did. Not. Care!

He didn't step back, so when she bent over to open the door and shove the baking sheet inside, he was *right there*. The long, hard ridge of his penis pressed against the crack in her ass.

There.

But not.

"Is there a valid reason you're tormenting me like this?"

"I'll stop if you don't like it."

"I like it. I like it a lot. I'd just like it to be faster!"

"Too bad. This is all about cooking the eggs slowly. Give them a slow swirl with the spatula. . . ." He moved his fingers inside her tight, pulsing sheath as he caressed her breast,

71

strumming the nipple with the edge of his nail, learning the shape and heft of her breasts in turn. "Slower. There you go. See how they're fluffing up? Glistening with all that succulent butter?"

Mia's head fell back against his shoulder, and she hissed out, "Bastard."

"Keep stirring. Don't let them burn."

"It's a good thing we're preparing scrambled eggs," she managed to pant out. "Because by the t-time we get around t-to eating the damned things, I'll be so old I won't have any teeth! They look ready. Can we—ah! Eat—" She hissed in a breath when the climax was so close, she knew she was about to crash and burn. A sheen of perspiration prickled her skin. Every nerve ending was like a little antenna tuned to the slightest brush of his fingers. "Now, damn y—"

Each rhythmic manipulation of his fingers, each twist and thrust, left her breathless, gasping for air as her body torqued higher and higher. The intensity built and built, like a roller coaster, dragging her higher and higher, swelling with each deep, slick stroke of his clever fingers, sliding over her clit, making that hot spot ultrasensitive.

Her hips moved restlessly, although he had her imprisoned between his body and the hard bar of his forearm. Almost sobbing, her internal muscles clenched tighter and tighter. Mia dug her nails into his forearm.

All thought went completely out of her head as he pressed the heel of his palm firmly against her clit, pulling her tightly against the rock-hard bar of his penis. As he slid his fingers deep inside of her, and with his rough, hard palm rubbing against her, she screamed as he brought her to a rolling, never-ending climax.

Sitting on mismatched chairs at the table, Mia vaguely gestured to the ceiling with her fork. "We can go upstairs and take care of your problem. I don't know a lot about cooking, but I think I can figure out how to keep your water boiling for a while."

He didn't smile. Did he ever? But his eyes lightened, and she almost caught a look of amusement in the inky depths. "That was your cooking lesson for the day. Maybe later you can teach me something."

Arrogant bastard, she thought without heat. "I'm never going to look at an egg the same way again." She forked up a pile of egg curds on the tines. Light, fluffy, and buttery. Mia hummed her appreciation as she swallowed. She was absolutely ravenous.

"Good?" he asked.

"Incredibly."

He reached down to fondle his dog's floppy ear. "Some things are well worth the wait."

"And some things can be accomplished in half the time." There was no point in reminding him what her request had been the night before. He clearly wasn't a man who took instructions well.

Dog and master were sweet to watch, not that Mia thought Cruz was sweet. *Picante* was more like it. As for Oso, Mia had no idea what breed he was. Medium-size, he had soulful black eyes, short golden-brown fur, and a long, expressive tail.

Fascinated by the way Cruz's large hand soothed his dog, Mia thought, *If I was scared, I'd nuzzle against your hand, too.* She sat transfixed, watching man and dog for a suspended moment, then got up to go to the cupboard and take down a bowl. Running water into it, she then placed it on the floor nearby, grateful to have something to do that didn't involve jumping on her guest and attacking his mouth.

"What kind of dog is he?" she asked, taking out the steak she planned to have for dinner that night, and on her salad for lunch tomorrow. She roughly cut it into large pieces and put the dog's breakfast on a china plate beside the water bowl. Resuming her seat, Mia glanced at the clock on the stove.

He'd kept her on her toes, off balance in more ways than one, for a good twenty minutes! She didn't even like foreplay. It had always been an irritating waste of time when she just wanted the main event.

Foreplay was going to be hard to turn down in the future, now that she'd acquired it. Who knew?

The dog came over to him, then rested his head on Cruz's knee, looking up at him adoringly. "Shepherd mix. What do you want me to tackle first?" he asked, leaning back in his chair.

Me, she thought, unbidden, and felt her face go warm. "I bought the house a month ago. I was looking for a fixer-up, because I wanted to try my hand at various home improvements. The house is solid apart from the roof, which the inspector apparently didn't bother to inspect. I have a list."

"I'll take a look."

Getting up, she crossed the kitchen, feeling his eyes on her as she took the plain yellow legal pad from beside the sink, then returned to the table to hand it to him.

"I presume the roof is the top priority." He indicated the three buckets across the room, one of which the dog was drinking from instead of the bowl she'd given him.

"Anything I can't do myself is a priority— No. No, that's not true. I'm in no hurry—I suppose I shouldn't have said that. You work by the hour, right?"

"Yeah, but I take exactly how long it requires to do the job." He held out his hand.

Just looking at his large tanned hand, with its ridge of callus at the base of his fingers, and the short, square nails, turned Mia on.

"Let's see that list."

She handed him the notepad. "I've contracted with a company in New Orleans to replace the roof. But they're backed up and can't be here for at least two weeks. I told them I'd let them know if I was still interested then." For all she knew, she'd be back in San Francisco.

Where would Cruz Barcelona be?

Who would he be teaching how to make French scrambled eggs?

It annoyed her that the very thought of him with another woman annoyed her.

"I can do some patching. At least enough to get rid of the collection buckets." Looking down, he frowned. "LTD? SWS? You've got those checked off already. What are they?"

Learn to drive: check. Sex with a stranger: check. "My to-do list." Snatching the pad from him, she flipped the page to the list of improvements she couldn't manage or didn't want to even try herself. "Here you go. Here's the to-do list for the house."

Mia drank her fill looking at him as he skimmed the long list. His eyelashes, straight and inky black, were tipped with silver. His mouth drawn with mostly straight lines, but tempting as sin. Broad shoulders stretched out his blue T-shirt, which clung damply to the stair steps of his abs before disappearing into his jeans.

Mia shifted on her chair, ostensibly to point to the paper he held. Moving was not a good idea, as it got things excited all over again. She leaned forward a little to let her T-shirt blouse out so he couldn't see her erect nipples. "Can you do all that?"

"Yeah." He glanced up at her. "I'd tackle the roof first thing, since the rain seems to have stopped . . . unless you have other priorities?"

"It would be nice not to have to get up all night emptying buckets. Excellent. When can you start?"

"Now."

All Mia's girl parts contracted, watching Cruz's deft fingers find just the right spot to make the dog close its eyes and lean against his thigh with a massive sigh. She knew exactly how the dog felt.

"Before you get started, I have a pole in the garage. I'd like it taken upstairs and installed."

"A pole?" He gave her a lazy, amused look. Still no real smile. Mia cocked her head, trying to imagine him laughing. She couldn't. "You training to be a firefighter? A high jumper? Ballet?"

"It's an exercise pole. It's in a green box near the garage door. Bring it upstairs, and I'll show you where I want it."

"I'll take care of it, then I want to tackle the roof while the rain holds off." He scanned the list. "I'll save inside jobs for when it's raining, and tackle the porch steps after I handle the roof situation. I'll need supplies. Noticed a hardware store on the way into town. I'll hit that when we're done here."

Today was a day of firsts. Mia had never let anyone set her priorities for her. She was a full-steam-ahead kind of girl. All ducks in neat, orderly rows, all tasks numbered, deadlines set. After last night, followed by this morning's shockers, she was prepared to throw them all out the window and substitute every one of her tasks for sex.

"I'll change and go into town with you—I need to pick up a few things at the market." He wasn't going to be satisfied with yogurt and eggs, no matter how slowly they were cooked. And his dog needed something other than her dinner.

"Change? We're not going into combat. You're fine the way you are."

Mia narrowed her eyes. No one ever talked to her that way. But, of course, he was right. "Looking 'fine' wasn't exactly my goal," she pointed out dryly. "But we're not going to the prom."

He cupped his coffee mug between his broad palms and gave her an assessing look. "Did you go to your prom?"

"No." Stanford Long had asked, and then not shown to pick her up. He'd just wanted to humiliate her and bring her down several pegs because she'd refused to sleep with him. If only her classmates had any idea how insecure she was, they could've saved themselves the effort.

She'd worn a Vera Wang strapless and a million dollars in jewelry. The most minimalist her stylist was willing to go. She'd sat on the bottom step of the double sweeping staircase waiting until after eleven, when she knew for sure he wasn't coming.

Mia hadn't mentioned the humiliating event to a soul, not even Todd. From then on, all dates were on her terms, or no terms at all.

"You must've been a pretty damn cute teenager."

"I—I was put together." Orthodontics, colored contacts, facials twice a week, stylist at the house every day—a Blush product from head to toe.

"'Put together'? What the hell does that mean?"

"Well-groomed," she told him wryly, desperately wanting to comb her fingers through that mane of dark hair hanging to his shoulders and falling over one eye. Thick and lustrous, it had a slight curl to it that should've made him look effeminate but instead made him look like a sexy pirate. "What about you?"

He was fit and athletic. Probably from working construction and not from working out in a gym. There didn't appear to be an ounce of fat on him; his muscles were rock hard and clearly defined beneath the still-damp fabric of his T-shirt. "I bet you were on every sports team."

"For a while, yeah. But no prom, or even the thought of one. I stopped going to school at fifteen, and spent most days with a street gang to further my education."

Mia was appalled. Her childhood had been devoid of affection, and even though her schoolmates were all in a similar income bracket, her shyness and her excessive wealth separated her from everyone else. She'd been excruciatingly lonely, but she'd always felt safe in that ivory tower. The thought of having that safety stripped away was unthinkable. "You ran away from home?"

"First my mother died, then my father died a few years later."

"That's terrible. Where did you go? Who took care of you?"

He gave her a surprised look. "I took care of myself. I wasn't going into the foster system. My father had a small construction company, and I worked for him after school from the time I was strong enough to hold a hammer. After he died, the company folded, and I did whatever construction jobs I could find. Paid mostly under the table, since I was underage, then I just kept going." He shrugged. "I'm bringing a shitload of experience to your table."

CHERRY ADAIR

"Good to know. And on that positive note . . ." She stood up. She didn't want to feel empathy for this man. He was a stranger, a sexy stranger, but a stranger nevertheless. If not for some lunatic trying to kill her so she had to bide her time here, she and Cruz would never have met. "Let me show you where that exercise pole is."

Chapter Five

 andy's Diner served frozen entrées and store-bought
baked goods. According to the sign in the window, all
of it was "homemade." If the coffee shop had been in New
York or San Francisco, it would've been cleverly marketed as
eighties-style kitsch. Mia suspected the cheap red plastic furniture and beige Formica in Sandy's Diner was just a result
of bad taste rather than a deliberate attempt. The place was
empty when she and Cruz stopped by on the way back from
the hardware store before returning home.

She'd happily driven her new truck to the hardware store.
Good practice, because the wide streets were pretty much
empty, and she tended to get distracted and go wherever her
eyes led her.

Mia glanced out the diner window, observing an elderly
couple walking by, holding hands. "Before coming here"—
she turned to look at Cruz across the table—"I had no idea
towns like this still existed."

His folded arms were propped on the table, and sunlight
made the dark hair on his tanned skin shine silvery. She liked
the look of his arms. Strong, muscled, tanned. A working-

man's arms. She dragged her attention back to his face, where the distraction was ten times worse. The man had his own gravitational field, and it was hard to keep her hands off him.

The light tangled in his five-o'clock shadow and tipped his eyelashes with the same silvery gloss as the hair on his arms. Mia had to lick her parched lips to get any words out. Breakfast seemed like a dream now. Watching his mouth move as he talked made every nerve ending in her body lean forward. She wanted to touch. Be touched. God. She hunched because she could feel her nipples hardening just from thinking about having him inside her again.

She cleared her throat. "Everyone knows everyone else's business, and a new, single woman in town is cause for gossip." She'd decided that the less interaction she had with the town's people, the better. The last thing she wanted was for anyone to recognize her from the news media.

"Let's see how fast they learn I'm parked outside your house."

His eyes weren't dark brown, they were a rich deep amber. The color of her father's best double-malt scotch, just much, much darker. "Parking isn't a crime," she pointed out. "Not even here. I don't think—"

"So," the owner of the restaurant addressed Cruz, having pushed aside the only waitress to get to their table, and effectively cutting Mia off midsentence. "You checked out of Gracie's to go stay at the old Broussard place, huh?" She held a notepad under a beefy arm and the coffeepot in one fist, her small inquisitive eyes darting between Mia and Cruz as she waited for the salacious details. "Pretty isolated out there for a single gal alone."

The insinuation floated over Mia's head. Sandy could use both Blush's Fountain of Youth intense hydrating gel and the Forever Young eye cream. And apparently she'd had her hair butchered by the same walk-in salon Mia had gone to, because her bleached hair looked as though a rat had gnawed at it. Lacquered and gelled, bleached and spiked, she thought she was something else.

"He's not staying *in* my house. He's staying *at* my house," Mia clarified, her tone cool, feeling bitchy and not giving a shit. The woman should take some etiquette lessons. "I've hired Cruz to do some repairs." She never explained herself. To anyone. But she didn't want to arouse suspicion in town while she lived here. She didn't give a damn what they said about her after she left.

"Are you going to bring us cups so we can have some of that coffee?" she asked, much more polite than she felt. "And menus and silverware, too, while you're at it?"

Without looking behind her, Sandy snapped her fingers at the hovering, painfully thin waitress, who, with the cook, watched them from kitchen doorway. "You hired my brother, then let this man fire him for no God-given reason. Just so you could have a good-looking man around the place? Marcel's a hard worker. You shouldn't have done that."

Mia gave Cruz a puzzled glance and raised a brow.

"Latour," he told her. "He was drunk at eight a.m."

"He's a good man." Sandy took a step closer so they got a

good whiff of her eau de cigarette. "He's got his troubles, but he's a good man. Got a wife and kid to feed. He wasn't yours to fire."

"Then he can come by tomorrow when he's sober," Mia asserted. When had Marcel come— Ah. The Jehovah's Witness.

Sandy cocked an ample hip, gaze fixed on Cruz as she said pointedly and completely out of left field, "That camper ain't got no faculties."

Faculties? Between the accent and the word, Mia was puzzled for a second. *Facilities*.

"And you would know this how?" Cruz asked.

"I just happened to be over at Te Jean's mechanic shop to pay for the outboard he fixed for my ol' skiff. He asked me to take a look in your camper, see if I could find *gros chat*, his big, mean, ugly cat who's always going missing. Sure hated to have it get stuck in your camper and die from the heat. That wouldn't be good, no. That would be a mess, yeah."

"You know what curiosity did to that cat, right?" Cruz said mildly, with a thin smile that should've warned the woman to shut up and do her job. It was a smile Mia recognized. She'd caught it in her own mirror a few times.

"*Mais*, it's why I was in the camper. Weren't you listening, man? You may be pretty, but you must have bad hearing."

"Cups, coffee, menus," Cruz said, maintaining his polite expression. "We can always take our appetites into Houma."

"Here's Daisy with your settings. I'll tell Marcel Miss Mia wants him to come by tomorrow." She shot Mia a pointed look.

"Only if he's sober," Cruz added, as Sandy stomped off.

Mia shook her head. "Charming."

"Isn't she, though?" Cruz absently shoved a shiny hank of dark hair off his face. It reached his shoulders but was clean and healthy-looking, and extremely touchable. Mia curled her fingers on her lap. "I'll keep an eye on Latour," he said, taking a pen out of his pocket. "Make sure he doesn't become a problem."

Oh, God. That look could make a woman's underwear vaporize. Mia crossed her bare legs under the table, shifting in her seat as she squeezed her thighs together to mitigate the throbbing ache. The pressure just made the ache worse. What would he do if she grabbed him by the hand, hauled his ass out of the diner, and suggested parking the truck in a nearby alley so she could get number eleven, *Sex in public*, out of the way?

Mia thought of something the woman had mentioned earlier. "Who or what is the 'Gracie's' you checked out of?" Some sexy blonde, she bet. Feeling a pinch that couldn't possible be jealousy, more likely hunger pangs.

He plucked a paper napkin out of the holder and doodled down as he talked. "My truck broke down yesterday. Had to have a place to stay while it was being repaired. Gracie's is the local B and B. Expensive. The bed in the camper will do me while I'm working out at your place."

Mia bit her tongue before offering that he could do *her*, in her bed, for a few days. "There's a bathroom downstairs; you're welcome to use it—whenever."

"Yeah, thanks, I was going to ask."

Mia thought of being in bed and hearing him downstairs, naked in the shower. Dear God, she was turning into a sex maniac.

She watched his hand as it moved quickly over the paper napkin. He wasn't writing, he was drawing. "Can I see?"

Wordlessly he handed it over. He'd sketched in incredibly few pen strokes a squinty-eyed, overweight rat with bouffant hair and a sly smile. "The likeness is amazing." Mia smiled. "You could do sketches like this for a living."

"It's just a hobby."

"May I keep it?"

He shrugged. "Never know when you might need to mop up a spill."

"You're being too modest. You have a real talent. Have you always been interested in art?"

"That isn't art, but yeah. I guess. I like some stuff I've seen, hate others. Art's subjective, isn't it?"

"It is. My cousin likes strange shapes and angles and what I call 'angry' paintings with bold slashes of bloody red and oddly placed eyeballs." Thinking of Todd made her miss him. She would've enjoyed sharing the Louisiana experience with him, though he would've gotten hives at Sandy's coffee shop. "I tend to go for color and texture. But I'm not a connoisseur by a long shot. I just like what I like."

"Elvis on black velvet?"

Mia laughed. "I'm more into dogs playing cards."

He almost smiled. His lips didn't curve, but his eyes lit up in amusement. "To each her own."

"Ready to order?" the waitress asked, pouring coffee. When they said they needed a minute, she said she'd get back to them, then scurried back to her vantage point with the cook and the owner, who glared at them while she talked on her cell phone.

"Nice to know I wasn't singled out." Mia straightened her silverware with a rueful smile. "Sandy doesn't like you either."

"She hasn't liked anyone since her boyfriend got her pregnant with quadruplets, then ran off with the local cheerleader in 1962."

"I guess Te Jean told you that, huh?" Mia laughed at his deadpan delivery. He made not smiling sexy. "Let's order before she poisons our food."

Cruz called the waitress back and they ordered burgers. He spread his arms out across the back of the banquet seat, perfectly relaxed. And why shouldn't he be? He wasn't pretending to be someone he wasn't, nor was he hiding in plain sight.

Mia mimicked his earlier pose, folding her arms on the table and leaning forward. She wanted to touch him so badly she could feel the nerve endings in her fingertips prickle with anticipation. "I've never lived in a small town, have you?" That was non-incendiary, wasn't it?

"No, and you can see why. Everyone is in everyone else's business."

It stunned Mia to realize that while she felt as taut as a bowstring just looking at him sitting across from her, three feet away, he was as relaxed as one of Blush's sexy male models, laid out like a buffet to sell cologne.

"What made you chose Bayou Cheniere to put down roots?" he asked, clearly in no hurry to return to the house to fix the roof.

"I was tired of big-city living," she began, easily telling him the lie. "Getting tired of the rat race."

"What do you do for a living?" He poured a waterfall of sugar into his cup, stirring as he watched her. It was almost as though he were searching through interesting files in her brain.

Mia shrugged. "Nothing too interesting. I work in a department store in Milwaukee." She'd toured the Blush departments of several stores there over the years. "Cosmetics. My grandmother left me a little money and I want to take some time to decide what to do with my life." Not too much information, if she wanted what she was telling him to sound believable.

"Louisiana's a big jump from Milwaukee."

"I figured a change was as good as a holiday." So not true. She was a fish out of water here, and intensely missed much of her real life. She was here because she had to hide and this was the most unlikely place anyone would think to look for her. If she didn't at least have the structure—however loose it might be—of her list to focus on, she'd already have gone mad.

She missed the rushing to meetings, the juggling of a hundred issues at once. The noise and electric heartbeat of San Francisco. While Bayou Cheniere was absolutely nothing like living in that big cold house on Nob Hill, the silence and isolation here for the past month made her feel the same as she had growing up. Alone. "I saw the ad for the house. It looked as if it needed some TLC, I had the time . . ."

Cruz shot her another not-quite-smile, which made her heartbeat kick up and her mouth go dry. "That place needs a lot more than a little TLC."

"I'll give her what I can and go from there." Mia realized she hadn't taken her attention away from his sexy-as-sin mouth, and that devastating promise of a smile dragged her attention back to his face. With a brief stop at the impressive outline of his pecs under his T-shirt, unfortunately now dry. "Are you a city or country boy?"

"Mostly city. Small towns have their own charms, but"—he shrugged—"not my thing."

She tried to detect an accent, but she couldn't tell if he had one or not. "And yet, here you are. Why?"

"Why not? I can do my work anywhere. Just figured between jobs I'd travel around, see the country. Experience different places and people. I was heading to New Orleans when the truck broke down. Bayou Cheniere is as good as anywhere. As long as I can put gas in my truck and eat, I figure I'm here as long as the work lasts."

"No permanent home?"

"The camper for now. So far I haven't felt the urge to put down permanent roots. I was in the military for a while. Got to see the world, in a manner of speaking."

The military could mean he was on permanent KP duty peeling potatoes. But somehow Mia didn't think so. He seemed always alert, even when he appeared relaxed. His bearing was that of a man quick in his reflexes, fast on his feet.

He shrugged. "I like the freedom to pick up and go whenever the mood strikes me."

"Leaving a string of broken hearts behind you?" Mia kept her tone light. Of course he left a string of broken hearts behind him. He was a man constantly on the move. But a man who looked and acted as he did would always have women falling at his feet. She'd be wise to remember that for the duration.

His eyes held hers. "I never make promises I know I won't keep."

"An admirable trait."

The waitress returned with their burgers, greasy fries, and more coffee, then ambled off slowly. Mia suspected that all three of the people behind the counter were straining their ears to hear their conversation.

He shrugged again. "What about you? What brought you to Bayou Cheniere, Louisiana?" He glanced out the rain-spattered window, then back to Mia. "Not the weather, I presume?"

She smiled, wanting to reach out to touch the stubble on his jaw. She'd felt it on her breasts and inner thighs the night before. She wanted to feel the abrasion again. Soon. Now.

"I don't mind the rain. This is a bit of a change of pace for me, I must admit. But I'm enjoying the differences."

"How long are you planning to stay here?"

"As long as it takes." Until whoever was after her was caught.

"As long as what takes? Getting the house in livable shape?"

"Something like that."

Cruz picked up his mug. "Let's drink to intriguing en-counters and interesting destinations. *Bon appétit*."

They clinked simultaneously raised coffee mugs.

It felt, Mia thought, feeling a little silly, exactly like a first date.

Two o'clock in the morning and no pounding rain to mask his footsteps. Cruz paused at the top of the stairs in the semi-darkness. He listened to the sounds of the house settling. A creak in the wall a few feet from him to the right. A groan somewhere near the window. The warm breeze added to the hushed night sounds. A tree branch *skritch-skritch-skritch*ed as it rubbed against the siding in the warm breeze. The rustle of leaves of the live oak outside her bedroom window.

While looking for her computer that afternoon, he'd taken care of the two creaking top stairs and the loose board outside her bedroom door. Mia had been down in the kitchen study-ing a Cajun cookbook as if it held the answers to the universe. She looked damned adorable in dark-framed reading glasses.

He could've driven a tank past her and she wouldn't have glanced up to ask him where he was going. The woman had a laser-intense focus. She was like that with sex as well. Totally immersed, totally focused. Having that single-minded inten-sity directed at him had been an incredible turn-on.

If this were a normal world, he'd be looking forward to another cooking demonstration soon. But normal it wasn't. He had a job to do. And he was here to fulfill his contract and move on. She'd be just one more household accident statistic.

So, no more sex with the mark, he decided resolutely as he reached the top step—the one that had creaked so loudly that afternoon—and set his weight down carefully, no sound. Moonlight streamed through the window at the end of the long corridor, making a white runner of light down the long hallway.

The woman turned him on at a level he'd never experienced before, which made her far too distracting, when he, too, had to be completely focused. Sex didn't usually muddy the waters, but in this case . . . yeah, it did. Big-time. It muddied already opaque waters. His dick had to stay in his pants.

Decision made.

He still wanted to ascertain the verisimilitude of his report so he could do his job, receive the balance of his payment, and disappear.

It was a sound decision, and one he'd stick with.

In the meantime, the more time he spent with her, the fucking less he knew her. Seeing was not believing. Hell, Cruz Barcelona was an affable, easygoing guy. It was a mask. A persona he donned like an old coat.

Amelia Wellington-Wentworth's coat was just a hell of a lot prettier.

He needed her computer.

No more sex.

For the next few days, he'd eat her culinary efforts, not fuck her, and find her damned cyber secrets.

The gumbo-style chicken creole she'd fixed for dinner hadn't been bad. She'd primly informed him, blue eyes alight with satisfaction, that his shock and amazement was damned rude. All it took to produce a decent meal was to read the recipe and follow directions. It was sort of like chemistry, and not brain surgery.

She'd been a lot more talkative at lunch in the local coffee shop than she'd been alone with him in her kitchen over dinner. There was something a lot more intimate with just the sounds of their cutlery on the plates, and darkness encroaching against the windows, than sitting in a bright diner with curious eavesdropping locals.

It was pretty damned remarkable to Cruz that they could have so much to talk about when neither was who they pretended to be. Their alter egos liked each other. Wasn't that a fucking kick in the head.

Unprecedented.

Propinquity, that was all it was.

Lust, more like it. He wanted to strip her bare and take her on the kitchen counter again. Or on top of that virginal white comforter, wrists bound to the metal headboard.

A decision had been made. He had four days. He'd never taken more than twenty-four hours to fulfill a contract since he began this business fifteen years ago. His gut yelled one thing, but thus far he'd seen nothing to repudiate what his research made no bones about. Just because she was a good lay didn't mean she was a good person. Just because she amused him with her intensity as she tried to drive that big-ass truck, or had self-deprecating humor, it didn't mean she wasn't responsible for the deaths and exploitation of thousands of children a world away.

She could not blame those deplorable conditions on ignorance. She'd personally visited those factories several times in the past year alone. In fact, she'd been to Blush's manufacturing plant in Guangzhou just three months before she disappeared from public view.

Cruz fucking knew she was guilty as hell. Knew it. And yet—God damn it. He couldn't put his finger on what the hell wasn't right with her, the situation, some damn thing. And what the hell did it matter, really? Hundreds of kids in her care were dead. Directly due to her greed. It couldn't be any clearer than that.

He wanted this over. One way or the other. The woman was preventing his retirement. Holding the promise of long stretches of sugary beaches and swaying palm trees hostage with those big blue eyes, firm ass, and quirky sense of humor.

And the remote possibility that she wasn't anything like the woman he'd researched before accepting the hit.

He'd searched upstairs while she'd been downstairs, then, when he returned to the kitchen, watched her typing away on the very computer for which he'd been looking. She'd closed it and shoved the laptop aside to bake a batch of cookies, then to prep dinner. Cruz had circled that damned computer all afternoon. But she hadn't left it on the table. When she went upstairs, she'd taken it with her. The middle of the night was his only chance to retrieve it.

The house still smelled of garlic, onions, tomatoes, and sweat-inducing spices as he made his barefooted way into her bedroom. The scent of tuberoses, as faint as it was, assaulted his senses the moment Cruz stepped through the door, making him instantly hard.

He could hear her soft, even breathing as he padded closer to the moonlit island of her bed. Mia was a small, curled-up ball beneath the sheet, just her dark head exposed, facing away from him.

There weren't a lot of places to hide a laptop, and he did a visual scan of the large room. Bed. Two bedside tables indicating she liked symmetry, two easy chairs in the far corner, a futuristic standing lamp and a small table. A couple of doors. Bathroom. Closet.

Since she had no reason to hide her computer, Cruz slid open the top drawer of her bedside table. He'd seen the fraternity house–size box of condoms there earlier and had choked back a laugh seeing them in three sizes. She was expecting to have a lot of sex, with several different partners.

He liked sex, so why shouldn't she? And why the fuck did the thought of her having it with a whole fucking platoon of partners piss him off?

He didn't have the goddamned time for all this mental masturbation. The computer was in neither of the drawers in the bedside tables. He headed for the bathroom. Here he needed the light. Shutting the door, he ran the small Maglite over every logical surface. No computer. Exiting the bathroom, he hit the closet. By today's standards it was tiny, but she didn't have much in the way of clothes. Jeans, T-shirts. He checked her underwear drawer again. He'd had a boner after searching it earlier that day. Skimpy, sexy, gossamer thin. Wearing this underwear would still leave her practically naked.

No sign of the damned computer, but he commandeered some interesting toys on his way out. He moved silently across the room to stare down at her for a moment. Half her features were limned by stark white moonlight now, the other half dark and shadowed, hidden, secret.

She was a study in black and white.

He had very few rules in his life: Meet a client face-to-face. Hit only those who absolutely deserved to die. Never get emotionally involved with someone he'd been paid to kill. Hell. Never get emotionally involved. Period.

He liked his privacy. In every aspect of his life. He preferred observation to participation.

He wasn't involved with Mia Hayward–slash–Amelia Wentworth, but everything about her intrigued him on a purely physical level. She looked sweetly innocent and vulnerable as she slept, nothing like the quick-witted smart-ass she was when she was awake and on the ball. This woman wasn't vulnerable. She was confident, self-sufficient, and so fucking sexy that she made his dick salute just watching her sleep.

Why was she hiding in this backwater? What was going on in her life that someone was paying almost a million bucks to have her forever silenced?

He knew why he'd taken the job. The business in China. She was the woman who imprisoned children in deplorable working and living conditions a world away, where no one could see how she made those obscene profits for the Blush company.

But was that all she was? Wasn't she also the personality she showed to the world? The woman whose personal foundation donated millions to various charities every year, who'd built a breast cancer wing at a San Francisco hospital? All PR?

Either, either, or.

One hundred percent trouble.

He looked at the elegant line of her slender back, her skin milky pale in the moonlight. Her choppy hair tumbled around her head, parting erotically on her neck. Cruz wanted to put his mouth there, wanted to slide his hand over her narrow shoulders and fill his hands with her breasts, then take her from behind.

He wanted to fuck her without seeing her eyes. Without imprinting her features onto his synapses.

He did not want to have to touch her. This was where a sniper had the advantage. A shooter didn't have to touch soft, supple skin or smell warm female flesh. He wouldn't feel the tickle of her hair, or have the overwhelming urge to bury his face in fragrant curve of her neck.

Knee on the bed, he leaned over her, then splayed his open hand on her slender throat. Her skin, warm, silky-smooth, and fragrant with the scent of sun-drenched tuberoses, filled his brain and shot directly to his already erect dick.

The faint throb of her pulse beneath his thumb was tempting as hell.

It would be so easy to kill her now, and fucking well be done with it.

Too bad strangulation wasn't his thing.

Eyes closed, Mia tried to remain motionless, but she couldn't prevent the shiver, a tiny heated flicker of reaction to his touch. Cruz's fingers felt cool on her skin, but that wasn't why she trembled as if chilled. She'd been aroused, anticipating, waiting for what felt like hours for him to come to her bed.

When she'd heard him come into the house, she waited for him to come upstairs. Just knowing he was in the house aroused her. Breathless, she'd anticipated the creak of the top step.

When that sound hadn't come, she'd fallen back to sleep. Waking to find his hand at her throat, the sheet covering her pulled taut by the knee he'd placed by her hip as he loomed over, didn't scare her. Although, with some weirdo trying to kill her in San Francisco, it probably should. But that life seemed far away and insubstantial, when everything about Cruz was in Technicolor and so alive even her hair follicles tuned in to him.

Without turning her head, she whispered, "Are you going to strangle me, or make love to me?"

"'Autoerotic asphyxia' not on your to-do list?" Voice low and husky, he nudged up her chin with his thumb while circling her throat with his fingers. A shudder went through her. His breath felt warm against her temple. He smelled of fresh air, virile male, and soap.

The threat of unnamed danger hung in the air like a seductive fog. At his words, a faint smidge of alarm seeped in. Mia's mouth went dry. "Not on any list I've ever made, and I'm pretty positive I'd rather not."

When she rolled over to face him, his hand stayed against her throat. He looked large looming over her, watching her, dressed like a burglar all in black.

Even though she could clearly see his features in the white glow of moonlight flooding the bed, a frisson of fear shot through her. His eyes glinted like those of a nocturnal animal spotting its prey, and those eyes were focused on her.

"Definitely not," she told him firmly.

"The carotid arteries—here and here—carry oxygen-rich blood to your brain."

That oxygen-rich blood surged pleasurably through her veins, as he exerted a little more pressure to the rapid pulse lying just beneath her skin. She prickled all over as he said, low, his voice thick and suggestive, "When they're compressed—like this. . . ." His fingers pressed a little harder than was comfortable, and her heartbeat kicked up several uncomfortable notches. "The sudden lack of oxygen to the brain, and the accumulation of carbon monoxide increases feelings of pleasure. . . ."

Mia wrapped her fingers around his wrist and tried to push his hand away. "Don't. I can't focus when I imagine I'm going to be strangled to death."

"Strangled to intense climax."

Her fingers tightened. She dug her short nails into his skin.

Hard. "My safe word is *Fucking get your hands off my throat, Barcelona*." She used the low voice Amelia Wellington-Wentworth had perfected for boardroom business. The *Don't fuck with me, or I'll fuck you over* voice.

He lifted his hand.

"My cousin died playing that game. It freaks me out." She *could've* had a cousin who played the game. It certainly freaked *her* out.

"How about this?" His obsidian eyes gleamed as he snapped one mink-lined handcuff around her right wrist and, before she could react, the other around her left wrist. Then attached both to a swirl in the wrought-iron headboard. "Better?"

Better was relative at this point. Where the hell had those come from? She was pretty sure not from his back pocket, since the black pants molded so closely to the curve of his ass. He was like a magician whipping out the cuffs. She hadn't seen that coming. Beneath the silky mink, the cuff felt hard and locked with a very final metallic clink.

Mia licked her dry lips. "I've never tried them, but I'm game." She had a pair just like them in her underwear drawer in her closet. She'd bought them online weeks ago, not having any idea when, if ever, she'd use them, but the titillation of thinking about using them had been fun.

Number twenty-three on her list.

Had he been going through her underwear? While that should have alarmed her, instead it confirmed that Cruz wasn't as immune to her as he liked to pretend. Perhaps he was thinking about her all the time, just like she was thinking about him.

He was a man of many talents

His lips twitched before he bent down to run his open mouth down her throat. "Do you want to pick another safe word?" he asked against her ear, voice amused. "*Fucking get your hands off me* is a bit long."

"How about *prick*?"

"That'll work." Smile wicked, he straightened and pulled his T-shirt over his head. She'd had sex with him multiple times, but she'd never seen him naked. Mia's heartbeat did a triple axel, and her mouth went dry.

Big, broad-shouldered, tanned, and with a sexy wedge of dark silky hair arrowing down to disappear into the waistband of his jeans, he was like something out of her deepest sexual fantasies.

Coiled power vibrated through him as he stood absolutely still. She wanted to stroke her fingers down those rock-hard abs, to free what pressed and pulsed behind the zipper of his jeans. His arms looked powerful, strong tendons snaked and twisted beneath his skin, bleached colorless in the moonlight.

Eyes black, mouth a thin line, he said, "Let's see what you have to offer me tonight." He tossed the sheet aside to get a full-length view.

The negligee she'd bought from a racy online catalogue was an absolutely plain tube. No ruffles, no embellishments. Just a simple, stretchy, sheer black sleeveless column clinging to every curve and valley, from throat to ankle.

Completely covered, her body was also completely exposed.

His gaze raked her from head to toe, and his smile turned superior and knowing. "Jesus. Better than naked. You expected me."

"You or a close facsimile," Mia teased, feeling giddy and breathless, and he hadn't touched her yet. "The UPS guy stops work at seven. I got bored waiting."

"I'm here to alleviate that boredom," he assured her softly, still damn well not touching her. "How would you like it?"

The tight buds of her nipples were painfully hard, and she was already wet anticipating his touch. "There's a menu?"

"Missionary-style? You on the bottom? Or me on the bottom?"

"Been there, done that." She shifted restlessly, arms drawn above her head by the cuffs. "What else you got?"

"I can eat you until you scream and pass out with pleasure."

"Scream and pass out?" She raised both eyebrows, practically panting with lust. "That sounds a bit braggy, but I'm willing to give that a try. Although I'd prefer to use my mouth on *you*."

"You like to be in control."

"Who doesn't?"

She saw the gleam of mocking triumph glimmer in his eyes as he murmured thickly, "You're not in control tonight, Mia mine."

Chapter Six

S he was not his, nor was she Mia, but those were minor points right now. She wanted him inside her. Now. "Are you toying with me like a cat with a mouse, or are you going to put your money where your mouth is?"

"Oh, I'm going to use my mouth all right."

"Will you be done not doing anything by the time my first UPS delivery gets here in the morning?"

"Are you always such a chatty smart-ass in bed?"

"Only when my mouth isn't otherwise occup—"

His mouth swooped down and crushed hers in a kiss that almost made her come there and then. It was wild and rough, a mating of mouths, teeth, and tongues, a mutual devouring that shocked her with its intensity.

The shudder that went through her body made her internal organs clench unbearably. Cruz Barcelona had some powerful sexual mojo.

One hand tangled in her hair, holding the back of her head in his palm, and the other swept in a rough, aggressive caress down her body to cup her mound. Her entire body felt like a giant sparkler lit up on the Fourth of July.

Mia found herself clasping her fingers together, wanting to use her hands on him, or herself, but, because of the cuffs, not having the capability. Cruz's tongue lashed against hers, giving no quarter as he explored her mouth. His hand closed around her breasts as he bit her lower lip, then licked the small sting before delving back to explore her teeth and tongue.

He lifted his lips a quarter inch from hers. "Breathe."

She couldn't. His kiss was sucking up all the oxygen molecules in the room. Desperate to touch him, she tugged at the cuffs. The headboard rattled. "Highly overra—"

His mouth was hard, his tongue relentless, while he kissed her as if he'd die if he didn't. At the same time he pinched her nipple between fingers that knew the exact amount of pleasure-pain to inflict to make her back arch. Mia's erratic breathing was swallowed by the kiss.

His hand followed the curve of her breast, explored the indentation of her navel, then cupped the curve of her hip as his mouth left hers. Her lips attempted to cling to his, but he took that clever mouth exploring. Along her throat. Over the upper curve of her breast. Taking her nipple in his mouth, he sucked hard through the gossamer-fine fabric. Her hips arched off the bed, and her head thrashed between her raised arms.

"Let me go." She twisted her wrists uselessly. "*Please*."

"Na-uh." He blew hot breath on the wet fabric, and Mia felt the sensation deep inside her. "You may be cool and calm, Mia, but your nipples haven't gotten that memo. They were hard just thinking of my touch, weren't they?"

She was far from damn well cool or calm at the moment. She had to touch him. Had to feel the flex and stretch of his muscles under her mouth. No. To hell with that. She wanted his lovely penis inside her, and she wanted it there *now*. "Fuck you," she panted as he tormented her to the point of distraction.

He laughed, then closed his teeth none too gently around her nipple. If he hadn't been lying on top of her, Mia's body would've broken in two as she arched. As it was, the pressure of his weight made her head thrash. Her fingers clenched around the wrought iron of the headboard, cutting into her skin.

"More," she demanded, finding it hard to drag in enough air. She didn't give a damn. More. More. Freaking more! Tugging at her bound wrists, she tried to break free so she could hold him where she needed him with both damn hands. The handcuffs, lined in luxurious mink, weren't simply decorative. They were damned effective at keeping her exactly where he wanted her.

She growled low in her throat in frustration. "Missionary—anything—is just fine. . . ."

His breath was hot and humid as he kissed her belly, filling both hands with her butt. He licked a damp circle around her navel through the diaphanous fabric so that she shuddered. His tongue skimmed the rim, then she felt his hot breath there. Her hips shifted restlessly. Eyes squeezed shut, she tried to stave off the climax hovering on the very edge of her consciousness. She was this close, and he still hadn't done anything. "N-now would b-be good."

Not in any hurry, knowing exactly what he was doing, the

son of a bitch took his sweet time. A habit of his. The glide of his mouth over the fine silk of her negligee felt as though he were drawing cool smoke across her heated body. Every nerve was sensitized, every muscle torqued tighter and tighter, and her head moved restlessly on the pillow as he kissed and licked his way down her body.

His open mouth explored her mound through the delicate fabric as he moved between her legs. His tongue explored the swollen damp seam until her head thrashed and she tried frantically to wiggle the fabric up her legs to give him free access. All it would take was one touch to her clit—*anything* inserted—and she'd melt into a puddle there and then.

He murmured "Uh-uh" against her heat, then bit lightly.

The cuffs rattled against the headboard as she bucked, trying to get him to get her nightgown the hell out of the way. "Do it. Please!"

The sharp nip of his teeth through the damp cloth at the juncture of her thighs made her cry out and arch her hips. Cruz ripped aside the thin fabric with hands and teeth.

Way past arousal, she was panting, her breath tight in her throat as liquid heat spread through her body. "That c-cost three hundred bucks."

"Open your legs."

"Dear God," she said, complying, "you're killing me. Just touch me. Even a finger will do the trick."

He chuckled, but he didn't touch. Fully clothed, he knelt in the V of her legs. "Knees up. Feet down. Do not come."

"N-not?" Holy crap! He must be joking. She was teetering on the very edge of a precipice; all she needed was for him to breathe on her, and she'd topple over the edge.

Mia had never been shy in bed. Never been modest when naked in front of her few-and-far-between lovers. Now, though, with his eyes intensely focused on her sex, with no more than moonlight lighting the room, and a sheer bit of fabric, she felt too exposed. Worse. Vulnerable.

She didn't realize that she had hesitated until he roughly shoved her legs in the position that he wanted them. Her first instinct was to close her knees but he had his hands there, making it impossible.

With her hands bound over her head and her legs immobilized, all she could do was watch him studying her damp folds. She started to come, and he wasn't doing anything but *look*. She felt the tightening of the first climax twist her body, and tried to keep her eyes open to watch him as it wound through her body, making her back arch and her body pulse frantically for release.

"Did you hear what I told you?" His voice was flat and harsh, his eyes so dark, so intense, she was sure they'd burn a hole in her skin. "Don't come until I give you permission."

"Fuck you."

"I won't fuck you if you come."

"Then use your fingers, damn you. Anything. *Touch* me, damn you."

His hot, humid breath caressed her belly as Cruz bent

his head, cool strands of his long hair caressing her skin. Mia sucked in a shaking breath, body tensed, anticipating his mouth closing on her. Instead he inhaled, breathing her in.

Body so tight she thought she'd shatter at any moment, her hips instinctively rose to get closer to his lips. "I hate you." Her voice wobbled with tension, and she meant it, as her body drew impossibly tighter and he did nothing more than fricking breathe in her.

The only sound in the room was their harsh breathing, and his was as ragged as hers. Her hips started moving as though he were inside her.

Cruz's dark eyes moved from her mound to her eyes, and he gave her a smile. Or maybe it was just a trick of the light, because she blinked and it was gone.

"You're gorgeous," he muttered before he slid down the sheets. He lay on his belly between her legs, using his shoulders to prop up her hips, and draped her legs over his back. He closed his lips over her clit, tonguing it as he slid two fingers inside her.

An orgasm hit her body in a rush of sweet release. He made it last, drawing it out like a maestro. Mia sobbed. The headboard rattled against the wall. Her heels dug into his back. Wave after wave hit her body.

She screamed as she came again, a never-ending succession of small and large, rolling waves that pounded into her until she arched and bucked against the pleasure-pain.

He was just getting started. Cruz's tongue, lips, teeth, and fingers brought new sensations to her. He pulled away when she was on the precipice, and increased pressure when she began to fade. She stopped counting her orgasms. She was melting. Dying from oral sex overload, if such a thing was possible. Drifting in and out of consciousness, and still he was eating her like a man who was starved, as though gaining sustenance from her juices, energy from her orgasms.

"You win," she said between breaths that didn't seem to provide enough oxygen. "I've screamed. I'm passing out with pleasure. You can stop."

In response, he shoved two fingers into her and bit her clit until she came with her most intense orgasm yet.

Finally, his face was over hers, his lips gleaming with her juices. He drew a deep breath, then closed his mouth over hers as he pounded his hard shaft into her. She felt his hands at her neck but couldn't think of anything but his cock filling her, exploding into her as she came again.

Cruz wrapped his fingers around her throat.

Mia passed out mid-climax.

It was a dirty trick, but he'd known exactly how much pressure to exert on her carotid.

More.

More would've killed her.

He'd pressed . . . less.

Last-moment decision.

Less.

She hadn't been hurt.

With the taste of her on his lips, he'd found her computer

on the floor on the other side of the bed, downloaded the hard drive, and was gone before she woke up.

Now he was in his truck en route to a busy McDonald's off the highway in Houma about fifteen minutes away. He'd left Oso in the house with Mia. He needed somewhere to access more intel away from prying eyes and to see what she had on her hard drive. No prying eyes and a solid, private Internet connection.

"Don't worry. I'll find her," Cruz assured the distorted synthesized phone voice of his client. Less than fifteen minutes after he pulled away from Mia's house, the call came in on the phone he kept in a lockbox under the floorboard of the truck. There was a gun in there, too, but he used that even less than he used the phone.

"I still have four days," he told his client, none of his irritation evident in his voice. He didn't like being rushed, and he sure as shit didn't appreciate being questioned or checked up on.

"With your reputation I expected it before then."

"Certainly," Cruz said, voice Sahara dry. "Give me her exact location and I'll take care of it immediately."

"She could be anywhere in the fucking world, for God's sake! Time's running out, asshole. Where are you now?"

"Somewhere she's not. I'll contact you when the job's done."

"You have until noon Friday or I'll hire someone else!"

Four days. Cruz disconnected. He was the best. He didn't mind being called an asshole—it wasn't the first time—but the client was pissed and panicky. Panicky meant not thinking clearly. The ticking clock was very real. He didn't have to like the client, nor was it necessary for him not to have the hots for his mark, in order to get the job done efficiently.

"What's happening on Friday?" he asked rhetorically, cruising down Highway 90 at just below the posted speed limit. Horse farms and cane fields filled the miles along the blacktop highway, and where there wasn't pasture or crop fields, there was bayou. "What will she do—or not do—that'll impact you?"

He had no idea who the client was. Couldn't, in fact, tell male or female on the phone. Cruz could recalibrate the synthesized voice with a little effort. But it wasn't the client who was the issue. The client wanted Amelia-Mia dead.

She was the issue.

Should've done it last night; then this would be a nonissue. He'd be on his way to the airport and a Brazilian beach.

First time he'd ever hesitated.

He tried to tell himself the hesitation was due to the odd feeling in his gut that the story his client had told him didn't add up. Or maybe it was just his dick insisting on some playtime. He was in uncharted territory with not knowing why the fuck he was hesitating.

There was no rational explanation for it at this point.

All he knew was that his dick sure was happy about it.

Cruz shook his head. He was getting sloppy. His gut—and most certainly his dick—had fuck-all to do with completing the job he'd accepted.

The only reason he hadn't finished the job was that murder opened up all sorts of drama he didn't need. He did accidents. Autoerotic asphyxiation, no matter how much fun, would bring the heat's spotlight on him, the strange new guy in town living outside her back door, his DNA all over her house. He could claim that was due to being her handyman, but now that he'd been all over her bedroom, in her closet, and in her bed, he doubted anyone would believe that he was just a handyman.

Fucking a woman sure could make someone suspect motive. Mia needed to have an accident, and now that he'd been stupid enough to do her every which way but dead, it needed to be a damn good, believable household accident.

He'd see if there was anything of interest on her computer, something that would finally convince him that she was exactly what and who he'd been told she was—a greedy, perverted, child-killing bitch—then do his job when he got back to the house.

After switching the bright yellow truck for a ten-year-old black Honda Accord he'd parked at a busy Walmart Supercenter, he drove to the fast-food place a few miles away, debated waiting in the drive-through line. He was hungry, and needed caffeine desperately. He'd had little sleep after he left Mia.

After finding the computer, he'd sat watching her until her breathing indicated natural sleep and not oxygen deprivation.

He'd gone back to the camper to sleep for a few hours, wanting to be back before she noticed he was gone for too long. Oso had already commandeered the narrow bunk, and Cruz had ended up hanging off the side of the uncomfortable mattress as the damn dog snored loudly right in his ear.

With the Honda smelling like grease and coffee, he pulled into the parking lot, already full with the breakfast crowd. Even this early, there was lots of movement: people lining up, cars coming in and out of the drive-through, people parked and talking on cell phones.

Great Internet access for the taking, and nobody to give a shit about one more guy wearing a cap, sitting in his car enjoying a couple of Egg McMuffins.

He inserted the thumb drive into his computer. No email, which was suspect, but not surprising. She'd done an efficient job of disappearing. The only things he found in her browser history were hundreds of how-to articles and various online purchase confirmations. There was a document with several hundred names on it, some of which had been struck through, and a to-do list with numbered items below in some sort of abbreviated shorthand.

Cruz tried to figure out what SWS and SIP might be, but he came up blank. Still, the list was the only incriminating thing on her computer. He copied the whole thumb drive onto his own computer to analyze later. "Fuck." Definitive proof, it was not.

In the end, the trip wasn't quite a waste of time. He checked his own computer. There was a reminder from his New York agent that he had another project to tie up. He hit Delete. More important than that other life were the two emails from an ex-lover whom he'd asked to put out feelers in Beijing. Lì húa Sòng worked in some secret capacity within the Chinese government. If anyone could give him answers, it would be her.

One had a grainy image of Amelia Wellington-Wentworth attached. Her arrival in Beijing ninety days ago. So that fact still stood.

She couldn't deny Blush's business dealings in China. She'd been there, several times this year alone. Since she'd been there, she must be aware of the illegality of hiring underage children as slave labor in horrific conditions. Slave labor without recourse.

The second email from Lì húa was a small news story in a local Chinese newspaper about an accident at a Guangzhou cosmetics manufacturing plant. Three days earlier a massive fire had broken out, more than three hundred kids had died, hundreds more suffered smoke inhalation and burns and were in critical condition. All because the stairwells had been blocked off so the kids couldn't sneak off somewhere to rest.

Fury swamped him. Jesus H. Christ. While she was playing house in Louisiana, had she been notified about the accident? If not, she was still responsible. If so, she was pretty fucking cavalier about the deaths of hundreds of children.

How the fuck did she live with herself?

Cruz started the car.

Decision made.

"You're up early," Cruz said, sounding annoyed as Mia walked into the kitchen. She'd had a moment when she'd woken at her normal 6:00 a.m. and Cruz and his truck were gone. But since he'd left the camper, and the dog's heavy head was resting on her hip, she presumed he'd be back. He wasn't the kind of guy—she didn't think—who'd abandon his dog and not say goodbye.

Of course, she didn't know that at all. For all she knew, she'd granted access to her house, and her body, to a serial killer. She should probably be worried about that. But that horse was out of the barn. If he *was* a serial killer, he would've done what he'd come to do by now.

The kitchen was redolent with the delicious smell of bacon and pancakes. "You made breakfast?" Anything less like a serial killer would be hard to find. Slouched on a bar stool, wearing nothing but low-slung jeans and what for him passed as a smile—in other words, he wasn't somber. Bare-chested and barefoot, his hair wet from a recent shower, he looked delectable.

All Mia's girl parts contracted, and she wanted to do him right there. Right now. "You were out and about early," she said, forking a pancake and a few strips of bacon onto the plate waiting for her beside the stove. Had he left her bed to go to another woman? She wondered if perhaps he had a local girlfriend, then was sorry she'd thought it. "I hope I'm not keeping you from a friend . . . ?"

"A friend?"

"Someone you know in town. I have plenty of time, if you'd rather start work another day."

"I don't know anyone in town. If you don't want me to stick around, say the word and I'll be out of here."

"Wow, you're touchy this morning. Did you get out of the wrong side of bed? Not my bed, but *a* bed?"

"I don't spend the night in any woman's bed. Unless we're still fucking when the sun comes up. But I consider that the night before."

Mia poured a mug of coffee, then added milk and sugar and leaned against the counter as she lazily stirred. He was snippy, and now she felt snippy. "I'll be sure to make a note of that."

"I had some errands to run before I got to work. I was going to make *baozi*, but I wasn't sure that would be something you'd eat, so I stopped for more bacon."

His mood switched off and on like a light switch. Mia immediately was wary. She read people pretty well—she had to. Was he hiding something? Lying? It was almost impossible to tell, he had such a poker face. "I'm a pretty adventurous eater," she said easily, sipping her coffee. "What's *baozi*?"

"Chinese dumplings, steamed or fried. Usually stuffed with pork, beef, and vegetables, with a soy- or chili-based sauce. Really good."

She sat down across from him at the island and imagined she could smell soap on his skin. She also had a quick flash memory of him on top of her right where her plate now sat, and felt her cheeks grow warm.

One look at his face told her that if he remembered that night, it wasn't having any impact on him now. So be it. After last night she'd felt her guard and natural caution slip down another notch or two. Now her shields were back. "I'll have to try them," she said easily, scooping up a handful of blue flower petals scattered on the counter. She put them beside her mug. "I like Chinese food."

"Ever been there?" he asked casually, holding his coffee mug in one hand as he idly fondled Oso's ear. The dog stood beside the tall bar stool, front paws on Cruz's jean-clad knee.

"No, but I'd like to go." Guy Stokes, head of manufacturing, had talked about opening a manufacturing plant in Beijing for a while, but they'd opted for Korea instead. "You?"

"Chinatown in various places, but never China. But I like Chinese food, too. Big fire there, I heard on the news this morning."

Mia supposed it was free association, but she checked. "In China?"

"Yeah, some big factory there burned almost to the ground. Three hundred kids under twelve years old who worked there in appalling conditions were killed. Doors to the exits were locked, apparently."

She pressed her palm to her chest in horror. "God, that's unimaginable. Aren't there laws against—well, laws in general there?" Mia could pretty much name every American law pertaining to employee safety, and the ones she didn't know, her staff did. And before Blush went into another country, laws there were put through the same diligent and rigorous process as at home.

"Kids work in unsafe conditions there. Families need their income—"

117

"I've read about this, Cruz, but can we change the subject? There's nothing we can do right this second."

"Yeah, you're right. Why should we give a flying fuck about little kids being subjected to inhumane treatment a world away?"

"That's not what I—" She decided then and there to add child labor laws to her taboo polite mealtime conversation, along with religion and politics. "I do give a flying fuck," she told him mildly. She didn't like that word, but had used it in and out of context more times in the last twenty-four hours than she'd done in her life. "But not here. And not now. I'd just like to enjoy my breakfast and start the day with something uplifting."

"We could hold hands and read the Bible together."

"What's wrong with you this morning? Do you want to discuss the hideous plight of those Chinese children? Fine. Give me facts, and numbers, and a solution. I have no idea what the hell you want from me, Cruz."

His expression was shuttered. "I imagine American-Chinese food and Chinese-Chinese food are vastly different."

Fine. If he was going to be impossible, she'd play along. "Let's make China a taboo subject, all right? I love Italian food. Preferably while sitting at a café on St. Mark's Square, pretending not to feed the pigeons."

"Never been there. Tell me about it."

They talked about food, and Europe, and the repairs to the house, but the conversation was strained, and Mia had no idea why. He'd been fine before she passed out from climax overload in the early hours this morning. What had happened between two o'clock and nine?

Mia was so relieved when the doorbell rang that she practically catapulted off the high stool. "That's Marcel. I'll go and get him started."

"Make sure the bastard's sober," Cruz cautioned. She heard him but didn't bother to respond as she went to the back door. Blush had hundreds of thousands of employees around the world. Her immediate staff in the San Francisco office was upwards of five hundred people. She didn't need advice from her handyman about the freaking gardener.

Latour brought his wife, Daisy, and their little boy, Charlie. Mia found busywork upstairs for Daisy, and sent Latour to get started trimming the trees on the graveyard side of the house. By the time she went back to the kitchen, Cruz was gone, leaving the dirty dishes in the sink for her to wash.

She had a list of projects she should be doing, but she felt lazy and out of sorts. Cruz's fault for starting her day on a weird note.

Sipping at an ice-filled glass of cold tea, Mia watched the little boy through the kitchen window as he wandered around the scrubby back lawn. The child seemed fascinated by the water.

About to go outside to warn him to stay away from the edge—and the ever-present alligator—she saw Cruz stride across the lawn.

He stood talking to the child for a few minutes, then

crouched down behind him. Picking up something from the ground, the man handed it to the child, then guided his arm. It took Mia a few seconds to realize that Cruz was teaching Charlie how to skip stones over the water.

The first couple of stones didn't go far, but Cruz kept talking and helping the child take aim at just the right angle. Eventually the stones skipped across the olive-green waters of the bayou. Mia smiled as she heard Charlie's triumphant yell through the open window.

She couldn't see Cruz's face, but he ruffled the child's shaggy hair and kept skimming stones. Mia stood in the kitchen for a good half hour watching them.

Cruz was good with children. A surprise. He seemed too contained, too serious a man, to bother with kids. Maybe it was just women he had a problem with.

Still, a man who had that kind of patience, and a willingness to spend time with a lonely kid, couldn't be all bad.

Maybe he just had a problem with *her*.

Chapter Seven

S he didn't want to talk about China. So she did have something resembling a conscience after all. Not much of one, though; she'd seemed more annoyed than appalled at the news of the factory fire. Presumably the kids were expendable and the factory could be rebuilt with little loss of end product.

No biggie.

Fuckit. He'd run out of excuses.

Cruz couldn't kill her now, with people wandering about the property and going in and out of the house. Latour had brought his wife with him. A rail-thin woman with downcast eyes and nails bitten to the quick, whom he recognized as the waitress from the diner the other day.

Mia hid her surprise at the gardener bringing his family and cheerfully put her to work cleaning upstairs. Latour's son—six? eight years old?—was a little shadow clinging to his mother's side.

Cruz actually liked small humans. More than he liked most adults, anyway. Charlie called him "sir" and Mia "ma'am," when he spoke, which was seldom, and so softly, one had to strain to hear him at all.

Cruz had watched the kid shuffling around near the water unsupervised, and had climbed down the ladder where he'd been about to start repairing the roof. The kid looked unhappy. Unfortunately he'd be a lot more unhappy if that gator slid up on the bank to grab some rays and found himself a small, slow kid to dine on.

He'd had as little to do with his own father as possible. In fact, when Cruz approached the kid, he flinched. A familiar and infuriating knee-jerk reaction to someone large and menacing looming over him.

Cruz had immediately crouched low, picked up a stone, and skimmed it over the scummy water, and kept it up as he made idle convo with the kid. Where'd he go to school? What grade? Did he know how to make a stone hop across the water?

He learned a lot in that half hour before Latour came around the house and demanded the kid come and help him.

Charlie's father got angry a lot. His mom cried. He hated when she cried; it made his insides hurt. When he was big he'd get a job to help Daddy with all the bills, then everything would be okay, and Mom wouldn't cry so much. And maybe his daddy would like him more, and not be mad at him all the time.

A familiar and painful mirror to Cruz's own childhood.

He knew how fruitless it was for a child to try to fix the problems of his parents. Latour drank, couldn't hold a job, and took it out on his wife and kid.

Cruz's father had been a functioning alcoholic. Violent, mean, and vindictive. He'd killed Cruz's mother, and Cruz was damned if he'd watch the same thing happen to this kid.

Unlike his own childhood, when his father's powerful and influential friends had turned their collective blind eyes to the cycle of abuse until it was too late, he'd keep an eye on the Latour family, and if he felt the situation warranted action, he'd step in.

Cruz went back up the ladder to his roof patching as Charlie worked alongside his father, picking up bundles of weeds in his skinny arms while Latour took a Weedwacker to the thick undergrowth on the bayou side of the house.

Cruz looked down on father and son for a few minutes. He added Charlie and his mother to the things he'd have to tie up before he left Bayou Cheniere, Louisiana. *I have your back, kid. Count on it.*

Mia, he knew, didn't give a tinker's damn about kids and their shit-awful plights in the U.S. or in China. She'd lied straight-faced. She was good at it. If he didn't have proof otherwise, he would've believed her.

The news reports he'd found had her in China, at the very plant where the children had died. But she claimed she'd never been there.

Son of a bitch. Cruz took out his frustration by pounding nails into slate shingles, skipping lunch, and feeling highly pissed off, without any mood improvement all day. He usually didn't think this much about killing people. Once he decided they were worthy of killing, the act of killing didn't fucking bother him. That he was bothered about killing Mia bothered the living shit out of him. The sun beat down. He scooped his hair back with a scrap of string, then tied his T-shirt around his head to catch the sweat. He enjoyed the sting of sun on his bare shoulders.

"You should at least drink something. It's hot."

Startled, Cruz whipped his head around to see Mia, eyes narrowed against the sun, only her head and shoulders visible above the eave.

He snatched the nails out of his mouth. "What the fuck are you doing up here? You'll break your goddamn neck, woman."

"Now see? I knew you'd be charming and happy to see me." Her voice was filled with amusement. "I've never climbed such a high ladder before. It's thrilling, in a terrifying way. Sort of like having sex with you when your hands are on my neck. Although now that I'm way up here, I'm not sure I can get down. I have cold lemonade in the kitchen—not fresh-squeezed; from concentrate—and a sandwich Daisy made, so it's really good. Are you going to stay up here and pout, or come down and take a break and rehydrate?"

"I'm a man. I don't pout. I have things on my mind."

"I'm a good listener."

"I don't need therapy. Get down before you fall."

"Will you come down and eat?"

"When I'm done with this section."

"Okay. . . ." She let out a little shriek as the ladder slid sideways a few inches. Cruz's heart slammed up into his throat, and he slid down the slope of the roof—to do God only knew what. She teetered almost forty feet above the ground, and he wasn't close enough to catch her before she dropped like a stone.

Grabbing the gutter with one white-knuckled hand, she bit her lip, squeezing her eyes shut as she and the ladder wobbled precariously, the metal rungs clattering against the gutter as she struggled to remain upright.

Cruz got close enough to clamp punishingly tight fingers around her wrist and could see the muscles in her arm flexing as she grappled to maintain purchase, feel the torque of the delicate tendons as she fought for balance.

Cold sweat bathed his overheated skin. "God damn it, why would you risk your life coming up here?"

"Hey, don't yell at me, I'm already having heart palpitations, buddy!"

Who the fuck isn't? "Can you get down by yourself?"

Sweat gleamed on her pale skin and, wide-eyed, she gave her head a small shake. "Can you magically put me on the ground? I just discovered I'm afraid of heights."

"Are you serious?"

"I really can't move." Her entire body visibly trembled, and she whispered, "Help."

He glanced over the yard. No one was in sight, for now. He could just push her. She wouldn't survive the fall, and no one would doubt that this was an accident. If she did survive, he could strangle her, quickly.

Fuck. Fuck. Fuck.

Damn it to hell. He just wasn't ready to kill her. Not yet.

"Stay where you are. Do not move."

"No problem," she mumbled, not moving even her lips.

Cruz slid down the shingles until his legs dangled on either side of her, his dick practically in her face.

Although she remained frozen in place, she gave a small smile as she stared at the bulge in his jeans. "Fascinating, but hardly the place, do you think?"

"Not the time to be a smart-ass. I'm going to climb over you. Hold on to the gutter and fucking stay still."

"Yes, sir."

"Suddenly you're good at taking orders."

"I'm better at giving them."

Yeah. He knew. "Hold tight and close your eyes." Without further warning, Cruz swung his body over the edge of the roof. The enormous irony of the situation was not lost on him. He might very well fall to his death saving her sorry ass.

His body slammed into her back as his feet found purchase on a rung several steps below hers. He closed his hands on the rung above her fingers, and got a mouthful of silky shampoo-flavored hair as he pressed her between his chest and the ladder. "Okay?"

"Couldn't be better." She rested her sweaty forehead on his forearm and took a shuddering breath. She wasn't faking it. She was terrified. "Can I open my eyes now?"

"I don't give a shit. Start moving down. One rung at a time, slow and steady. I won't let you fall."

"Wow. Good to know." She moved one foot down to the next rung in slo-mo as a full-body shudder ran through her. Which ran through Cruz.

She was terrified, so why the hell was *his* heart beating

so hard and fast? "Clearly you didn't think this through," he said, giving her time to calm her erratic breathing.

"Clearly not."

When there was absolutely no sign of another move, he snarled directly in her ear, "Move your goddamn feet. Now!"

"You can huff and puff until the cows come home, Barcelona. But it's not helping when you sound as though you'd rather toss me down on my head and get this over with."

No shit. "I have no patience for stupid people who make bad fucking choices. Move this hand down." He nudged her fist with his elbow until she released her death grip.

It was a painstakingly slow process moving her down the ladder. "Lean against me and wipe your hand on my pants," he instructed when her sweaty fingers slipped for the second time.

Death by sweat. He should add it to his repertoire.

She stopped. "Sorry." Dropping her head back to rest in the curve of his shoulder, she breathed a shuddering sigh. Her hair smelled of tuberose, lemon, and sexy, sweaty woman.

Get the fuck over it. Her. *Jesus.*

Her white knuckles maintained a shaky death grip on the rungs. "Can't open my fingers." Her lips barely moved.

Cruz sighed as he pried one hand off the rung beside her head. She sucked in a breath. "I've got you." Taking her wrist, he swiped her palm down the side of his jeans. Her bones were fragile, slender under his hand. It wasn't too late. . . .

"Great. Who's got *you*?"

"Same person who always does. Me." Replacing her hand

on the rung, he waited until her hold was secure, then switched hands himself and repeated the wipe-off with her other hand. "Halfway there. Move it."

They were still more than twenty feet from the ground, and the pained squeaks of the wobbling ladder confirmed what he already knew. Their combined weight exceeded the ladder's capabilities. If he didn't get her down quickly, they could both topple to the ground.

"I'd just like to stay here another minute or five."

"Didn't ask what you wanted. I've got things to do. I'm not going to hang from a goddamned ladder sweating for the rest of the day."

Mia rested her head on the rung near his hand. "I don't like being scared. I'm usually a very brave, daring kind of woman."

He waited.

She didn't move.

"Mia?"

"Give me a min—"

Angling his head, Cruz kissed her. No points for finesse, but several points for distraction. The position was awkward; the angle of his head almost jettisoned him off the ladder with her. But it did the job. Her fear tasted sweetly of lemonade as her tongue met his—fear evident in the caution when usually she'd dive in headfirst.

Her lips clung as he shifted his head. "When you kiss me my toes curl." Her voice was husky.

Her foolish trust rocked through his nerves and irritated

the piss out of him. *I'm here to kill you, woman. Be fucking afraid.*

"Let your toes curl on terra firma," he told her, unmoved. "Left foot. Right hand. Get down in the next sixty seconds and I'll let you tie me to the bed tonight." The lie tripped easily off his tongue. He didn't bother trying to figure out why the bull made him feel like shit.

It would make for an excellent alibi. Except he'd already decided to keep his fucking hands and dick away from her. Again. If she'd just stop watching him with hot blue eyes when she thought he didn't notice, and if he could just fucking stop thinking about the erotic things she did with her mouth, and the way her sleek body felt under his . . .

If her expression over breakfast earlier hadn't shown him she was remembering that first night in graphic detail, her rosy blush as she set her plate down on the center island had. It had taken everything in him to maintain his mild expression and not grab her, strip her, and screw her hard and fast.

No. More. Fucking.

Concentrate on the business at hand.

Brazil.

Her chuckle was strained, but she did move. "You're on."

With a tall glass of cold tea sweating on a coaster next to her, Mia highlighted portions of the booklet that had come with the *Sensual Pole Dancing* video, which was on Pause on her laptop as she read. She had "a secure pole, determination, and the desire to let go of her inhibitions." All of the above, and then some, thanks to Cruz.

While she highlighted, she enjoyed the low, constant roar of Marcel's lawn mower out on the front lawn, and the hum of the vacuum cleaner upstairs as Daisy cleaned. The little boy stood near the water, throwing sticks—she presumed at the alligator. She stood for a moment to see if he was in any danger. His feet, in tiny worn, faded blue tennis shoes, were at least eight feet away from the water's edge. The gator was nowhere in sight.

Satisfied that he wasn't in imminent danger of being eaten, Mia sat and resumed studying. Head on his paws, Oso lay panting under the table. Absently she rubbed his back with her bare foot; his sleek fur felt soft against her skin. He gave a loud groan.

She grinned, remembering the silky mink being stroked against her skin; she knew how the dog felt. She reached down to fondle his ear, as she'd seen Cruz do. "You're a very handsome boy, you know that?" He nuzzled her hand, and her heart melted a little bit. "Maybe Cruz will let me buy you when he leaves. Would you like to come home to San Francisco with me and live in a big house? The garden's pretty. I think you'd like running on that big lawn. You could chase the peacocks."

She'd never had a pet. When she was growing up, her father had made abundantly clear that the multimillion-dollar purebred horses in the family's racing stable weren't pets, his hunting dogs weren't allowed in the house, and her stepmother was highly allergic to cats, dogs, ferrets, parakeets—anything that squawked, purred, or barked.

And now she was so busy with business-related social events that she'd never ever considered a pet an option. Somehow Mia couldn't quite picture Oso fitting into that other life.

She needed to make some changes when she got back home.

She played the next bit of choreography and shook her head at the contorted position of the instructor, who was entwined, upside down, around the pole. Frankly, the contortions the woman's legs were in looked painful and not in the least bit sexy. Years of yoga classes might aid in this new endeavor, but Mia was pretty sure her body didn't bend that way; and, unlike the instructor in the video, she doubted her ability to smile while in any of those uncomfortable-looking positions. She hit Pause and found the corresponding text in the booklet.

Although pole dancing was definitely on the list, she was distracted by the sounds of other people being industrious, and the glorious sun-shiny afternoon—which, by the look of the sky, wasn't going to last much longer. And, of course, she was distracted by him. Cruz. Even though he wasn't in the room, he was nearby.

She couldn't concentrate on freaking pole dancing knowing that he might walk through the door at any moment, shirt off, muscles moving beneath tanned, damp, glistening skin. If Cruz's earlier promise of letting her tie him up was true, she couldn't wait for the Latours to leave.

She'd felt like an idiot earlier. She was genuinely petrified once she'd climbed to the top of that ladder. Who knew fear could be so incapacitating? Yet, the moment Cruz put his arms around her, she felt safe. Safer, at least. And, she now realized, it was the first time she could remember that she'd not only needed someone else's help but had accepted it willingly.

Tapping the orange highlighter on her chin, Mia glanced outside, checking on Charlie again as he played on the bank near the water. No sign of Cruz. The ladder was gone, and she didn't hear him hammering on the roof. His truck and camper were parked in the side yard, next to her truck.

The child's dark head was bowed, and he'd stopped throwing sticks. Shoulders hunched, hands shoved in his pockets, he looked the picture of dejection. Mia wondered if she should go outside to talk to him. But she knew nothing about kids, and besides, both of his parents were within shouting distance.

"Oso, do you want to play? Go outside to Charlie." She gave the alert dog an encouraging push with the side of her foot. "Go on. Go play with Charlie. Good boy!"

The dog streaked out of the kitchen, his nails clicking on the wood floor as he dashed outside. Had he understood her? She rose to see if dog and boy were together. They were. Oso danced around the little boy, tail wagging like crazy. Mia stood there for a full minute watching the two greet each other, one shyly, the other with manic exuberance.

For a moment everything looked normal.

Until she looked behind the happy pair to the dark and

dangerous bayou, perilously close by. Nothing was ever as light and carefree as it appeared.

Dark clouds hung low in the sky and the odd light on the trees and water made the colors almost surreal, much like her favorite Turner painting, hanging in the entryway of her house in San Francisco.

Hot and muggy outside, it wasn't much better inside, since she didn't have air-conditioning. "I should get an air conditioner," she said, talking to herself as she sat on a high stool at the island just as Cruz walked into the kitchen.

He'd ditched the shirt he'd tied around his head, and his hair hung to his broad shoulders. Wearing jeans and still barechested, he looked delectable. Tanned, fit, and sweaty. Mia wanted to jump his bones.

"You planning on being here long enough to need one?" he asked, opening a cabinet, taking out a glass, and walking over to turn on the tap. Turning his back to the sink, he chugged the water, then refilled the glass. Fascinated by the way his throat moved, Mia had to try to remember what the conversation was about. He looked like one of the hunky half-naked male models in an ad for Seduction, Blush's top-selling male cologne. Better.

Models imitated men like Cruz. Good ones came close, but none that Mia had ever laid eyes on—and there had been many—ever managed to pull off the raw masculinity that Cruz exuded. Seduction? Yes, he could sell that. Easily. It was a great scent. But the reality was, this man could sell anything by the gallon if he ever appeared in an ad.

"I need one now." Tucking the booklet under her computer, she closed the screen and gave him a bland look. Which was no easy task. She wanted to race across the kitchen and jump into his arms like a motherless monkey, take him down to the peeling linoleum floor, and screw his brains out right there in the middle of the kitchen. She gave him an appreciative up-and-down look, lingering strategically now and then.

The prospect of making *him* vulnerable and at her mercy had fueled all sorts of creative and erotic thoughts for the last hour.

"There's lemonade and tea in the fridge, and Daisy made you a ham sandwich for lunch. Which I ate, because I told you lunch was ready three hours ago, and I was hungry an hour ago. You snooze, you lose, Barcelona."

"I'll grab something before I go back outside." He opened the fridge and took out the jug of tea, then filled his glass with ice and poured. Finding the sugar, he dumped a stream straight into his drink.

Mia shook her head. "I see diabetes and massive weight gain in your future." There wasn't a spare ounce of fat on him anywhere. Just tanned, sleek skin pulled taut over impressive bands of muscle. The man was in his prime and didn't need to flex those biceps to look like sex on a stick.

He chugged half the tea before saying, "Roof's fixed. But I'd get that NOLA company to come and replace it sooner than later. Those patches are only going to hold a season."

"Hmm." Noncommittal. Mia had no idea where she'd be in two weeks. Todd could call her at any second and tell her it was a false alarm, or that they'd caught a deranged ex-lover, and it was safe to come home. She wasn't sure what she'd do with the house. Sell it? Keep it as her secret hideaway? Bronze it because this was where she'd met Cruz and had the best sex of her life?

Watching her with dark, intense eyes, he leaned against the sink and silently finished his drink.

A little chill breathed down her neck as he assessed her. He didn't give the impression that he was bowled over by her sex appeal. More like he was analyzing a weighty problem and didn't like his options. Mia was intuitive, a handy skill when managing so many people at Blush. There was a vibe about him this afternoon that hadn't been there last night, although, now that she thought about it, he'd been a bit weird when she almost killed herself on his ladder earlier.

"Everything okay?" Of course, she didn't have a hell of a lot to base that feeling on. She didn't know the guy at all, really. Wanted, had the hots for, but didn't know what went on behind that bad-boy attitude and those rock-hard, rippling abs. Maybe it was her imagination.

Daisy walked into the kitchen lugging the vacuum cleaner, which looked bigger and heavier than she was. "I've finished upstairs, Miss Mia." She gave a little relieved huff as she set it down, then wheeled it out of the way of the doorway. "What would you like me to do next?"

The large house was practically empty; Mia was waiting until the painting and wallpapering were done to have the furniture delivered. There was nothing much to speak of to dust, and she didn't care if there was a layer of dirt on the floors in the rooms she never used. She had not even thought about having someone in to clean. But Daisy looked as though she needed the work.

"Thanks, Daisy, great job upstairs. There's nothing else I can think of for you to do today. Would you like some lemonade before you go?"

"The windows," the woman offered a little desperately, shaking her head at the offer. "I can clean them windows."

Mia didn't care about the windows, and she really, really wanted the couple to leave so she and Cruz—

"Just the ones on this floor," Cruz told her, a smile curving his mouth. Mia felt a jab of unreasonable and therefore annoying jealousy. Cruz pushed away from the counter to grab a handful of the peanut butter cookies Mia had baked that morning. "I don't want ladies climbing ladders." He gave Mia a pointed look that shot through her all the way to her girl parts, and despite the fact that there was no smile for her, she still had a flash of how his hard body had felt as he pounded into her.

The fact that she was horny, that she wanted to be laid. Again. By him. Was aggravating. He wasn't here to service her sexually. Unfortunately. And if the son of a bitch wasn't willing, then who was she to force herself on him?

As soon as he went outside to work, she'd call the Bon Temps agency and have them send someone over tonight. Then she'd lock the front door. If Cruz needed to pee, he could go in the damn bushes. Perhaps the alligator would bite off his penis.

Apparently being horny and spurned made her childish as hell. Mia didn't give a damn. She was the boss, and it was time she reminded him she didn't do rejection. Well or otherwise. He'd had his shot, now it was time to assert her authority.

"Thank you, Mr. Cruz." Daisy gave him a quick, shy smile. "I'll get my cleaning supplies and get right on i—" Her face drained of color, and she grabbed Mia's forearms with both hands when they heard a loud cry from outside. "Charlie—"

"He's fine. Just playing with Oso." At a blank glance from Daisy, Mia clarified, "Cruz's dog."

Daisy snatched her hands off Mia's arm as if burned. "Sorry."

"That's okay, for a moment there I was startled, too. Come and look." Putting a gentle hand on the small of the other woman's back, Mia slid off the stool and edged her to the window. "Look how sweet they are together."

"He's playing," the child's mother said in wonder as she watched Charlie laugh and throw a stick for the dog. Barking, Oso raced across the grass to catch it on the fly.

Mia smiled at the cute picture they made. The boy in his too-large secondhand clothes and, Mia suspected, too-small shoes, and the sweet-tempered mutt so happy to have a boy to play with.

"Boys and dogs seem to be a winning combination."

"Yes," Daisy said quietly. "It's nice to see him laugh. It's been . . . I'll get my cleaning things out of our car," she finished abruptly, and speed-walked out of the room.

With a frown, Mia watched her leave the kitchen, then

glanced over at Cruz, who'd polished off the entire plate of cookies as he watched the little drama unfold. "Was that a little strange, or was that a little strange?" Maybe she was reading things into the other woman's reactions that weren't really there.

Maybe she was just full of assumptions about everyone around her, and being out here in the middle of hell-and-gone from anywhere civilized had tampered with her judgment of people.

Cruz rinsed the plate at the sink, then dried it with a dish towel. His domesticated actions were strangely erotic to Mia. It was the deft movement of those large, tanned hands skimming a towel over— Oh my God. She had it bad. What would it be like to have him wash her? Dry her? Mentally she added those to the list.

Dragging her attention to his face instead of his hands, his buff abs, his hairy chest, she mimicked his stance, crossing her ankles and leaning her hip against the counter. Only about eight feet separated them, and she could smell his skin. Soap and clean sweat. She wanted to lick him all over.

"I suspect she's abused," he told her, eyes narrowed and serious, jaw flexing. He looked both grim and pissed off.

"Dear God. At first I thought the marks on her upper arms were smudges of dirt, but they were fingerprints, weren't they?"

Cruz continued to look out the window at Charlie and Oso. He didn't reply, but his big hands clenched. She'd hate to ever see him truly pissed off enough to use them. And she'd never want to be on the receiving end of that unleashed anger.

Her heart skipped a couple of beats. He was strong. Bigger and more powerful physically than she was—and if he ever raised a hand to her, he'd find himself wearing a cast-iron skillet around his neck.

The muscles in his bare back flexed as he watched the pair outside. He had a magnificent back, satiny skin stretched over broad shoulders tapering down to a narrow waist. Not a mark on him. One would think he'd have a slew of tattoos, or at least scars. But there wasn't anything to mar his smooth, taut skin. And, despite his bad mood, Mia was still tempted to lick a path from the small of his back up the ridge of his spine, then sweep aside his hair and bite his nape.

Instead, she returned to the counter and planted her butt in her stool. He could come to her. Or hell could freeze over. Whichever happened first.

"From the way the kid acts, I suspect the mother isn't the only one." He twisted the towel in his hand. He turned back to watch her from unreadable dark eyes that ate the light and gave no clues to what the hell he might be thinking, or how his mood had turned from hot to cold.

He was unreadable, but Mia, on some instinctive level, felt that some of his anger was directed at her.

"You're still in a pissy mood."

"Not much to smile about when you figure out that a woman and her child are being abused by some drunk asshole."

139

"I agree"—she drew a deep breath—"but it seems like you're pissed at me."

Dark eyes bored into hers. "Only if you're abusing women and children."

"Well, then, that's a relief. Because the answer is no. Never have, never would." Mia followed the direction of his gaze, to Charlie and Oso, and reminded herself that as intimate as they had been, and no matter where their mouths and bodies had touched and tasted each other, they were still strangers. She really didn't know anything about him and he certainly didn't know anything about her.

"But still . . ." Cruz turned back to her, his tone grim as he gave her a strangely pointed look. "Charlie has it better than kids in, say, China, for example, doesn't he?"

China again? Mia shook her head. "That's an incredibly cold and insensitive thing to say. One has nothing to do with the other."

"Sure it does. Kids are kids. All deserve to be treated well. Whether they're on U.S. or Chinese soil, right?"

Instead of lick him, she now wanted to slap him. She had no idea what his problem was, only that it was annoying her. "Did you have an Asian girlfriend who dumped you or something?"

His face seemed to darken more, if that was possible, and Mia sucked in a breath. Whatever was pissing off Cruz or going on in his head, she was glad she wasn't the source. No good would come of it.

Her fists clenched, and she was suddenly afraid. She didn't know him. Didn't know a damn thing about him. He was an unemployed handyman, for God's sake, and she'd let him into her house. She quieted her rapid-fire heartbeat, stood as tall as she could, and asked, very quietly, her eyes intent on him so that she could read him as he answered, "Have you ever hit a woman?"

He started as if she'd struck him. "Jesus, Mia." When she added nothing, merely sat there watching him, he settled back against the counter. "No. I have not."

Something in his stance, his face, told her that was the truth. She relaxed slightly. "What should we do about Daisy and her son?"

"Not a damn thing. Not only is it none of our business, but we're not even sure she *is* being abused; she might just be clumsy."

"And she might not be clumsy at all. Her dick of a husband might be hurting her. So, yes, we are ninety-nine point nine percent sure he's hurting her. But you're right. I'm going to damn well make sure I've assessed the situation correctly before I take action."

"Fire Latour and you'll be rid of the problem."

"Fire Latour and the problem will be ongoing, and I won't know about it, so I can't take action. My God, don't you have any compassion?"

"I'll leave the hearts and flowers to you. I've got work to do."

Mia stared at his awe-inspiring damned back as Cruz stalked out of the room. Then shook her head as she heard his heavy footfalls disappear down the hallway, followed by the slam of the back door. "Asshole."

Chapter Eight

L ong day. Made longer by trying to function with a boner
that only pounding into Mia would alleviate. Cruz knew
he couldn't put off killing her any longer. He had to do the
job. Shoving his wet hair off his face, he turned on his computer. After he'd spent the afternoon with a steamer, strip-
ping wallpaper, he'd declined her tempting dinner invitation,
opting for a cold shower in her downstairs bathroom and time
with the information he'd placed on a thumb drive.

The camper still smelled of the previous owner's cigarette
habit and was cramped as hell. Especially with Oso as close to
his feet as possible without actually occupying the same space.
Cruz absently leaned over to give the dog an ear rub as his
computer booted up.

The camper, like the dog, were merely props.

Once the job was done, he'd abandon the camper and return the dog to the pound. He didn't do attachments. He'd
already delayed the inevitable too long.

Earlier, she'd rattled the doorknob of the bathroom when
he was taking a shower. Damn it to hell. He was relieved that
he'd thought to engage the lock, at the same time berating

himself for being a pussy. The only way he could accomplish this fucking job was to keep his hands off her and his dick where it belonged, and the only guarantee of that was to bolt a flimsy hollow-core door? Yeah. Pussy. With a capital *P*. Well, this time tomorrow it would no longer be an issue.

She was the witch with the pretty, shiny red apple. Delilah with the scissors hidden innocently behind her back. The beautiful vampire sleeping at night, mouth closed, fangs covered. It was damn impossible not to want to touch her. And more. Cruz knew fucking her "one more time" could cause him to overshoot his deadline by several years.

No. More. Sex.

Kill her now.

Brazil waited.

Balance of the money padding an already healthy offshore account.

No regrets.

No entanglements.

She met his stringent criteria, even though she claimed she'd never been to China. He was staring at the proof on his monitor. In the photo, Mia-Amelia stood in the customs line at Beijing International. He compared a side-by-side image of her on arrival in Switzerland a month earlier. Same straight nose, same stubborn chin, same slender throat, same classy chignon, her dark hair swept up off the slender column of her throat. Cruz enlarged each image, then frowned.

Glancing at the Beijing airport images, Cruz realized something was missing. Where were the three sexy freckles on her collarbone? At this angle he should be able to see them clearly.

He went back to the Swiss image.

Three freckles on her creamy skin, evident even on the slightly grainy enhanced version of the airport security tapes.

Covered with makeup? A doppelgänger for security purposes?

Absently he brushed a trickle of water off his forehead, then glanced up to see that his damned roof leaked, too. Great. He went back to his file on her and checked out several dozen of the candid shots taken by the paparazzi over the past six months. Three freckles in every one. So she didn't habitually cover up the small, sexy marks with cosmetics.

He looked at the screen full of photos.

All Amelia. But not.

With everyone gone, the house was way too quiet, even though she had her iPod attached to her Bose computer speakers. Blasting Pink's "Raise Your Glass." Fast and upbeat was exactly what Mia needed tonight. Edgy female rock and roll, fun and upbeat, that she could dance to as she stirred batter. Lemon bars.

Mia had offered to cook Cruz dinner earlier. He'd politely, too politely, declined. So he was still cranky and adamant on his rejection policy, apparently. So much for his offer to let her be in charge tonight. If she was really in charge, she'd order him to get his naked ass upstairs and wait for her.

He'd come in when it started to rain in the late afternoon,

and had used the steamer on the entry- and hallway's hideous wallpaper. It had been a pleasure to watch him every time he passed the open door as he worked, his sweaty muscles flexing. At seven he'd taken a shower. Interestingly, when Mia tried the door handle, the bathroom door had been locked.

Shocked, Mia had stood out in the hallway staring at the door. What man didn't want sex? Even if he was annoyed about something? And, damn it, shower sex was on the list. She was ready for him when she heard the water turn off.

Draped in a barely-there purple negligee this time, she'd perched her butt on the chilly kitchen counter, feeling a little silly vamping when he wasn't even there to see her sexy pose.

She shook her head as Pink's "U + Ur Hand" reminded her that she'd been just fine before Cruz Barcelona sauntered into her damn life, and maybe that's why he'd locked the door. He was taking care of that lovely erection all by himself. Selfish bastard.

She slid the baking sheet into the oven.

Without coming into the room, he'd yelled that he was leaving, and slammed out of the house to go to his cramped camper and the company of his dog. Mia had slid off the counter, deflated. Wow. Not very flattering, but clearly he had something serious on his mind. Unless he was no longer interested in having wild monkey sex with her.

Seriously? He'd lost interest? So soon? Possible, although she'd seen the heat in his eyes when he was watching her earlier. He'd quickly shuttered the look.

She hummed along to "Perfect" as she removed the fragrant pastry from the oven. She had mastered baking. Time to move on. No more eggs either. She needed new cookbooks pronto. She didn't need a song to tell her he was less than perfect.

Hell, maybe she wasn't as good a judge of character as she'd always believed. Perhaps, being isolated like this from Blush, she was losing her edge. Or maybe it was the heavy humidity that was making her brain soggy and her raging hormones scream for more sex with Cruz that had her brain misfiring.

She went upstairs to blow out the candles and change into shorts and a tank top. So much for her romantic seduction plan. His loss. Some men didn't want the challenge of a powerful woman. Maybe he felt threatened. Maybe he didn't want to jeopardize his job by sleeping with the boss. Maybe she was a big disappointment in the sex department. Who the hell knew what the man was thinking?

Back in the kitchen, she fixed a salad and put wild monkey sex out of her mind. But her body, constantly on edge when he was around, wasn't so easy to convince.

Pink belted out "Blow Me." "Hmm. Blow me one more kiss? A farewell screw would be even more welcome," Mia muttered. "But will I get it? No, apparently not!"

Damn it, she wasn't asking for love and marriage. All she wanted was more of what he'd already given her. Mindless, awesome, sweaty sex. Was that too damn much to ask?

"Focus. Think about something else." She forked a red, ripe cherry tomato into her mouth and chewed, thinking now of the marks on Daisy's arms and her alarmed reaction when her little boy had screamed.

Mia wondered again if she should at least say something as she poured herself a glass of crisp Riesling. She looked kind of pathetic in her reflection in the black windowpane. Sitting alone, eating off fine bone china, drinking good wine from a crystal glass, mooning like a teenager over some itinerant laborer—

She shook her head. That line of thinking was ludicrous, and she knew it. If the man didn't want to have sex with her, that was his prerogative. She couldn't do anything to lead that particular horse to water, but she could do something about Daisy.

Offer—what? Counseling for her husband? Herself? Shelter? Mia wasn't sure what, if anything, she should do in this situation. And she and Cruz could be way off the mark. Daisy could just be a shy woman who bruised easily. She could have fallen and someone had broken her fall by grabbing onto her, just as Cruz had grabbed Mia when she nearly fell off the ladder. She looked at her own wrist, not totally sure there wasn't a bit of bruising there. Or on her neck from their rough lovemaking the other night.

She ate dinner in lonely, quiet splendor with her pretty china and a crystal wineglass. No music, just the gentle whirring of the ceiling fan and loud rhythmic croaking of the frogs, and all the chirps and cheeps and grunts that the crickets, alligators, and other swamp creatures were making beyond the closed windows. The insects and wild things were content in the heavy night air, while the man who was always on her mind seemed discontented.

Though he hadn't been that way last night. She thought of how his eyes smiled when the stern line of his lips didn't. How the lamplight limned his skin, and how his dark hair brushed against her cheek as he applied his mouth with great deal of attention to detail when kissing her.

No, the man wasn't always so angry and unhappy, she reasoned, deciding it was best for her sanity not to think anymore about all the wondrous things his large, callused fingers delicately stroking her breasts did to her.

Mia shook her head and looked around her mismatched, outdated kitchen and smiled. Better to think about the major remodel. The kitchen was dreadful, with those crazy psychedelic butterflies and hideous Formica countertops and fruity curtains, but it was starting to grow on her.

Not the décor—that had to go. But the very fact that it was her kitchen to do with as she pleased, without crabby-faced Chef Simon asking what it was she needed. It was homey and comforting, and she needed nothing other than pride in knowing that she could fix herself a decent meal without relaying what she wanted through five people.

She could count on the fingers of one hand how many times she'd been in the kitchen in her San Francisco home. As beautifully designed as it was, even with every top-of-the-line modern stainless steel appliance, it was unwelcoming and cold.

She wondered what sex would be like on the large expanse

of Carrara marble on the kitchen island in her house in San Francisco. That would certainly put a twist in Chef Simon's apron. And that led to her thinking about the velvety smoothness of Cruz's penis in her hands, and the salty taste of his skin. And made her wonder, with a surge of heat, what he tasted like there.

After cleaning up—which took all of a minute—she went upstairs with her phone, iPod, computer, and notebook. Time to call Todd for an update, and then "It's you and me, baby," she told the pole bolted into the floor and ceiling and gleaming in challenge. The uncovered window nearby would serve very well as a mirror should she want to observe herself sliding around all over the place in an ungainly, uncoordinated heap.

On the other hand, she might be better off using another kind of pole to get rid of her horniness. But business before pleasure. Which reminded her that Cruz had said much the same thing the first time they met.

And just thinking about that made her hot all over.

Throwing herself down on the bed, she turned off the music and punched in her cousin's number. There'd be time later to decide which pole was going to get the workout.

She didn't need Cruz Barcelona's hands and mouth on her. She could bring herself to orgasm easily enough. Had plenty of experience in that department, actually. Problem was, she wanted him, and longing for a particular man was a new experience for her. One that wasn't on the list.

Todd's phone rang three times. "You know it's midnight here, right?" He didn't sound the least bit sleepy.

Rain pounded the black square of the window and formed pretty diamonds as it ran down. She turned onto her stomach and crossed her feet over her butt. "Aw, poor baby, did I wake you?"

"No, I'm reading what Davis and Kent have to say about the LBO—"

The leveraged buyout was all but a done deal, which would be finalized at the end of the week. "Why are they saying anything? You have my proxy. You sign on the dotted line on Friday and it's all done but the champagne toasting and wild frivolity."

"You've never been frivolous in your life."

"Working on it," Mia assured him.

"D and K insist you sign in person. I'm insisting you bloody well *don't*. They agreed to a compromise. They'll send you the paperwork when the time comes, and you get a notary. Get a post office box as far away from you as makes sense and give them the address. They can *mail* paperwork as soon as that's in place."

"Then can I come home?" As soon as the words were out, she suddenly realized that she didn't want to return to San Francisco quite yet. Not now, anyway. The house was just starting to come alive. She wanted to restore it to its former beauty, to accomplish something while she was in exile.

"Sorry. No. Enjoy the sun, use lots of Tropics, SPF fifty, and stay put until Basson gives us the okay."

Miles would find whoever was trying to kill her, and he'd take care of it. The head of security had been protective of her father, and had watched out for her as soon as she was old enough to sit at the boardroom table. But Mia had assumed that the threats were in direct relation to the LBO. Once the deal was done and the papers signed, the motivation to kill her would be over. Wouldn't it?

"Okay, talk to me."

"We leaked the announcement last night that we're considering selling the company. Korea is interested, to say the least." His tone was dry. Korea had been trying to buy them out for years. "Company shares rose fourteen point three percent on NASDAQ this morning at opening bell."

"That won't hurt us. Just gives me more clout."

"The press is having a field day, however. And everyone is speculating you're in hiding until the dust settles."

"Of course they're speculating. The press is skeptical because they're trying to figure out if I'm selling, going under, or reorganizing. They know it means Blush will fund some kind of venture with borrowed money. The shares are going up because we won't be selling stock to the public, and there's a feeding frenzy. I'm not worried."

"Davis and Kent planned to take the company private for two hundred dollars a share." There was a pregnant pause. She heard the clink of bottle to glass as Todd poured himself some wine. "They were outbid."

Mia's heart slammed into her ribs and her eyebrows rose. "By who—whom?"

"Everybody," Todd said dryly. "All the big dogs want in on the action. Morgan Stanley, Merrill Lynch—pretty much all of Wall Street. No winners: all bids have been rejected so far."

"As long as I win, I don't give a damn. Question is, how did anyone find out what I'm doing? There's enough misinformation floating around to muddy the waters. If not, throw more mud. We'll be fine. But damn it to hell, I want to know who leaked confidential information. Their side or ours?" There were only a handful of people total who knew what she planned.

"Basson and D and K's equivalent?"

"No." She didn't want either Blush or the investment company's security people involved in this. "Get someone smart, efficient, neutral, but loyal to us. Call Black Raven Security and have them put their best people on it. And, Todd, while you're at it, have them see what they can find about this alleged killer who's after me."

"Basson's already on that." He paused. "Are you saying after thirty-five years of loyal service, you don't you trust him?"

"The only person I trust right now is you."

Todd chuckled and took a swallow of whatever it was he was drinking. "Jesus, babe. About fucking time you got paranoid."

"I want this over."

"Yeah, I'm sure all those cabana boys are wearing you out." He paused, his voice changing from mocking to serious. "Kidding aside, be careful. I don't want anything to happen to you. I like being second in command way too much. All the perks, none of the responsibility. Don't trust anyone, even me. Promise?"

"I was going to invite you . . . here. For a little vacay."

She heard the glass hit a little too hard on the table. "I don't want to know where you are! For fucksake, Amelia—"

"When this is over, then?"

He let out a sigh and she could hear him swallow, ice tinkling against the sides of his glass. So he was drinking something stronger than wine. "It's a deal." Todd paused. "But they want more financial data—the buried-deep-down, confidential data that we typically don't release."

Mia tapped her unmanicured fingernail on the back of her phone. Not being there during this crucial pivot point for Blush was irresponsible of her, but what could she do when her life was potentially on the line? It left her feeling exposed on more than one front. "Fine, give them whatever they need. But first have Black Raven plug the leak. And remind them they signed a confidentiality agreement. Things are already volatile enough. Any more stuff in the press and they'll say it's not a rumor."

"I'll put a lid on it."

"One more thing. When you talk to Black Raven, have them run a background check on a Cruz Barcelona."

"Sexy. Is this your hot contractor?"

"I want everything they can dig up as soon as possible. I'll contact them directly for the results. Tell them they have twenty-four hours to find out everything about him from birth to today."

"Intriguing. You got it. Candice dropped by the fortieth floor this morning to see how I was doing in your absence."

Mia let out a mirthless chuckle at the thought of her father's self-centered trophy wife giving a crap about anyone but herself. "How *are* you doing in my absence?"

"I'm being a brave little toaster," he said with a laugh. "Between us we have enough assistants to run the world. I'm fine, but you know that, or you wouldn't have left me in charge. Candice was fishing to see if I'd let the cat out of the bag about who's doing your surgery and what you're having done. I hinted at boobs. Either she doesn't read the *Wall Street Journal* or she's just oblivious."

"Bless her heart. Shallow as a puddle. You know she'll just keep pestering you until I get back, don't you?"

"Annoying bitch," Todd said without heat.

Mia laughed. "Maybe, but she's very decorative."

"She is that. A decorative bitch."

"I know she can be annoying, but I think she's lonely in that big house. Oddly, I think she really cared about my father. She misses him, and wants to be part of something. We've talked about this. Have Allison give her a job."

"Isn't being on the board of directors enough?" The annoyance in his tone grew, and she heard the gurgle of liquid being poured over ice.

"You know it's just a title; she doesn't have any power. She doesn't *want* any power. Just somewhere to go a couple of times a week where she can wear her pretty outfits and shoes and boss people around for her amusement. Find her something to do, sweet pea, then she'll get out of your hair."

"I'll talk to Human Resources tomorrow. She wanders

155

around here like a damned lost fart in a thunderstorm. I'll tell Allison to give her an office with a door. Speaking of closed doors, how's your hunky sex slave?"

"I wish. He's brooding at the moment."

"Does he ride a motorbike?"

Mia laughed. "No. Would that help him not to brood?"

"Brooding and motorbikes go together. Very sexy."

"How about brooding and campers?"

"Not quite so sexy."

"You'd be very, very surprised, cousin." They talked for a few more minutes and then hung up. Mia rolled over and looked up at the water-stained ceiling. Just because Cruz was sulking/annoyed/distracted didn't mean she couldn't persuade him to change his mind.

She could knock at his door. . . . Bake a pie? Take too long. He seemed to like her cookies. Too bad he'd eaten them all that afternoon. She could cut up those lemon bars—

She eyed the discarded sheer purple garment tossed on the foot of the bed.

Fresh-from-the-oven lemon bars and a wet negligee? Mia grinned. Skip the bars. If the negligee didn't lure him out of his cave, he was made of granite.

And she would never, ever try to seduce him again.

Cruz whipped his head around to get his rain-drenched hair out of his eyes. Both hands were occupied fighting the slick tarp he was attempting to stretch over the damn leaky roof of the camper. Uphill battle. His wet fingers slipped, and the tarp became a fucking sail billowing in the wind, slapping him in the face and almost knocking him over the side.

Have you ever hit a woman? Jesus fucking Christ. It had taken every atom of Cruz's self-control not to go outside the second he'd seen the bruises on Daisy and her reaction to her child's screams, and show Latour what it felt like to be beaten on by someone stronger and bigger than himself. It was like fucking seeing what his old man had done to his mother all over again. Unacceptable. He'd look into the situation before he left tomorrow, then take action. But that wasn't for Mia to know. Not that it mattered what she knew, since she wasn't going to live to see the sunrise.

As for him striking a woman— Hit as in killed, yeah. But strike a woman? Never. He'd never raise a hand to anything, or anyone, smaller and weaker than himself.

He'd make Mia's death quick and painless. She wouldn't know—

But *he'd* know. He'd always know. Fucking hell. What a shit job to perform as his swan song.

The gator's deep, forlorn croak echoed in the black cypress swamp. The bullfrogs bleated with a hollow, resonant sound that dissolved into the gator's croaking bark and the tinny thunder of the rain pelting the metal of the camper. The tarp vibrated in his hands as rain slid icy fingers down his bare skin. Pulling a shirt on to climb around outside would've been useless and only gotten his one pair of extra clothing soaked. The muggy heat of the day was squashed by the deluge after dark. It was cool but not cold.

It was pretty damned hard to imagine lying on a beach in Brazil while cold rain sluiced down his neck and his dripping hair slashed across his eyes, making it even harder to see.

Suddenly Oso erupted into frantic barks. His excitement rocked the small camper, causing Cruz to stagger several steps to maintain his balance on the curved roof. "What the fu—"

"Hey! Need help?"

Mia. Illuminated by the only light source, face upturned, drenched to the skin. Bare-assed naked. What. The. Hell.

"Oso! Quiet! What are you doing out here?" Naked.

"Coming to help you?"

Since she couldn't see the camper from inside the house, he doubted that was her original intention. His dick rose in eager anticipation. Down boy! "I don't need h— Fuckit!"

The tarp flexed as if it were alive, snapping and whipping at him as he fought the updraft, wrestling the blue beast back to the roof, where he anchored one corner with his bare foot. Tying this son of a bitch down was going to take all his ingenuity and a good deal of strength. He didn't know why the fuck he was even bothering. He'd slept outside, cold and wet, many times and survived.

By this time tomorrow . . .

"Go back inside."

"You won't be able to secure that in this wind," she shouted up at him, her skin shiny and wet and mouthwatering, even with those gorgeous curves mostly hidden in silvery shadows of slashing rain and darkness. "Get down and come into the house before you slip off that thing and kill yourself. Oso wants to come in, too."

The dog, on hearing her voice, whined frantically to get to her. Cruz knew the feeling. Oso would be inside, standing at the narrow door, tail wagging, tongue lolling. He was male, wasn't he? Cruz figured the only difference between himself and the dog was that his tail was in front.

He could stay up here being an ass and looking like an idiot, or climb down and go with Mia into the house and get it over with. He'd planned on waiting until she slept, but awake would be better. Not for him, but for any police investigation—if they suspected foul play. Which they never did.

Cruz climbed down. The only reason he felt leaden was because of the slipping and sliding of his bare feet on the wet metal rungs of the ladder, not because of any doubt in his mind that Mia deserved her fate. Although the absence of those three freckles stuck in his head. By the time he was on the ground, she'd sprinted back inside the house, leaving him to follow or not follow.

Fuck. He wasn't made of steel. What red-blooded man wouldn't follow a naked running woman? The predator drive was coded into his DNA.

He quickly checked on the dog, left Oso dozing in the camper on a dry corner of the narrow bunk with a rawhide chew sticking out of his mouth like a cigar, then raced across the wet grass to the back porch.

The open door spilled golden light onto her watery footprints on the worn wood floor, and the new patches. If he'd decided to hang around, he'd sand the deck until it felt like satin underfoot, then give it a couple of new coats of paint. . . .

But he wasn't hanging around. He never did once the job was complete.

Running his hand through his hair, he squeezed out as much moisture as he could as he walked inside. The house still held the heat of the day—no savory smells of dinner, but something tart and sweet filled the air. She'd offered him dinner, and when he'd declined she probably didn't bother to heat up the kitchen.

She heated *him* up. What the fuck was she doing, running around bare-ass naked in the middle of the night? She was just asking for trouble.

She was nowhere in sight. The stepladder he'd used earlier when applying the wallpaper steamer was propped against the wall near the foot of the stairs, the drop cloths still spread on the floor and shoved against the wall along the stairs. The unplugged steamer was filled and ready for the next round, supposedly in the morning.

When he'd be comfortable ensconced on a private jet to Brazil.

The setup couldn't be more perfect.

"Mia?" Hopefully she'd gone upstairs to get dressed. It would be hard to dress her, but he'd have to if he wanted the fall to look accidental.

She stepped out of the downstairs bathroom halfway down the long hallway, a towel in one hand. "Just getting a dry

towel. The one you used earlier is still wet, so we can share."
Padding toward him, she rubbed the towel over her dark hair,
making it stand out like a dark, spiky halo around her head.
She looked hot, sexy, and fucking adorable.

She wasn't naked.

Better.

Worse.

The skimpy bit of transparent, clinging wet fabric looked
as though she'd been wrapped in purple plastic wrap. Every
curve, every hill, every valley, plain to see. The dark wedge
of her pubic hair shadowed the juncture of her inner thighs.
Cruz's tongue stuck to the roof of his mouth, and his trai-
torous and noncompliant dick rose uncomfortably inside the
tight, wet denim of his jeans. He told his dick no, in no uncertain terms. It told him to fuck off.

Even he had a line he wouldn't cross.

Tonight he'd do his job.

Chapter Nine

*Y*ou should go up and put on something dry." He was damned annoyed at how husky his voice was as she walked toward him like a stealthy cat stalking its prey. Slow, deliberate, sinuous steps that took her forever to get close enough to touch him. The scent of wet tuberoses made him almost dizzy with lust.

"Better grab a hot shower while you're at it," he instructed, voice harsh. "I'll take one too while I'm here, then get out of your hair."

A slip in the shower would work even better than a fall off a stepladder. Falls were the number one cause of unintentional deaths in the home.

Shower.

Stepladder.

Either.

He wouldn't have to dress her if she fell in the shower. A bonus.

"I'm not cold—just the opposite, in fact."

Her wet skin gleamed like pearl as she held out the hand towel. Cruz did not want to touch her. He looked at her extended hand as though she carried a machete and was about to chop off his arm. Less fucking painful than trying to control his rampant erection with no hope of release.

He was hot for her. That was a given. Great body, beautiful face. Undeniably smart and witty. He liked her, God damn it. Genuinely liked her.

But he always finished what he started.

Cruz knew he was grasping at straws as to why he hadn't done it. Yet.

Cool, wet, gossamer-thin fabric brushed his bare chest as she stepped up against him, tilting up her chin so she could meet his eyes. "You're dripping on my floor." Her voice, husky and low, poured over him like hot honey. A fucking aphrodisiac that filled his senses until all he could think about was tasting her, touching her, fucking her until neither of them could move for days.

Damn it to hell, he couldn't think straight when she was near him.

The hard buds of her nipples nestled in the hair on his chest as she dropped her hand clutching the small, useless towel. He didn't need it. No doubt any water on his body had already turned to steam.

He didn't grab her, but it was damn hard not to put his hands all over her sleek curves and valleys. Hands balled, he resisted her lure with everything in him until he shook with the effort of it, and sweat prickled his skin.

"I'll clean up when you're upstairs." He kept his voice cool, controlled, impersonal.

No attachment. No emotion.

Clenched fists at his sides, he noticed that Mia was mimicking his no-hold policy, arms at her sides, posture tense. Good. Fine. It would just throw gasoline on his fire if she put her hands on him.

Ah. Hell. She put her pale, elegant hand on his chest. Lightly, just a brush of skin against skin. Cruz felt as though he'd been branded, and jerked instinctively.

She touched his jaw, then glided a finger across his mouth. "Come upstairs—we can shower together."

"I prefer my showers alone," he lied. Shower sex had always been good. He knew damn well it would be incredible with her.

Face flushed, she frowned slightly, and for a second she looked away, face shuttered.

Damn it. He'd hurt her feelings. He was being too callous. She wanted him, and he was rejecting her. He could just say no instead of making up shit. He was hurting her feelings, and he didn't like it. As soon as he thought that thought, though, he almost groaned.

You're here to kill her. Why the fuck are you concerned you're hurting her feelings?

Hell, was it so wrong to want to give the woman one last fuck before she died?

Undeterred, and unaware of his thoughts, she slipped her hand in his. It felt incredibly fragile. Fragile. Vulnerable. And—God damn it—trusting.

Cruz realized that her skin flushed, not with embarrass-

165

ment but when she was aroused. What kind of man was he that he had been with this woman for two days straight, having some of the best sex of his life, and not noticed this sweetly endearing trait?

The sight of her pink cheeks made his pulse race. As his fingers automatically tightened around hers, he knew he'd made the worst mistake of his life. He should have killed her when he first laid eyes on her. Now he was always going to remember that blush, that sweet, innocent hint of pink in her cheeks that revealed that she wanted him. Ironic that the last job of his life was the one that would tear at him the most, when the first was long forgotten and the ones in between had become nonevents.

His brain screamed time to get this over with, but he stood there, frozen.

Very deliberately he let his gaze wander over her: short hair damp from the rain, glossy under the too-bright lights, the telltale flush on her cheeks, the sparks in her blue eyes.

Horny and pissed were an irresistible combo.

His jaw went rigid with the effort not to touch her.

She gave his hand a little tug as she backed away. "Come upstairs with me."

Eyes gleaming fever bright, he was clearly aroused just looking at her, which gave Mia some satisfaction. But the bulge behind his zipper was no match for his annoying willpower. Why he suddenly *needed* damned willpower was a mystery to her. It was as annoying as hell.

She wanted him, God only knew, but she damn well wasn't going to beg him. She'd made her intentions abundantly clear, going several extra miles to show him just how much she wanted him. But she wasn't willing to club him over the head and drag him to her lair to have her wicked way with him. Although the idea had enormous appeal.

Either he wanted her or he didn't. Now was the time to show her. One way or another.

Just as she was about to release his seemingly reluctant hand, he started moving his large, sexy bare feet. The man did *not* look happy as he started to follow her up the old, worn stairs. She wasn't exactly dragging him, but it felt like it.

She glanced over her shoulder. "Are you coming or not?" She made sure it sounded neither needy nor belligerent. She felt both.

He gave her a cool, assessing look that made her reconsider her precipitous decision to seduce him. His reluctance, when she was so eager, was humiliating. Any self-respecting woman would just tell him to fuck off right now.

She took the next step up. So did he, but his pace was slower than hers. Less eager. The light in the hallway and on the stairs was as far from romantic as it could get. She'd told him to toss the cheap chandelier, and now there was nothing but the naked 100-watt bulb hanging above them. Hardly flattering after her drenching.

His slow pace, with his hand in hers, almost pulled her off balance on the smooth, slick stairs. Mia had to do a little jog down two steps, then back up one to keep her balance. Another move like that and she'd accidentally knock them both down the damn stairs. She bit the corner of her lip, now half-irritated and half-amused at his reluctance. Slewing her eyes to look at him, she gave his hand a firmer tug. "I've never seen anyone *trudge* before."

"You know the alternative."

"That I finish the walk of shame by myself, and get out an appliance? Don't do me any favors, Barcelona. All cats are gray in the dark. And as much as I want it, I'm not going to go all cave girl on your ass and force you to do something against your damned will." Mia didn't bother to keep the sarcasm out of her voice this time.

She'd never seduced a recalcitrant male—probably because she'd never encountered one before. But she doubted even a guy with Cruz's steely determination would be unwilling if she had her mouth on his penis and his balls in her hand.

The smell of soap on his skin made her insides mushy and her brain forget she was the CEO of a multibillion-dollar corporation, used to bossing people around and having them jump to do her bidding.

Had he ever asked anyone "How high?"? She doubted it. She talked a good game. But they were halfway there. And it wasn't a plastic dildo she needed between her legs; it was his lovely hot, thick penis. She'd like to handcuff him, have him lying spread-eagled on her bed, and then see who begged for mercy. The idea had an enormous appeal.

Suddenly he stopped dead in his tracks; his fingers lost

their hold on hers. Pulled off balance, her heart kicked as her bare feet no longer had the solid surface of the wooden stairs beneath them. There was nothing, just air. Empty space.

Heartbeat crazy fast, arms flailing, she reached to grab anything stable to break her fall. Nothing. Too far from the banister. Too far from the upper landing.

Cruz was the only thing between her and fifteen hard steps below. Shock made him appear impossibly far away, as if he'd moved out of reach in the blink of an eye. "Cruz!" For a second, one awful, long second, it seemed as though he wouldn't catch her, that he was going to just stand there as she tumbled to the foot of the stairs in a broken heap.

Then strong fingers grabbed her upper arm and he yanked her in hard against the solid, safe plane of his chest. Air whooshed out of her lungs on impact. Mia clung to his waist, holding on tightly, face pressed to his chest. The jolt of adrenaline made her heart kick, and cold sweat prickled her skin. It was a near miss, and she could've been seriously injured if he hadn't grabbed her.

"Good catch." Her voice rushed out on an exhalation of fear and air. She looked up to observe his tight lips and the muscle flexing in his jaw. He drew deep breaths as if he, too, had had a near fall. The unflattering single lightbulb overhead made Cruz look more dangerous, more ruggedly handsome. The light cast shadows on his face, making his eyes appear darker and more deep-set. It formed shadow muscles on his bare chest and accentuated the flexing of his biceps.

Mia shifted to break free of his tight hold. So he'd saved

her from a tumble. Didn't mean he wanted to engage in wild monkey sex with her. She had more pride, more dignity, than that. She was making a fool of herself, and she knew it. Her skin still felt hot and prickly all over. And only partly because of the slip.

"This obviously isn't working for you, and I don't need to drag you up the stairs. Or pull you down, for that matter. I still have the number of the Bon Temps agency . . ."

In response his arms tightened, almost cutting off her air. Fine with her. Right now her legs felt weak—she could use the support. "Far be it for me to coerce you into doing something you're clearly reluc—"

Without telegraphing what he was about to do, Cruz grabbed her by upper arms. He slammed her back against the wall, hard enough to knock her breath out of her as he grasped her by the wrists to hobble her hands over her head in the hard shackle of his fingers.

All lovely and sexy, but by his expression he was considering flipping her over the banister rather than kissing her. "Look, Cruz, I—"

With a small shake of his head, he swept a rough hand from her hips, to her waist, to her breast, sparking small flashes of burning need in their wake as he kicked her feet apart. Standing between her legs, he loomed over her, blocking the light, stealing all the oxygen in the room as he said dangerously, "Anyone ever tell you you talk too damn much, woman?"

Seeing his eyes change from disinterested to predatory

slammed her heart against her ribs. "Not anyone who wanted to keep their job—" The pissy words dried up at the look of intent in his face.

Catching her face in one large hand, he crushed his mouth down on hers, forcing her lips apart. There was nothing gentle or seductive in his kiss.

Plowing rough fingers through the hair at her temple, it was as if he wanted to crush her skull. He fisted a hank to hold her head still so he could deepen the kiss.

Barely allowing her to drag in a sip of oxygen, he kissed her again and again. Deeper, harder, bringing her up on her tiptoes as he crushed her between his rock-hard chest and the wall.

Mia moaned, on fire as he pressed his thigh against the pulsing juncture of her thighs. The merciless press of his hard chest against her aching breasts, the heat and slip and slide of his tongue ravishing her mouth, giving no quarter. He was everything she wanted and needed. Her air. Her water. The solid ground beneath her feet.

Breathing was overrated. He took her mouth aggressively, the cavern of his mouth scalding hot, his tongue promising untold pleasures to come. A delicious and effective way to shut her up.

Mia sank into the kiss. He tasted so good. So familiar. So damn perfect. His skin burned hot against her naked, acutely sensitive breasts, and the hard jut of his penis from behind the prison of his jeans rocketed her lust from just *I want* to *Give me. Now.* She wanted him so badly, she could barely breathe. Her heartbeat thumped hard against her breastbone, then sent off tendrils of surging heat to every atom of her body like sharp electrical currents running along the pathways of her veins.

After playing the cool virgin all day—*him*, not her—his onslaught shot her sadly ignored libido from zero to a hundred in seconds. Mia wanted to climb his body as he murmured low, sexy words in her ear and nuzzled and licked his way around the shell of her ear.

She fought to free one hand from the shackle of his fingers, still anchoring her wrists high above her head. Liberated, she went exploring, fumbling blindly to forge a small space between them. Bracing herself with one leg wound around his, she managed to undo the top button of his jeans. Still kissing, she pulled down the zipper, the exercise made infinitely more difficult because he was pressed, penis to mound, against her, and she was so focused on his avid mouth, she kept forgetting what her hand was supposed to be doing.

"Upstairs," she managed when they broke apart to drag in oxygen, their chests heaving as they gulped air.

"No time." Large hands skimmed down her sides and slid the wet, stuck-to-her-skin nightie up over her sensitive breasts and then over her head. It hit the wood floor with a wet slap. Then his mouth was back.

Thank God. She'd rather kiss Cruz than breathe.

She vaguely remembered what her clumsy fingers were trying to do, and struggled to tug down the zipper. As he made love to her mouth, his teeth scoring her lower lip, his tongue dueling with hers, she inched that damned zipper down. His erection made the task that much more difficult, and that much more distracting.

She arched her back when his palm cupped her breast and he unerringly found her nipple, teasing it between his fingers to pain-pleasure until she whimpered with greed.

More. More. More.

She'd known how badly she wanted this, but Mia hadn't realized the depth and scope of that need. It spread through her, a living, breathing emotional need that shocked her to the core as she rose on her toes to meet him.

With a hard thump of her heartbeat she realized that Cruz was the first lover she'd ever had who was equal to her in every way. It made their encounters even more intoxicating to know that he wouldn't back off. Wouldn't back down. That he'd give her everything she wanted, and knew the things even she didn't know she needed.

It was incredibly strange to have that clarity of truth, considering she knew this man intimately on one level but not at all on another.

Licking her lips, she breathed hard through the spirals of arousal swirling through her body. "I have . . . fresh . . . thousand-count Egyptian cotton sheets on the bed—"

He cut off the inane words with a kiss. Fine with her. She loved the slide and slip of his tongue mating with hers. She loved the pressure of his body crushing her to the wall. After several minutes, or perhaps a week, he lifted his head. His smile predatory as he skimmed his palm down her thigh, then curled his fingers under her knee. "Up," he murmured thickly against her throat.

The hair on his chest teased her breasts and Mia felt the flex and power of his biceps against her side as he drew her leg up high.

"We can't have sex standing halfway up the stairs!" she told him, the sternness in her voice not as effective as usual because she was having a hard time breathing, let alone talking. Standing on her toes, she curled her knee over his hip, opening herself to him, and urging him more tightly against her with her heel on his butt. With little purrs deep in her throat, she scraped her teeth along the prickle of his unshaven jaw. "If we do this here, we'll break our ne—"

"No ifs about it—" His entire body shuddered as he pushed the hard length of his penis deep inside her in one powerful thrust, pinning her to the wall with his driving weight.

The instant orgasm rolled though Mia in enormous waves and she went deaf and blind, all pure, hot, sizzling sensation.

"Yes," he grunted, face tight, eyes black, as he pumped into her, hard fingers gripping her butt. "Just. Like. That." He took her mouth in a soul-eating kiss, mimicking with his tongue what he was doing with every thrust and parry of his hips.

Another strong climax broke over her, in her, around her, leaving Mia panting and gasping for breath as she dropped her head to his shoulder and tried to drag air into her starving, heaving lungs.

A few minutes later, as her internal muscles squeezed and contracted, his climax made his body jerk and shake. They were both sweaty and panting, clinging to each other like leaves in a storm.

"Jesus. Jesus. That was too fucking fast. No time for foreplay, woman."

"My foreplay was thinking about this all day. I'm amazed I lasted as long as I di—" The lights blurred and turned. "What the hell are you doing?" His fingers gripped her butt, holding her in place. She strengthened her hold around his neck and locked her ankles at the small of his back to keep him inside her.

"It seems pretty obvious. Carrying you upstairs. Didn't you say you had sheets?"

Eyes closed, Mia laughed against his sweaty throat as he took the stairs two at a time. He was still inside her. Still hard. She had to tighten her internal muscles hard around him as well as her arms and legs as he took the stairs. "*Fresh* sheets."

"Then a shower is called for."

She briefly thought of her large luxury spa bathroom in San Francisco, with its rainfall showerheads and personal body sprays and miles of white marble tile. "No water pressure," she warned as he crossed the dark bedroom and went into the small bathroom with her twined around him like a jungle vine. She flicked the light switch on in passing. Too bright. She needed dimmers everywhere. "I'll have to add dimmers to my to-do list," she said.

"Add it to *my* to-do list," he told her, making her smile and kiss the prickly underside of his jaw. Tightening an arm around her to secure her, dipping her dangerously low, he leaned in to crank on the old shower.

It spat at him. Tightening her hold on him, inside and out, Mia laughed as he straightened. "Better make that a priority, Barcelona. Grab my hairbrush off the sink and hit the pipe a couple of times; that usually does the trick."

What the fuck was he doing? The goddamn job should be over by now. Instead, he'd broken her fall, he'd fucked her, and now he had her hairbrush in his hand, banging it against a pipe and having more fun than he'd had in . . . forever.

Sex was never *fun*. It was a release. It was a guarantee of a decent night's sleep. A way of blowing off steam. It was a few minutes of oblivion when necessary.

Sex with Mia was a roller-coaster ride, naked, at noon.

Hitting the pipe didn't do the trick, so they showered in cool water that spluttered at them as they stood tightly together in the narrow, chipped cast-iron tub. It was worse than trying to shower with a water pistol.

"This is going to take days." He liked the feel of her ass crack tucked against his dick, and the slick, soapy glide of his fingers over her breasts.

"I hope not. I'm cold. We need to hurry up and jump into bed to warm up."

"It's ninety degrees outside."

"Then we should build a decent shower outside. I'm cold

now. Don't even think of hanky-panky in here," she warned, slapping a hand over his as he skated his palm over her mound. "There are more death-in-shower accidents than anywhere else."

Yeah, he knew. He'd been responsible for several of them.

She twisted to look over her shoulder. "Is there soap on my back?"

They'd spent several minutes soaping each other, making sure there wasn't a patch of skin or an erogenous zone untouched. Cruz didn't feel cold at all. In fact, he was surprised that the dribble of cool water didn't turn to steam the moment it came into contact with his skin.

He slid his palm over her belly, circled a soapy finger around her navel, then skimmed his hands back to her breasts. "I'll check after I finish washing your breasts." Her nipples— peaks hard due to his stimulation, he suspected, rather than the cold—nudged his palms, ultrasensitive and responsive to his every touch, no matter how light.

"I believe they're squeaky clean now." Her voice was dry as she rolled her head against his shoulder to look up at him with sparkling blue eyes filled with laughter and heat. Spiky-wet, long black lashes fluttered flirtatiously as she leaned back against his chest, cupping the backs of his hands where his finger stroked her breasts.

Turning adroitly in his arms, she slid down his body. Kneeling in front of him, Mia took his penis in her hands, then slipped the head into her mouth. It wasn't the first time she'd given a man oral sex. She knew just how to apply pressure as his penis hardened, how to suck so that his erection became rock hard.

Using superior skills, she squeezed and stroked, sucked and licked, her head bobbing against his belly. Cruz plunged his fingers into her wet hair, holding her against him, his eyes squeezed shut as pleasure washed over him in waves.

Cupping the back of her neck, he guided her head so that her mouth mimicked the thrust and counterthrust of intercourse.

Her skin felt cold.

He reached under her shoulders and lifted her up. "You're freezing."

"Since when does that matter to a man getting a blow job?"

Stepping out first, he helped her over the edge of the old-fashioned tub and cranked off the dribble of water. Her skin was pebbled and pink, her nipples tight, rosy buds, and beads of water sparkled on her pubic hair. "Since tonight," he told her, wrapping her in a towel.

"Well, I wasn't finished there, mister. I want a do-over."

He briskly rubbed the towel over her from her shoulders to her upper thighs, and considered the job done. "You and me both." Picking her up, he carried her into the bedroom and stretched over her on the fresh white sheets.

Lazily she parted her legs, and he slid into her wet heat. Missionary style was not something he often did. It was too intimate, too slow, too face-to-face. It was a style that invited connections that he normally resisted. Now, though, he kissed her as he thrust in and out, their eyes open, their gaze locked on each other.

She came not once, not twice, but three times before he did. Each time she moaned her release, his arousal built. When she finally screamed his name, he exploded into her with an intensity that stole his breath.

He woke up an hour or so later, hard again, and slid inside her as she slept. She woke up to his penetration, welcoming him by wrapping her legs around his waist and arching into him.

He slept only until arousal awakened him. Each time he reached for her, she welcomed him, and his desire for her had no boundaries. He'd never had so much sex in one night in his life, and when he wasn't making love to her, he held her, slept with her, felt her breath, relished the silky sensation of her skin on his.

When the morning sunlight hit his face, he groaned, because she should be dead, and he should be many miles away.

Chapter Ten

"*M*iss Mia, you want me to do anything for you in the house?" Daisy kept her face averted as she clutched the leafy branches to her chest. It was barely nine in the morning, and wet-blanket hot already, yet she wore a brown fleece sweatshirt over her jeans. Sweat darkened the neckline, and her brown hair lay flat and lifeless against her head.

Mia, dressed coolly in shorts and a skimpy tank top, hesitated. Latour, working nearby, cast his wife a threatening glance before his gaze snagged on Mia's. He held her gaze for several hostile beats before going back to trimming a shrub whose boughs were so heavy, they were nearly touching the ground.

A shiver of revulsion cooled Mia's skin. She returned her attention to Daisy. "Yes, would you come inside now?" She had to raise her voice over the buzz of the trimmer.

Daisy shot a glance at her husband, but obediently placed her armload of sticks at her feet as carefully as if they were a baby.

Oh, shit. From Daisy's sucked-in breath and how stiffly she moved, Mia could tell it caused the woman pain. "Let's go into the kitchen. I made sweet tea." Turning her back, she headed back to the house, anger seething under the surface.

"Oh. You shouldn't do for me, Miss Mia. Just ask, I'll be happy to make it . . ." Her voice trailed off fearfully. "Next time?"

Oh, crap. She thought she was being fired. "Thanks, next time I will. I don't quite have the hang of the simple syrup. You'll have to show me. Let's see if Cruz left us any chocolate chip cookies. I'll give you some to take home to Charlie."

She gave Cruz a meaningful glance as she went down the hall. He'd already painted the wall going up the stairs a soft, warm, misty gray, and was about to start on the opposite wall. He shook his head and raised his eyes.

He'd told her not to interfere, but how could she not? It had been obvious, just observing Daisy through the kitchen window earlier, that the woman was in a great deal of pain. Mia suspected at least a broken rib. Possibly worse.

She wasn't just pissed, she was enraged.

Cruz clearly wasn't used to dealing with a hundred staff problems a day. She was. And while Mia kept herself out of her employees' personal lives, this was different. She couldn't turn a blind eye to outright abuse. It was unacceptable on every level.

Daisy's steps behind her were slow and deliberate.

"It's way too hot to be working out there in the full sun. Sit down," Mia told her, keeping her voice upbeat. "I'll pour."

"I like the sun. It's full of vitamin D," Daisy said defensively as she pulled out one of the ladder-back chairs at the table by the window and gingerly lowered herself into it.

"Oh, I wasn't criticizing, it's just—" Criticizing. Crap. "I really appreciate what you've been doing around here, and you're way too valuable for me to lose you to heatstroke." Shit, that didn't sound any better. "I like you, Daisy. I don't want you to get sick."

Feet in clean but worn tennis shoes, pressed together, Daisy sat very straight, her hands clenched in her lap.

Mia took her time pouring the tea into two ice-filled glasses, enjoying the smell of fresh paint and the green smell of newly mown grass drifting in on the muggy air coming through the open windows and doors. Out in the hallway, Cruz was up on the ladder. It was sweaty work. His strong back flexed as he wielded the roller. She appreciated the fact that he liked wearing as few clothes as possible in this heat. Sweat gleamed on his skin, making it look like polished satin. She couldn't get enough of him. She wanted to run her tongue up the grove of his spine, then bite him. All over.

Turning back, she carried the glasses to the table. "Let me know if it's sweet enough," she told Daisy cheerfully as she sat down.

Daisy curled her fingers around the base of the glass and gave Mia a small smile. "I'm sure it's exactly right."

Mia realized that with better care and the aid of a few Blush cosmetics, the other woman would be pretty and look years younger. Now she just looked worn to a nub and absolutely exhausted. Used up.

For once, Mia was at a loss for words—especially now, when diplomacy was called for. She needed a moment to formulate exactly how to approach the delicate and serious matter, and got up again to get the plate of cookies.

"He didn't eat them all. But that's only because I hid half the batch. Yay for us." Sitting down again, she pushed her closed computer aside and made busywork of lining up a small stack of folders nearby. "I'm teaching myself to do things I've never tried before." She gestured toward the folders, the small stack of DVDs. "Baking seems to be pretty easy. It's scientific. Proportions, measurements, chemical reactions . . . Do you like to cook?'

Daisy smiled slightly. "We like to eat, and Marcel never did take a liking to being in the kitchen. Woman's work. Men like their dinner on the table at six, don't they?"

Mia circled her drink with both hands. "I don't really know. And honestly? I wouldn't care. If he wanted dinner at a certain time, I'd tell him to make us both dinner at six."

They shared a smile.

When Daisy started to lift the full glass, she grimaced, then quickly dropped her hand back into her lap and subsided against the chair back.

"Daisy, do you need to go to the hospital?" Even for Mia, the statement was too direct, but she was afraid subtlety would be lost on the other woman if she was dealing with what Mia suspected she was.

Daisy's shoulders remained hunched, hands tightly clasped in her lap. "No, miss. Thank you for the tea, but Marcel needs me to help him outside." Muddy brown eyes rose to meet Mia's. "If you don't have work for me inside . . ."

"Daisy, is Marcel hitting you?" Mia said flat out.

Daisy looked appalled at the suggestion. "Marcel loves us. He'd never hurt us."

It was a lie. Mia didn't need a psychology degree to tell when someone was prevaricating, and in the brief moment when Daisy lifted her head to make eye contact, the bruise on her check, badly disguised by sweated-off, wrong-color makeup, was so pronounced that Mia felt a wash of fury rush through her at the obvious lie. The other woman didn't have a black eye, yet—but her lids were swollen, that eye bloodshot.

"Daisy, come and stay here with me," she said with quiet urgency. "You and Charlie. He can't hurt you here."

Daisy's fingers clenched and unclenched. "You don't know me. Or him."

I've seen bullies in three-piece suits wearing that exact same look on their faces before they rip into a weaker opponent. Fists or wiles. A bully was a bully. Mia covered the other woman's hands with her own and said gently, "I don't need to know you to want to help you."

Daisy abruptly pushed away from the table, and Mia's hand dropped to her own lap. "My hands are dirty, I'll wash them outside. I have to go."

"If you change your mind about me helping you, will you come to me?"

"I've been married for ten years. Marcel is a good man.

He loves us." Back stiff, she walked to the door, then turned. Every tense line of her thin body showed that she was braced for something unpleasant. She dragged her gaze up to Mia's face with obvious effort. "Are you going to fire us?"

"No! Of course not."

Daisy's shoulders relaxed some. "Thank you, Miss Mia."

A few minutes later, Mia watched her crouch gingerly to pick up the shrub clippings off the ground. Latour was nowhere in sight.

"He'll hit her again," Cruz told her grimly, coming to stand behind her chair. He didn't touch her, but she felt the heat of his body and instinctively leaned back, her hair brushing his belly. He smelled of clean sweat and paint. It was an awesome smell, manly and industrious, and it made her girl parts want to dance.

"Well, I'm going to figure out a way to make the son of a bitch stop."

He placed his hands on her shoulders, and the weight and strength was strangely comforting. "You can't stop a man like that with threats, and you can't harbor them here. Offering her help will only make it worse for her in the end. He'll find her and the kid and take them back home, then he'll teach them not to run sniveling to someone else for help."

Mia turned her head to look up at him. "Are you talking from experience?"

His eyes grew hollow, dark. "My father whaled on my mother for years. He was a bully and a coward, but no one could stop him from getting to her. Not that anyone really tried, but no one would have been a roadblock. He did whatever the fuck he wanted with impunity."

She got to her feet. Her heart, already pounding uncomfortably from the conversation with Daisy, beat harder at his shuttered expression. Mia put her hand over his heart and felt the solid, steady flub-dub beneath her fingers. Looking up, she met his dark gaze. "Did he 'whale' on you, too?"

"Until I got big enough to stop him from fucking with both us." He shifted so her hand dropped away. Mia curled it into a loose fist at her side.

"You mentioned your mother left when you were very young . . . ?"

"She didn't *leave*. She *died* when I was fourteen. I could never prove it, but I think he beat her to death, then shoved her over the balcony to the pool deck to cover his tracks."

The coldness in his voice made the small hairs on her body stand up. Was her young son the one who'd found her?

"God—"

"Had fuck-all to do with it. Not sure where He was when she needed Him."

Filled with empathy he wouldn't appreciate, Mia merely said, "Did the authorities suspect him?"

"His best friend was the police commissioner, and he played golf with three senators. He knew their mistresses and their under-the-table deals, so no. They didn't 'suspect' him. I was the only one not fooled by the face he showed to the world. He supported a dozen charities, and was a big supporter of the police and firemen's funds. He was a sick fuck, and bad to the bone."

Oh, Cruz. She'd never heard anyone tell such a gut-wrenching story with such an impassive expression on his face. Her heart hurt for him, and tears stung the back of her eyes. "Is he still alive?"

"He was murdered when I was around eighteen." He said the words without emotion, without flinching, without revealing anything about what his father's murder meant to him. The absolute stillness with which he held himself—the abyss of darkness that suddenly filled his eyes—chilled her.

"Murdered? That's terrible." She met his eyes. "Did *you* kill him?"

"Can't say the thought didn't cross my mind three times a day. Never caught the guy. Rumor had it someone put a hit on him."

Mia noted that he didn't deny it. "As in a contract killing?"

"Yeah, that's what the cops believed."

"And did you think the same thing?"

He held her gaze. The dark void became even deeper. The gravity in his expression told her that she'd never know everything he knew about his father's death. Did she really want to? "He had one of the largest construction companies in Chicago. He was unscrupulous, dishonest, and had a lot of secret enemies, had the cops bothered to look. They didn't."

He touched her cheek, and Mia wanted to nestle her face in his palm. As it happened, he didn't leave it there long, just long enough to leave a phantom imprint. "If I don't get the rest of that paper off the walls out there, I'll never get the painting done."

She wanted to tell him there was no hurry. But, of course, he might have places to go that didn't involve having incredible sex with her and scraping off wallpaper.

He turned to leave. "Let the Latours work out their own issues, Mia."

"I'm surprised you can say that after your own childhood. Wouldn't you have been grateful if someone had stepped in?"

His face went tight. "What difference would it have made? I was right there, and I couldn't help. She refused to leave him. He refused to stop abusing her. In the end he killed her."

"You were a child. Powerless. I'm not a child, and I have resources she doesn't have. I'll put them at her disposal."

"Leave it alone."

She wasn't going to leave it alone. As soon as she had a sensible plan of action, Mia would deal with Marcel Latour, one way or another. "Leaving it alone is an interesting suggestion, but one I'm not going to take."

"You shouldn't take on other people's problems," he told her unsympathetically. "You'll only make their lives worse."

It occurred to her that this man did not know her at all. That had been okay until last night. Sex on the stairs had been just sex. Perfect, lust-driven sex. What had happened after they'd showered, though, and what had happened throughout the night had been as close to making love as Mia had ever experienced.

This man, who had held her for hours throughout the night—who'd made love to her again, and again, each time more tenderly, more completely—knew nothing about her. *And whose fault is that?* She had no one but herself to blame.

She wanted Cruz to know her. To *see* her. When they walked away from each other, as she knew they eventually would, she wanted him to know exactly who and what he was walking from.

"I can handle Latour, but how would you know that?"

He shrugged. "I guess I wouldn't."

"I need to fix that. There are things I need to tell you."

"I'm standing right here."

"No." She glanced at the couple standing close together outside in the garden. Latour was leaning forward, Daisy making herself as small as possible. Mia forced herself to look away, because if she didn't, she'd go out there and interfere. Big-time. "When the Latours leave. This is important."

"Do I need a shirt and tie for this conversation?"

Mia slid her arms around his bare waist. His skin felt hot and smooth as she lifted herself up on her toes to kiss him lightly on the mouth. "No," she said, dropping her arms, moving back to the table. "But it's a keep-your-pants-on kind of conversation."

Cruz fielded an irate call from the person who'd hired him. Assured him/her he was still looking, and would find Amelia in due course. He coldly informed his employer that he didn't need to be checked up on and he would notify him/her when the job was done, then he disconnected.

He hadn't meant to tell her anything about his past. None

of her business, and dangerous as hell to share confidences in his line of work. He'd never done that before.

Foolish, but then, who was she going to talk to in the depths of Louisiana?

After a quick shower downstairs, he detoured to grab a couple of glasses and her preferred chilled pinot grigio. Carrying the glasses upstairs, he shoved open her bedroom door. "When am I going to see you on that stripper pole?"

She'd dried her hair into a sleek, sophisticated style and applied cosmetics to make her eyes look piercingly blue and mysterious. Dressed in white shorts and a blue-and-white-striped top, she looked cool and fresh and delectably sexy. "It's an *exercise* pole."

"As long as you exercise naked, I want a front-row seat."

She took a glass from him. "Thanks." Indicating the two upholstered chairs she'd dragged out onto the long balcony that ran across the back of the house, she stepped outside and sat down, cradling her wine.

Cruz flicked off the interior light so as not to attract insects, but also so they weren't sitting ducks on the balcony. He followed her outside, pausing to look out over the dark trees and water. There was unseen danger out there. Animals, for sure. He didn't sense human eyes, but he was alert to any unnatural sounds. The evening had cooled some—high seventies, he figured. Comfortable.

The sound of insects chirruping and clicking accompanied the occasional splash from the dark waters of the bayou. The damp air smelled delectably of tuberoses.

The reflection in the dark window beside her gave him an interesting front and side view. She had a patrician profile he hadn't really noticed before. Caressing the bowl of her glass, she waited as he dropped into the other chair.

Whatever she was about to tell him, she was nervous. He wanted to lean forward and cover her fingers with his. To tell her whatever the hell it was she thought would piss him off, or scare him off, he'd heard and seen it all. She believed he'd killed his old man, and she was still sympathetic to the kid he'd been. What she hadn't figured out was that he'd grown up at sonic speed. He didn't need her sympathy.

He crossed one bare foot over his ankle as he leaned back. "I feel as though I've been called into the principal's office."

Her smile didn't reach her eyes. "I bet that happened a lot."

"You'd be surprised," he said dryly. "I was a pretty good kid. At least for a while."

"I wish . . ." She didn't complete the thought. He could practically hear the gears and pulleys in her agile mind turning.

"You've never been anything but direct with me. What's going on? What's so important?"

She drew in a breath. Let it out slowly. "I haven't been completely honest with you. I haven't lied exactly, but I've kept something important from you, and I want you to know. . . . My real name is Amelia Wellington-Wentworth."

He'd waited too long to kill her. Way too long. He knew her now. Killing her was off the table, and he knew it.

Her hands went up to her hair, as if she wanted to pull it away from her face. Something he imagined she'd done unthinkingly before cutting it. Her hands dropped to her lap. "I'm the CEO of Blush Cosmetics. I live in San Francisco, and I've been hiding out here for a few weeks because my security people think someone is trying to kill me." She paused, presumably to give the information time to sink in. "They're trying to figure out who and why."

His pulse quickened when he heard that Amelia and her cohorts at Blush knew there was a hit on her. He'd been hired after she left for Europe. He'd looked for her there, followed her circuitous route back to the United States. Tracked her to Louisiana. She'd had five aliases in two months.

All he'd been paid to do was kill her. Why she was living in a decrepit plantation, trying out cookie recipes, dancing on a goddamn stripper pole, and fucking her handyman were tangential issues that hadn't mattered to his end goal.

He drank his wine, wishing it was a single malt instead. "I imagine a CEO of such a large company has a lot of enemies." Even a handyman would know the name of Blush Cosmetics. It was synonymous with cosmetics and health care products and was international. Only someone living on a deserted island would be oblivious.

"I didn't think so, but apparently I was wrong." She shrugged her slender shoulders and took a fortifying sip of wine, lowered her glass, then brought it back to her mouth for another sip. "At this level there are plenty of false friends and true enemies," she said prosaically. "When you're vulnerable, you can never let your guard down. And I let my guard down."

She had cause to be cynical, but since he'd made no attempts on her life, he had to wonder who had. Perhaps he wasn't his anonymous client's first choice. Had his employers come to him *after* another contractor failed to take Mia out? Was that why his deadline had been set so precipitously, and his hiring so close to a fixed deadline?

It was a damn good thing they weren't playing truth or dare. Because if Amelia knew the truth—that he'd been the hit man sent to kill her—she never would have let him in the front door, let alone into her bedroom with the stripper pole.

Cruz crossed his ankle over the opposite knee and leaned back, assessing her. She didn't sound or look spooked about having someone trying to kill her. Annoyed, yeah. But not running scared.

She should be, damn it. She had no business telling him—a perfect stranger—any of this. Well, maybe they weren't strangers, exactly. She might trust him with her body, but she had no basis to trust him with this kind of information.

"What made your security people suspect someone was trying to kill you?" *And when?*

"Apart from the regular threats a beauty-based business gets from animal rights groups, activists, and the like?" She indicated the seven-inch scar on her upper arm with her wineglass. "This. Someone took a potshot at me from the building across the street from our Blush headquarters seven weeks ago. If I hadn't shifted to close my laptop, the bullet would have struck the back of my head." She took a sip of wine. As she swallowed, she squeezed her eyes shut.

"You were damn fortunate someone didn't take into account that movement."

"The bullet shattered the window behind me. It sounded like a bomb exploding." Her eyes were dark, glassy, lost in memory. Cruz imagined that this shocked, frightened look couldn't have been much different the night she was shot at. "The sparkling shards of glass looked like a waterfall breaking over me. It seemed to happen in slow motion, yet it was over in the blink of an eye. Weird and surreal."

Jesus fuck. Did she have any idea how damned close she'd come to being a statistic? Cruz's fury rose. Crap. He never lost his temper. Never let shit get under his skin. And now . . . Fuck. "Your security people raced in and—"

She shrugged. "Not much they could do. I had small cuts all over me. They administered first aid, patched me up, then waited for the police and paramedics to show up. It was only after they arrived that I discovered I'd been grazed by the bullet.

"I was too shocked to faint, and too pissed off to puke, but not too anything to stop shaking. I have to tell you, I wasn't feeling anything close to brave at that point. It took me days to stop looking over my shoulder. And loud noises still make me jump. But I damn well won't live in fear."

He'd noticed. "What did the cops discover in the other building where the shooter was?" Nothing, he bet. A sniper had made that shot. It could be any one of a dozen contractors, and none of them would leave even a shoe scuff to indicate their presence. Not like himself, who'd already left his fingerprints and DNA all over the fucking house.

"It was from a neighboring fortieth floor, under construction for new occupants, in the building directly across the street. From the distance and the almost pinpoint accuracy, they know it was a professional sniper. That said they weren't surprised that not a single clue was found over there."

Professional. No clues. No surprise.

Mia downed the rest of her wine, then cradled the glass against her chest. "The bullet recovered from my office was an HSM230 from a .338 Lapua Magnum sniper rifle. I did some research. That's a weapon used by police and military snipers. Not something anyone could buy off the street. Whoever shot at me meant business."

Cruz knew that the HSM230 cartridge was designed to arrive at a thousand meters with enough energy to penetrate five layers of military body armor and still make the kill. A plate glass window and a pretty head of hair in a French twist would be as easy to crack as a hot knife cutting through butter.

The effect would be just like what had happened to his mother. Nothing left to make an identification. Cruz's finger tightened on the stem of his glass. The effective range was over one mile in the right shooting conditions. Cruz had made a kill shot with the same rifle in excess of 2,000 meters. But realistically 1,500 meters was within the range of a trained sniper. Shooting between two buildings, a street's width apart, was child's play, no matter what the conditions.

"They could've just been a bad shot and aiming for some-one else in the building. . . ." Like hell. Anyone in the business would know they hadn't, and he felt a rise of ire. If they'd hired him out of the gate, the job would be done, no questions asked, because he wouldn't have used a goddamn sniper rifle. She'd have had a fall, a car accident, a fall in the shower. A sniper was just sloppy and asking for an investigation.

Lemon and Muncie? Good, but not as good as he was. Not by half. And the attempt had been botched. The two men weren't Rhodes scholars, but their marksmanship had always been impressive.

Which made him question the integrity of his client, es-pecially if he wasn't their first choice. Had they started cheap and worked their way up the ladder to the top and to Cruz Barcelona?

"It was after ten at night. Other than the cleaning crews, I was the only one still in the building."

He reached over, took her glass, and picked up the wine bottle. "Who knew you'd be working late?" he asked, pouring.

"Everyone. Thanks." She took back the filled glass, then pulled her bare legs up under her. "I'm habitually always the last one there, unless I have a function to attend, in which case I usually end up back at the office before I go home. Or I just sleep downtown. I have a pied-à-terre on the next floor up."

"Jesus, Mia. Didn't your security people instruct you to mix up your routines? Being consistent and predictable is an assassin's dream."

She frowned, her finger rubbing over the rim of her wine-glass. "Well, it's freaking inconvenient to try to mix things up all the time." She sounded testy. "I'm a from-point-A-to-point-C kind of girl, with no time-consuming detours."

"That stupid habit almost got you killed. What else?"

"What else?" she said, finally sounding annoyed, and set her empty glass on the table beside her. "Wasn't being shot at enough?"

"More than," he said dryly. "Were there other attempts? Before or after that?"

Chapter Eleven

"Three weeks before the shooting incident, my limo driver had an accident," Mia told him, sounding remarkably cool for a woman who had a hit man after her. Or *several* hit men. Cruz was getting more and more pissed the more he heard. What the fuck was going on? He had to do some investigation of his own. See how deep, how far-reaching, the threat was.

Well, for fucksake. This job was *supposed* to be easy. Quick. Right now he should be in his sunny oceanfront studio in Brazil. Painting, eating moqueca de camarão, and drinking Skol beer. But something about this whole situation wasn't right, and now he was in too deep to let it go.

"Something manipulated in the engine, they said." Mia held out her glass for more wine. Cruz poured, and she leaned back in her chair, cradling the glass between her breasts. Lucky glass.

"My assistant went to the event in my place while I was incapacitated with the flu. By some kind of miracle, neither Kevin nor Stephanie was badly hurt, thank God. But the car was totaled."

"Nothing suspicious there. Accidents happen." In this case, Cruz could certainly have engineered such an accident.

"Yes, they do. And we wouldn't have thought anything about it if the executive elevator hadn't dropped several floors three days later. Immediately followed that night with everyone at my table at a charity event getting serious food poisoning. It was so bad, nine people ended up in the ICU at the hospital. I was barely recovering from the flu and wasn't hungry, so I just moved my food around and sipped water all night, otherwise I would've been there with them."

"You were damn fortunate." Fucking with food was Clive Benzie's MO. He was good, damn good. A master at his art form, in fact. He would've calculated her weight and metabolism to a tee. Benzie didn't make mistakes. He made sure a dozen or so other diners with the same meal were affected, but the person he wanted dead always ended up dead. Unless his target was too damned sick to eat.

Tampering with anything mechanical—car, elevator, train, or plane—was Joel Shram's specialty. Anyone could've dicked with the car, but Cruz's gut told him the car and elevator were Shram.

Cruz was starting to see a pattern here he didn't like.

Was it possible that whoever had hired him had three people on the job simultaneously? Did they want Amelia/Mia dead so badly that they'd hired, at great cost, three professional hit men?

Talk about overkill . . . and irony, since she was still very much alive.

"How did you end up in Bayou Cheniere?"

"My head of security, and my VP of marketing, advised me to disappear while they figure out the who and why."

"Did they also tell you *how* to disappear?"

She moved the almost empty glass onto the armrest of her chair. If he didn't know her so well, Cruz would've thought she was completely relaxed. But he did know her, and he was shocked to realize how well he knew her tells.

"Miles did," she said, absently swirling the last inch of wine in her glass, her index finger tapping the glass, a nervous habit he'd observed before.

"Miles?"

"Miles Basson. Head of security. He explained the steps to me in detail. He walked me through changing my ID and my appearance, and how to drop out of sight." She drained her glass. "But I'm not a fool, Cruz. As much as I trust him, I wasn't going to be led anywhere. I left San Francisco and found people in various places who made me false identities. They went from mediocre to damn good. And I kept moving until I figured I'd diffused my scent. Then I did a U-turn and bought this house from a broker via the Internet. Nobody knows where I am, and nobody will until it's safe for me to go back home."

Too damned bad. I know where the fuck you are.

"Has it occurred to you that the two people you trust the most could be the ones trying to kill you?"

She gave him a pained look. "Miles worked as my father's personal security for thirty-five years. He's on point and one hundred percent trustworthy. I've known Todd, my cousin, from the day he was born. I trust both men with my life."

"Literally. Because these two men are the only people who know you're in hiding, right?"

Rubbing the glass over her cheek absently, she nodded. "But don't know *where*. And everyone else has been told I'm taking a long-overdue vacation." She smiled slightly. "My stepmother thinks I'm getting plastic surgery."

"On what, for God's sake? Your tits are amazing, your ass is prime, and you're too damn young to need any face work."

The press thought she was having plastic surgery, too. Hadn't they looked at the thousands of photographs they'd taken of her? And had this stepmother leaked that factoid?

"Anyone else in this close inner circle? This stepmother? Does *she* have any axes to grind with you?"

Mia shrugged. "It's hard to tell with Candice. Her face doesn't move, so it's hard to read any nuances." She smiled. "She's two years younger than I am. We're not BFFs, but we're not enemies either. She's quite extraordinarily beautiful, so she's certainly not jealous. And my father left her extremely well-off, so I doubt she has an issue with money. She was kind of pissed at me a few years back, but that wasn't about me per se. Our advertising agency didn't want to use her as the face of Blush. They chose Amanda Dupris, a sexy twenty-year-old redhead with amazing skin. Candice was not happy, and let everyone know it. But that was two *years* ago. I doubt anyone would carry a grudge *that* long, or *intensely* enough, to hire a hit man."

"Depends on how badly she wanted it. How about someone in your office? Your assistant?" She shook her head. "Board of directors?"

"No. But I'm sure they're speculating. I've been orchestrating a leveraged buyout behind the scenes for several months, and the paperwork is almost ready to sign."

Bingo. It would've been good to have this vital piece of information before he'd accepted the job. "Who's handling the buyout?"

"Davis and Kent."

One of the biggest investment firms in the country. "Top-notch players. Does anyone at Blush know about this?"

"Only Todd is in my confidence about the LBO."

"It doesn't take much cross-referencing to figure out that this cousin is the only one of two people to know you've gone into hiding, and he's the only one of the two people also in on the LBO." She was shaking her head. "Are you sure you're willing to trust him with your life?"

"Yes. One hundred percent. But, that said, not even Todd knows where I am right now. No one does." She gave him a small smile that did weird shit to his heart. Cruz ignored the sensation. "Except you."

Fuck. "Someone doesn't want you to own the company outright. What's the family dynamic here?"

Absently she stroked her thigh. Self-soothing. Cruz wanted to do it for her. Mesmerized, his gaze followed the path of her fingers on her smooth, pale skin. "Great-grandfathers Duncan Wellington and Christopher Wentworth started Blush together almost a hundred years ago. A member of each family has been on the board for all those years with equal shares. It's made for interesting family dynamics."

Her palm cupped her knee, then slid to her calf. Cruz's attention snagged on the path of her fingers, and the glide of her small hand on her own silky skin made his dick pulse.

"In the late eighties, my mother, Sonya Wellington, married Richard Wentworth in a wedding extravaganza to rival royalty. People still speak about the spectacle—or, as I later saw it, a brilliant business merger. Sonya was my father's second wife, and he was in his mid-sixties when she got pregnant with me.

"Before Sonya's death from an aneurysm, he met a young model working in Blush's advertising division. She became his"—she made quote marks in the air— "personal assistant." Candice Jensen was two years younger than I was. He married her and made her his number three—so she's now Candice Wentworth—two days after my mother died. Eighteen months later he inconveniently died of a massive stroke, leaving his new wife a place on the board and a nice block of Blush stock. Damn rude!" Mia said mildly. "Rude and mildly frustrating. Candice can't/won't make a decision without the other board members lighting a fire under her Jimmy Choos. Which in a week won't make any difference, because I'm negotiating a leveraged buyout of all the shareholders so I have complete control of the company back in my own Blush Super Satin hands."

"Why do you want that kind of control?" *So that no one asks questions about the factory and everything going on a world away, in China?*

Mia went back to running her hand up and down her calf. "I don't want to go through hoops every time I want to put money into my foundations. The stockholders want accounting, the board has opinions. I have plenty of money. I want to put it where it'll do some good. With no shareholders, I can do whatever the hell I want with my money. As long as I pay my employees fairly, it'll be nobody's business but my own. Everyone involved—board, shareholders, investors—will get an enormous payday when I do the buyout."

He wanted to shake her. "Surely you're not that naive. Not everyone is satisfied with great wealth. Some people want the power and prestige that goes with owning a chunk of a multinational, incredibly successful company. Someone is willing to kill you to stop the buyout."

"But nobody— Hell. Not true. Todd told me a few days ago that he thinks bits and pieces of information have already been leaked. . . ."

"He has telephone contact with you?"

"It's a burner phone."

"Even a burner phone's location can be traced with the right equipment bought from a goddamned chain electronics store. Who's your biggest shareholder?"

"Me. By far. On my father's death, his shares went to me, Todd, and his first and third wives. But even before that, I've always been the majority shareholder. My mother, grandfather on my maternal side, and my paternal grandfather all left me their shares."

"Enemies?"

"Business competitors? Sure. Personally? I hate to think so, but obviously someone hates me enough to want to get rid of me."

"Permanently."

"Yeah," she said dryly. "I already got that part."

"When are you signing the papers?"

"Friday."

His deadline. All of it made sense now. Todd was the number one suspect. And frankly, knowing it was her cousin who wanted to bump her off so he could have all the toys to himself pissed Cruz off. Put together with the double, it didn't take much to figure out he was being played. He hated being played.

"Three days from now?"

"Right."

"Then I'd better make sure you're safe."

"God, Cruz. I don't want to put *you* in any danger."

Oh, the irony. "No one knows where you are, right?" But if *he* knew, someone else would eventually track her down. She'd disappeared, but anyone with enough brains, resources, and incentive—several million dollars' worth of incentive—would find her.

Cruz almost laughed. Who said fucking didn't addle a man's brains?

He'd just gone from hit man to bodyguard.

Cruz seemed to be taking her revelations in his stride. Mia wasn't sure if that was a good thing or a bad thing. She tried to gauge his thoughts, but as usual his expression was shuttered and still.

The doorbell rang, making her jump. "That's the first time anyone's rung the bell." She gave him an inquiring look. "Are you expecting anyone?"

"No. And certainly not at nine at night. Don't worry, I doubt a hit man would ring the doorbell. I'll go see who it is."

Mia uncurled her legs and got to her feet. "I'll go with you. Hang on." She dropped to her knees beside the bed, brought out the Beretta and a box of cartridges, then got to her feet. "James Bond's gun." She placed one bullet at a time into the top opening of the magazine, pushing and simultaneously sliding the bullet back against the magazine wall until all fifteen rounds were loaded in the magazine. "I figured, why not?"

Cruz watched her engage the safety switch without comment, then noted, "Bond's gun was a Walther PPK."

She slid the magazine into the well and heard the click indicating it was locked into the weapon. "*After* he had the Beretta—"

Someone leaned on the doorbell. It was old, and sounded like a car horn. Very annoying. Mia made a mental note to replace it as she grasped the serrated area of the slide, then pulled it to the rear and released it, chambering the round. The safety was still on, but the weapon was ready to fire. "Okay, okay, we're coming!"

Cruz held out his hand at the top of the stairs and yelled over the doorbell, "Give me that thing."

Mia hesitated. She'd had years of target practice experience. "Do you know how to use it?"

"Military, remember?" He wiggled his fingers. "I've shot one a time or two."

Mia handed it over, then ran down the stairs. At the bottom she told him, "Do not shoot off any of your own body parts. In fact, try not to shoot at anything. It's probably a neighbor wanting a cup of sugar."

The front door was completely boarded up, so visitors had to use the back door on the bayou side to enter the house. A new front door was on the house to-do list. She waited for a break in the raucous ringing, then shouted, "Who is it?"

She glanced at Cruz when there was silence. "Hey," she yelled. "What do you want?"

"I'm— It's me. Ch-Charlie, Miss Mia."

Mia exchanged a look with Cruz, who stuck her gun in the back of his jeans and motioned that he was going outside and around the house. "I can't open this door, honey. Cruz will come and get you and bring you in the back, okay?"

"Okay." His voice sounded small and scared. Mia's stomach instantly went into a knot. "Are you hurt, sweetheart?"

"A little bit—" His voice shook as he started to cry, great tearing sobs that broke Mia's heart. "Can you go help my mama? Plea—" He broke off with a high-pitched scream.

Mia almost ripped the plywood off with her bare hands,

and it was only the deep sound of Cruz's voice murmuring to the child on the other side of the door that made her sag with relief.

"I've got him. Stay put until we assess the situation."

Mia nodded, her heart pounding with the spike of pure adrenaline racing through her body.

"Mia?"

"I'll be in the kitchen." She raced down the hall. Daisy needed help. Medical for sure. Mia yanked open a cupboard and took down the small first aid kit from the shelf. How bad? More than a Band-Aid bad? Hospital bad? The police?

God. Her blood chilled.

Had Marcel killed her?

Cruz came into the kitchen with Charlie wrapped around him like a little monkey. Skinny arms clutched around Cruz's neck, and twig-like legs wrapped around his waist. Other than tiny Superman underpants and one filthy sock, the child was naked and crying hysterically.

Cruz rubbed a large, soothing hand up and down Charlie's narrow, bruised back. When he looked at her she saw the same horror she felt reflected in Cruz's eyes. The most unguarded emotion she'd seen from him since they'd met.

"Grab your shoes, purse, and whatever cash you have, and haul ass." The calm in his voice was in direct contrast to the fury in his eyes. His hand didn't stop soothing the child while he talked. "We'll be in the truck."

Mia flew up the stairs, gathered shoes—hers and his—the

bundles of cash she kept in a small safe under the carpet in the closet, and, just in case, the full box of ammunition for the Beretta.

She hoped to God they wouldn't have to shoot anyone tonight.

Nothing incensed Cruz more than someone abusing a child or a woman. There was absolutely no excuse for anyone to hurt someone smaller and defenseless. Hurting someone big and mean was another matter entirely. Icy anger made him revel in exacting payback from Latour for his wife and son—and for himself. He took the assault personally. His damn fault. He should've listened to Mia and this would never have happened. Either Latour would've met with an accident, or Daisy and Charlie would have been out of his reach.

Marcel Latour was in for an unpleasant surprise.

After passing Charlie to Mia, Cruz backed the truck from under the carport and swung into the street. "Do you know how to get home?" he asked a now sniffling Charlie, who sat on Mia's lap even though there was plenty of space, and a backseat, in the large vehicle.

Mia wrapped him in a large black-and-white scarf, then snuggled him up under her chin, rubbing his back as Cruz had done.

The child, head on Mia's chest, nodded, then swiped his hand under his nose. Mia handed him a wad of tissues. "Tell Cruz how we get to your house, honey."

Thank God Charlie knew his way home.

It was three miles from Mia's place. The kid had walked three fucking miles. In the dark. Wearing only Superman skivvies and a sock. He was six years old, for fucksake! He should've been tucked up in bed, with a night-light on, dreaming about superheroes.

"Turn here by the green house. Turn up there by that big tree." The little boy sat up straighter and pointed. "That's my house! That's my house!"

Charlie jerked his head around to shoot Cruz an accusing look as they cruised by the small house. A light shone from a side window; the rest of the house was dark. And there was no truck parked on the street outside. "Stop! I told you! That's my house right there!"

"I know," he told the kid calmly. "But we're not going to park outside the door, okay?" Cruz cut the lights, then circled the block again. "Where does your dad park his truck?" Latour had a beat-up Chevy filled with an untidy collection of gardening tools.

The boy pointed to his house. "There."

"On the street, outside your house?"

Charlie nodded.

No truck was excellent news. Unless Latour had taken Daisy somewhere. To the hospital, perhaps? Unlikely. There'd be questions and police involved.

He parked beside an empty lot five houses down, then popped the door and stepped outside. The air was hot and muggy, and smelled like garbage. The good news was that all the streetlights were out. Shot out, taken out, or no power.

End result, a patchwork of pools of illumination directly beneath the streetlights. Everywhere else was murky. There was enough ambient light to see fine, but at least Mia's truck wasn't spotlighted, and the shadows of the big overgrown bushes in the empty lot hid it from view of the Latour house.

"Stay put," he instructed. "Lock the doors, slide over to this side. I left something in the door pocket. Don't ask questions. Use it if necessary."

He quietly closed the door, then waited for Mia, with Charlie attached, to slide over under the steering wheel. He motioned for her to lock the door, then pointed down. Her eyes widened when she felt the gun in the side pocket, and her head jerked up. "No!" She shook her head over Charlie's. "You need it more than I do!"

Cruz shook his head and walked away at a fast clip. If anything happened, she'd have Charlie and herself to protect. He hated to leave them in the big, shiny, fancy new truck without him. The neighborhood was crap. Run-down or abandoned houses, weed-infested yards. No kids' toys anywhere. A couple of old fishing boats up on blocks. A radio blared obscenity-laden hip-hop as he passed a dark house. Even from the street, the distinctive smell of pot was strong. A couple of dogs started barking several streets over. A motorcycle revved somewhere, then peeled away, scattering gravel.

He'd spent some gnarly nights in places just like this when he was a kid. Not slept, just rested, eyes open, always alert. Waiting to be robbed, or killed, or forced into some illegal activity at gunpoint. It was a shit way to live. Charlie deserved better.

As he passed the small house next door to the Latours' place, Cruz recognized the sweet smell of ether and a strong ammonia or cat pee stink, indicating a meth lab. No surprise.

He glanced up and down the street for any movement. A cat darted across the street. That was it. Him and an alley cat. Brothers.

The decision whether to knock or just walk in was made easier when he saw that the front door was half off its hinges and hanging askew. Foot and fist. A lot of rage there. It told the story of a man locked out of his own house.

Cruz clenched his fist, hoping the bastard was there to meet him. He slipped between the door and the shattered jamb, heart racing now. A man that mad at a door would do a lot worse to his wife.

He was ready for Latour, but it was his wife Cruz was searching for.

"Daisy? It's Cruz Barcelona. From Mia's house," he called softly, allowing his eyes to adjust to the darkness inside. The room was small, ten by ten. A sagging sofa turned on its side. A shattered wood pallet. A broken lamp. There'd been a fight here. One-sided, but a fight nevertheless.

"Daisy?" Cruz walked farther into the room. He could see almost the entire kitchen off to the right. He strode in. The tiny room was lit by the open refrigerator door, the contents dashed to the floor. He took an all-encompassing look around. No Daisy, but the obvious signs of a man enraged. Every door and cabinet flung open, the contents scattered in broken bits and pieces over the linoleum floor.

213

An open door off the living room stood ajar. Cruz pushed it open all the way. A shadeless lamp lay on its side on a TV table beside the bed. The light he'd seen from outside. "Daisy?"

"Thank you, Jesus." The voice, thready and weak, came from the other side of the massive bed, which took up most of the floor space. Cruz was beside Daisy in seconds.

Crouching beside her in the confined space, he tried to assess her injuries. Blood covered the entire left side of her face, and more seeped out of what was obviously a broken nose. One eye was already swollen shut, the other turning colors. Her mouth was swollen on one side, and her hands were covered in blood. Cruz hoped she'd killed the asshole. He'd pay her legal fees.

The rage he felt was off the charts. "How badly are you hurt?" he asked gently. The light was shit, but he saw enough. Blood. Copious amounts on her face and clothing. Bruising. Contusions. A black eye.

Terror. Resignation. Hope.

Her hand, curled on her hip as she lay on her side, twitched, as if she wanted to pull him closer. "Charlie?"

"Mia and I have him. He's safe." She let out a whimper that pierced his anger. Fuck fuck fuck. She reminded him so much of his mother that for a moment the two women were superimposed over each other in his mind's eye.

Cruz sucked in a heavy breath. He had to focus on what the hell was going on now, today. He was no longer a child. This was not his mother. And he had to get her the fuck out of this house before Latour returned. He yanked a thin comforter off the bed, and paused as he calculated the best method to get her wrapped and up off the floor.

"I'm going to put my arms under you very gently and pick you up. I'll try not to hurt you any worse, but we have to get you out of here."

He'd hurt her more, and he was fucking sorry for it, but she needed medical treatment, and he had to get her away from here.

"Don't let Charlie see me. . . ."

He took that as permission and carefully wrapped her in the thin quilt to lessen the possibility of his hands accidently hurting her when he picked her up.

She cried out as he lifted her in his arms. She was as light as a child. She smelled of blood, vomit, urine, and bone-shattering despair.

"I'm s-sorry," she choked out, tears diluting the blood on the side of her face as she tried to keep her head upright.

"You have nothing to be sorry about," he told her, keeping his tone light and calm. "Lay your head on my shoulder, Daisy. I won't drop you, I promise."

"I'll g-get bl-blood on your sh-shirt."

"I've always hated this shirt. There." Her head dropped to his chest. More because she couldn't remain sitting upright than because she was willing to be a burden. "We'll be in the car in a minute, and you can see that Charlie is all right."

I'm going to find you, you fucker, then show you exactly how being beat to shit feels like. "I'm sorry this hurts," he told her as he carried her out of the house, his steps fast and as even as he could make them as he strode down the cracked, weedy sidewalk.

He saw Mia's pale face inside the cab of the truck, and by the time he reached it, she'd unlocked the back door and jumped out to meet him.

Her eyes sought his. Cruz indicated that it was bad.

"Charlie fell asleep," she whispered. "Lay her on the backseat. I'll stay back here with her."

Daisy was barely conscious as Cruz and Mia laid her down, the comforter over her. Mia climbed into the backseat, lifting Daisy's head to her lap, whispering "God damn that fucking son of a bitch" under her breath. Then urgently, "Go, go, go!"

Cruz got in, buckled up, and took off. Beside him, a little boy in Superman skivvies, wrapped in a designer scarf, slept the sleep of the finally rescued.

Chapter Twelve

*M*ia loved the feel of Cruz's heavy arm draped over her shoulders as they drove home from the hospital in New Orleans, her head resting on his shoulder, her arm across his waist. She especially loved the way he absently rubbed her upper arm now and then as he drove. She loved the way he smelled, too. No cologne, and his shower soap smell long gone. He just smelled male and sexy, and whatever it was, it was a siren song to Mia's hormones.

She felt like a teenager. Not that she'd ever been in a truck with a bad boy as a teenager. Then it had been arranged dates and limos. She liked this much, much better.

She was exhausted but not sleepy, and almost in a hypnotic state from the vehicle headlights coming toward them. Even at three in the morning, the road was busy.

It had been a risk driving that far with an injured woman. But Cruz hadn't wanted to risk Latour's being able to find his wife and son at any of the local hospitals or shelters, and Mia had agreed. Leaving them anywhere close to Latour wasn't an option. They'd taken them to Ochsner Medical Center in New Orleans.

Daisy required surgery to repair the life-threatening internal hemorrhaging, plus her cheekbone, arm, collarbone, and ribs were broken, her shoulder was dislocated, and she had multiple contusions, cuts, bruises, and scrapes all over her body. Marcel had beaten her almost to death.

Mia barely knew her, but seeing Daisy in that hospital bed with tubes and wires attached to her made her sick to her stomach, and so angry she didn't know how to handle the rage inside. Through it all, Cruz had been cool, calm, and collected. He seemed both stoic and resolute.

Mia had stood by anxiously as Charlie was checked out. Her eyes welled with tears when he cried, and it took everything in her not to sob with him. Lost, terrified, she was the only thing in his little life he could hold on to, and his little hand had amazing strength as he clung to her through every test and examination.

The diagnosis was that Daisy was malnourished, traumatized, and bruised, but otherwise in decent health. Charlie had fallen asleep in Mia's arms as they sat out in the waiting room waiting to hear about his mother.

Cruz had been taken aside by the police, followed by two women from Social Services and a woman from a local women's shelter. He'd signed paperwork and given them his and Mia's information. Then he'd sat with Charlie as she had her turn. Every step of the way, she was tempted to give them her true identity, but Cruz had warned her not to. Her fake ID was excellent. There was no need to give them more than that.

As soon as Daisy was released, she and Cruz would find a safe place for her and Charlie. They had no idea if she had friends or relatives who would give her and her son safe harbor. But even if she did, Latour would find them there.

She'd gotten fake identification; certainly she could do the same for Daisy and Charlie. "They're going to be okay, right?" The first words she'd said since they'd returned to her truck.

"Yeah," Cruz responded to her question, his chiseled mouth in a grim line, a muscle in his jaw ticking as he clenched his teeth. Mia's anger was hot. Cruz's anger was Arctic cold. "They're going to be fine. They have the best medical care. You heard what the doctor said: with proper care, and away from danger, she'll recuperate just fine."

"Physically, not emotional. I'm sure that'll take time. I want better than fine for them, Cruz. We should've brought Charlie home with us— No. You were right. That would be the first place Latour would look for him. He's safer in foster care until we can go and get him. But what if they don't—"

Cruz dropped a kiss on the top of her head, and the intimate touch instantly calmed her frayed nerves. "Stop worrying. They know what they're doing, and it won't be for long. I told him one of us would call him every day."

"He'd be less scared if Oso was with him, don't you think? I wonder if that's allowed. I can drive him over tomorrow."

"Call and ask in the morning." Mia felt his warm breath on her forehead as he said softly, "I thought you didn't like kids."

Puzzled, she looked up at his chin. "What a weird thing to say. Why on earth would you think that?"

His shoulder shrugged beneath her head. "Hmm. Must've been something you said."

"I doubt it. I like children. Not that I've been around many, but those I have been around I enjoy. I like the way their mind are so open to learn new things. Their little brains are like colorful butterflies flitting from topic to topic. I find children fascinating. At least the few I've interacted with."

"Wow, I had you pegged wrong, didn't I? If you like kids so much, why don't you have a bunch of them?"

Mia laughed. "I said I like them, but not in multiples. I wasn't thinking of producing a litter."

"So you plan on having children, Miss CEO of Blush Cosmetics? When would you have time?"

"Not right now, especially with the LBO happening," she admitted. "But yes, eventually. Men run multibillion-dollar corporations and have families—why can't I?"

"No reason. So love, marriage, and two point five children for you sometime this decade?"

She smiled. "I've never really given it much thought. My life is pretty packed to the brim as it is. But eventually I'd like to share my life with someone special, I suppose." She snuggled closer, enjoying the warmth and strength of him beside her. "What about you?"

"The only thing I know about love is that it's usually a business arrangement. I'd never bring children into a business arrangement. They'd become possessions and bargaining chips. Love and business shouldn't be considered the same thing."

"And yet it almost always is. A woman marries a man for

financial security, and a man gets married to continue his line and have a pretty ornament on his arm. Not so bad. My parents were married for more than twenty years before my mother died. They were fairly compatible."

"Compatible? What about passion?"

"Well, clearly they had sex. At least once anyway," Mia said dryly, eyes closed. She inhaled deeply, loving the smell of him. Whether he was fresh from the shower or at the end of a long, sweaty day, his masculine pheromones shouted to her phero-mones, *Come and get me*. "What about you?"

"What about me? Sex once in twenty years isn't my style, but one doesn't have to be in love to have mind-blowing sex. We both know that."

But one could be halfway there if one allowed it. "Have you ever been in love?"

"No."

"Do you believe in love?" she asked curiously, sitting up-right and running both hands through her hair as they ap-proached the house. It was the first time in hours that she'd given her appearance a thought. In fact, tonight was the first time in several months that she'd even bothered to put on makeup at all.

"Doesn't exist, except in advertising to sell anything from your fancy Blush perfume to Ferraris." He pulled her truck under the carport and cut the engine. She'd left all the lights on in the house when she'd run out, so pools of golden light dotted the wide expanse of non-lawn. It looked welcoming and safe.

"Wow. We're both cynics." That was kind of depressing. She'd never given her cynicism any thought at all until now. "Well, I do believe in love. Pretty much three out of four songs for hundreds of years have been about it, so it must exist, right?"

"Maybe for some people." He could almost have added, *But not for people like us.*

Mia realized she wanted everything love could bring into her life. As mysterious and closed as he was, she was already more than halfway in love with Cruz. She wanted to lie on a blanket in the sun with him and eat strawberries. She wanted—

It was good to want things. But her life was chaotic enough as it was, without adding a man into the mix.

Her sigh shook a little as she gusted out a breath.

"You okay?" Cruz asked.

"Just really, really wired."

"It's all that adrenaline racing around your body. You'll feel better after a good night's sleep . . . or a hot night of sex."

"Right now I'm not sure I can do either, thinking about what he did to her and Charlie."

"And I'll sleep well only when I know Marcel's been arrested. If they found him." The police hadn't, as of half an hour ago. "I'll call Detective Hammell again when we get inside."

Mia didn't care that they'd already called twice in the last hour and a half. "I hope they throw the book at the pig."

She wanted Latour arrested. Just seeing Daisy lying in that hospital bed with a breathing tube and a brace around her neck had shot Mia's blood pressure sky-high. "I hope someone in prison thinks he's pretty," she told Cruz, tone grim.

"They'll get him on aggravated second-degree battery. He'll be there awhile, so there'll be plenty of opportunity for him to make friends and perhaps get a taste of his own medicine." Cruz's voice was tight. "He not only used his fists, it looks as though he gave Daisy that orbital fracture behind her bruised eye by striking her with the lamp base. He wasn't battering her. The sick fuck used brute strength and a weapon to try to kill her."

He hadn't told her that at the hospital, and now she pictured what it must've been like for Daisy. Tears prickled behind Mia's eyes, and she began to shake with a potent combination of anger, fury, and a deep-seated desire for justice. "I've never said this in my life, but I want him to die."

Cruz's fingers tightened around the curve of her shoulder. "They'll be hard on him. Prisoners don't take kindly to wife beaters."

"Then I hope he's the only beater in there, and they're all bored and looking for a punching bag."

He looked down at her, and Mia's heart did a somersault at the tender expression in his eyes. Probably the moonlight. Possibly the adrenaline. Definitely the sexy man beside her.

"Bloodthirsty. Hell, I feel exactly the same way."

"I know, right? This has brought out a whole different side of me. But, honest to God, any man who puts the people he should protect at risk deserves to die." She popped the passenger door.

As soon as they got out of the truck, the muggy heat slapped them like a hot, wet blanket. She waved away the persistent mosquito buzzing around her head, and Oso started frantically barking from inside the camper.

"Let's go liberate the beast, then hit the sack." Cruz wrapped his arm around her shoulders as they walked through the carport into the backyard, where his truck and camper were parked near the house. Mia slipped her arm around his waist and listened to the throaty moans of the frogs and the dog's happy barks as their feet crunched on the dead grass. She'd miss this place when she was back in San Francisco.

Maybe she'd keep it. Hire a property manager to ensure all the repairs got done. She could come here for vacations— No. She couldn't: (a) she never took vacations, and (b) every time she set foot on the property she'd remember Cruz.

No. When this was over, eventually she'd sell the house, and not give it a second's thought. Would their time spent together be a fond memory, or would thinking about him tear off another little chunk of her heart?

She'd deal with the aftermath as she did every other crisis, decision, and big event in her life. By analyzing it, researching her options, weighing the facts, and making an informed, rational decision.

Except she had no facts about Cruz other than what he presented to her, and, God help her, she couldn't make any rational decisions because everything she knew and felt was based on her visceral physical response to him, and pure emotion.

She knew that any man with his sexual appetite had a bedpost somewhere notched with all the nameless women he'd had sex with.

Even in his passion he was cool and controlled. He kept himself so well guarded, it would take a lifetime to really get to know him. Mia knew she didn't have lifetime, or anything close to it. He was more drifter and less the kind to stick around, especially since she'd told him the truth about who she was. She couldn't picture Cruz mixing in high society, not when he wore the bad-boy persona so well. Not that he couldn't, she suspected; he just wouldn't be bothered to make the effort.

Her business in San Francisco would be concluded in days. Todd and Miles would figure out who was trying to kill her, and she'd go home. Where did that leave any chance of a relationship with Cruz?

She knew she wouldn't sleep for what was left of the night. She had a lot to think about. At home, when her mind was too full to sleep, she went into her gym and worked out until she pretty much dropped. There was no gym here, and with Cruz in the room she wasn't going to try to master that stupid pole.

Instead, she'd lie beside him, memorizing his sleeping face all night. Because dollars to doughnuts, one day, sooner rather than later, Cruz would be long gone when she woke up.

"What are you reading?" Mia looked adorable, and sexy as hell, wearing black horn-rimmed glasses and a frown of concentration as she leaned against a mound of pillows. Her laptop was balanced precariously on the mountain of her knees and a book was propped against her thighs.

She wasn't naked. Thin, fire-engine red straps curled over creamy bare shoulders. The snowy sheet covered the rest.

Pulling the glasses down her nose, she gave him a sweet smile that caused some weird shit in his chest. Which was damned odd. He'd been aloof and cold inside from childhood. His mother's death had closed off what little emotion was left. He had never considered his lack of emotion an issue. Never even noticed one way or another.

But a smile from Mia made his insides feel as if the block of ice was slowly thawing.

Cruz felt a jolt of panic at the sensation.

Maybe, once he was satiated by her, he'd lose this odd ache he felt when she smiled at him with complete trust in her eyes.

"Tomorrow I thought I'd try my hand at making something incredibly valuable and stunningly beautiful with my potter's wheel."

He had a flash memory of some movie with two people slippery with clay. . . . "Does it have to be either to have value to you?" he asked, toeing off his shoes and pulling his T-shirt over his head at the same time.

Like a naughty schoolmarm, she gave his bare chest a hot look over her reading glasses. "No. But anything worth doing is worth doing well." Her twinkling eyes returned to his face, and she gave him a smile he was sure wasn't intended to be seductive, but the end result was the same. "I might have an aptitude for it. Who knows?"

Cruz unzipped his jeans, not in the least surprised to discover he had a boner. "You won't know till you try."

He slipped between the smooth, cool cotton sheets, then rolled to his side to face her, propping his head on his folded arm. She had all the pillows. "Are you going to be at that all night?"

"Why?" She gave him a serious look. "Do you have anything else in mind?"

"Sleep?" They could both use it. It had been an action-filled day.

She closed her computer and slid it onto the bedside table, followed by the book she'd been reading. "You should go on a regime of vitamins," she said over her bare shoulder as she turned off the light, plunging the room into darkness. "No stamina." She slid down beside him, stroking her smooth foot over his hair-roughened calf. "Would you like a pillow?"

He pulled her flush against his chest, burying his nose in the damp strands of her hair. He'd never smell tuberoses again without thinking about her. "I'll rough it tonight." Her nose nuzzled under his throat as she slung an arm across his waist. Mia was practically straddling his body. "Ever been camping?"

Not unless she considered sleeping with one eye open under an overpass camping. "No. You?"

"Uh-uh." Delicate fingers traced his rib cage. "Ever ridden a bike?" She found his nipple, then removed her finger to lick it before returning. The sensation of her wet finger tweaking his nipple, which had never been, in his entire life, an erogenous zone, made his dick jerk and weave like a divining rod to get inside her.

"Yeah. The kid I stole it from beat me within an inch of my life." His father had knocked him unconscious and put his mother in the hospital for not controlling her son. "I was nine. Last time I stole anything." Cruz stroked his hand up and down her slender back in slow, even caresses. Her skin, impossibly soft, heated with every brush of his hand.

She laid a string of kisses down his throat and played with his now hard nipple, rolling it between her fingers as he'd done to her. "I stole a lipstick from a grocery store when I was about the same age," she admitted, pausing. "Does this feel good?"

"Don't stop," he said hoarsely, skimming his fingers down the crack of her ass and making her shiver.

"My father was livid, and made my assistant take me back to the store to return it with a letter of apology. He wasn't pissed I stole it; he was pissed because it was a Revlon lipstick. Brand loyalty was important at my house."

Her father sounded like a dick. Abuse by any other name . . . "You had an assistant at nine years old?"

"I've had an assistant since I was born." Her tone was dry. "Babies have incredibly busy social lives; someone has to keep track of all those playdates, dance lessons, and birthday parties."

"Wow. Poor little rich girl."

"I didn't know any differently. How about—"

"My turn." Time to switch gears and not go down memory lane. "Ocean or mountains?"

"Ocean."

"Me, too. Drive or fly?"

"Fly."

"Yeah, I like to get there faster, too. You on top or on the bottom? No, let me answer that for you."

"How's the view up there?"

"Spectacular."

"Your eyes are closed."

"How do you know? It's pitch-dark."

"Do you realize this is the first time we've made love in the dark?" *Made love*. He hadn't even been about to say *fucked*. How had the L word slipped out? He never used it in any context, ever. And certainly never thought it.

"I like it. Eliminating one sense makes the others more intense."

"Would you like to use one of the hundreds of condoms you have in the drawer?"

"It's a bit late for that, isn't it?"

He brushed his lips over hers in a light, tantalizing kiss. "Before you, I'd never had sex without one." Never been tempted. And now he knew why. He was hungry to feel her slick, hot juices surrounding his dick as he pumped into her. Rationality was a distant annoyance. Caution thrown to the wind, he was consumed with the idea that he'd have her with nothing but lube between them. His balls tightened.

"Neither had I. I love the way you kiss. I love how smooth and firm your lips feel against mine. I love how hot the inside of your mouth is, and the taste of you. When you kiss me, it's as if there's an electrical charge running directly from my lips to my womb. It makes me hot and shivery all over."

He tangled his fingers in her hair at her nape, letting the

strands part and drift in a silky fall over the back of his hand. "Are you aware that when you're hot and shivery all over, you're blushing all over?"

Her hands clutched his shoulders. "I don't blush."

He kissed the shell of her ear, then trailed his lips down the side of her throat, his fingers still buried in her hair. "You have your own personal heat wave when you're turned on." He smiled against the rapid pulse at the base of her throat, then moved his mouth slowly to where he knew those three cute freckles were.

"You being turned on turns me on." The want, the need, he felt for this woman blew his mind. The smell of her skin made him light-headed, and as hot as a pistol. And yet, making love to her slowly was its own reward. Strong yet fragile, she was a match for his fierce and fevered passion.

Cruz kissed her luscious mouth slow and hard and deep, and felt her shudder through his own body. Everything male in him responded to the small sigh and whimpers she made.

His hands drifted over her body, her contours, hills and valley so familiar to him now, yet new because he was taking his time. Savoring her. Knowing that, after the horror she'd seen, she needed to be treated with gentle, loving hands and deep, sweet kisses.

Now he knew he was never going to kill her. Now, instead of being irritated that he couldn't resist her, he was free to relish every second that he was with her. He fondled her breast, loving the weight and shape in his hand.

"Too light." Cupping the back of his hand, she pressed his fingers down hard. His thumb rasped her nipple, just the way she liked it.

Her abdomen was flat and firm, her skin as soft as the smoothest satin. He kissed the little dimple of her navel, then swirled his tongue where he had kissed.

A primordial instinct made him want to brand her, claim her as only his. Fucking insane.

He had other commitments. So why think beyond the moment with her?

She dug her nails into his back, her hips undulating against him. He grabbed one of the pillows, stuffing it under her ass. Rising above her, he settled himself between her thighs and slid into her slowly. She was wet, slick with juices, and the slow movement of her hips in counterpoint to his set him on fire.

Sweat glued their skin together, and his breathing came hard and fast.

Her head rolled back and forth on the pillow.

His teeth ground as he tried to hold back, to give her as much pleasure as he could before they went over the edge together. All his attention was on Mia's responses: he knew her body so well, knew when she wanted him to touch her breasts, when she wanted his hand between them to touch her clit.

She cried out his name when he kissed from her breasts to her neck, then nibbled at the soft skin beneath her ear.

He moved with urgent power, primal in his need to come at the same time as Mia but so aroused by her he worried he'd come first. And that would be a first. He never lost control. Without the drumbeat of a killer governing his thoughts, she aroused him too much.

"Don't stop," she whispered, sensing that his urgency was driving him to the brink. "Please. Don't stop."

Her sheath clutching him tighter and tighter, he gritted his teeth, trying to make it last. Impossible.

"Let go, sweetheart. I'll catch you." Reaching between them, he found her clit in the swollen folds and rubbed it lightly; then, when she moaned and her hips bucked against him, he rolled her clit between his thumb and his index finger.

With every slow thrust into her, he applied more and more pressure on her clit. She screamed his name as she came. He nibbled at her neck, then let go, thrusting hard and exploding into her, biting her, branding her as his.

For now.

Chapter Thirteen

The bedroom smelled of sex and fresh paint when Mia emerged from a tepid shower. Cruz had woken her with coffee, a juicy kiss, and two slices of peanut butter toast, then informed her he was painting. They'd decided to complete the parlor so that she could get the furniture delivered before she left. Mia didn't tell Cruz the "before she left" part of that decision. Her lips had clung to his as he leaned over her, arms braced on either side of her head as he gave her a lingering good-morning kiss.

They'd spoken to the police. The bad news was that La-tour still hadn't been apprehended. But the good news was he had no idea where his wife and child were, so at least they were safe from him. He couldn't run forever. Then they called Charlie's foster mother and spoke to her, then to Charlie. He sounded subdued, but he was safe, and they assured him he'd be reunited with his mom soon. They also told him they'd pick him up later for a short visit to the hospital. Yes, they'd bring Oso.

Soon was a relative term. Daisy was in bad shape. But she'd mend, and as soon as that happened, Mia planned to fly her and Charlie to San Francisco. They could start a new life there, far away from Marcel.

All of that had happened less than an hour ago. Mia heard Cruz murmuring to Oso, and the dog's happy barks as she flung open the window to let in a warm breeze and the green smell of the bayou.

She dressed in tight black exercise shorts and a stretchy pink tank top, and made up the bed with fresh linens. Today she was determined to master the pole. Moving her computer within easy reach at the foot of the bed, she cued up the first exercise video.

Once Cruz was done in the parlor, Mia planned on contacting the furniture company in New Orleans to have that room's furniture delivered. Tomorrow, she had to go to the rented mailbox in downtown New Orleans to pick up the papers sent from David and Kent and have them notarized. Once those were returned to the investment company, and the money changed hands, she'd be the sole owner of Blush come Monday close of business.

Then she could go home. Maybe.

Sole ownership of Blush wasn't a guarantee of her safety. And Miles still hadn't ascertained who, if anyone, was trying to kill her. Maybe it was all a big tempest in a teacup, and they were being alarmist? Mia wished to hell she knew. If her death was to prevent the LBO, it would be too late once she signed the papers. And if it had nothing to do with the leveraged buyout, she had no idea who was trying to get rid of her. Would she ever know?

She sat on the foot of the neatly made bed. What if she never discovered who was trying to kill her? Would she stay in Louisiana forever? While this new life was surreal, her life in San Francisco had insidiously become the paler version of her reality.

Blush was her life. It was her birthright, her passion, her entire life from the day she'd been born. It was as if some unknown entity with enormous power had thrown her life up in the air like juggling balls, and they were falling back to earth in slow motion.

It seemed ludicrous to be trying to teach herself to swing around a pole when she didn't know where she'd be after this weekend. Tomorrow, Friday, the buyout would be officially over. That was finite.

Bayou Cheniere, Louisiana, wasn't where her life was. She belonged in the cosmopolitan city with her people around her, her meetings, her business dinners, and the opera.

And Cruz? How did he fit into her real life?

He knew all her secrets, and it felt right to trust him. She felt safe with him. What she'd do with that, Mia didn't know. But for now it was good to know she had him at her back.

One more day and the LBO would be a done deal. Then Saturday and Sunday before the investment brokers received the paperwork back. Then she'd have to decide if she wanted to remain in Louisiana hiding, or go back to San Francisco and face this situation and take a more hands-on approach.

Decisions had to be made.

She always felt better when she'd made a decision and took action.

But right now, all she had to think about was mastering the pole. She looked over the detailed text description for the move that was being demonstrated on the video, and skeptically eyed the jar of iTack2, which apparently was going to help her stick to the pole like a baby tree frog. Now or never.

The pole felt cold against her bare arm and hooked leg as Mia perfected the first handhold. He'd called her "sweetheart." Was that a universal endearment when he couldn't remember the woman's name? Her stepmother called everyone, even those she'd just met, "honey" because she never listened when introduced, so she didn't know anyone's name. She'd been married to Amelia's father for almost three years and had called her stepdaughter by her name perhaps twice. Candice still called her "honey." Even when she came to the office.

She paused, one ankle hooked around the base of the pole, her hands— Where was her left hand supposed to be? Leaning over the keyboard, Mia backspaced to see that section of video again. The moves were basic, so-called easy. Maybe she needed the knee-high, high-heeled boots the instructor wore?

To "Blurred Lines," she imitated the slinky, catlike walk of the instructor and approached the pole again. "Okay, pole. Front hook spin. Ready?" Leg hooked on the pole, Mia hung from it like a monkey and executed a sort-of, kind-of spin around it. Her biceps protested. She did it again. And again. Easier each time.

She attempted a back hook spin and nearly dislocated her

neck. "Skip to the next." Fast-forwarding the instructional video, she slinked back to the pole. Thank God no one was watching, because she was pretty sure she looked like an idiot. She imagined Todd watching her, and could almost hear her cousin saying, "Dance like no one is watching. Feel the music."

Okay, new music. She started up "Closer" by Nine Inch Nails. The lyrics were rude, crude, and offensive as hell, and the beat primal and sexy. Mia blocked out the words and let the driving rhythm take her.

"God, that's sexy as hell." Cruz's large hands circled her bare waist as he came up behind her. "I'd consider the class money well spent."

Mia gave his wandering hand a small smack as he explored her breast. "I haven't done anything but wrap myself around this thing. Come back later when I have half a clue."

"I can stay and help. For a start, I think you have on too many clothes."

"Don't you have something to paint?"

"I do. But I need to run to the hardware store for another gallon for the trim, and might as well pick up those plumbing supplies. Want to come with me? We can stop for lunch at Sandy's, or go into Houma."

Mia shuddered at the name of the coffee shop. "Maybe she knows which rock her dickhead brother is hiding under."

"She wouldn't tell me if she did. Don't worry, the cops will find him. Coming or staying?"

"Staying. I'm on a learning curve with my pole dancing.

You're on your own with picking out thingamajigs and other doohickeys. Get a rain shower jet while you're at it."

"Not enough water pressure, unless you get new pipes and a bigger water tank."

"I'll add those to my list."

He cast a quick amused glance at the pole. "Maybe I should stay to supervise. You might climb too high and need help getting down."

Mia laughed and pushed him with her palm on his muscular chest. "Go. Anticipate all the cool moves I'll show you later."

"Don't break anything."

She turned up "Tainted Love," the pounding beat perfect for getting in the mood.

An hour later, sweaty and triumphant, she'd mastered a dozen moves, including hanging upside down like a bat. The problem with the basic inversion position wasn't getting into the position; it was unknotting herself and getting on her feet instead of sliding down the pole onto her head. Currently she was twined, ankles tightly crossed, gripping the pole tightly between her legs, watching the video upside down, the blood rushing to her head.

The plan was to loosen her hands and tuck her head in a graceful slide, supported by her legs. Except that she couldn't quite get the knack of opening her hands. Eyes closed for a moment, she visualized the graceful, head-tucked slide.

Mia had just started to let go with her hands, when she felt a hard hand on her ankle, and wrinkled her nose because Cruz smelled different—like stale pizza and booze. Her heart jerked in warning. "That was quick. Did you change your m—"

Starting to twist herself right side up, she opened her eyes. The smile disappeared as she was unceremoniously, and violently, yanked off the pole, saving her from doing it herself. It didn't hurt any less.

Landing hard on her hip, Mia looked up at Marcel Latour with dread. He stood over her, his flushed face contorted in a rictus of fury. A vein bulged in his forehead. His dirty orange T-shirt was the same one he'd worn all week, and it smelled like sweat and desperation, and was covered with food stains and, she realized sickly, his wife's dried blood. Clearly he'd had enough liquid courage for him to barge into her house with blood in his eye.

Her heart slammed up into her throat, and her mouth went dry. Mia scrabbled backward on her butt, trying to get her feet under her. Cold sweat prickled her skin at the feral look on his face "You have no business being here. Leave. Now. Get out of my damn hou—"

Unshaven, with bloodshot eyes and heavy stubble, he was mean drunk and furious. With shocking speed, he grabbed her throat and hauled her to her feet, his fingers digging into her skin like painful steel bands. Her heart leaped, then started pounding hard and fast.

Her throat hurt from the pressure of his fingers, and it was hard to drag in a breath between him cutting off her air and sheer, unadulterated panic. Mia grabbed his forearms, digging her nails into his skin, trying to break his hold. She gagged. Black spots danced in her vision and her ears roared as she struggled like a fish on a line to break free.

Bringing his face right up to hers, he shouted, "Where the fuck is she, bitch?" Boozy spit flew with every word.

She gasped for air as she dug her short nails deeper into his forearms, trying to break his hold on her throat, shoving as hard as she could, her legs flailing uselessly. His grip and the violent shaking just got harder and more out of control.

Her panic and fear rose like a black tide, wiping out all reason. She screamed in fear, in fury. But there was no one to hear her. She was an animal caught in a trap, and fought as hard as she could to break free. Nobody had ever put their hands on her in anger in her life. And while theoretically she knew what she should be doing, her brain went completely blank in the face of such violence.

"How did you get into the house?" Mia gasped inanely. The back door locked automatically. Why hadn't Oso barked? How long until Cruz came back? An hour? More? She'd lost track. All she knew was that this man had beaten his wife and almost killed her, and he'd have absolutely no compunction doing that, or worse, to her.

The Beretta was under the far side of the bed. It was loaded—all she had to do was get to it and flip the safety.

Marcel backhanded her, snapping her head so she fell backward, held upright only by his fingers clamped around her neck. The metallic taste of blood filled her mouth, and her heartbeat was manic as tears of pain stung her eyes. She blinked the moisture away, struggling with all her strength to get free.

She kicked his leg but, barefoot, it didn't have any impact. He was an arm's length away, so she couldn't bite or head-butt him or knee him in the balls. All she could do was use both hands and her nails to lessen his grip on her throat.

It would be pretty pathetic if she was murdered by a drunken, wife beater instead of a highly paid assassin.

Stop being a damn girl, Amelia Elizabeth!

Thinkthinkthink. Don't panic. Think.

"You fucking told her to leave me! Take my kid? Who the fuck do you think you are, you sanctimonious bitch?"

"I offered to help h—" Oh, crap. Wrong thing to say. He swung back the hand on her neck, giving her a nanosecond to suck in oxygen, then backhanded her again, his full body weight behind his arm. This time she saw sparkling silver dots in front of her eyes as she staggered back to slam into the wall. The impact jarred every bone of her body. She used the palms of her hands on the wall to steady herself because she couldn't get her footing enough to maintain her balance.

"*I* help her, you fucking rich bitch!" he yelled, grabbing the front of her tank top, his nails scratching her chest as he dragged her upright and began shaking her like a rag doll. "She doesn't need someone like you putting fancy ideas in her stupid brain, now, does she?"

"If Cruz finds you here, he'll kill you." The words came out of her mouth as a threat, but Mia realized she believed them. If Cruz saw this man with his hands on her, he'd take immediate action.

But Cruz wasn't here. And by the time he did get back, it

might be too late. She wasn't prepared to wait to be rescued. She absolutely had to get her shit together and be smart if she had a hope in hell of surviving this.

"You think I'm scared of your pussy lover boy?" he scoffed, fingers clamped at her throat tightly enough that she felt dizzy and light-headed and the black dots returned. "A drifter?" His voice came at her down a long tunnel as blood pounded in her ears. "Where's your phone? Call Daisy and tell her to get her ass back home where she belongs. Tell her she'd better goddamn be there when I get there, or she'll be good and fucking sorry."

She barely heard him over the fast drum of her heartbeat. "My phone's d-downstairs. Why don't you go ahead and go home? I'll make sure she's there waiting for you."

"I don't believe you!"

"Do you want me to call her? You can tell her yourself." If she could get downstairs, she had a better chance of getting out of the house. The garden was still so overgrown, she could hide in a dozen places, or go over the wall and hide between the mausoleums in the graveyard next door.

But Latour knew the garden better than she did, and the crumbling stone wall was six feet high. She'd have to run like hell. Down the gravel driveway, and—

"Give me your phone!"

"I told you. It's downsta—"

The horrible pressure of his fingers around her throat eased, and she sucked in half a breath of blessed relief. But it was just a momentary reprieve. "You lie!" he screamed, grabbing a handful of hair at her temple and flinging her across the room.

Mia tried to break her fall, but she slid across the carpet on her side, then banged her head against the leg of the bedside table and saw stars. There was no time for pain, or rationale. She was operating on pure animal self-preservation.

"Everybody carries their phone with them wherever they fucking go! Give it to me—"

She blinked rapidly to bring him into focus, stupid and dizzy with pain and sheer, unadulterated terror. As he walked toward her, she scrabbled under the bed like a crab in the confined space, her breathing harsh and erratic. She had to get to the other side, grab the gun—

Hard fingers grabbed her ankle and yanked hard as he used his body weight, attempting to drag her out from under the bed. Mia flipped on her back, using her free foot to wedge up against the bottom of the box mattress to prevent him from pulling her free.

The lockbox was perhaps two feet away from her outstretched, straining fingers, but felt like a hundred miles. Sweat stung her eyes, and adrenaline raced through her body, making everything feel surreal and in slow motion.

Hurryhurryhurry.

Curled up in the narrow space between the bedspring and floor, with her free foot she used the hard edges of the box spring to anchor herself while Marcel pulled and twisted her other foot to pull her free. All the while he was screaming invectives and threats. Mia didn't bother listening. It was all noise. She shut it out. She shut out the pain he was inflicting on her ankle, and the way the wood slats hurt her foot and hand wedged tightly against the frame.

She. Was. Not. Letting. Go. Fuck him. If he wanted to kill her, he'd have to crawl under the bed with her.

She knew she had to be proactive, but for once in her life she had no idea how. The knowledge that she was helpless to deal with the situation scared her almost as much as the situation. If she could just have a few minutes to think—

Her fingers screamed with agony as he pulled, but she maintained her grip on the hard wood frame. Stretching her arm overhead to reach the lockbox, every muscle and tendon, like rubber bands about to snap, screamed in agony. She felt as though, any minute, she'd be snapped in two.

Still holding her bare foot, Latour lay on the floor now. His voice echoed in the confined space, so enraged, so out of control, that he was inarticulate. His fingers scrabbled up her leg, his nails scoring her bare calf as he tried to use her leg as a fulcrum to force her out from under the bed.

Lashing out with her wedged foot, she kicked him in the face. As hard as she could under the circumstances. There wasn't much power behind it, but for a moment he released her other ankle enough, giving her time to slide away from his flailing hands.

Sweat dripped into her eyes, and Mia's manic heartbeat tripped, then raced even faster as her fingertips brushed the metal box just as Marcel dug his fingers into her foot again. *God, oh God, oh God.* The crazy son of a bitch was crawling under the bed after her. She let out a cry of pure fury. The man was like a damned zombie.

"Hi, honey, I'm home— What the fuck!"

Cruz. Mia almost puked with relief.

Cruz yelled out the teasing greeting before he entered the bedroom. What he saw when he walked in chilled his blood. The bottom half of a man, in filthy jeans and work boots, protruded from his side of the bed.

Dropping the plastic bag of plumbing parts, he dashed across the room, grabbed the man's legs, and dragged his ass out from under the bed.

His blood chilled as he wrenched Latour off the floor, and decked him before he stood upright. Twisting a fistful of the man's shirt in his left hand, he yelled, "Mia, where the fuck are you? Are you all right?"

"Yes."

Latour swung a fist, trying to reach him. Cruz just held him at arm's length, so his punches went wide. The guy cursed a blue streak. "You can't do this. I have my rights—"

Cruz punched him again, getting satisfaction from the crunch of cartilage and the instant gush of blood from Latour's nose. "You don't have any fucking rights, dickwad. You lost them the moment you broke in and committed assault. Call the cops," he told Mia.

"M-my phone's d-downstairs." Disheveled, glassy-eyed,

Mia emerged on the opposite side of the mattress, the gun box clutched in a white-knuckled grip as she staggered to her feet.

Latour continued to fight Cruz's firm hold on him as Cruz watched Mia from the corner of his eye. She seemed to be whole. He didn't see blood, but he saw the dark smudge of bruises beginning to form on the delicate skin of her throat and along one cheek.

Latour's boot hit him a glancing blow on his knee. "You can't steal a man's family. I have my rights!"

Cruz kicked his legs out from under him and planted a heavy foot on his throat the second the dickhead hit the floor. "Use mine." He tossed his phone on the other side of the bed close to where she stood.

It took every ounce of control for Cruz not to shatter the man's skull like a fucking watermelon after what he'd done to Mia. Not to mention putting his wife in the fucking hospital, and scaring the shit out of his kid. But then it wouldn't look like an accident, and he couldn't afford for the police to dig too deeply into his handyman persona and find out who he really was.

"She's mine, dammit!" His breath wheezed as he tried to suck in the small sip of air Cruz allowed him in a moment of generosity. "You and your damn Yankee bitch got no business here. We take care of our own. You fuckers better tell me where she is or I'll kill the both of you with my bare hands," Latour shouted. "You're nothing but a vagrant and she's"—Latour pawed at his face, catching clots of blood that dripped from his nose as his gaze fell on Mia—"and she's nothing but—"

Cruz didn't want to hear another word from this asshole. He put his foot not so gently over the man's mouth and broken nose. Latour gave out a pained, muffled shriek and his eyes rolled. "Not such a fucking macho man now, are you? Don't like someone bigger, stronger, and smarter than you getting the upper hand? Too bad, shithead. You're going to jail for a long, long time. Get up." Cruz hauled Latour up by twisting his hand behind his back with slightly less force than necessary to break it, then held him tightly as he struggled and blubbered.

Mia, white-faced, hands shaking, reached across the rumpled bed, snatched up the phone, then punched out the three numbers with a hand that shook.

"Detective Hammell, please." Her legs gave out and she dropped to her knees, elbows braced on the mattress as she waited.

Cruz wanted nothing more than to scoop her up into his arms and hold her. But he had a little lesson to teach Latour before the cops arrived.

"I'll be right back. Stay put." He heard her speaking to the detective as he frog-marched the struggling Latour down the hall, arm twisted high on his back.

Five minutes later, Cruz was back in the bedroom, Mia on his lap, his face buried in her hair. Her sob wrenching up through her chest tore at her throat.

"Hey. I've got you. You're okay. I've got you."

"I'm so f-fricking . . . furious!"

Well, that was better than scared or in pain. He'd considered knocking Latour unconscious, but then the bastard couldn't feel any pain, so he'd opted for him to sit it out until the cops arrived. "He'll be in custody soon where he can't hurt anyone."

"I'm f-furious at m-myself! I can't believe I allowed that—that low-life piece of shit to terrorize me. I'm strong and smart and resourceful, damn it."

Cruz gently brushed his hand over her hair. "Jesus, sweetheart, he was drunk, has fifty pounds on you, and was determined as hell. You did what you could to prevent him killing you. I'd say that was a win."

"I know how to shoot. I should've shot the son of a bitch."

Cruz didn't point out that the gun's lockbox was secured, the key in the bedside table.

"I hate that I froze instead of fighting back. *Hate* it. I took self-defense classes, for God's sake. I know how to defend myself. To be honest, I shocked myself. I would've thought I could've handled that situation, if not with ease, then with smarts. I failed myself on all counts."

"Different in a real-world situation when your adrenaline is pumping and your opponent has nothing to lose. Don't beat yourself up about it."

"Believe me," she told him, voice grim, eyes flat, "my pity party is already over. I'll never be caught like that ever again. Forget learning how to frigging pole dance. I'm going to master self-defense and kick the next attacker's ass. Better yet, I'm going to learn how to become an expert marksman so I can shoot whoever is coming after me."

"Excellent sentiment. But there won't be a next time. I

won't leave you alone again when a crazed wife abuser's on the loose."

She frowned. "There are plenty of other threats out there, and you know it. Someone might still be trying to kill me for one, in case you've forgotten. You won't always be with me, will you?"

Fortunately, it was a rhetorical question. She obviously knew the answer. "I won't leave you until the matter's resolved," he told her, yet it was the hardest promise he'd ever made. He had to leave her, and he had to do it as soon as he knew she'd be safe. Urgent departure was required, because if he didn't leave her soon, he'd never be able to. He enjoyed being with her too much. And that thought scared the crap out of him. One day she'd find out what he was. Then she'd hate him. Hate everything about him.

"Then for your sake I hope everything is resolved by Monday. I have to decide where to go from there."

Cruz had a not-so-short list of priorities to focus on. All essential.

1. Keep Mia alive.
2. Find out who'd paid for the hit before they hired someone else to finish his job.
3. Deal with them.
4. Discover who else had been hired.
5. Stop them.
6. Save Daisy and Charlie.
7. Deal with Latour.
8. Don't fall in love.

Detective Hammell and two other cops showed up twenty minutes later. "What happened to him?" he asked Cruz, who leaned against the counter, drinking a cup of tepid coffee.

He'd worked Latour over, so that, besides his bloody, swollen nose, he had lacerations and bruising on his arms. Sick of listening to the man whine and berate him, his wife, Mia, and the entire universe for how shitty his life was, Cruz had used duct tape to bind him to a bar stool, then slapped a piece over his mouth. Latour's eyes were feral over the silvery tape.

Cruz shrugged. "Drunk. Fell down the stairs. I have one for you. Why isn't he in jail?" Hammell, a slightly overweight fifty-something with a hangdog expression and light eyes that had seen it all, cast Latour an unsympathetic glance. "Cousin twice removed is police chief. Posted bail."

Shit.

As his men cut away the tape around his chest, arms, and legs, the detective gave a nod of approval. "Nice job," he told Cruz as the last of the tape was tossed aside and Latour was secured with cuffs. "He'll probably trip again a couple of times on the way to the squad car. He's pretty tanked, and some people are just accident-prone."

Cruz's lips twitched.

Chapter Fourteen

*A*fter Mia grabbed a shower and applied some antiseptic to the scratches and makeup to the bruises Latour had inflicted, they loaded an ecstatic Oso into her truck. Cruz drove, and they went to pick up Charlie from his foster family in Metairie, a suburb of New Orleans located on the south shore of Lake Pontchartrain, then headed to the hospital.

Because of the heat, Cruz stayed with the dog in the air-conditioned truck, letting Mia and Charlie go in together. His heart twisted as the child slipped his hand into Mia's as they walked.

She was wearing a summery dress the color of crushed strawberries that bared her shoulders, and high-heeled strappy sandals that showed off her toned legs to perfection. He knew where each and every bruise was, but she'd covered the smudges with makeup, and from where he was sitting she looked flawless, fresh, and sexy as hell.

Charlie tugged on her hand, and they stopped at the entrance to the hospital. Mia paused to crouch down, smoothing back Charlie's hair as they talked. After a few minutes, the little boy flung himself at her, his arms tight around her neck.

Mia soothed his back, then rose and took his hand again. They disappeared inside.

Cruz swallowed the damn lump in his throat. "Now what?" he asked the dog, sitting upright and alert in the passenger seat. Oso swiveled his head to give him what Cruz was sure was an inquiring look. "Never mind." Oso cocked his head.

Never mind because Cruz had no intention of putting anything emotional out into the ether that could come back later to bite him in the ass.

Just like he didn't tear up at pictures of cute cats and dog tricks, seeing Mia showing an unexpected maternal side shouldn't have any emotional impact on him. He didn't do sentimental, and he never noticed shit like that.

Cruz turned up the air, cooling the cab and directing a vent in Oso's panting direction. "I need to make a couple of calls, then how about we get out and stretch our legs?"

Clearly realizing there'd be more waiting, Oso sighed lugubriously, then lay down with his head on his paws to stare as Cruz took out his phone and speed dialed Lì húa Sòng in Beijing.

"What updates do you have on the factory?" There was a twelve-hour time difference, and since he knew she was a night owl, he wasn't concerned about waking her at eleven at night.

"Even for you this is no civilized greeting, *bǎobèi*," she responded tersely, still using the endearment she'd used years ago when they'd been lovers. "Five more children died. The investigation appears to be closed. Faulty wiring, unsafe conditions, not uncommon in situations such as this. As of yesterday, Blush China is back in business. More children hired. Everyone working extra hours to make up for the loss of time."

"Jesus. That's cold. Will the families be compensated?"

There was a pause. "No. The children were disposable. Most came from— Never mind. No. There will be no compensation. On the other matter. I did facial rec on the woman at the airport."

Lì húa Sòng's government contacts had proven invaluable over the years. Cruz no longer wondered in what capacity she worked, just that she had pull and could get answers. Just as she'd never delved into what he did for a living. They'd lived in the moment, and both, he'd thought at the time, been content.

"And?" Cruz clenched his fingers on the steering wheel. *Don't tell me conclusively that the woman was Mia.*

"Very similar features and bearing, but the woman who visited here was not Amelia Wentworth."

He straightened in the seat. "All three times? You're sure?"

"Positive. I believe the woman who came here wore expertly fabricated prosthetics."

Jesus. With the sudden lightness of relief came the grind of concern. Someone had gone to extraordinary lengths to implicate Mia. Who? Why? "*Xiè xiè nǐ bāng wǒ, Lì húa.*"

"You are most welcome." There was a pregnant pause. "Why she so important this woman? Are you sleeping with her, Cruz?"

"You lost the right to ask that question many years ago," he reminded her gently.

"This is true," she said with quiet regret. "I wish you well, *qīn ài de nǐ*. Call me if there is any other service I can provide."

He was no longer her dear, and Cruz was sorry to hear sadness in her voice. He knew he had been the love of Lì húa's life, but he'd had nothing but a deep respect and fondness for her when they'd been lovers. He'd been with her for half a year, then left Beijing when—after pressing him for a more formal relationship—she announced her engagement to a family friend. He hadn't been heartbroken, he'd just moved on.

There was no chitchat or catching up. They said goodbye and Cruz wondered if he'd ever speak to her again.

"I'm not the hearth-and-home kinda guy," he told Oso, clipping on a leash to take him for a walk while they waited for Mia and Charlie to return. The dog's eyes tracked his every move, and his slowly wagging tail became an entire body wiggle, with lashing tail and perked ears.

Cruz found a tree-shaded grassy area and let the dog sniff around. Had whoever hired him tried at first to discredit Amelia/Mia and, when that hadn't worked, put out the hit? It didn't make sense, but neither did the way things had gone down. The factory fire had only happened this week. He'd taken the job and been paid a shitload of money as a deposit weeks ago.

It made sense if this was all about her leveraged buyout. If someone wanted to prevent that from happening, they could feasibly want her discredited so the stock prices went down. The same if she unexpectedly died.

But by tomorrow all the speculation would be over. Once she signed those papers, it would all be over.

"Which means," he told the dog, who'd stopped exploring to come and sit at his feet, looking expectant, "that if I was going to kill her, I'd do it before she got her hands on those papers, right?" Oso wagged his tail just as Cruz's phone vibrated in his back pocket. He checked the number. The person who'd hired the hit. Cruz turned off the phone.

"I think you were supposed to turn two streets back," Mia told Cruz. Charlie sat between them, but he kept squirming to scratch Oso's head.

"We have to stop at the store." Cruz pulled into the parking lot of a PetSmart. "Oso wants a ball."

She raised an eyebrow at him over Charlie's dark head.

"*A ball?*" Charlie's voice went up several octaves. "How come he wants a ball?"

"He's got a boy," Cruz said, expression serious. "Every dog needs a boy and a ball, right? Hop out on this side, kid."

"*I'm* a boy," Charlie whispered, cheeks flushed, eyes bright as he turned to Mia as if for confirmation.

Her heart squeezed; there was so much longing, so much hope, in that look, and yet the child was already anticipating that this would not go as hoped. "Perfect," she told him cheerfully, eyes stinging behind her sunglasses. "And you're *exactly* the right boy to help Oso pick out the best ball in the whole store."

Cruz lifted the little boy out of the truck and shot a smile at her, a real smile that showed the long dimple in his cheek and sent rays of light to every part of Mia's body.

Opening the back door, he grabbed Oso's leash and let the dog jump out, all happy panting and wagging tail. "Let's go find him the best ball they have. It might take some time," he told Mia, straight-faced. "Kick back and turn up the air. We have men's work to do here."

"Yes," Charlie told her, peering at her very seriously as he stood on tiptoe so he could see into the big truck from his position beside Cruz on the curb. "Men's work."

A couple of hours in a local park, a stop at a fast-food burger place for Charlie, and the boy and dog were worn-out.

Cruz had a quick talk with Joann Follmer when they dropped Charlie off at his foster family. Permission asked for and granted for an overnight stay for Oso, and they left the two playing tag in the front yard. "That was sweet of you." Mia threaded her fingers through his as he drove away. "Oso will protect him and help him not be so scared when he goes to bed tonight."

"Every kid has the right to not be scared *every* fucking night."

"Don't yell. I agree with you one hundred percent."

He parked the car in a lot behind Café Du Monde, then guided her along the walkway that bordered the Mississippi River. She said she'd never been to New Orleans, but he'd been here several times. The noisy crowds starting to wander between the bars, nightclubs, and tourist-crowded restaurants over one block to Royal Street. While many of the shops had already closed for the day, some were still open, selling everything from shot glasses and sunscreen to Mardi Gras masks. Here and there the hum of conversation and clinking of dinnerware and the sultry, soulful sounds of jazz music came from the open doors of restaurants, and tourist groups milled about, waiting for tours of the French Quarter to begin.

It was the kind of city through which all kinds of people traveled, a hard-hitting city with a high enough crime rate that locals were immune to shocking news and officials were too busy to care much about murders that looked like accidents. It was a great place for a Cruz-style hit.

Mia's fingers tightened in his. Her personality was so big, it always surprised Cruz how small her bones were. His fingers closed around hers as they walked along the river, then turned onto Conti, a side street that led toward Royal. They wove between the musicians and street vendors who dotted the sidewalks along the gated gardens of St. Louis Cathedral.

He knew just where he wanted to take her to dinner, and had called ahead and set it up. For now they joined what felt like a party as they strolled the streets of the French Quarter. "You made Charlie's day," she told him. "If not his year."

"Yeah, well, it shouldn't take a damned tennis ball and an hour in the park to make a kid's day."

"When I talk to my cousin tomorrow, I'll ask him to set the ball in motion for a place for Daisy and Charlie to live. Something temporary until she can get her feet under her. I'd offer to let her stay with me for a while, but something tells me she'd refuse."

Not if he had anything to do with it. But that was a ways off. Daisy needed to stay put for several more weeks. And the longer she was stuck in that hospital bed, the more chance Latour had of finding her. Even with the round-the-clock security Cruz had hired. "Hungry?"

"Not yet. Oh! Look, a fortune-teller." She tugged his hand and walked faster, toward an antique store that fronted on Royal Street. The shop had closed for the night, and the covered entrance, slightly off the busy sidewalk, became premium space for the woman, who had purple streaks in long, inky black hair, a crimson halter, and a flowing blue skirt.

She couldn't be more clichéd if she tried. Cruz allowed himself to be tugged along. Mia happy was worth spending time with a tarot reader or whatever she was going to profess to be.

Her table was covered with a black velvet cloth, on which sat tarot cards, rocks, a crystal ball, and a dozen flickering tea lights. A black cat on a rhinestone leash sat at her feet, licking its paws. Very atmospheric.

Mia tugged at his hand, a little harder this time. "Come on."

"You're joking, right?"

"It's just for fun." She paused, giving him a quick quizzical look. "Scared?"

"Terrified," he told her dryly. "I'll pass." He was sorely tempted to pull Mia along, away from the street performer, but once she'd made eye contact with the woman, it was too late.

"You want your fortune read by Madame LaBelle, pretty lady."

Mia plopped her butt in the chair. "Yes."

With a small shake of his head, Cruz took up position behind her chair.

"What kind of reading of the cards would you like: something fast and quick, or something more in-depth?" The woman's gaze never left Mia's. "Five dollars for a past, present, and future reading, twenty-five for the full spread of the cards."

"The simple read, please."

Cruz handed the woman five bucks. "If she's a mind reader, she wouldn't have to ask," he whispered as he reached over her shoulder to hand over the money. The woman took it as fast as a Venus flytrap snapped up a hamburger. She spared Cruz a back-off-and-shut-up glance, then focused on Mia.

While it appeared that Cruz's attention was focused on the two women at the table, he was minutely aware of the people milling around them. Of the cars, the music, the smells, and the lights.

The fortune-teller took the worn stack of oversize cards beside her and set the stack in the middle of the table between her and Mia. "Lay your hands on the cards and think about the questions you want answered. When you are ready, pick whatever three cards you wish and lay them out facedown next to each other in front of you."

Mia did as she was instructed and cupped her hands around the deck of cards, then slowly slid three random cards out of the deck.

"Good. Now let us see what the cards have to say." The fortune-teller touched her finger to the first card on Mia's left. "This is your immediate past. It shows what has laid heavy on your heart and shaped the point where you are today." She flipped the card and an image of a knight surrounded by fallen, slain enemies and five swords. "The Five of Swords. There is someone close to you who is making decisions, heedless of what others need or want. They work behind your back with hostility and trickery to get what they want and gain advantage in the situation. You have been lied to by those closest to you."

Faux fortune-teller or not, this was a fucking heads-up that he should've told Mia the truth by now. She deserved to be told. *Oh, by the way, I'm the hit man hired to kill you, but I've changed my mind.* Yeah. That would go over well.

"And this one?" Mia pointed to the next card while Cruz admired the way the lights gleamed on her hair and highlighted the curve of her cheek. It also gleamed on the long red scar on her upper arm. A harsh reminder that if it wasn't him who did the job, they'd send someone else.

Time was short.

Tonight. He'd tell her tonight when they got home.

The woman flipped the middle card. "This is your present."

"Well, that's cheerful," he murmured, and Mia shushed

him. A skull, its empty eye sockets staring back from beneath a metal war helmet, didn't need much explanation in Cruz's opinion.

"This is the Death card."

Mia shivered. Fake psychic or not, this was a bad idea under the circumstances. "I'm starving, let's make tracks. We have a reserva—"

"Do not fear it." The woman grasped Mia's hand, her rings winking in the candlelight. "While it can mean literal death on occasion, more often it is the death of things, situations, and people you have outgrown. A cutting of ties. Those who have lied to you or hurt you being tossed out of your life. A sudden transition into something better."

Cruz disagreed. Death meant death in his book. Plain. Simple. Final.

Mia flipped over the last card herself. "Tell me about my future."

"The Ten of Cups. Happiness in your domestic life. People who have experienced trials and tribulations together finding a successful moment of peace." The woman glanced up at him. "It's also the card of weddings."

Okay, for a moment, just a moment, Cruz thought she had something possibly going for her card reading. Two out of two wasn't bad. But she was so wrong on the third card, he couldn't maintain his willing suspension of disbelief any longer, not even for Mia's benefit. Weddings? Happy domestic bliss? Not. A. Fucking. Chance.

Then he had a revelation that sobered him instantly. Yeah.

Mia could have that. But the man couldn't be *him*. Wasn't that a fucking kick in the balls? She'd get her happily ever after, her long life. But he wouldn't have any part in it.

No point spilling his guts, he acknowledged. He'd do his thing and walk away. Same as he always did. It was a relief, really. He wasn't into confessions or declaration. Clean, sharp. Done.

Mia stood, thanked the woman, then wrapped her arm around his and nestled her head against his shoulder as they continued their stroll up Royal Street. "You know, she wasn't that far off."

Cruz made a noncommittal grunt.

"Right now, the only person I trust one hundred percent is you."

Mia couldn't have executed a cleaner shot straight to his gut. Guilt hit with the precise hot aim of a bullet.

He steered her into a restaurant and hoped like hell the bar was well stocked.

"This is nice." Mia smiled as she rejoined him at the table and slid into the banquet seat. Mr. B's restaurant was crowded on a Thursday night. She had no idea how Cruz had managed to get them a corner booth almost right away. People spilled out onto the street, cups in hand, having a party of their own on the crowded sidewalk as they waited for tables.

She'd reapplied Ready To Go red lipstick and a spritz of Blush's Aphrodite before leaving the restroom, then ruffled her fingers through her hair to give it a sexy tousled look. "Almost like a date."

He didn't return her smile, but Mia superimposed the smile he'd given her earlier over his serious features. He was so guarded, he was hard to read, and he hoarded his smiles like a miser his gold. "Whatever that perfume is you're wearing must make your company a fortune. I watched men's heads turn as you walked by—poor bastards were salivating."

Holding his gaze, she scooted a bit closer. "I only want one man to salivate."

"Then you've achieved your goal. That stuff is an aphrodisiac."

Taking his hand, which lay on the table, she weaved her fingers through his. "Thank you for everything you're doing for Daisy and Charlie," she said quietly.

Their corner was slightly quieter than the rest of the restaurant, but she leaned against his arm, enjoying the tensile strength and the heat of his skin. "I was so freaked out at the time, that it didn't occur to me to hire security to keep her safe."

"You covered her medical bills."

Mia played with his fingers. He had nice hands, with broad palms, long fingers, and nicely shaped nails. She stroked a finger along the ridge of calluses at the base of his fingers. "She doesn't have family. And I want her as far away from here as possible. They won't release her for several weeks, by which time I'll be home, and can do what needs to be done. It depends on how long they keep dickface in jail."

His lips twitched. "'Dickface'?"

She shrugged. "I couldn't think of anything bad enough."

"'Dickface' works just fine. They'll add time for his assault on you; breaking and entering, too. He has a cousin who's not taking his incarceration well. Even with your charges, Hammell told me they could only do a twenty-four-hour hold until Daisy presses charges and he has his day in court."

"Hard to do when she's so out of it. I think she knew Charlie was in the room, but she didn't open her eyes. It killed me that he had to see his mother like that. The bruising was so much worse today than it was yesterday, and Charlie freaked out seeing all the tubes and hearing the beeps of the monitors."

"If he hadn't run all the way to get us, their story would've ended up very differently." His leashed anger was evident in the tightness of his jaw and the way his fingers flexed in hers. "His being a drunk has little to do with the violence. He'd be like that without the booze. Alcohol just exacerbates the fact that he's an angry, weak man who preys on those smaller and weaker than himself."

Mia realized that he was also talking about his own father, and she turned their hands so they were palm to palm, her hand cradling his.

"Being a husband and father isn't about strength," she said quietly. "It's about making the right decisions for your family; it's about fully assessing situations before you put your family at risk. We can both relate to Charlie, because neither of us had a father who treated people with dignity or respect. Yours was like Latour: he ruled with his fists. My abuse was a lot more subversive. But in the end we were both colored by who our fathers were. I'd like to be a part of helping Charlie learn that there are men who are good and kind, and that not every male in his life is angry and violent."

The waiter appeared as if by magic. They ordered bowls of seafood gumbo, grilled redfish, and a bottle of crisp pinot grigio.

"What happens tomorrow?" Cruz asked as the waiter left with their orders.

"I go to my mailbox place and pick up the papers. Sign them in front of a notary and overnight them back to the investment company."

"I thought no one knew where you were." Cruz straightened, suddenly alert.

"I contacted the investment company directly, via email. I had to give the private-equity firm an address to send the papers. Don't worry. The mailbox rental place is here in New Orleans, and they have a notary. I'll be in and out in a flash. They open at nine. I'll drive in, and be back home for breakfast."

"Not showing your hand would be better yet. This is still too damned close to Bayou Cheniere for my liking."

"Well, the papers have to be signed, and Todd and Miles won't let me return to San Francisco to sign them there."

"Now at least three people know you're in New Orleans?"

"No. Although, as I told you, I trust them one hundred percent. I only gave the equity company the address, and directly to the personal email of the man in charge of my LBO."

"Michael Ordway."

"Ye—" Her eyebrows rose. "How do you know his name?"

"Because you've been convinced someone is trying to fucking kill you, and while you only want to know the *who*, I fucking want to know the *why*."

"That doesn't answer the question, Cruz. How do you know Ordway's name?"

"You told me the name of the company. I know this much about you: you'd only deal with their top man. Ordway is that man. He's savvy, well respected, and a shark for his clients."

Mia mulled that over. She wasn't accustomed to people second-guessing her, nor was she used to someone stepping in to protect her. It felt odd. Good, but . . . odd.

He brought her hand to his lips and kissed her fingers, a sweetly romantic gesture that made her heart kick up pleasantly. "Trust me. I only want to keep you safe. Let's forget business," he murmured, his breath humid on her skin, "and for a few hours, other people's problems, and just drink our wine and enjoy our meal."

"Excellent plan."

He reached into his back pocket, and withdrew a piece of lined paper, which Mia recognized as from her pad in the kitchen. She smiled. "So, instead of heavy dinner-table topics, you want to talk about construction and plumbing? Let's move that hot-water tank to the top of the list."

He unfolded the single sheet on the table and smoothed it with his free hand. "Let's talk about *this* list."

Chapter Fifteen

A re you blushing?"

"Of course not."

"Intriguing." A small smile curved the firm line of his mouth, and his eyes glittered. He ran the back of his fingers down her cheek, making her shiver. "What does SWS mean?"

"We have plenty more interesting subjects to talk about—"

He raised an eyebrow. *What the hell.* "Sex with a stranger."

He didn't look shocked. "I presume this check mark is for me?"

"Other than the entire football team at Stanford, that night of a drunken orgy, yep. You're the only stranger I've ever had sex with."

Dipping his head, he closed his mouth on hers. Her lips and teeth parted to allow him entry as her body melted. Oblivious to the crowded restaurant, to the noise, to any observers, her hands fisted in his hair and she sank into the taste and texture of him.

He gathered her close, fingers tangled in her hair. Mia was always in such a state of heightened awareness around him that she was turned on instantly.

He was the one who released the hold first. Dazed, she blinked up at him. The look he gave her could melt the polar ice caps. He tucked her hair behind her ear.

"Eighteen: PD? Pole dancing, I'm guessing. How about number one, LTD?"

Her lips still buzzed, and her heartbeat thudded in her pulse points. "Learn to drive. Eleven is pump gas, and thirteen was buy a car. I thought the truck was more kick-ass." Her smile felt strained. She was preternaturally aware of his every small movement, from the flick of his silver-tipped black lashes to the stern line of his mouth. That long dimple was nowhere in sight, but just knowing it was there, to emerge if and when he gave her a real smile, was tantalizing. Her body leaned toward him like a flower toward the sun.

"You skipped number eight." He pointed. Just looking at his big hand on the light tablecloth made Mia feel as though she were in the tropics. Flushed, and covered in prickly heat that made it feel as if she had on far too many clothes.

SIP. Sex in public. The idea, intriguing and titillating when she'd jotted down her long to-do list a month ago, now seemed silly at least, and downright embarrassing at worst. Especially with Cruz's hot eyes inches from hers, daring her to give up all her secrets.

"Sun in—" She couldn't make up anything fast enough, especially when his eyes were filled with heat and humor.

He saw right through her.

"Liar." Cruz grinned, flashing white teeth and that elusive

long dimple in his left cheek. His rare smile did something strange to her insides, turning them to liquid fire, which in turn suffused her skin with heat. He was a dangerous, dangerous man.

"This first letter definitely stands for *sex*. . . ."

Mia kept her mouth closed. SIP could represent just about anything.

"In public?" His smile turned devilishly predatory. "Seriously?"

She gave him an innocent wide-eyed look as her pounding heart kicked up into overdrive. "Not in this lifetime, Barcelona."

He gave her a wicked look that made her nipples peak and her mouth go dry. "I'd hate for you to not fulfill your wildest fantasies, sweetheart."

Sweetheart? "Learning to drive wasn't a fantasy, smart-ass. Nor was learning how to bake cookies for that matter."

"That's because you seeded all the fun stuff in between."

"Not intentionally. I never expected anyone else to read this." When she reached for the paper, he quickly folded it along the same fold lines, picked it up, and put it in his back pocket. "Give it back."

"No. I'm keeping it as a memento."

Mia shook her head. "To put in your scrapbook?" She couldn't imagine Cruz being sentimental.

"I've never been one to keep trophies." His voice was dry. "Too incriminating."

"I can imagine— What are you doing?" she asked, startled, as he ducked under the table, completely disappearing from sight under the shroud of the tablecloth.

"I dropped my napkin."

"Ask for another one when the waiter—" She'd never seen anyone disappear beneath a table to pick up a napkin. His palms glided up her thighs under her dress. Her blood heated, and she felt a thrill of excitement. Surely he wouldn't . . . No way! *Cruz? No way!*

"I'm bored waiting for dinner." His voice was slightly muffled. "I thought I'd snack while I wait."

Mia looked around the crowded, noisy restaurant as his hands skated up her thighs. Goose bumps rose on her skin. "You can't be . . . be—" Hooking his fingers into the top band of her bikini panties, he slid them down her hips, until the crease between belly and thigh prevented them from going any farther.

"Oh! My. God! *Serious.*" She was already wet, already highly aroused, already flushed from head to toe.

"Lift."

"Hell no!" She pressed her butt down harder on the seat to prevent whatever he intended to happen next. The pressure in turn made her body throb and pulse. Her mind, her strongest erogenous zone, did the rest. "You're cra—"

Cruz's breath felt hot and humid on her hip, followed by the cool nip of his teeth against her skin. Then Mia felt, rather than heard, the small *riiip.*

She sucked in a shock breath. Sure everyone in the

restaurant must've heard rending fabric. "That's my favorite pair!"

"I'll buy you two dozen," she thought he said. Hard to tell as he kissed his way around her navel, his voice muffled.

A quick, frantic perusal of the diners around them showed that no one was looking their way. But for how long? They were in a booth in the corner, so only the tables in front of them would be able to see—what? Mia almost giggled. God. What if other dinners saw Cruz's feet protruding from beneath the tablecloth?

Dear God, this was an arrest just waiting to happen. And yet—heated blood roared through her veins, and the sensation of Cruz's smooth lips exploring her tummy while the people at the next table drank their wine and laughed and talked was such a turn-on that she pretty much didn't care.

She contemplated, for about two seconds, that getting arrested at this juncture could possibly ruin her LBO. But it would be worth it. She was beginning to realize that she was willing to give up just about anything for Cruz.

The next table over was practically an arm's length away. If she concentrated, she could hear snippets of the two elderly couples' conversation. All it would take would be for one of the sweet-faced grandmotherly types to turn her head, glance down . . .

Mia had a flash image of the scene from the movie with Meg Ryan pretending to climax in a restaurant, and tried to press her knees together. Cruz was having none of that as he wedged his shoulders between them, separating her legs, and at the same time sliding the damp scrap of fabric across her labia so that she jerked in response to the stimulation.

The waiter stood beside the table with their bottle of wine as Cruz teased and tormented her with his mouth, his tongue hard against her clit, so that all Mia heard was her own heartbeat in her ears.

"May I pour or would you like to wait for the gentleman to return?" She didn't hear him—she read his lips through sex-hazed eyes.

"No—I. Go ah-ahead and pour, I'm sure it's fine." Mia was positive if she picked up the glass to sip her wine to ease her dry mouth, she'd snap the delicate stem. She curled her fingers on the edge of the table as Cruz's tongue slid in and out of her slick folds, lingering, sucking, blowing.

What seemed like a nanosecond later, the waiter returned with dishes of—who cared? "Should I return these to the kitchen to keep warm?"

She shook her head a little frantically. If she were resting on a pillow, her head would be thrashing. The waiter gave her an expectant look, the plates held aloft as Cruz's tongue found her clit. The first brush of his hot mouth right on the exquisitely sensitive tight bud made her whimper. Deep, throbbing pleasure sharpened, then widened in concentric circles, pulsing through every nerve.

Oh, shit. The waiter was still standing there, plates in hand, still looking at her. "J-Just leave everyth-thing. Tha—" Her eyes crossed and she forgot what she was saying as she started to crest, but she should've known Cruz wasn't done torturing her, as he let the pressure build, then drew back.

She took a shaky moment to gulp down half a glass of wine. The waiter was halfway across the restaurant before she could function on any level once again. People were leaving, more were arriving. The restaurant was bustling on a Thursday evening, and the tables were all full and close together.

"He *knows* you're under there!" Mia hissed under her shaking breath.

She was close to panting, but it was impossible to catch her breath when he kept driving her higher and higher. Pushing her up Everest, then leaving her hanging on the highest damned precipice with no oxygen.

"Nuh-uh," Cruz's negative murmur vibrated against her inner walls.

Sucking in a shuddering breath, Mia shifted her hips restlessly as he lifted his head, kissing a damp path up and down her inner thighs while he explored her butt crack with inquisitive fingers.

"Ahh." One hand behind her, the other in front. An all-out assault. Her breath snagged, then stopped all together. A slow slip-glide. Up. Down. Up-down. In tandem. Over. And over. Until she was quivering, on the edge of her seat, nerves torqued impossibly tighter and tighter. "Our w-waiter's coming!"

"Then you'd better come before he does, hadn't you?"

"Stop that. Get up here before—argh!" He bit down on her inner thigh at the same time he lodged two fingers deep inside her slick channel to the hilt, his palm rubbing against her clit. Mia reflexively squeezed her thighs around his big hand as he finger-fucked her.

His dexterous fingers found every pleasure pathway, every sensitive, slick, quivering bundle of nerves. Helpless to stop her small, broken whimpers, Mia bit her lip. Blood roared in her ears and she went blind as the orgasm rolled through her with the power of a freight train, leaving her sensitized and climaxing like a pot brought to a rolling boil.

Cruz turned on the radio in the truck, then adjusted the volume to cool jazz as they headed home.

"You know we'll never be able to go to that restaurant ever again," Mia told him, not sounding too worried about it.

"*I* can." He smiled. "They'll only remember you."

Mia punched his arm, but since he had her snugged under his arm and against his chest as he drove, the hit didn't have any impact. Cruz had never been a cuddler. When he was done with sex, he was done. But this felt . . . nice. Except for his cockstand, which had caused a major issue when he'd wanted to leave the restaurant earlier.

With a laugh, Mia curved her fingers around his imprisoned erection and gave it a friendly pat. "I gave you my purse to carry. But I believe people will remember you, because you walked like a cowboy after a long ride across the prairie. People were staring at your crotch all the way down Bourbon."

"If it was me they were looking at, not you, they were thinking only a manly stud would dare carry a pink purse."

"It was really nice of Joann to let Charlie keep Oso for the night," she said, wisely changing the subject. She'd already warned him that they would not, under any circumstances, have sex on the side of the road, and to cool his jets until they got home.

His jets were a far cry from being cooled. He was hot and horny as hell. A permanent state, he'd come to realize, when he was around Mia.

He sucked in a breath as she started unzipping his jeans. "Weren't you the one who insisted on waiting until w— Jesus, woman! I'm going eighty," he felt compelled to point out.

"Eighty-four, actually," she said, tugging, and having a hard time getting the last few inches of zipper down over his rampant hard-on. Her diligence paid off as he sprang free. Her relief wasn't half as heartfelt as his own.

"Keep up the good work—don't mind me. Oh, my—" She sucked in a breath as she slid her hand around him. His dick leaped with happiness in the firm grip of her fingers. "Aw, this is sweet. You left him unwrapped for me?"

Yeah, he went commando. A man had aspirations. Cruz choked back a laugh. "'Him'?"

"Sure," she said, pulling up her knees, then turning to him, tucking herself into a position where her face—and, thank God, that beautiful mouth—was just inches from his dick. "He looks like a Jack to me."

"One-eyed Jack?" he laughed, but his laughter faded as she closed her mouth on him. The wet glide of her tongue and sharp nip of her teeth catapulted his discomfort at prolonged arousal into instant preorgasmic bliss. He eased his foot off the pedal slightly as she gripped the base of his penis with her hands and squeezed, sliding her mouth up, then down. She narrowed her lips so that the wet, soft heat of her mouth mimicked the sheath of her hot, tight vagina.

Getting a blow job from Mia while driving was almost as good an idea as giving her oral sex in a crowded restaurant. Having her mouth on his dick while she had an orgasm was an even better idea. He was more than able to drive with one hand, so he reached around her, pulled her dress up, then shoved two fingers inside her as his thumb found her clit.

She gasped when he buried his fingers in her vagina, but she didn't let go of his dick. Instead, she squeezed tighter with her hand and sucked harder with her mouth as he moved his fingers in and out of her moist heat, feeling the benefit of her pleasure on his shaft as she lost control.

Her every moan reverberated through him, every gasp brought him closer to the edge. He'd planned to pull out of her mouth right before he came, but her loss of control was contagious. He could barely keep the big truck in his lane as she bobbed her head up and down, sucking and scraping her teeth along the vein on his shaft, swirling her tongue around the head as if she were licking an ice cream cone.

He pushed his fingers deeper, feeling the wet pulse and throb of her pussy gripping as she trembled with an orgasm brought on by the relentless movement of his thumb and his fingers.

Mia wrenched her mouth from his dick. "Pull over, pull over!"

Cruz slewed the truck to the grassy verge and shut off the engine. While the engine pinged, she came back down to finish the job. Without meaning to, he exploded into her mouth in a powerful, uncontrollable orgasm that stole his breath and made his entire body buck.

After several minutes, while both remained frozen in position, Mia righted herself. "Give me your shirt."

Without comment, Cruz yanked his shirt over his head and handed it to her. She delicately wiped her mouth, then offered it back to him with a wicked glint in those glorious blue eyes.

"Thanks, but you keep it."

"I'll probably bronze the shirt and my dress to look at when I'm in the senior center one day. I'm going to slide way over here and hug this door. You drive. We'll listen to some cool jazz for the rest of the drive, and not look or touch."

How could a woman as powerful, as advantaged as Amelia Wentworth be so fucking adorable? "Yes, ma'am." He turned on the radio.

"Oh, shit." She jerked upright. "Did he just say *Blush*? Hang on—" Mia reached over to crank up the volume.

"Stock prices plummeted by more than seventeen percent after the FBI report became public earlier today. Megagiant cosmetics company Blush is under heavy fire after China Labor Watch released their findings after a six-month investigation in conjunction with the FBI and the National Crime Agency. Child endangerment—pornography—exploitation. After a massive fire knocked out half the factory building, killing hundreds of children this week."

Shaking her head, Mia turned the radio off, and muttered, "I don't *have* a damned factory in freaking China!" Without being asked, Cruz handed her his phone. "Thanks."

"Who are you calling?"

"Todd. . . . What the hell's going on?" she snapped when her cousin answered. "Calm down. Just calm down. This is just a misunderstanding. . . . *Okay*, I hear you. But I didn't know anything until thirty seconds ago. Just heard the news. No, I *know* we don't, so how could the FBI and these other regulatory groups get it so wrong? We don't. You know we don't." She paused to listen. "That's impossible. What's Legal doing? Damn it! You're scaring the crap out of me, Todd. I'm coming home to deal with this."

Over his dead fucking body. Cruz heard the cousin argue with her. Not the words, but the tone was clear. "*My* life. Of course someone wants the stock prices to plummet. If I'm discredited—"

Todd voiced his opinion. Cruz wished he could hear more than blah-blah-blah. He'd like to be a fly on the wall for the whole convo, but he certainly got the gist.

Confirmation that Blush didn't have, nor had they ever had, a factory in China. Someone was working damn hard to discredit not only Amelia Wentworth personally but the ethical standards of Blush as a company.

This was confirmation that someone wanted her dead. And since Cruz knew for a fact the hit was still in effect, why discredit the company at the same time?

Because that someone wanted to buy Blush at a bargain-basement price and get their biggest obstacle out of the way at the same time?

She moved the phone from her ear. "Okay if I give Todd this number?"

"You called him. He has it."

"Right." She rubbed her forehead. "Davis and Kent over-nighted the paperwork today." She was back to talking to the cousin. "I'll get it back to them by Saturday. Then none of this will matter." Mia pressed two fingers between her eyes. "I had to. If I hadn't given them my location, I'd have had to come home— Dear God, they do? Of course they do—they think I'm a criminal! They might know I'm somewhere near— Fine. I'm *not* telling you where. A major city, and nobody knows what name I'm using here. It's a big place."

She squeezed her eyes shut and a pulse throbbed at the base of her throat as her cousin talked. "Yes. Of course I will. Use the apartment if you want to. Even you have to sleep eventually. Call me at this number if anything changes. Love you."

Closing her fingers around the phone, she sat clutching it for several minutes in silence as Cruz ate up the miles to the house. "Blush doesn't have a factory in China."

"So you said."

"My name is on the factory building's lease, in a city I've never even heard of. The press have 'proof' I visited China.

They have a copy of my passport with the travel stamps 'proving' I visited on numerous occasions." She used the phone to rub her temple. "They've closed down all my business there pending the investigation. For God's sake, this doesn't make any kind of sense. My legal people are working on it. Todd and my personal staff are still at the office. He said it's chaos. Thank God he thrives under chaos. Even my ditzy stepmother is there 'helping.'"

Mia choked back a laugh that had a tinge of hysteria in it. "Someone is going to extraordinary lengths to ruin my life."

Someone wants to do more than that, sweetheart.

"I'd like to know how anyone found out. But of course it's impossible to keep this kind of secret. Todd already told me something had leaked to the press last week. But the price of Blush shares went up. Now they're way down."

"I think we should turn around and go back to NOLA, stay in a hotel tonight," Cruz told her, glancing over to see the strain on her face, illuminated by oncoming traffic. "You'll be there first thing to go to the mailbox place to sign the papers. How about spending the night in an anonymous hotel? It'll give us time to reassess the situation. One thing at a time." And he wasn't going to leave her side for a second until this was over.

"We're five minutes from the house. I want to sleep in my own bed tonight—although, honestly? I'm not sure I *will* sleep with all this going on. I guess it all boils down to what this person, or people, *want*. If they hope to drive the stock price down, and then scoop up the company, they're SOL. Once I sign the paperwork for the buyout, they won't be able to even get their hands on shares, because I'll own Blush outright."

"Who owns Blush if that's the case, and you die?"

She rubbed her arms as if chilled. "It reverts back to the publicly held company."

"So everything you've done up to this point is a wash, and it goes back to the way it was?"

She shrugged. "Todd has no interest in sole proprietorship, and he's my only blood relative."

Cruz closed strong fingers around the back of her neck, feeling the tension there. He massaged gently as he asked, "What about your stepmother?"

"Candice? Not blood. And not in my will, anyway."

"You're a wealthy woman. Who *is* the main beneficiary in your will? Who gets your personal fortune?"

"My foundation gets everything." She paused to give him a look so sad, so poignant, that Cruz felt his hard heart develop another small crack. "Isn't that freaking pathetic? I've made Blush my entire life for as long as I can remember—and yet, when I die, not only will I die alone, I won't have anyone to pass the baton to."

"You're not going to die," Cruz told her grimly as he turned off the headlights when he turned onto her long, dark gravel driveway. "You'll live a long life and have a herd of kids playing with makeup the moment they start walking."

"So, girls or drag queens?" Mia's lips twitched. "Todd will be thrilled."

Chapter Sixteen

Mia suddenly noticed he was driving without headlights, and straightened. "What's wrong?"

Cruz had a gut feeling. A bad-as-shit feeling as they rolled down the driveway to the carport in the dark. "Not sure. Something's off." The hair on the back of his head lifted, and his heartbeat slowed, which in turn clarified his sight and hearing. This was how he felt when he was about to kill. Sharp. Focused.

He scanned the open expanse of scrubby lawn, the ghostly Spanish moss hanging unmoving from the trees. Moonlight glinted on the water of the bayou and painted black-lace shadows on the scrub grass beneath the trees.

The dark shapes of the beat-up, piece-of-shit truck and camper lay dense and impenetrable beside the house. Nothing moved, yet he felt the threat of danger nearby. He trusted his gut.

He unscrewed the dome light. "Drive down the street. Come back in ten minutes, if the porch light isn't on, call the cops."

"I'm not leaving! Don't give me that damn look, Cruz Barcelona. I won't leave you here alone."

It was almost comical that she feared for *him*. He knew she wouldn't leave, and sighed. Stubborn woman. "Then stay in the truck and lock the doors, and slide over in case you have to drive. I'll check the house."

"Give me your phone."

He lifted his butt to get it out of his back pocket and handed it to her. "I've never known a woman not to have a phone."

"At home I have a dozen. Here my burner phone lives in the sugar canister in the kitchen."

She'd already unsnapped her seat belt and turned to watch him with pale, worried eyes as she whispered, "Be careful."

"Don't call the police unless I'm gone for longer than ten minutes."

"Ten minutes? Are you insane? That's *forever* if there's some deranged killer inside the damn house!"

He wanted to say, *They should be scared of me.* But she didn't need to know the truth of what he was. Not yet. Not until he knew she was safe. "Ten minutes. Do *not* leave this vehicle until I come back for you or the police arrive. Promise me."

"I promise."

"Let me see your fingers."

Her smile was faint. "I'm not crossing them. Ten minutes or the police. Got it. But not a second more. I'm not going to hesitate if I don't see you in ten minutes or less." She chewed her lip, not in fear, but concern.

Their gazes locked. Both of them knew the chances were high this was no burglar. There was practically no furniture or anything of value in the house and the place was too isolated to be just a random act. Whoever was inside was looking not for something but someone.

"Whoever is trying to get you out of the way wants to make sure you don't sign the papers."

With the FBI and the press closing in like rabid dogs, and everything about to be finalized with the buyout of her business, tonight was the night if anyone was going to off her. This would be the golden hour. Or in the time it took her to sign the papers and for them to be overnighted to San Francisco.

If *he* was going to do the job, it would be tonight.

"Don't go in. Look, if they're a trained killer, it's stupid to take the risk."

"I served in the military, remember? Trust me, I can take care of myself."

She placed a hand on his forearm. "Still, you don't have to do this. We should call the police." She shook her head at his closed expression.

"That's where you're wrong. Whoever is in there doesn't know who or what I am, or that I'm coming in alone. I've got the advantage. Just stay here. Stay safe and don't distract me."

He exited the vehicle, then waited for the door lock to engage. Followed by buzzing mosquitoes, he slipped through the dappled shadows to the accompaniment of the deep-throated croak of frogs, the occasional growl-roar of the alligator, and the splash of some night creature in the water.

He detoured to his truck for his gun. He'd removed the interior light long ago. He found the hidden compartment and the box under the floor by feel.

The SIG Sauer fit comfortably in his hand. He didn't use a gun often, but that didn't mean he didn't know how, and the custom 250 felt like an old friend in his hand.

He set his watch for nine minutes twenty-six seconds.

When he stepped up onto the back porch, he knew which floorboards creaked and where to step. Moving quietly to blend with the shadows, Cruz pushed open the front door with the muzzle of the semiauto.

Not latched. Sloppy.

A sense of the air being displaced, and a faint trace of stale sweat, told him his gut was right. Someone *was* in the house.

While there were no lights on, there was enough ambient light from the moon so that he could see fairly well as he moved from room to room. He had excellent night vision, and his eyes quickly adjusted.

Silently he searched the first floor. No sign of an intruder, and nowhere to hide. Upstairs, then.

He'd never be caught on the second floor of someone's home. Too hard to escape. Too easy to become trapped. Moving cautiously up the stairs, Cruz grabbed a screwdriver lying on top of a paint can and tucked it under his shirt against the small of his back. His hands were his best defense. But a stabbing tool came in handy on occasion. And if all else failed, the SIG would do the job.

By the time he was halfway up the stairs, he knew who lay in wait for him. The stink of booze and sweat was unmistakable. Latour.

Cruz tucked the SIG away beside the screwdriver as he

strolled into Mia's bedroom. "Why aren't you in jail, you sack of shit?"

Latour, who'd been riffling through drawers in the bed-side table, straightened and spun around, shocked as hell to see him. His nose was swollen, both eyes were purple and swollen almost shut, and his puffy lower lip sported crusted blood around a gash. He was drunk enough to be dangerous, but not unsteady as he glared at Cruz from puffy, slitted eyes.

Latour's fists curled at his sides. "I want my *wife*."

"And you think she's in a six-inch-deep drawer?"

"You can't keep her from me, asshole! I'll find her, and when I do, she's going to learn some respect!" Fist raised, he rushed forward, and Cruz sidestepped. The man crashed into the doorjamb nose first with a wild shriek of pain.

Cruz grabbed the short sleeve of Latour's orange T-shirt to spin him around and raised his arm. "You hurt my woman, you fucked-up son of a bitch." His fist glanced off the man's cheek, but he heard the satisfactory crunch of bone as Latour staggered backward, then righted himself and charged him like an enraged bull. "Mia didn't know you had that fucking knife with you, but I did."

He stabbed Latour's forearm with the screwdriver as the other man jumped on him from the side. Latour threw a punch, Cruz sidestepped, and Latour's fist punched Mia's stripper pole instead. He let out a howl of pain, then spun around and attacked with his fists and feet. He was strong and determined, but with the limited floor space between the bed and the window wall, he didn't have much room to maneuver. While Latour was enraged and out of control, Cruz wasn't even breaking a sweat.

Cruz collared him with his forearm around his neck from behind. Latour struggled and tried to pry his arm away from his throat. "News flash, dick: You'll never see Daisy and your boy ever again. I'll make sure of it. And. You. Will. Never. Hurt. Another. Woman."

Cruz tightened his arm around Latour's neck while using his free hand and palm to grip him by the forehead. There was an art to strangling a man so it looked accidental. Cruz was a master. Careful not to leave scratch marks, he used the pads of his fingers and his strong palm and twisted, hard, feeling cartilage, tendons, and bones give way with the pressure. He kept twisting until he broke Latour's neck with a final snap and the son of a bitch collapsed.

With Latour still in a headlock, he flung open the window, then, like a bag of sand, tossed the bastard over the sill. He waited until he heard the thud on the ground, then glanced down the forty-foot drop. From the awkward angle of Latour's body, it was evident he'd broken his neck in the fall. Accidents happened.

He slid the window shut, then worked fast to straighten the bedspread and stuff everything scattered on the floor back in the drawer of the table, and turned on the light to survey the room. "Good enough."

After carrying the long ladder he'd used for his roofing project around to the other side of the house, he propped it below the bedroom window, against the house, and near the body.

He tapped on the truck's window to indicate that he was alive and well. Mia flung open the door and practically bowled him over.

He'd been gone for seven minutes eleven seconds.

The next morning she looked fresh and chic in a royal-blue sundress that bared her shoulders and the three sexy freckles on her clavicle. When the mailbox store opened at nine, Mia and Cruz were the first customers there. "I rented this when I first arrived."

"Who did you give this address to?"

"You asked me that last night. *Nobody* until yesterday, when I gave it to the investment company. You're more paranoid than Todd and Miles combined."

If anyone wanted to find her, she would've been found, just as he'd found her. But there'd been no indication that anyone else had. Yet. He'd expected something last night. She'd shared this address with one person. That had been twelve hours ago. Someone could be here from anywhere in the world by now.

After Latour, no one else had shown up, though he'd been on high alert all night, watching her sleep as he listened for every sound.

The young guy behind the counter, with serious acne and an Adam's apple that bobbed every time he surreptitiously glanced over at Mia, mumbled "Good morning" as they headed to the wall of small, numbered brass doors.

"Not even Todd has this address," Mia said over her shoulder, key in hand. "At his request, I might add. Only Michael Ordway, at the investment company. For all he knows I flew here just to get my mail. This is my box right here."

But when Mia unlocked it, it was empty. "That's weird. Ordway assured me he'd overnight the paperwork so I could sign and send it back today."

"Maybe your friend over there hasn't put everything in the boxes this morning."

"I'll ask."

Apparently, all mail and packages delivered that morning had already been placed in the correct boxes.

"Perhaps there was a mistake, and the papers will be here on Monday."

Mia looked grim. Cruz knew this deal must be in the multi-billions. Not something that some lackey would mail. "I'll call him when we get back to the truck. I want to go back home—for some reason I feel really exposed here."

"I can't imagine why," Cruz said dryly, tucking her hand in his elbow as they left. As soon as they were in the truck, he handed her his cell phone.

"Michael, the paperwork you sent yesterday didn't arrive," Mia said, sounding not like Mia but like Amelia Wellington-Wentworth. "What's the holdup on your end?"

Cruz started the truck and eased into traffic to head back to Bayou Cheniere.

"Repeat that," she said tightly. A quick glance showed him her pale face and tight jaw. "Yes, I was aware that investment and brokerage companies were conducting evaluations and

analyses on us, but their interest was based on pure speculation. This is very different? And it happened when? Yes,
maybe things would have been different if I was there, but,
considering the circumstances, it was *necessary* for me to disappear." She nodded. "What happens now?" She listened for
several minutes.

"Up my offer by ten—all right, *twelve* percent. Keep upping my bid until I win. Yes, until they drop like flies. Call me
at this number with developing updates." She rang off and
stared at the traffic ahead of them on the freeway. Cruz noticed that her breathing was a little heavier than it had been
before the phone call.

"What was that about?"

"Dark pool liquidity." Her voice was sharp as she shifted
to face him. "The reason for all that negative press with my
face being splashed across the news resulting in Blush stock
prices plummeting? *That's* what the hell *that* was all about," she
said bitingly. "A private forum has been buying large blocks of
stock in secret all week. It was a setup. The bastards bought
low, cashing in on Blush shares slipping on the market because of all the bad press. Then went to Ordway yesterday
with a better offer than mine."

"No rival investment brokers?"

"Perhaps them, too. But this is an anonymous, *private*
group."

"Any idea who they might be?"

"No. But you can bet I'll damn well find out who's going
behind my back!"

"I doubt it's personal."

"Really? It feels extremely, damn well personal to me. More so because only a small handful of people I trusted even knew I was doing this."

"Now what happens?"

"Now I wait to hear if upping my bid will get me my own damned company."

Cruz looked as grim as Mia felt. "We're going away for a few days until the dust settles."

"Go where?"

He shrugged a broad shoulder. "Anywhere you like. Podunk? South of France?"

"Right now I live in Podunk," Mia said with a small smile. "I'm not running. Ordway knows how important this leveraged buyout is to me. He's got his orders. He'll keep raising my offer until I'm able to buy the remaining stock. The others will drop out."

"And if they don't?"

"Then I'll have a very, very, freaking very expensive company on my hands when this is done. They won't win. I'll make damn sure they don't. And when this is all over, I'm going to find out who was part of the dark pool and make them very sorry they screwed with me."

Mia was already considering how she'd compensate for the rising cost of the buyout. She might have to sell off one of the divisions, cut staff . . . close some of the retail stores. . . . Whatever she did, *her* belt would have to tighten. She'd liquidate her personal assets, of course. Sell the houses, the plane, the horses, the cars. "The question is, who are the people making up this damned dark pool? Who's putting the money into this forum to buy the stocks?"

"We'll make a list when we get home of who has the money to pool or singularly fund it. We'll include everyone you can think of, including the least likely."

He was thinking about Todd, but Mia merely said, "Yes, let's."

That list had to be put on hold when they got back to the house, because Detective Hammell and several plainclothes detectives were waiting for them.

"Oh, Lord, what now?" Mia asked rhetorically, seeing two police cars and the group of men standing and talking in her driveway.

She hopped out of the truck when Cruz stopped, walking around the front of the vehicle, hand extended. "Detective Hammell, what can I do for you?"

His huge hand swallowed hers for a brief shake. "Sandy said Marcel was in a lather last night after he was released on his own reconnaissance, pending his court date. After the police chief himself posted bail. Seems like he told his sister he was coming here because he thought you were harboring Daisy."

Mia waited. Hammell knew where Daisy was.

"Drunk as a coon dog," he continued. "I came here looking for him. Did a walk around your property. Apparently he tried to gain entry to your house at some point last night. Fell off the ladder. Broke his fool neck."

A black van pulled up behind the police cars, and two men got out with a stretcher. One of the suited men directed them to the back of the house.

"I didn't hear anything last night." Mia glanced up at Cruz, her cheeks burning at the thought of what they'd done after the fear of the possibility of an intruder had subsided. His under-the-table oral sex on her and the blow job she'd given him in the truck had only whetted their appetites for more. "Did you?"

"Not a thing." He gave her a significant look. They'd made love for hours, and she'd been pretty vocal. It creeped her out that Latour might've been watching them through the window.

His gaze followed the men with the stretcher. "Where was the ladder?"

"Around back, third window."

Her bedroom. She suddenly felt nauseated. She sagged against Cruz, and welcomed his arms around her.

"Dog didn't bark?"

"We left Oso with Charlie for a few days," Cruz told him.

"Latour didn't knock on the back door or yell trying to rouse you?"

"No." Cruz put his arm around Mia's shoulders, tucking her against his side. "We had dinner in New Orleans after spending a couple of hours with Charlie. We went to bed pretty much right after returning."

We went to bed was a little more information than Mia was willing to share, and her cheeks felt hot.

BLUSH

"Well, if you remember anything, give me a call. Gotta go tell Sandy. That should be a noisy conversation," the detective said dryly. "Hate to talk ill of the dead. But he was a mean, drunken rattlesnake. Other than his sister, no one will miss him. Solves Daisy and little Charlie's issues effectively."

"Yes," Mia agreed. "It does." She was relieved that Latour was permanently out of Daisy's and Charlie's lives. "Let us know if you need anything," she told the detective. She didn't want to be there when they brought Latour's body around to the front of the house. "We'll be inside."

After Cruz made a pot of coffee, they sat at the center island as Mia gave him the list of names she'd compiled on her computer. People she worked with, people she did business with, personal, professional—the list went on for pages and pages.

"This is long, but I can't imagine my nail girl or the pool guy wants to overthrow me," she told Cruz. "Besides, I don't pay or tip them that well."

Of course, he didn't smile. "I'm not ruling anyone out. Even the manicurist or pool guy could've been brought into the forum if they provided insider info instead of cash." He slid off the stool. "I'm going to go get my computer. We're doing a background check on all of these people. See if we can find any kind of pattern to all this—"

"I have Black Raven doing background checks. You can't find out as much as they can."

"I have resources they might not have. My military contacts can help me get into files they might not have access to. If

295

we double up on info, no loss. I'm not sitting around waiting. Once we do that, we can eliminate some of them."

Mia took a sip of now cold coffee and pulled a face. "Most, I imagine." She got up for a refill, holding the pot aloft. "I feel the same way. I'd rather duplicate our efforts than sit here twiddling my thumbs, waiting for something to happen. Coffee?"

Cruz shook his head, so Mia returned to the island with her coffee. He came up behind her, swept her hair off her neck to press a lingering kiss to her nape. "God, I love the smell of your skin." With a hand under her chin, he turned her head to face him. "It smells like sex on crisp, clean sheets or on fresh spring flowers."

She smiled, looking into his darkening eyes. That was the sweetest thing he had ever said to her. It was raw and real and unguarded. She lifted her lips to his and kissed him.

Straightening, he brushed her cheek with his thumb, eyes holding hers, dark and filled with promise. "That'll hold me until I get back."

Mia watched him exit the kitchen with his long, loose-limbed stride and go out to his truck to retrieve his computer. "Who are you, Cruz Barcelona?" she murmured under her breath.

She'd asked Todd to have Black Raven do a search on Cruz the minute she'd regained her senses enough to decide to hire him. She was stringent with security and with knowing everything she could about the people around her. Even, or especially, a new lover. Had all the changes she made in her world here along Bayou Cheniere resulted in that or was it her odd sensual relationship with Cruz that changed that about her?

She picked up his phone, tempted to see whether his cell had any revealing activity, but she controlled the urge. While she felt sanctimonious for not doing so, it was really because she had only minutes to complete the call to Black Raven. She had to call information for their office number in Denver, then hung on impatiently until Somerville answered.

"Anything else on Barcelona?" Mia asked the second the agent came on the phone. Her eyes were fixed on the door, waiting for Cruz's return, and her heart pounded as if she was doing something illicit.

"Nothing of note," he told her, cutting to the chase. "No arrest warrants. Idaho driver's license. That's about it."

"Employment history?" she asked as she heard the back door open, then close.

The report on Cruz had come back clean. No arrests. No prison records. No parking tickets, for pity's sake. He'd gone to high school. Done a stint in the military and been working on his own as a handyman since he got out. The guy looked like a freakin' saint on paper.

The problem was that his background was *too* clean. In her lengthy experience in the business world, no one was that good. Everyone had secrets or had done things they weren't proud of. And, given his strength and skill set, and the way she'd seen him handle Latour the other night, she had a niggling feeling that perhaps Cruz Barcelona wasn't his real name at all. Maybe he was in the witness protection program.

"Not that we could find. But that's not uncommon for a man who moves around. Cash-under-the-table jobs aren't that difficult to come by."

"Don't search on his name. His father had a large construction company in Chicago. Thirty, thirty-five years ago. Father was connected. Politicians, police chief. Wife died under suspicious circumstances when son was in his teens. Suicide, or murder. Keep looking. Go deeper," she said, lowering her voice, knowing Cruz was nearing the kitchen. As soon as the words crossed her lips she felt awful for saying them, yet, another part of her was glad she couldn't take them back. This was what she should do, what she was supposed to do, to protect herself. Still, it felt wrong.

"Will do," Somerville said just as Cruz came into the kitchen, his laptop in hand. After setting it across from her on the island, he strolled over to pour himself some coffee, then sat watching her, eyebrow cocked inquiringly.

"I'm emailing you a list of two hundred and twelve names," she told Somerville, not missing a beat. "I want a thorough background check on all of them. Expedite this, I need it right away. I want as much as you can dig up by Sunday night. Yes, I know. Weekend. Only two and a half days. I'm sure you can handle it. Tell me when you're ready—I'll give you a thumbnail with what I know. I'm looking for any and all ties of the people on this list to one another. Also, I want to know if they have been involved or are involved in illegal activities, and have hidden bank accounts. Large sums moving in or out of it, too. Ready?"

She met Cruz's eyes across the counter and began: "Todd Wentworth . . ." She gave the Black Raven agent any details she knew about each person. She was so tempted to cross off Todd and another dozen people she was sure weren't involved. Just like she had been tempted to drop the check on Cruz. She didn't. It didn't matter what she thought. Cruz was right. Everybody had to be vetted. Even him.

It took three hours.

Cruz made another pot of coffee, made her a sandwich, which she didn't eat, and massaged her shoulders. Then he worked at God only knew what on his own computer, a frown of concentration on his face as his fingers tapped away at the keyboard.

Mia fanned her face with a sheet of paper from the stack beside her. She liked paper, a lot of paper, and printed every new list, every new bit of information they dug up on someone. And since that involved more than two hundred people, there was a shit storm of paper on the table, on the floor, stacked beside a printer that had come out of one of dozens of boxes in the otherwise empty living room.

"We have cool fog in San Francisco," she told him, reading as she talked. "Even in the summer. I'm not used to this 'muggy' stuff."

Her dewy skin looked as if it tasted of flower petals, and her hair clung damply against her neck, curling seductively, beckoning him closer. He ignored the temptation. He'd tossed his shirt over the counter hours ago, and wore khaki cargo shorts and nothing else. She'd changed into a red tank top and white shorts earlier. Cruz enjoyed the way the ribbed cotton accentuated her unfettered breasts, and the sharp buds of her nipples caused by him looking at her.

Giving him a sultry look that spiked his blood, she blew a breath, which fluttered her bangs. "I'm going home tomorrow."

His heart did a double tap. *"Away somewhere safe? Yes. Home to San Francisco? Hell fucking no."*

She raised a dark brow. "I beg your pardon? Who put you in charge of me? I appreciate you being protective, I really do. But this is my decision."

Damn it. He'd put *himself* in charge of her. And until this shit was resolved to his satisfaction, and he knew she was safe, he was going to be her shadow. And then, like a shadow, he'd be gone at the right time. The thought wasn't nearly appealing today as it had been a week ago.

"You already know dark pool shit is swirling back there. It would be incredibly foolish to tempt fate. You say you'll keep bidding up until whoever is in that pool finally runs out of capital and gives up? Stay here until that happens." *Stay here with me* was left unsaid.

Picking up one of the pens littering the table, she seesawed it between her fingers. Papers, pens, and cold mugs of coffee attested to their persistence and focus for hours. A glance outside showed that night had fallen, and blackness pressed against the windows with their ridiculous half curtains covered with fruit.

"I can't let other people, Todd in particular, fend off questions and innuendos without me," Mia told him, putting down the pen and accordion-pleating a piece of paper to make herself a hand fan. "However this is resolved, the press will be like scavengers picking at the bones of everyone involved. No matter what, this isn't going to end up neat and tidy. It's not fair, not to mention irresponsible, of me not to be right there in the middle of things."

She tried out her new fan. It barely ruffled her bangs, and she tossed the sheet of paper onto the table. "Blush is mine. I have to be there to defend my company from the wolves."

"You're not irresponsible, you're agitated that you aren't in control of the situation. You have PR people whose job it is to make sure there's no negative press and, if there is, to mitigate it. Let them do their jobs."

"I want to know who it was impersonating me in China. Hell, I want to *go* there. See what the situation is with my own eyes."

"When the danger has passed, sure. But right now you have to stay put."

She chewed her lower lip as she pretended to consider it. But he knew better. She wasn't going to stay in Bayou Cheniere, Louisiana, no matter what he said. He saw in the firm set of her jaw that she'd already made the decision to go home. Cruz felt a strange surge of panic.

Getting up, he went to her and scooped her up in his arms,

turning her to face him, her legs on either side of his hips. She couldn't mistake his erection as he settled her astride his lap.

Loosely crossing her wrists behind his head, she gave him a stern look, made sexier by the black-rimmed glasses perched on her nose. Sexy librarians had nothing on sexy women CEOs.

"We still have half the people on the list to go through."

She'd hired an independent security company to do *that* job. But she was still doing her own legwork. Cruz was observing Amelia Wellington-Wentworth in action. The powerful, take-no-prisoners CEO was sexy as hell.

"Did you ask the Black Raven people to do a background check on me, too?" Cruz asked, sliding his palms between her tank top and shorts. Her skin was damp, silky smooth, and the heat of her skin intensified the fragrance of tuberoses, making him dizzy.

Mia lifted her arm so he could draw the fabric over her head, then settled her wrists back on his shoulders. Looking at him over the edge of her glasses, she said, "Of course, wouldn't you have done the same?"

There'd be nothing to find. Cruz Barcelona had a sketchy but realistic past. He'd paid a great deal of money to make it so for Cruz Barcelona and the dozen other well-worn aliases he'd used over the years for his job. They were all solid. "Of course. You'll find out more about me if you ask the right questions yourself."

Her smile was faint as she lazily ran her fingers through his hair. "But would you tell me what questions to ask?"

Placing both hands on her lips, he lifted her from his lap so she stood between his spread knees, and pulled down the zipper on her shorts. "Under the right circumstances, yeah." He was still undecided whether he'd tell her any part of his truth before he left.

He loved the soft fluff he revealed as he eased the fabric over her hips. Sliding her shorts down her legs, he leaned forward to kiss her satin belly, breathing in heady musk and the rich scent of her skin.

It was as though the very essence of her had bonded permanently with his DNA. The realization should scare the hell out of him. But she fascinated him too much for that to happen. The sex was off the charts, but it was her kindness and willingness to learn new things that captivated him. She had charm, compassion, and a steel rod for a spine.

Kicking her shorts aside, Mia said sternly, "Lose those clothes, buddy." While he stripped, she unfastened her bra so that she stood gloriously naked between his knees.

Cruz ran his hands up her hips, urging her forward. "This can't possibly be comfortable, Barcelona." Mia spread her legs over his lap.

He eased her down on his erection and she wrapped her arms around his neck as they moved together. "Nice and slow."

"For the moment." She smiled against his neck, and his penis jerked in response to the flex of her internal muscles.

"Let's go to bed," he said, feeling her vaginal walls pulse around his dick. "We can finish this list in the morning. By which time they might have some answers—"

There was no warning. One moment he was nuzzling her damp throat, planning what he'd do with her naked body when they got on a horizontal surface, and the next the window beside them shattered. Glass showered them in a slow-motion rain of sharp fragments, followed instantly by the high-pitched whine of a bullet as it whizzed inches from Mia's head.

Chapter Seventeen

The bullet struck six feet behind them, exploding into the wall in a burst of sharp fragments of wood and plaster.

Cruz, having seen movement outside from the corner of his eye seconds before the strike, was already yelling "Get down!" as he wrenched her off him, off the chair, and onto the floor in one violent, jolting move. Covering her with his body.

In a low crouch, he shoved Mia's shapely naked ass ahead of him across the linoleum floor, then pressed her against the solid barricade of the center island, his body forming a shield.

No more shots. For now.

Mia stared at him blankly as he scanned her face, her naked breasts, her satiny belly, and the dark fluff between her legs for injury. Her cheeks were drained of color, her eyes all pupil. Glass sparkled like diamonds in the messy strands of her dark hair. Several tiny cuts on her throat leaked bright red blood, but other than that, she appeared unharmed.

"Are you hit?" He kept his voice low and calm as he ran both hands up her back, over her arms, then finger-combed her hair, dislodging glass, which pinged like hail as it hit the floor. "Mia? Are you hit?" A calm came over him and he went into work mode. Cool. Focused. All his senses wide-open to receive data.

"My heart's manic, but I think I'm okay. We should call Detective Hammell. What's a hunter doing way out h— Oh, my God! The hit man found me!"

The hit man had found her a week ago.

They'd hired another one. One who'd get the job done, no questions asked.

Fuck.

This time they'd sent a sniper.

Who?

Several options. Cruz knew what *he'd* been paid. If it was anyone comparable, they wouldn't miss next time.

He had to make sure there wasn't a next time.

She sucked in a breath as if in pain, but no cry escaped her lips. Instead, she ran searching hands over his chest in return. "Are you hurt?"

"No. I'm fine." His shorts were still around his ankles. He contorted his body to yank them up. "Go upstairs, get the Beretta, and stay hidden until I come for you."

"What?" She blinked him into focus, eyes suddenly sharp as she grabbed his wrist in a life-or-death grip. "No! Where are *you* going?"

His SIG was in the drawer right above his head, and he was already opening it to fumble around inside. "Outside to put an end to this." He checked the clip and took off the safety.

"You don't have shoes on," she observed, sounding shell-shocked but also pissed off as she crouched there, naked and vulnerable.

Her vulnerability scared the crap out of Cruz. He pushed the fear aside. It wouldn't do her any good. Someone was out there. Someone who'd probably watched them having sex while he took aim. Someone who'd come to do the job he hadn't completed. Someone who wasn't going to be swayed by beguiling blue eyes and perfect tits. Someone who was already executing his backup plan.

Cruz tamped down his fury into a nice, neat, manageable ball of cold rage. Colors became brighter. Sounds crystal clear.

Time to go hunting.

"Listen up. Get your ass upstairs. Stay away from windows, keep the lights off. Get the Beretta and hide in the closet. Shoot the first person who comes through the door. No matter who the fuck it is."

"The first person who comes through the door better damn well be you. Put shoes on, for God's sake, and be careful." Her fingers tightened on his wrist. "I love you," she told him thickly. "I've never in my life said that to another man other than Todd. Come back in one piece, or I'll kill you myself."

Heard. Computed.

"Don't even *think* about coming outside, hear me?" Not waiting for a response, he put a hand on her shoulder, needing—wanting—more. He was already fucked. It was no longer just about sex. That entanglement was bad enough. What disarmed him was the unexpected emotional connection that somehow had been forged between them. No time to think about that now. If ever. He didn't know who waited outside for him. "When I turn off the light, move your ass. Low and fast."

Slithering across the floor, he used the jamb to shield his body as he reached up to flip the switch. The kitchen was plunged into moonlit darkness. Not dark enough. Cold moonlight shone through the broken window. He gave her a shove on the ass. "*Go. Go. Go!*"

She went. He listened to the soft thump of her feet taking the stairs, then raced down the hall when he heard her footfalls over his head as she ran into the bedroom. His work boots were on the porch. Not that he would've cared if he had to go out there barefoot. But he didn't have to.

Closing the back door behind him, he waited for the click of the lock. The door was flimsy as hell. Not the original solid oak. One good kick and the lock would break. Hurriedly he shoved his feet into his boots, allowing his eyes to adjust to the speckled moonlight. Scrub grass. Shadows, the glint of water. The smell of swamp and greenery accompanied by the roar of the gator.

Even though she listened for the slightest sound from outside, Mia jerked in response to the muffled crack of a gunshot in the distance. Her heart leaped into her throat, then started to feel as if it were skittering frantically inside her chest.

Don't even think *about coming outside, hear me?* he'd yelled.

Was a numb nod a promise?

She *had* run upstairs, naked and shivering. And she had the Beretta. Loaded, safety off. But she wasn't damn well hiding in any frigging *closet*. One, because she'd be trapped in there if some bad guy came hunting for her, and two, this situation was *her* problem, not Cruz's. She was damned if she let him put himself in danger to protect her. No matter how sweetly chivalrous the gesture.

She paused just long enough to pull on black jeans and a long-sleeved black T-shirt and dark boat shoes and grab up her purse. She wasn't likely to hurt anyone with a pen, but the laser pointer might come in handy.

Mia's fingers tightened on the butt of the gun as she took the stairs two at a time at breakneck speed in the dark. Easing open the back door, she listened for any unnatural sounds. Just bugs, crickets, and the occasional splash of water. For now.

She sprinted across the rickety wood deck and took the three broad stairs in a running leap before the next barrage of gunshots sounded. Where were they?

Somewhere amidst the overgrown garden? No. The last shot had sounded farther away.

On the street? From behind the high stone wall of the graveyard? The shot sounded incredibly loud in the thick, muggy moonlit darkness. There were three other dilapidated mansions on the street. All empty. Spooky dark now. Overgrown landscaping just as her house had been. Cruz and the gunman could be damn well *anywhere*.

Her entire being was her elevated heartbeat as Mia ran,

hugging the deep shadows of the high bushes on the left side of the long driveway. Gravel flew up to sting her ankles, sockless in her shoes. Tree branches grabbed at her arms and snagged in her hair as she moved through the dappled darkness.

The next loud report made her body jerk in reaction. That was followed immediately by another. A shout of pain, the pounding, uneven beat of running footsteps on something hard. Cement?

Years of jogging stood Mia in good stead as she ate up the distance, but her adrenaline and fear had her heartbeat pounding faster than it ever had in her life. Even advanced exercise classes at the gym or her tyrant personal trainer pushing her body to the point of collapse could not have prepared her for this full-out, panting sprint with her own and Cruz's lives at stake. With strength and power beyond her human capacity, she raced to the end of the too-long driveway where the giant oak spread its branches to lay down a black shadow-blanket on the ground.

Into the moonlight once again. Every blade of grass, every rock and stone thrown by her foot strikes in stark, high-relief black-and-white. She was a flesh-and-blood and breathing ghost in a world of shadows and moonlight. It was surreal. It was unimaginable fear.

Her labored breathing sounded loud in her ears as she veered left, her feet pounding down the hard-packed dirt that ran parallel to the high, crumbling stone wall surrounding the cemetery.

The lacy wrought-iron gate stood ajar. Frozen that way for decades. Surely not enough room for a man to squeeze through, even if he was determined. She was smaller, and a lot more single-minded. She slipped through the hard lace, eyes searching, ears pricked, manic heartbeat uneven, and *loud*. God, it was loud. Her fingers tightened painfully around the grip of the 9mm semiautomatic as she slowly scanned the surrounding area.

City of the Dead. Great. As if this whole thing wasn't scary enough. Gravel roads and walkways intersected between the crypts. She tried to walk on the grassy weeds.

Where were they? Mia stopped, flattening her spine against a brick mausoleum as she listened. Muted voices. Male. Cruz having a conversation with the shooter? The voices gave her a direction. She darted across to a mossy angel on a pedestal. Paused to catch her breath. Dear God, she needed to breathe—her abused lungs struggled to take in more air. She covered her mouth with her hand and inhaled through her nose, trying to regulate her breathing, then crept out of that shadow and made for the next. Underfoot, gravel, weeds, dead flowers, broken bottles.

Another barrage of shots came from the right, indicating the end of the conversation. She headed that way, keeping low now, slinking between monoliths of cement and marble.

Old death and new death.

Eyes dry and constantly scanning the area for danger, she prayed. *Please God, let Cruz be okay.*

Pleasepleaseplease.

• • •

Four hit men sent for Mia, for fucksake? Whoever had hired *him* had hedged his bet. Talk about overkill. Cruz knew where they were; he'd seen four muzzle flares in the last five minutes.

The tomb city had street-like rows of high marble and cement edifices, allowing anyone to hide behind the structures standing fully upright. Knee-high weeds grew in thick patches on the narrow paths of crushed shell between the eight- and ten-foot-high tombs. It crunched underfoot, no matter how lightly one stepped. Some of the doors stood ajar, perfect hiding places.

A dozen snipers could easily remain concealed here for hours. He didn't *have* fucking hours. Perhaps not even minutes. All it would take was one killer to double back to the house—

Cruz focused. Take out the four he knew about, trust Mia had done as instructed. Get back to her alive.

Who was he dealing with? Strengths? Weaknesses? Skill level?

Richard Lemon. Cruz ID'd him when he got a brief glimpse of the guy's frizzy orange hair as he darted behind a large headstone before getting off two shots in quick succession, covering his shit-for-brains partner so he could get closer. Dick's clown hair made him easy to spot among the moldy, mottled-gray tombs. Dumb fuck should have worn his customary knit cap.

The moonlight spotlighted Lemon's partner as he disappeared off to the left behind a tall tomb with chipped plaster and a watchful guardian angel perched on top. Medium height. Bent shoulders. Thin, dark hair, dramatically receding hair-line, bald spot. Beak of a nose. Kevin Muncie. Yeah. That fit.

The ex-military sharpshooters usually tag-teamed. They were crack shots. If a client wanted a clean hit, they were the two to do it. They weren't the brightest bulbs in the pack, but they knew the business end of their Lapua Magnum sniper rifles.

They'd never met, but Cruz had studied them, seen their pictures and rap sheets, just as he did with anyone in his line of work. Knowledge was power.

Their MO: gunshot to the back of the head. Always accurate. They were good, damn good. When they were sober they were considered the best snipers for hire. But word on the street was Muncie had a drinking problem, and Lemon liked his nose candy. As indicated by their miss tonight, one or both of them were impaired.

Or the shooter had been one of the unknown others.

Fuck. Who were the other two, and where the hell were they? The hair on the back of his neck prickled, imagining them sneaking into the house to confront Mia. . . . Cruz's heartbeat kicked up, pounding in his throat, and he consciously lowered it.

Four men working together? Or a fucking coincidence that they'd all converged tonight? One of the quartet thought he'd be the last man standing for the huge payout after they hit Mia. Or planned to make sure he was. It occurred to Cruz that there might be more than just the four of them.

Which begged the fucking question: How had the four killers found Mia in this backwater? She trusted the cousin, Todd, and Blush's security guy. Neither, she claimed, knew her present location.

Michael Ordway at Davis and Kent had received the mailing address in New Orleans *yesterday*, but had not put anything in the mail because of the new development. One of the three men had betrayed Mia. One of them wanted her dead. One of them had hired at least five hit men to do the job: himself and whoever else was out here. Clouds drifted over the bright light of the moon, creating moving shadows in the black-and-white cityscape to deceive the eye.

Time to draw everyone out into the open where he could deal with them. Fast. "Give it up, Dickhead," Cruz yelled from behind an enormous ivy-covered mausoleum with a kneeling angel at prayer atop the arch over the ornate, rusty scrolled wrought-iron door. It was the biggest and most elaborate crypt in the forgotten Louisiana country cemetery. "This hit is mine. Fuck off. Go back to your hole in Laredo."

Lemon's hiss of surprise sawed through the thick night air. "How the fuck do you know where I li—"

"Shut it, asshole!" Muncie hissed. Much closer now. Up ahead fifty feet.

Cruz listened to the asinine exchange as he tuned in to other footfalls. A slight breeze came up to ruffle his hair with damp fingers, sending a swirl of leaves rustling down the walkway in front of the concrete bone house. Between the lightly dancing leaf shadows across the way, he glimpsed, rather than heard, a man hiding two hundred feet north of his location. He was crouched near a dark gray crumbling tomb with *Debeneaux* engraved along the top face of it. A family crest was centered below the name.

Two solid granite panels sealing the tomb had etchings of the people's names and birth and death dates engraved on the front. It looked decades newer than the shadowy pockmarked tomb behind him. Cruz crouched in a wedge of denser blackness, as still and dark as the shadow itself.

The man sneaking up behind him smelled faintly of Brut cologne—moron. His tread disturbed the small twigs in the damp weeds. Under two hundred pounds, slight limp. Thus far he hadn't gotten off any shots. Maybe the guy was smarter than Lemon and Muncie. Maybe. Maybe he was smart enough to bring a handgun to the party instead of a long-distance rifle. Maybe.

He'd be dead before the night was over.

Definitely.

"Looked pretty fucking cozy to me, back there in the kitchen," Lemon taunted, revealing his exact position. Cruz stepped back lightly, moving slowly, his feet making very little sound on the hard stone surround of the crypt. "What happened? Suddenly decided you'd rather fuck the mark than off her? Maybe we'll take a turn before we finish the job. No hard feelings."

"Apparently the client didn't trust you." Cruz used his shoulder to get his hair out of his eyes. Sweat from the muggy heat prickled his skin. "I was hired to do what you two couldn't. Did you snipe her in her office seven weeks ago? Couldn't make your mark from two hundred feet? Fuck, man, you're slipping. The job should've been done, and you two could be holding hands, sipping mai tais in the Bahamas right about now." Cruz thought of the long, livid scar on Mia's arm. Thought about how close she'd been to death, and felt the thick, cold chill of his blood pumping through his veins.

"We're not g—"

"He's baiting you. Shut the fuck up, Dick," Muncie snapped. Feet scraping across the same stone surround where Cruz stood. "He's yanking your chain."

"We were *all* paid to do the job." Cruz didn't bother to lower his voice. He wanted their attention diverted here— away from the house—so he needed to keep the party going in the graveyard. "She'll only die once. And I'm the one who'll do the job. She knows me. Trusts me. And I'm smart enough not to bring the cops down on me. The rest of you will still have your dicks in your hands when I finish the job. You won't get another opportunity to get off a shot," Cruz said easily, attuned to the stealthy footfall coming up on his left. No point masking his location.

He knew if he could see Muncie ahead of him, the guy in back of him saw *him*. "Piss off," he told Lemon. "Keep your up-front money and walk the fuck away while you have the chance. I won't offer again."

"Who the fuck are you?" Lemon shouted, moonlight glinting off the long barrel of his Lapua.

"The man who's going to collect the balance of my fee, and

put in a request for the balance of yours as well. Still banking in the Caymans, Dickhead?" A wild guess.

"Holy fuck! How do you know where we—"

"Jesus, Dick!" Muncie groused, sounding even more incensed as he crouched low, the Lapua Magnum cradled in his arms like a baby, forming an elongated silhouette on the stones behind him. The guy needed a shower and a gallon of deodorant. He reeked of cigarettes and stale perspiration, a surefire gotcha.

They sure as shit weren't going to get lucky tonight.

Cruz tested the ledge of the stone foundation that ran around the base of the mausoleum. Solid. Muncie and his nose a lighter black in the shadows. Moonlight glared on the small bald spot on the back of his head, making a nice bull's-eye. Cruz stepped closer to the man without making a sound. He edged almost within touching distance, directly behind him. Oblivious to his imminent death, the man bitched, "You're telling the prick everyth—"

A sniper rifle was no contest in close combat, and the hand was faster than a bullet in this case. A quick, practiced twist of the guy's neck, and Muncie was permanently out of the picture. Not the way Cruz liked to do things. But it was expedient, and he felt a pulse pounding with growing urgency to get back to Mia. He didn't like that she was alone and unprotected in that big, empty fucking house.

"Kev?" Lemon prodded after several minutes of throbbing silence. He sounded justifiably nervous.

Cruz ignored him. Someone else was closer. Someone weighing in excess of two fifty, judging by the sound of his stealthy footfalls. Heavy smoker by the sound of his ragged breathing in the thick, muggy night air. Number three? Smart enough not to join in the convo as he closed in on Cruz's location.

Cruz stepped over Muncie's slumped body, keeping his back to the stone wall, turned the corner, then waited in the deep shadows, breath held. He didn't have long to wait. Number three's sausage-like fingers curled around the stone corner less then a minute later.

Cruz grabbed his thick wrist, yanked hard, and jettisoned him out in the open.

Arms outstretched for balance, and with an involuntary yell of surprise, the guy stumbled into the narrow dirt alley between the tombs and into full, stark white moonlight, a small handgun still clutched in his hand. Antonio Romero. Cruz knew him to be a small-time contractor with no conscience and a rep for brutality.

The moment the big guy fell to one knee, Lemon got off a head shot. Romero toppled. The blood pooling beneath his head looked black against the gravel. Lemon gave a victory yell. "See that, Kev? I got him."

Cruz shook his head. Idiot. The muzzle flash gave him pinpoint accuracy as his own shot followed Lemon's within a half a heartbeat. "Wrong him, Dickhead."

Three down. One to go.

The fourth man, silent and now invisible, lurked. Cruz scanned the surrounding area for any telltale movement. But the still, mottled darkness revealed no secrets.

The hair on the back of his neck lifted at the faint, almost imperceptible brush of a soft-soled shoe on rock. By the weight of his movements over the crushed shells and patches of weeds. Light. Agile. Sure-footed. But when Cruz tuned his sharp hearing toward the sound, all he heard was the susurrus of the breeze through the trees and a distant croak of a frog.

Cruz's own breath was as quiet as he'd trained it to be. He didn't move so much as a muscle. He might not know where number four was, but number four knew, he was sure, with pinpoint accuracy where *he* was. All Cruz had to do was patiently wait for the man to come and get him.

If there were more fuckers sent for Mia, Cruz would deal with them. If or when the time came. He hoped they weren't there now, because for the moment he had his hands full with upping the body count in the city of the dead.

Mia hid behind a half-open stone door. It was dark and creepy as hell wandering around the ancient graveyard alone, especially with bullets flying. She was scared out of her mind. If not for hearing Cruz's familiar voice, the one solid, comfortable, *good* thing in this bizarre situation, she would've had some smarts and hightailed it back to the house to wait for the police.

She'd heard some of the conversation, but hadn't processed it. Mostly they'd just been unintelligible words exchanged. Until she'd crept closer. Just enough to know Cruz was still alive. Hard to catch her breath in the circumstances, especially with the weight of the dark, damp night air pressing in on her.

She flinched at the sound of a bullet hitting something solid, followed by a cut-off cry.

"See that, Kev?" a man shouted, sounding pleased with himself. "I got him. Money in the bank, dude. Money in the bank!"

Oh, God . . .

"Wrong him, Dickhead." Cruz's voice cut through the darkness.

Mia released the anticipatory breath she'd sucked in. What the hell was going on? Cruz clearly knew these men. A few phrases seeped into her consciousness. *This hit is mine. Fuck off. Go back to your hole in Laredo.*

She'd *thought* that was Cruz's voice, but sound bent at night, especially when she was scared out of her mind.

He certainly wasn't friends with them—not from the tone of their voices and the exchange of bullets. But they all seemed to know one another. It didn't make any damned sense.

She had been waiting for the other shoe to drop, anticipating it for months. She knew someone would come to kill her. That day was now. Thank God he had missed—again. Cruz had saved her. Now he was out here alone in this awful, creepy, desperate place trying to protect her. Who would protect *him*?

The police were on their way. She'd called them while running. Seven minutes, she'd been told. Hadn't seven minutes come and gone a dozen times since she'd made the damn call?

Hoping to hear sirens, and lots of them, she heard nothing but frogs, and leaves rustling, and the distracting, hard thump-thump-thump of her blood pounding in her ears. Mia wiped her damp palms on the legs of her pants and tried to press herself closer to the stone door so she could get a better view without exposing herself.

Comeoncomeoncomeon.

She could delay a boardroom decision on her own for several hours, but she was at a loss as to what to do now. A fairly good shot, she wasn't so sure about her skills in this weird black-and-white real-time situation. Could she shoot the assassin and make it count? Even given the dire circumstances. Could she *shoot* an actual human being? This wasn't the instance where she could hope to wing him. If he was a killer, he meant business—and his business was to make sure she was good and dead. It was either him or her.

She chose him.

She lifted the barrel of the Beretta another fraction of an inch. She might have only one chance to take him down. And as much as she'd rather be back at the house following Cruz's directive, this wasn't his fight to fight. He was the innocent bystander. She knew he could take care of himself, but if he got hurt, she'd never forgive herself.

This hit is mine. Fuck off.

She leaned forward a fraction more and peered around the sharp stone edge of the door. More voices. Cruz and the killer. *Ignore them.* There'd be time to make sense of the surreal conversation later. Now she had to know her surroundings as well as she knew her own body. There, on the ground in the moonlight, she saw a dead man sprawled in the open space between the rows of crypts, a shiny black pool on the gravel as it spread out from beneath his head. Another man slumped half in, half out of the shadows.

Dear God, there was more than one. More than two. Someone else was still out there with Cruz. She sucked in the hard breath squeezing her lungs. The coppery smell of blood and a drift of whispered new death made the hair on the back of her neck prickle in warning.

This hit is mine.

This hit is mine.

This. Hit. Is. Mine.

A muggy breeze tinged with the musty odors of swamp and rotting things ruffled her hair, and she shivered as if cold, dead fingers stroked her cheek. Crap. She wished she hadn't put *that* image into her mind. There was enough non-woo-woo shit going on to freak her out without thinking about ghostly skeletal fingers touching her.

Hit. Mine.

It was downright fucking unnerving. She wanted to run. Run out of this haunted graveyard, run from the gunfight with what might be an army of assassins trying to kill her. . . .

And leave Cruz to fight her battle for her? Hell no.

She'd identified Cruz by his long hair and the shape of his darker shadow on the shadowy wall behind him and, after getting confirmation by the sound of his voice, kept him in sight.

Her eyes narrowed. *Shit shit shit.* There was a shadowy figure sneaking up behind him. Her gun felt heavy and unwieldy in her tense grip, but she tightened her fingers and slowly—very, very slowly—raised the barrel, training the muzzle on the man's thick silhouette. Her hand trembled from the weight and the gnaw of fear and indecision.

Mine. Mine. Mine.

This hit is mine.

Was it possible? Was Cruz *the hit man? Dear God.* She didn't want to believe it.

The tableau across from her had Mia riveted, dry-eyed, as she followed the man's stealthy approach. Didn't Cruz hear him? Sense the killer was there? In the time they'd spent together, she had learned that he had the hearing and instincts of a panther. He had to know, she reasoned. So, was Cruz fucking insane standing there, just waiting for the man following him to shoot him? Damn it. Maybe he wasn't aware this one time when he most needed to be. The guy was less than twenty feet from him with a gun pointed at his head.

Her racing heartbeat made her dizzy with fear. Sweat itched a path down her temple and made her fingers, clamped around the grip of the Beretta, slick. Dear God, the man lifted his arm and out of the shadows and the moonlight caught the blue-gray metal of his gun.

He was going to shoot Cruz. The moon and all of the ghosts now shoving their dead, stubby cold hands on her back urged her to *do* something.

Flicking on the laser pointer she used in presentations that she'd grabbed at the last second as she was running from the house, she shined it between the two crypts.

The small red dot gave Cruz's stalker a laser-bright bindi right between his eyes.

Chapter Eighteen

T his is the police," Mia shouted with authority, holding the dot steady between his eyes. He wouldn't see the dot, but he'd see the beam and think it was a laser gun sight. If nothing else, her action would warn Cruz and give him time to protect himself.

"We have you surrounded. Drop your weapon and come out into the ope—"

Her foot came down on a loose stone as she shifted her weight to adjust her weakening gun hand. The incredibly loud blast of the bullet exploding into the cement door inches from her head almost gave her a coronary.

Stone and concrete flew off the wall behind her in a stinging shrapnel of sharp fragments and dust.

The first shot was instantly followed by another blast, which added another tone of ringing to the first high-pitched whine in her ears. Staggering backward, she stepped farther into the pitch-dark crypt, pressing herself against the mossy door. She froze. Not breathing. Not blinking.

"Mia!" The voice sounded muted and far away.

Her lips moved, but no sound came out. A black streak

moved swiftly, seen out of the corner of her eye. Mia cowered back as Cruz grabbed her, wrapping his strong arms around her and almost squeezing the breath out of her.

"Jesus, woman—what the fuck were you thinking? Are you hurt? Did he get you?" He carried her out from behind the door into the moonlight, then set her on her feet to run his hands from her head over her shoulders, and over her breasts.

"You think he aimed for my boobs, Barcelona?"

"This isn't a fucking joke. You could've been killed." His voice was rough, and furious. He gave her a hard shake for good measure. "You could be dead because you didn't do what you were told. These guys were professionals."

"Go to hell, Barcelona. I came to help *you*." She stopped abruptly when her bravado leaked out, and she pressed her face against his chest, wrapping her arms around his waist.

His arms came back around her and he held her tightly against him, his fingers tangled in her hair. "I could've lost you tonight."

"I could've lost *you* tonight," she countered, tightening her arms around him. Inhaling the scent of his skin steadied her. But her heart still beat too hard and too fast, and her knees felt rubbery, as if they might give out at any moment.

She shuddered in the safe haven of his arms, holding him tightly. He had raced out to save the day without even a shirt as protection. Idiot! Her heart still beat in a fight-or-flight drumbeat, sweat prickled her skin, and her knees felt like jelly.

Swallowing fear-induced nausea convulsively, she gripped the damp, sweaty skin above his jeans and held on for dear life.

"The police are here," he said over the top of her head, his hand rubbing up and down her back soothingly. With her head resting on his chest, Mia was vaguely aware of sirens and saw flashing lights behind her closed lids. Took them long enough.

"Take this." He slipped his gun into the back of her jeans. *This hit is mine.*

The weirdest sensation came over her. Absolute bone-chilling cold. Freezing, brittle-cold, as pieces, like small ice cubes, fell into place. She stepped carefully out of his arms.

The minute she looked up at him, Mia knew. "You came here to kill me, didn't you?"

"If I'd wanted you dead, you'd be dead."

He didn't deny it. All she could do was blink up at him as the pain of betrayal flooded her body so painfully that she had to steel herself not to fall to her knees.

Police officers with flashlights and guns drawn flooded the graveyard.

"*You*, come with me," Detective Hammell instructed Cruz the moment he came abreast of them. "You got a piece?" he demanded. Cruz handed him his gun. "Dumb-shit move coming out here to confront the bad guys, son. How about you, Miss Hayward? You got yourself a weapon, too?"

Mia handed him her gun, which he took with a head shake. "Officer Durant will get you back to the house and take your statement, ma'am."

Without a word, Cruz turned his back and walked off with Hammell.

As furious, confused, and scared as she was, she wasn't ready to be interrogated by the police. What had just happened, what she'd just learned, was too raw, too new, too damned *unprocessed*, for her to discuss with anyone other than the person who'd made her feel all those damn things.

"Miss Hayward?"

She gave the young officer a blank look before she gathered herself and blinked him into focus. Late twenties, bobbing Adam's apple. Eager. She almost groaned. "Let's head back to the house."

It was considerably easier, and a lot faster, to walk across the brightly lit graveyard in a direct line. Officer Durant loaded her in the back of a squad car, something that had not been on any of Mia's lists, and without any conversation drove her the short distance to the house.

All the lights were on, and there were already officers inside and outside, processing the scene.

She headed down the hallway. "I need a dri—" She came to an abrupt halt in the doorway. There were people everywhere.

"Kitchen's a crime scene, ma'am," Officer Durant said kindly. "Is there somewhere we can talk?"

"The parlor, but I don't have any furniture."

"That's all right, ma'am, this isn't a social call."

No shit? "Right."

Even though she rarely drank hard liquor, Mia wanted

a drink now, but instead she flipped on the light in the never-used parlor. The scarred wood floor gleamed, thanks to Daisy, and a dozen packed boxes stood against the wall. She turned in a circle, then just went to the middle of the room and folded her arms at her waist. God. She wished her brain would get into gear. She had no idea what Cruz was saying to Detective Hammell. She had no damned idea what *she* was going to say to explain the scene in the graveyard.

Officer Durant flipped open a notebook. "Your full name?"

Shit, she couldn't even answer the first question honestly. On the short drive back to the house, she'd debating telling the police the truth, and why she was in Bayou Cheniere. But if she did *that*, then she'd have to say that there was a hit man after her, and if she said *that*, she'd have to tell him that Cruz was that man, and if she told him *that*, then he'd question her sanity in welcoming a hired killer into her home. "Mia Hayward."

Drawing on Amelia Wellington-Wentworth, Mia stiffened her spine and channeled her old self. The one who didn't believe bullshit from a man bent on seduction. Who saw through lies and half-truths and dealt with them accordingly. Who hadn't fallen in love with a man like Cruz fucking Barcelona.

Once Durant got the basics down, most of which were applicable only to Mia Hayward, with no mention of Amelia Wentworth, he asked her to explain in her own words what had transpired earlier.

Mia gave him a brief summery of the events. No, she didn't know the men. No, she had no idea why they were there. Cruz had run out there, and she'd called the police and followed with the gun. Guns. Yes, in hindsight she knew it had been a foolish thing to do. Yes, she was extremely lucky Mr. Barcelona had been there, and that neither of them had been injured.

He closed his notepad, Adam's apple bobbing. "Thank you, Miss Hayward. If we have any more questions, can we find you here?"

"I might have to return to San Francisco for business. I'll give you a number there if you need to contact me." Mia gave him her personal cell phone number, hoping like hell he hadn't been observant enough to notice the gleam of nervous sweat on her skin. The minute everyone left, she'd call for her private jet to pick her up in New Orleans. She didn't care what time she got back to San Francisco. Only that it was tonight. She wanted this over once and for all.

For a few minutes she considered changing her name again. Disappearing somewhere else where—hopefully—no one would ever find her. But where would that be? And for how long? She was damned if she'd hide away for the rest of her life. She was sick of being scared, of not being able to trust anyone. She had people who depended on her. Someone was behind the takeover of her company. Someone was pulling the strings of the people sent to kill her. There was China to deal with, and a company she loved needed her back at the helm.

If another killer came for her, he could ring her damn doorbell in San Francisco. She was done hiding.

She'd take every precaution. But she wasn't running away again.

She was going home.

She accompanied Officer Durant into the hallway just as Cruz and Detective Hammell came down the stairs.

Cruz hadn't bothered with a shirt, but his hair was tied back. He looked quite civilized, if one didn't look at his lying, killer black eyes. He was not in handcuffs, so he'd told his own damn version of the truth. She gave the back of his head a cold look as he walked outside with the officers.

The back door closed. Good. It locked automatically. Mia stood in the doorway to the kitchen and looked around. "What a damn mess." Broken glass, crap scattered all over the floor. She stalked over to the narrow closet and pulled out a broom, then stood there looking sightlessly at cleaning products and a yellow bucket, her finger curled around the door.

Every bit of bravado seemed to leak out of her and her hand tightened around the edge of door when her knees felt too insubstantial to hold her. She just couldn't make her feet move. Just stood there, staring straight ahead.

"Whose life *is* this?" Even her voice sounded different. *She* was different. The whole experience. Hit men. Cruz. People assaulting her in her own home. A woman she liked, battered and hospitalized while her little boy lived with strangers. "How would my life have been different if I hadn't run in the first damn place?"

Why hadn't Cruz killed her on one of his tries in San Francisco? Why hadn't he killed her at any time in the past week? She wasn't *that* damned good in bed.

Resting her forehead on the side of the door, Mia closed her eyes. Was Cruz in custody? Had they taken him away to charge him with attempted murder? She didn't care. She hoped he was locked in a tiny, urine-stinking cell with the worst of the worst.

She straightened her spine. First things first.

Retrieving the burner phone from the jar, she jabbed out the home number of her assistant as she ran upstairs. "Steph, send the jet to pick me up in New Orleans. Yes. *Now*. Take this number in case you have any problems." She had about four hours to pack up what she wanted from the house and get to the airport.

There wasn't a damn thing she wanted from the house.

Tossing a few things into a carry-on bag, she took the small case downstairs. Actions taken, she felt marginally better and got out the broom. Attacking the glass on the floor, she righted furniture and picked up the papers scattered across the kitchen. There was a hole in the cabinet and wall where the bullet had struck.

"Let's take a moment to take *that* in," Mia muttered grimly. The impact to her skull would have— "Yeah, *that*."

She presumed that the police had photographed the broken window and the shards of glass all over the floor and removed the slug from the wall. She'd observed the officers scouring the shrubbery outside the window with bright lights, looking for footprints and shell casings. Through the window she could see panning lights from the direction of the graveyard. So they were still over there.

She poured herself a tall water glass of wine and, after righting a bar stool, sat down facing the door with the glass, the bottle, and the small LadySmith revolver she'd had hidden in one of her suitcases. She raised the glass to her mouth and took a gulp just as Cruz walked in.

"This has been a hell of a day." Son of a bitch was still shirtless. Not playing fair. But then, had he ever? She forced her gaze to stay on his face. "Why don't you go up and take a hot shower and get some sleep? I'll finish cleaning up here."

So tense she thought she might shatter, Mia gave him a cold look as she leveled the double-action revolver right between his eyes. The matte silver gun was small. But if necessary it would do the job. Her hand was absolutely steady, and so was her voice. "You lied to the police about who and what you are, didn't you?"

"Are you going to shoot me?"

There were five rounds chambered. That should be enough. "*I'm* asking the questions. But a heads-up, Barcelona? Don't tempt me, because right now, if I did shoot you, it would be justifiable homicide, and I wouldn't mind spending a quiet twenty to life in jail." It was only fifteen ounces, but the longer she held the revolver, the heavier it got. Tightening her fingers, she adjusted her aim. "What load of BS did you feed Hammell?"

"I gave him my real name and occupation."

"Really?" She arched her brow. "Wow, and he didn't cuff

you and haul your lying, criminal hit man ass to jail on the spot?" Adjusting the barrel of the gun to point at the middle of his chest, Mia topped up her glass without looking.

She took a drink. "You weren't just winging it. You knew what you were doing. You moved and reacted like a professional." She looked into his eyes, looking for a reaction, got none.

"I told you I was in the military—"

"Why don't you stop bullshitting me, and tell *me* who and what you really are?"

Chapter Nineteen

*C*ruz walked across the room and leaned against the other end of the center island. She knew. Now she wanted confirmation. He wanted to give it to her. Should have before she asked. His emotions balled into a tight jumble of self-directed anger in his gut, which he hid behind a mask of pure calm. Just like he always did. Why the hell hadn't he told her before now? Before she overheard him talking to the others in the cemetery?

Panic. Fear. And a boatload of guilt. *Fuckfuckfuck.*

He should either have told her yesterday, or walked. Instead he'd been self-indulgent and lied to himself, believing he was being chivalrous. He should've explained the Mia situation to Hammell, and he would have taken her into protective custody. Could've. Should've but didn't.

"How much did you hear?"

"Enough to know that you assured those guys you were going to do the *hit* yourself. Is that true?" She swallowed, threw her shoulders back, and looked him directly in the eyes. "Did you come here to kill me?"

"Yes."

She flinched, her fingers tightening on the gun. "Who hired you?"

"I don't know." He crossed his arms over his chest, right where it felt heavy and achy, right where the bullet would hit. At this distance she wouldn't miss.

When she brushed aside a strand of hair that fell onto her brow, Cruz noticed her hand shook a little. She was maintaining, but at what cost? He wanted to go to her, comfort her, hold her.

"How much were you paid?"

"Fifteen million dollars." He waited to see the moment the hate and disgust came into her eyes. It hadn't—yet. There was plenty of emotion, though. "Half down. Half when I completed the job."

Her eyes widened a bit. "Wow. In the world of sleazy hit men, is that a big paycheck? Don't bother with an answer. But just an FYI? I'm worth considerably more alive than dead."

"It wasn't about the money," he said, keeping his voice calm and his eyes steady on hers.

She stared him down, the rage, the hurt, the full gamut of emotions, tamped down tight and with the lid on. "It's always about the money." She frowned. "It's easy for you to say it's not about the money when you already have seven point five million in your bank account. That's what half down means, right?" He nodded. "Why not just get the next seven and a half mil? Why make love—have sex—and hang around? Are you that cold and heartless to make love to me, act like you care about me, and then kill me?"

Her voice wasn't as steady as it was a moment before, and Cruz hated hearing the slight waver in it. It tore his insides into sharp, jagged pieces knowing he—not the other assholes in the cemetery—had done this to her. *Him*.

"Is this what you do? *Make love* with the people you're sent to kill before you kill them?" *Now* he saw the disgust in her eyes, the anger. Worse, he saw the pain of betrayal.

"Is tonight the night? The police will wonder about it if they come over tomorrow and find me dead in the kitchen and you long gone. That will tip them off that *you're* the bad guy after all."

"I told you not to trust me."

"So this is *my* fucking fault?!" Her eyes narrowed, her face flushed with anger. "You asshole. You told me not to trust you, then you did everything in your power to make sure I did." Her voice was bitter. Her long, toned legs were crossed, and her foot bounced in irritation. "Is that how you get the job done? Seduce the victim and then shoot them? I'm right here." She stood abruptly, knocking the stool over behind her. She spread her arms out from her sides, her eyes never leaving his. "Go ahead. Do your worst. I'm too damned tired to run. You're a professional: I'm sure you can draw that gun you claimed you got off one of the killers faster than I can fire mine. Oh, wait. You don't have a gun, do you? Hammell took it."

She couldn't hate him any more than he hated himself right in that moment. "How many times do I have to say it, in how many ways, until you get that I mean what I say? Listen to me, Mia. Listen to my words. Look into my eyes." He waited to make sure she was listening. "I . . . am . . . *not* . . . going to kill you."

She glared at him, the gun still pointed at his heart. "Your words are empty. I wouldn't know until it was too late, would I? And news flash, buddy: you don't get to do pained and exasperated tonight."

"Mia . . ."

"You know that's not my name. You knew who I was from the moment you walked into my house pretending to be someone else." She placed the gun on the counter. "Don't. I don't want to hear your bullshit. All I want from you is information. That first night—you came to kill me. What changed your mind? Did you decide to get in a quick fuck to sweeten the deal?"

His eyes met hers. "Yes. I saw you dancing, and I . . ."

"Thought: 'Here's a dumb-ass, desperate chick, too stupid to hide under the bed, knowing a killer was after her? Bet she'll just fling open the door and her legs and welcome me in'?"

His jaw tightened as she leaped to the most negative conclusions she could. Hell. He didn't blame her. "No. I thought: 'Here's a beautiful, uninhibited woman, totally unafraid and without artifice.' That's what I thought."

"Were you responsible for all those 'accidents' in San Francisco? The car? The elevator? The food poisoning?" Her eyes narrowed dangerously. "Are you the one who tried to shoot me in my office?"

He shook his head. "I wasn't hired until you were in Switzerland. I followed you back from there."

"So those guys in the cemetery were responsible for all those events?"

He nodded. "A few of them. They were pros. And I doubt they were the only ones after you. Someone is damned serious about wanting you dead, Mia."

"Rumor has it I'm quite hard to kill."

He laughed at that. Understatement of the year. "If one knows you—*impossible* to kill. I've been conflicted ever since I met you, even though I was strongly motivated."

"The fifteen million bounty?"

He shook his head. "I told you. It isn't about the money." He ran his hand in frustration through his hair, pulling out the band. How could he explain to her why he was a hit man when he had never given voice to his mission before? "Shit, Mia. I'm struggling to find the right words here."

"How about you find the truth."

He took a step closer to her and stopped when she looked like she was about to pick up the gun again. "Mia. I've never spoken the truth about this to anyone before." He sucked in a breath, needing air to clear his head. "I've never killed anyone who hasn't deserved it. Never. I do my reseach dillegently. Which was why I couldn't kill you. I knew something was off."

"My *clothes*," she said dryly. "If I hadn't hauled you into the house and told you not to say anything, would you have killed me that night? Or were you just thinking the fuck was a bonus?"

He stared at her until she shifted impatiently, hanging on,

waiting for his answer. "Yes," he said honestly, "it was exactly that. It was nothing but a fortuitous fuck that first night. I'll give you that. But I knew almost instantly that you weren't the person I was told you were."

"And why was that?"

"You didn't come across as an amoral, sadistic bitch who imprisoned children in your Chinese factories, who had a secret sex ring online."

Mia pressed her fingertips to her temples and half closed her eyes. "I told you Blush doesn't have business interests in China—" Her eyes opened wide and she snapped her fingers. "Ah, that was what all those Chinese hints were about. You couldn't possibly have believed that—"

He put up a hand, stopping her right there. "These people are good. They had evidence—pictures, property records, news articles. A private detective followed you for a *year*, Mia. Yet something told me within minutes of meeting you that you weren't the person in the dossier given to me.

"So, I started trying to disprove, or prove, what they were telling me. I also knew that if I didn't do the job I was paid to do, they'd send someone else." He paused, knowing he had to tell her everything. "Which they did, several times. They wanted you dead by tomorrow morning. That was *my* deadline. And clearly the deadline for the others, too. If one didn't kill you, another would. When you gave Davis and Kent the mailbox address, you also gave someone the opportunity to wait for you and follow us back here. I've been trying to figure out who hired me."

"And all the others," Mia said bitterly. "Whoever hired all of you is pretty damned determined to kill me. There were how many tonight?"

"Four."

"*Five*, with you. At *least* five people paid a fortune to kill me. Who's to say there aren't another half dozen hit men lurking in the damned bushes? Who the hell has that kind of money and hatred for me?"

"They might be lurking, but it isn't gonna happen."

She raised a brow.

"I won't let anything happen to you, Mia. I'll do everything in my power to protect you and keep you safe. Think, sweetheart. Think. You should know, somewhere in here"—he touched his head—"and in here"—he touched his heart—"you have to know that you can trust me. That you can trust my word."

Tears shimmered in her eyes. Not that she'd let them fall, he knew. She was too angry. Worse, too hurt to allow him to see her vulnerable. He rubbed his fist over the ache in the middle of his chest.

She swigged the rest of her wine and put the glass back on the counter with utmost care before meeting his gaze.

"Your word isn't worth a damn thing. You're a criminal. A killer. Hell, for all I know, you're lulling me into trusting you again and you'll kill me if I let down my guard."

"You've turned your back on me more times than I can count and you're still here. I told you, you have my word."

"The word of a killer?" The tone was cutting, but he understood why. Trust was a hard commodity to come by in both his profession and hers.

"The word of the man who's come to know and care about you."

"You care for me? How noble. People care for plants. They care for what they're going to have for dinner. Do they walk away from seven and a half million dollars for things that they care about? I don't think so."

She was right, but he couldn't say the words that he'd never said to anyone before. He was already saying things that he'd never admitted to before. He more than cared for her.

In his pause, she continued, "What if the police figure out who you are? Wait. Who are you, anyway? Is your name even Cruz Barcelona?"

He shook his head but still didn't give her the truth of his identity. "Nobody knows who I am or what I look like. All transactions go through an email account I have routed all over the world."

"You idiot! I saw your face that first night. *I* can identify you!"

"*You, yes*. But none of my marks has ever been in a position to give my description to the authorities."

"I'm leaving tonight. Are you going to try to stop me?"

"You can't go anywhere on your own. You know that. Not until we asertain wh—"

"There is no damned *we*. If you're not going to kill me right now, leave."

Maybe he was hedging his bet to negotiate with whoever hired him to get paid all of the other assassins' money too.

Dear Lord, she didn't want to believe that was true. She wanted to believe what he said, but hadn't he told her not to trust anyone? She couldn't even trust her own heart that was crying out for him to hold her. Him. The man who would've killed her if he hadn't banged her first. But as warped as it all was, what he said kind of all made sense. If Cruz, or whatever his real name was, believed he was doing the right thing, it did ring true. Could he really have this steadfast code of honor that ran deep into his core, causing him to kill to carry out his own brand of justice.

Mia looked at him. Really looked at him for the first time since they had met, seeing him for who he was, not as the handyman or even as her lover. She saw him and heard all that he had told her in their time together. And she remembered how he had acted, responded, and desired her. The pieces clicked into place.

She knew this man. She knew who he was.

"You keep killing your father," she said quietly, emotion keeping her from speaking any louder. She felt hollow, emptied out. "Is that it, Cruz?"

He gave her a startled look. "I never said I killed my father."

"You said there was a *hit*."

"I never said *I* was the one who did it." His eyes were bright. Wide. Perspiration started to bead on his brow.

343

"You didn't have to." She took a step closer. "I know you." She took another step. "You avenged your mother's death. You found something you were good at." She stopped with four feet between them.

Everything in her wanted to hold him, but she stood her ground. She was ready to meet him halfway. But he wasn't budging. Either physically or emotionally. *Close the gap. Come to me. Show me I'm more than a way to scratch an itch. More than a job on your scorecard.* "You said you only killed people who were evil to the bone. You protected their victims. They were people who preyed on the small and weak. People like you were as a child. Am I right?"

Cruz plowed his fingers through his hair. "Jesus, Mia—"

"I'm right, aren't I? Your instincts told you I wasn't who I was painted to be. And you couldn't kill me. You couldn't do it now if you tried."

He groaned and shut his eyes tight for a moment before locking his gaze on her. "I have feelings for you."

"I was falling in *love* with *you*."

For several minutes she thought he'd turn tail and leave. But he stood there. Features tight, but blank and unreadable. Strong emotion held his body rigid before he spoke. "This is new territory for me. I never go into a new territory without surveilling and researching every angle. Yet, here I am."

Not enough. And not a damn answer. Disappointment made her chest feel heavy, and she folded her arms around her waist, hugging herself when what she needed were Cruz's arms around her. "While you figure that out," she said coolly, unwrapping her arms and moving across to straighten some papers on the center island, "I have more immediate problems."

Instantly the cool, calculating killer was back, his eyes sharpened, his body tightened. Emotions clearly weren't his strength. "Stay here. I'll find out who's behind the hit and shut them down."

"That's not in your job description, is it? And you weren't paid to *protect* me. My safety or lack thereof isn't your concern. And frankly, I'm damned if I'm going to stay here and wait for you or anyone else to solve my problems. I've got a life to live, Cruz. I'm going home to finish my business at Blush. I'll go through legal channels and prosecute to the fullest extent of the law everyone involved in this. Then I'll go back to what I was doing with my life before *this*, and *you*, came into it."

"I'll be your bodyguard," he said a little desperately.

"I'm not stupid enough to go into this unprotected. Not now, when I'm aware of the reality of these attempts." She'd hired Black Raven to accompany her back home. They'd be on her jet when it arrived in New Orleans, and with her every moment until the people responsible were exposed and caught. "I neither need nor want your services. You've proven to be a security risk, and unreliable. I don't trust you. I won't *ever* trust you." *Come over here. Grab me, kiss me, and tell me you love me.* Clearly, that wasn't going to happen.

"You can't be so stupid as to—"

"Not stupid. I run a multibillion-dollar company," she told him, jaw tight. "I control every aspect of my life with efficiency and purpose. Not you or anyone else. I haven't reached this level of success by trusting every—hell, *any*—good-looking guy capable of giving me a decent orgasm."

"I care about you. I don't want you hurt."

Was that enough for him not to wake up in the middle of the night one night, and for him to decide he'd like to have the other 7.5 mil?

"How you feel is immaterial to me. I want you to leave now."

She'd never see him again once they went their separate ways.

He grabbed her arm and pulled her up close to him until there was full body contact, as if that would keep her next to him. "For God's sake, Mia, this isn't a fucking business merger. This is life and death. You can't go back to San Francisco."

Anger welled up. Anger and hurt and yearning, all mixed up in one huge fucked-up nightmare of a tangle. And there was only one thing she could do to unwind it "Tie things up? Then what? *You* don't give me permission for *anything*, Cruz. It'll take time to resolve a multitude of critical issues and time to unravel who was responsible for hiring you and your co-horts."

He winced, clearly not liking her to compare him to the other assassins in the cemetery.

"You aren't the only one who wants retribution and justice. I want it, too. And I'm going to make damn sure I get it, no matter who's responsible."

But they both knew what would happen after their good-byes had been said.

His fingers tightened on her upper arms. "What about us?"

"There's an 'us'?" She kept her tone insouciant as she stepped away, the feel of his fingers burning like ten individual brands. Instead of rubbing the sensation away, she braced her hands on the counter behind her. His gaze dropped from her mouth to her breasts, making her heart leap in response. No, not this. He wanted her physically. But Mia was greedy. She wanted it all.

"I'm not sure what you're talking about, because I didn't get that from what you said. I said I loved you. *You* said you cared for me. That doesn't add up to an 'us'. As a matter of fact, I'm not sure I'd ever believe that you're capable of giving or receiving love. Does someone who kills for a living feel love? Do you even feel anger or hate, Cruz?"

"Damn it. You know we have something."

"What's the definition of that something, Cruz? Maybe I'm obtuse. Spell it out for me."

"I care about you," he repeated, eyes black and unreadable, tension in every line of his body.

"Hmm."

She walked back to the table and the piles of papers she'd haphazardly returned to the surface. Brushing off a sparkle of glass, she found a business card and a pen. Turning over the card, she scribbled on it, then handed it to him between two fingers—almost a challenge. "I wrote the number to my direct line on the back. Maybe I'll want to talk to you in three or four months. Maybe not."

She took a last look at his face, even though looking and not touching ripped out her heart.

It was better this way. She couldn't not love him, despite who and what he was. And he was incapable of loving her the way she wanted and deserved.

She walked past him, close enough to smell his pheromones and near enough to observe the muscles under his eyes flinch as she kept going. At the door to the kitchen, Mia picked up her carry-on bag, then straightened and made herself turn to face him. "Goodbye, Cruz."

After following a convoluted flight plan through five different cities so that no one would be able to follow her, Mia arrived in San Francisco with the security detail of four men sent by Black Raven. The first thing on her list was food. She planned to hole up and get these matters resolved once and for all. And the fewer people who knew she was back in town, the better.

It was one in the morning, three days after she'd left Cruz. She hit a twenty-four-hour market that was empty other than herself and her security team, and a gum-chewing guy who talked on his cell phone as he rang up her purchases. He was more interested in the men with her than in Mia herself.

She was taking a risk returning to the city. Probably a big risk. But she had to see this through to its conclusion, and returning was her only option. And at this point she didn't trust anyone other than the heavily armed men accompanying her. Two carried her groceries; the others kept their eyes moving as they walked into the empty lobby of the Blush building. She was made to wait while one of the men distracted the security guard so that she could enter the elevator undetected. Within minutes they were in her pied-à-terre on the top floor.

Mia felt as though she'd been gone for years instead of months. She was home, but she wasn't taking any chances of things going south. She had things to do; the security company's sole job here was to make sure she was safe and unharmed and able to do what she needed to do. Their counterparts in Denver were still doing intense background checks on everyone she could think of.

After unpacking the groceries, she made herself a cup of tea and carried it into the study, leaving the men to their own devices. The small study-library would be her war room. She needed answers, and she wouldn't stop until she had them.

Starting a new list brought her a strange sort of peace.

While she sorted through the most likely suspects who wanted her dead, she'd stay in, prep her own food, and not trust a soul. Five men had been hired to kill her. Ludicrous. It was overkill. But if someone had hired *five* hit men, they were desperate, and therefore dangerous. For all she knew there might be more hit men lurking where she least expected them to be.

Now hyperaware, she was taking no chances. First thing on her agenda was taking a meeting via Skype with the investment firm. She'd set that up for first thing the following morning.

At 9:00 a.m., two of her personal lawyers, Chris Deacon and Roslynn Carpenter, plus her CPA, Claire Fine, were included in the conference Skype call. They made damn sure she had the highest bid, and that the bidding was officially closed.

Blush was hers.

She crossed the successful leveraged buyout off her list as if it were butter on a grocery list.

A billion-dollar tub of butter.

The security people wanted to stay with her until they ascertained who had hired the hit men. Yes, the buyout was a done deal, but anyone that strongly motivated might have another agenda. They'd stay until they figured out the who and why.

They were there, but unobtrusive.

There was no time to think about Cruz, although her body had muscle memory and she ached for him. She was on full-speed, hyper-CEO mode. Things had to be resolved systematically, and once and for all, before she could think of the future without the man she loved.

She was trying damn hard to get over him.

The police, waiting for word from her, closed in at the investment company to investigate where the illegal leak had come from and to establish who made up the black pool. From that black pool would come whoever had put out the hit on her, Amelia was certain.

It took her three days, and dozens of phone calls, before she was ready to go down to the executive floor. The news of her return spread to the other thirty-nine floors, and to the press, like wildfire. Within an hour, practically everyone who was anyone knew she was back.

Returning to Blush headquarters turned out to be anticlimactic. People told her she looked well rested after her vacation. Some said she'd been missed. She had a long list of things she wanted to accomplish in the first week, and in typical Amelia Wellington-Wentworth style, she got right down to it.

Mia had more agents from the private security company come into Blush to "work closely" with her own people. They were there to observe and report. She was done with this shit of jumping at her own shadow and sleeping with one eye open. Having that many killers after her did that to a girl.

Security was doubled while she, Black Raven Security contractors, and the police closed in on who had hired the hit men. Black Raven was taking a much harder look at some of the players. So far there was no definitive proof, but they assured her they'd have something solid for her in a few days. The police, too, were looking at the same information Amelia had given them the day after arriving back in San Francisco.

The Black Raven agents with her had handed her an envelope with the report on Cruz. The envelope, still sealed, was in a drawer next to her bed. She wasn't ready to look inside. Would whatever was in the envelope make him love her? He wasn't *capable* of love—realistically she knew that. But did an *I care about you* trump living a life without him?

Before she dealt with anything related to Cruz, she had to take care of herself and Blush, and that meant talking to Todd.

"Welcome home, honey!" Her cousin strode into her office with arms outstretched, his gray suit immaculate, his hair just long enough to be sexy, his blue eyes, so like hers, bright with concern. While they were never demonstrative in the office, her door was closed, and she walked into his arms, crazy happy to see him.

"God," he said thickly. "It is *so* damn good to see you. I've been worried sick."

If he had an inkling of what she'd gone through in Louisiana, he'd have a coronary. "Are you crying into my hair?" she teased, giving him an extra squeeze around the waist before forcing a wobbly smile of her own.

"Who wouldn't cry into this hair?" He let her go but held her at arm's length, critically inspecting her from head to toe and back again. "Dear God, was it chewed off in a fit of passion by that sexy lifeguard at the beach?"

Her hair had been halfway down her back when she left. "No beach. No sexy lifeguard. But that's a whole other story."

Perched with her hip on her desk, a large, raw-edged slab of black granite, she turned to take in Todd's sartorial splendor. As always, he was a sight for sore eyes. She'd missed him. He was cousin, brother, father confessor, best friend, and then all his other hats for the company.

Her right-hand man.

She didn't need a written report to assure her of his loyalty to both her and the company. He was the one person in this whole mess she'd trusted unequivocally from the start.

Tall, elegantly thin, her cousin had the Wellington aquiline nose and the Wentworth blue eyes, and gorgeous, thick, wavy blond hair. Mia smiled. "No matter what, you always look like a Jane Austen hero."

"I don't believe in having tragic love affairs, but I'm more than willing to hear the salacious details of yours."

"I own Blush." Mia dusted off her hands. "Highest bid. Done deal. I got the paperwork an hour ago."

Cocking his head, he narrowed his eyes and said tentatively, "Congratulations?"

"Yes. We'll celebrate later. Let's finish this thread before we start tugging at the next. I have a private security firm, and the police, checking into who was part of the black pool. We all agree that the hirer of the hit men will be found swimming in that murk."

"Makes sense— Wait—hit *men*? Plural?"

"Four that I know of." She left Cruz out of it.

"Holy crap, Amelia!" Todd paced her office. "*Four* of them? I'm going to wrap you in cotton batting and keep you under my bed until we figure this out."

"Too hot, and difficult to make phone calls," Mia said briskly, sliding off her desk and grabbing her notebook. She tore off the top sheet. "And definitely not my style. Take a look at this list. Tell me what you think."

Todd took the sheet of paper and retreated to one of the red leather easy chairs in the elegant seating area across the room. He glanced at her as he sat down. "Shouldn't we call Basson in for this meeting?"

She got up to join him, perching on the arm of another

chair, foot swinging as she crossed her legs. May in San Francisco was downright chilly, and she was dressed in a beautifully tailored black Armani skirt suit with a narrow pencil skirl, a man-style white shirt, and red Jimmy Choos with six-inch heels. A far cry from cheap cotton shorts, a Walmart T-shirt, and bare feet.

She felt more in control here. She was back where she belonged, but even after three days it was as though this life didn't quite fit. Her life. But not.

"Miles was behind this. The police are interrogating him in my private conference room right now," she told him, tucking her hair behind her ear. "I believe he's been working in conjunction with someone in-house to get rid of me in a depressingly permanent way."

Todd nibbled at his bottom lip. "Shit. You know, I've never particularly liked him. But he was trusted by your father—and mine, for that matter. You'd better be damn sure. He's worked for Blush for thirty-five years. A wrongful-termination suit would be costly, to say the least. What does Legal say?"

"To be very, very sure before I press charges. I, the Black Raven people, and the police are sure. As is Interpol."

"Fair enough." He glanced at the sheet in his hand. "Only five names are uncrossed." He glanced across at her. "Pretty much *none* of these would be on my list of suspects, to be honest."

"They weren't on mine at the start either," she admitted. "But by process of elimination . . . As Arthur Conan Doyle said, 'Once you eliminate the impossible, whatever remains, no matter how improbable, must be the truth.' One or more of those people is working with Miles."

"Improbably so, you must admit."

"Yes. But possible, *you* must admit."

Todd stretched his arm over the back of the chair. "I'll trust your judgment on this." He paused. "I don't see my name anywhere on this. I thought you were checking and double-checking anyone and everyone. I shouldn't be an exception just because I'm your favorite cousin and you love me madly."

"You're my *only* cousin, and I do love you madly. I also trust you like no one else. But even so, I had you just as thoroughly investigated as everyone else. So the answer to that question is, your name *was* on the long list, and I *did* put you through exactly the same scrutiny as everyone else."

"Good," he said briskly, unoffended. "I always knew you were a smart woman." He rattled the sheet of paper. "You have people dealing with these five and Miles?"

Mia nodded.

Todd settled back comfortably. "Good, then you have time to tell me every small detail about this delicious, hot affair of yours."

Chapter Twenty

*T*he cab pulled up on Market Street across from the impressive glass-and-steel high-rise that was Blush headquarters. Cruz handed the driver the fare and exited the yellow cab. The Financial District of downtown San Francisco was busy at midmorning with well-dressed pedestrians clogging the sidewalks. Cars, buses, and trolley cars moving up and down the steep hill added to the commotion.

A soft, ethereal, drifting fog had pedestrians huddling into scarves thrown over overly optimistic summer clothing in early June. Wearing jeans and a white dress shirt, Cruz's body temperature soared in anticipation of being with Mia. Thirteen days without seeing her, breathing her fragrance, or hearing her voice.

He knew a "Fuck off" when he heard one.

But Cruz was clinging to the hope that he still had one ace in the hole.

He couldn't wait another twenty-four hours to see her.

Like a junkie waiting for his next fix, his addiction to Mia thrummed through him, better than effervescent bubbles in the finest French champagne.

He took a moment—yeah—he was procrastinating and he knew it. He looked up at the forty-story rose-quartz-colored glass building with its soaring modern lines. An elegant pink-and-black-striped awning belled over the enormous front doors, which were flanked by two man-sized glossy black jardinières, with some sort of fluffy feminine pink flowers and lush greenery. The words *BLUSH TOWER* curved the span of the awning in elegant copperplate script.

Understated. Classy. Impressive. Very Mia.

It was insane how nervous he was about seeing her here in her natural habitat, on her turf. Going to other people's turf to get the job done was what he had always done. This was different. Completely different. This wasn't work. There was no neutral zone for him to regroup here or anyplace he could neutralize to give himself the advantage.

He'd never been this nervous about seeing a woman in his life. Cruz dragged in a ragged breath of cool, foggy air. Standing across the street like a nervous kid on his first date wasn't going to get the job done. He'd mentally rehearsed his bullet points, mapping out every action just as he would if this had been a hit. He'd only get one shot.

This was a risk. Bearding her here where she was on familiar ground, surrounded by loyal employees. She was either going to be damn happy to see him, or pissed. There'd been no closure, no deadlines, no promises made.

What they had had been dropped into a big black hole.

She was furious. Hurt. Felt betrayed.

He got that. He was one hundred percent at fault.

They had to work through it. He refused to give up on them.

That was unacceptable.

He'd mentally given the press three days to find something of more topical interest than Amelia Wellington-Wentworth's takeover of her own company. She'd triumphed. Of course she had. Cruz had never doubted her dedication, power, and tenacity. Now the headlines were about some actress's sex tapes being released on the Internet. No mention of the attempts on Mia's life, nor any mention of any arrests.

The person who had set out to kill her was probably laying low now, since Mia couldn't be stopped and she got the company. That didn't mean Mia was out of danger. Cruz knew it. He was also certain her security team knew it, since he spoke to Black Raven daily about Mia. Hell, at first Sebastian at Black Raven refused to speak to him. Then, after Cruz made him an offer he couldn't refuse, he allowed him in the loop. Information for information. Cruz had resources and availability to intel that even the impressive Black Raven did not. He made sure her team kept Mia safe. And he made sure they didn't tell her that he was doing it.

Now it was time to come back into her life. Time for him to make his move and stake his claim on the CEO of Blush.

Three cyclists pedaled by, then he had to wait for a damned lumbering bus to pass before he stepped into the street. Cruz stuffed his fingertips into his back jeans pockets as he started across the busy street. Should've worn a suit. . . .

The bus moved to reveal the approach of a discreet black

town car. His heart thumped in anticipation. He made a suicidal dash through traffic to the center divide just as the limo eased to the curb right in front of Blush's doors.

His heart leaped.

Mia.

An angry driver honked and swerved around him, and the muted clang of a cable car as it headed downhill toward the bay reminded Cruz where he was. She exited the car. The diaphanous fog took the sheen from her dark hair, and the beautiful cream suit hugging her curves was unfamiliar. He was used to seeing her mostly bare. His Mia. He wanted her on his Brazilian beach. Naked.

God. He just . . . wanted her. He was so tired of the hurting and longing. He was tired of the hole in his world that could only be filled with Mia. Now all he had to do was convince her that they *would* make this work. Demonstrate the depth of his feelings for her. He knew she needed him to say it. He felt it, but that wasn't enough.

He checked for oncoming cars, then stepped off the median into the street again.

"Mia!" Her name burst from him joyously. Love. Holy shit. He *loved* Mia. He loved this woman. His life was nothing but pain and awful feelings without her. She was all the good things he wanted but never had. Love.

He loved Amelia Wellington-Wentworth. Mia. Now that his mind knew what his body had known all along, he couldn't wait another moment to tell her. Cruz had never known such happiness, elation. He moved toward Mia. *"Ameli—"*

Thip. The sound of a silencer was familiar to his ears. Stumbling to a stop, he stared with horror and complete incomprehension as blood sprayed from the bullet shot to the back of her head. She crumpled to the ground and fell out of Cruz's sight.

"Jesus! No." Heartbeat manic, Cruz vaulted over the shiny black hood of her car. She was sprawled facedown on the sidewalk. Blood pooled beneath her in a sickening, ever-widening red puddle.

"No!"

Nearby, a pedestrian screamed, a high-pitched sound that echoed deep in his soul. Cruz fell to his knees on the sidewalk beside her, gathering her limp body to cradle her in his arms. *"Please . . ."* He felt individual ribs on her narrow back through her linen jacket as he clasped her tightly to his chest.

A sob wrenched its way up his raw throat as scalding tears blurred his vision. White blurred into red.

"No," he whispered hoarsely into the wet, sticky mess of her hair as he pressed her slender body tightly against his chest, rocking her, eyes squeezed shut. Tears burned like acid on his lashes.

She'd been hit. God fucking damn it. She'd been hit. The stupid fucking LBO had gone through, and she'd *still* been hit. His nightmare.

A torrent of grief flooded his body in a dense black wave of anguish too intense to contain. "Mia!" His voice was broken, hoarse.

The press of people and the susurrus of their voices were beyond Cruz's ability to separate or even comprehend.

Running footsteps. Sirens. Noise. Screams.

As a kid, he'd mourned the violent death of his mother, been ripped apart emotionally for years afterward, but this . . . this was worse.

Someone grabbed his shoulder, shouted something unintelligible. Shrugging him off, Cruz growled low in his throat, holding her even tighter as they tried to take her from him.

She's dead, he wanted to yell.

He'd never see her shining blue eyes laughing up at him again. He'd never see that private smile she gave him like a gift when they lay naked and satiated. He choked back the raw pain and it sounded like the cry of a wounded animal.

The overwhelming urge to look at her pressed like an anvil on his chest. He wanted to feel the silk of her hair against his fingers as he pushed it off her face so he could see her beauty one last time. But he knew, with sick bile rising in his clogged throat, that if he did, he'd never sleep again. Hell, he probably wouldn't anyway.

"The paramedics are here, buddy," some guy said sympathetically as the siren shut off abruptly. He smelled it then. Not tuberoses. Blood. Death.

The clang of the gurney, rapid footsteps on the sidewalk, someone talking on a comm.

The man tugged at his shoulder. Cruz shook his head. Tightened his hold. He'd promised to protect her.

Promised. He had failed her. Failed *them*.

There wasn't a damn thing on this earth that could ever fill the void of her loss. Or mitigate his overwhelming guilt for allowing this to happen on his watch. Fuck him. Fuck. Him.

They had to pry his fingers off her. Had to shove him aside, a police officer holding him back, so they could lay her onto the gurney and check her vitals. The EMT turned to look at Cruz and sadly shook his head. "Don't—" he cried, anguish making him feel wild and feral as they zipped up the black plastic bag with a grating death knell sound so final, so gut-wrenching, he couldn't draw a breath. "Don't," he whispered soundlessly, crouched where he was on the crowded sidewalk.

Frozen. Paralyzed with grief. Dry-eyed.

They wheeled her away. His eyes tracked her until the doors slammed shut. He stared after the ambulance until it disappeared. No siren.

He couldn't move.

People milled about like dark ghosts on the periphery of his vision. He was aware of the police presence, of people taking pictures with their phones, of the cool fog lifting, and of the sun's light, but not of any feeling of warmth.

The small black void where his heart had once been expanded to fill the rest of him.

Numb and feeling wooden, Cruz gave his statement to the police. The limo driver had taken off. They had an APB out on him. What the fuck did it matter now? Finding her killer wasn't going to bring her back. Time stretched, then was truncated. Nothing felt real as he stood there on the heatless sunny street, pedestrians washing around him as if he were a rock lapped by the tide.

He'd never hold her again, never bury his face in the fragrant crook of her neck, never—

No familiar, heady scent of tuberoses.

His gaze dropped to the wide bloodstain on the sidewalk, then swiveled to look at the tinted windows of her building. His heartbeat suddenly started to gallop.

Turning away from the detective who'd just closed his notebook, Cruz sprinted to the wide double doors, shoving the cold pink glass open with both hands. A curved black marble counter, manned by two surprised-looking security guards, stood between him and the two banks of elevators across the wide expanse of the checkered black-and-white floor. "What floor is Miss Wentworth on?" he asked without slowing down.

"Sir, you can't—"

"What the fuck floor is she on?"

"*Forty*, but you can't—" The rest of his words were lost as Cruz ran past him. A security turnstile was no deterrent. He vaulted over it, then hauled ass to the closest elevator—thank God for the express elevator. The doors closed as one of the security guys came barreling after him, yelling for him to stop. Cruz slammed his palm on the button for the fortieth floor.

The elevator rose smoothly as his heart pounded manically. A glance in the surrounding copper-framed mirrors showed a man who'd seen hell, and wasn't sure he'd live to tell about it. His eyes looked wild. The entire front of his white dress shirt was stained red and clinging wetly to his skin.

"God, this is crazy, but let me be right."

There was so much adrenaline surging through his body, Cruz's head felt off-kilter. Dropping back, he leaned his shoulders into the corner, squeezing his eyes shut, his knees no better than melting wax.

Pleasepleaseplease.

Amelia stared in deep disgust as the police slapped the handcuffs on the man who had tried to kill her . . . multiple times. In multiple ways.

How could Miles have done this? How could he have betrayed her? How could he have betrayed her father? And the company he'd protected for more than thirty-five years?

She glanced at the others who'd been gathered in the conference room prior to Miles's arrest. Local police and, interestingly, Interpol as well as several of Blush's attorneys, Todd, her assistant Stephanie, and several key Blush executives.

There was a laundry list of charges against Miles Basson and Candice Wentworth, her stepmother.

"You deserved everything we dished out and then some," Miles shouted, tugging at his cuffed wrists. One of the plainclothes detectives put a restraining hand on his shoulder.

Mia tugged down her short red jacket over her bold red sheath as she rose from her chair to circumvent the long conference table. She took long, even strides on her favorite bone-colored Louboutins to stand in front of the man who wanted her dead. She slapped him hard across the face. "You were more than a trusted employee to me and my family." She kept her voice calm, her breathing steady. "My father respected you. Entrusted his family with you. He thought of you like a brother. I feel nothing but disgust for you. Not for what you did to me, but what you did to my father and everyone at Blush."

"You'll regret turning me in to the police, you self-entitled, *fucking* bitch." His already florid face went dark red. "Your father's rolling in his grave, knowing what you've done to me."

My father would've emasculated you first, then killed you slowly with his bare hands if he'd ever discovered the man he trusted was sleeping with his wife, and paid to have his only child killed. "I haven't even *started*, Miles." Amelia gave him a cool look, then added, "Not yet. And when we find Candice—which we eventually will—she'll be caged like the animal she is, too."

Where in the hell *was* her stepmother? The fly in the ointment was that no one had seen Candice. The police had sent out an APB. Miles, her lover for freaking *years*, according to Black Raven's investigators, claimed he had no idea where she was.

"If we hear from her," she told the lead detective, who had Miles by the upper arm and was shoving him toward the door, "we'll let you know immediate—"

"*Mia.*"

At the raw sound, Mia turned toward the door, knowing who it was before she saw him. She would always know his smooth, deep voice. It was the same voice that haunted her dreams and left her longing every night. It was the voice now that had her heart racing.

Cruz. He stood in the open doorway, his hand on the doorknob. White-faced, wild-eyed, white shirt rolled up on his muscular forearms, covered in . . . oh my God. It looked like blood. Jesus. Was that his blood? He stared at her as if he was seeing a ghost, his skin two shades paler than it should have been, his eyes haunted.

"Dear God—" Shoving her way between handcuffed Miles and one of the detectives, she ran to Cruz's side and slid a supportive arm around his waist. His features were so drawn, so pale, she wedged her shoulder into his armpit to keep him upright in case he collapsed.

"Where are you hurt?" she demanded, running a frantic hand over the wet bloodstains on his shirtfront. "Cruz, where are you hurt?"

If he'd been shot or otherwise seriously injured, he would have needed a hospital. Anything else could be treated by Blush's top-notch staff clinic on the fifth floor. But she didn't know how serious it was.

"Todd! Call an ambulance! Steph, get the nurse up here right *now*. Everyone else, out!"

Tightening her arm around Cruz's waist, Mia tried to steer him over to the closest chair. Had he been in a car accident?

"Were you *shot*?" She met the eyes of the lead detective. There'd been no attempts on her life since she'd returned, but that didn't mean the threat wasn't still out there. His face was a hard, expressionless mask. His feet seemed planted where he stood. "Not me. I'm not injured. A woman—" He shuddered, tightening his arms around her like steel bands.

The detective hung up his cell phone. "I believe your stepmother was shot outside the building. They have the perp in custody. I'll be in touch." He strode from the room.

"Come and sit down," she told Cruz gently.

Oblivious to everyone around them, Cruz cupped her face, seemingly drinking in her features with his eyes as he whispered in a thick, agonized voice, "I thought it was you, Mia. I thought you were dead."

She turned into him, fitting herself against him. "I'm fi—"

He made a wild sound in the back of his throat, his chest vibrating against her breasts as his mouth cut off her words.

A lie. She might not be bloody, but Mia was far from fine. Missing him had left a hole in her heart impossible to fill with work, playing detective, or wrestling her company back from the bad guys.

Vaguely she heard Todd say with his usual calm, authority, "Everybody out. Come on, move it, people."

Cruz lifted his head; his dark eyes glittered as he looked at her mouth. "Where?"

"Upstairs." Not releasing her hold on him, she angled them toward the door. "This way."

Arms wrapped around each other, she led him from the conference room. Todd stood near the elevator. Behind him were at least two dozen titillated employees watching them avidly.

Todd put a hand on Mia's arm as they passed. "Still need the medics?"

She gave Cruz an inquiring look. He shook his head. "I told you, I wasn't hurt. Is this Todd?" At Mia's nod, and without waiting for an introduction or making small talk, he said grimly, "I think Mia's—*Amelia's*—stepmother is splattered down on Market Street. She was wearing a prosthetic to make her look—" He shuddered. "You might want to have your cop friends check it out."

"They are," Todd told him, his eyes slewing to Amelia. "Why do you look as though you feel sorry for the conniving bitch?" He pitched his voice for their ears only. "She hired the hit men, so in the end she paid for her own death. She brought it on herself."

"I know. But still—poor Candice. Not that I wish death and splattering on anyone," Mia said grimly, her arm tightening around Cruz's waist. "What a damn irony that impersonating me again is what got her killed. That's incredibly sick and sad at the same time."

"It brings closure," Todd pointed out.

Cruz's arm locked around her. "There isn't closure with everything." He looked at her. "Yet." He kissed her on top of her head and nudged her toward the door. Her assistant ran over and pressed the button to open the doors on the private elevator. The doors slid open silently, revealing plush carpet, soft lighting, and mirrored walls. With a sappy smile, Stephanie dashed out of the way as they stepped into the car.

Mia slapped her hand on the touch keypad and the doors slid closed.

Cruz walked her backward, shoved her against the mirrored back wall. "You, Mia mine, are not like anyone I've ever met and I won't lose you again." He kissed her as the elevator slowly rose. His kiss was hard, starving, desperate. The sensual, mint-flavored invasion detonated an explosion of lust and intense longing inside her. She'd missed this—missed *him*.

Looming over her, his face shadowy, he kissed her again.

Panting, Mia took each side of his bloody shirtfront and ripped. Ripping damp fabric was no easy task, but she was strongly motivated. Buttons popped, some pinging on the wall as she bunched what was still buttoned and drew it up the ridges of his belly.

Cruz yanked off the short jacket, then found the long decorative gold zipper running down the back of the red sheath and peeled it over her shoulders.

The dress dropped to pool around her feet.

His eyes flared as he looked down at the sheer wisp of red fabric covering her breasts. Nothing was hidden. Her nipples, hard and pink, jutted out, eager for his touch. His lips twitched with amusement. "This is how you dress under your conservative business clothes?"

"I was thinking about you when I dressed this morning. I've dressed for you *every* day since I saw you at the house." *Forever ago*. Tangling her fingers in his hair, Mia drew his mouth back to hers as he glided his hand beneath the gossamer-thin fabric of her demi-bra. The scorching contact of his hand on her breast made her gasp. Her nipples, painfully hard, welcomed the rough friction and rasp of his callused fingers.

Cruz lifted his head, leaving just enough space between their mouths to speak. His voice was raw and filled with so much anguish, it brought stinging tears to Mia's eyes. "I saw the world without you, and it was a grim, bleak fucking place I didn't want to inhabit."

Taking his hand, she pressed it between her breasts, over her rapidly beating heart. "I'm here. Very much alive."

His back was reflected in the opposite mirror, his muscles flexing like polished, satiny copper over steel. The mirror felt cold on her practically bare ass. His skin burned hot inches from hers. Skimming her hand between them, she unerringly slipped the button at the top of his zipper free. His penis was a hard ridge behind the denim—not easy to liberate, but not impossible. Mia managed one-handed to tug his jeans partway down his thighs. No underwear for Cruz. "Thank you—this makes it so much easier." She curled her fingers around the satiny length of his penis.

"I was thinking of you when I dressed this morning." He arched his back as she stroked her thumb over the damp tip. The veins under the satin pulsed and throbbed, which in turn made her even wetter.

Mia saw herself in the mirror behind him. The twin scraps of sheer red enhanced rather than hid what she had for him.

He made a leisurely trip from her breast down her mid-riff, making her dizzy and her legs feel as insubstantial as jelly.

"We're not making any stops, are we?"

"Do you really care?"

"Nope. Don't give a flying fuck if your entire company watches us right now."

It terrified her that she didn't either. "Then it's a good thing this will take us directly to the apartment." In about three seconds . . .

She wrapped her legs around his waist, digging her six-inch Louboutin heels into the taut curve of his flexing ass. His penis jumped and twitched in the firm grip of her fingers.

Filling his hands with her butt cheeks, he lifted her completely off her feet as the doors slid soundlessly open. Mia crossed her ankles in the small of his back as he stepped directly into her living room, flooded with sunlight.

"Nice." He dismissed the thirty-million-dollar view of the San Francisco skyline. The pale gray-blue walls, the sleek Ultrasuede furniture of the same color, the tasteful artwork. All of which melted into the vast sky seen through towering ceiling-to-floor, wall-to-wall windows.

Smiling, Mia dragged her mouth off the pulse she was exploring at the base of his throat to mumble, "Bedroom's that way." Then, after a quick tilt of her chin, went back to kissing his throat.

The next thing she knew, she was falling through space as

Cruz followed her down onto the plush cushions of one of the deep sofas overlooking the view.

He grinned down at her. It was the first genuine smile she'd seen from him. Her heart did cartwheels as he brushed a strand of hair off her cheek. "*This*," he said, nibbling a path from her ear to her mouth, "will do nicely, Mia mine."

Chapter Twenty-one

No mas." Mia flung both arms out in surrender. "That was amazing." The words came out in short, choppy bursts, and her chest heaved as she struggled to breathe. "If we live through the next few minutes, let's do it again. Exactly like that."

Cruz chuckled, too spent to respond. He took almost as much pleasure in holding her warm, satiated body as he did in the act itself. Almost. He loved the hot comfort of skin against skin. The feel of her erratic breath against his damp throat, and the clutch of her vaginal walls holding him deep inside her. He was still partially erect, and the pulse of her muscles made him hard, again, in a minute.

Glued together by sweat, they lay together. He nuzzled her damp throat and laid a string of kisses across her shoulder, then abruptly twisted his body to lever Mia up and over. Her legs settled between his, her soft breasts plumped on his chest. The smell of her, hot come and tuberoses, was indelibly stamped into his synapses. Her unique fragrance was as heady as if he'd drunk too much scotch. He had the same altered perceptions and euphoria as he imagined a drunk must feel. Although he'd never abdicated that much control in his life.

She rested her chin on her double fists as he smoothed aside sweat-damp strands of hair sticking to her cheek. "I'm drunk on you, you know that?" He loved her like this. Soft, satiated with sex, intensely focused. The hand on her head trailed a light touch down her damp back. "Every damn thing about you is intoxicating. Heady. Addicting."

"It's rarely flattering to a woman to be bare-ass naked in direct sunlight. You, on the other hand, look like a bronze god. It's incredibly unfair."

She was absolute perfection. Her skin creamy and fine-grained, the three freckles on her collarbone beauty marks he adored. "I can see why," he teased. "Want to go into the bedroom and draw the drapes and hide under the covers?"

She punched him not so lightly in his rib cage, and he took her smaller hand, going palm to palm as he threaded his fingers through hers. Then stared for a moment at their clasped hands. "It amazes me how capable this small hand is."

"It's not my hand that's capable, Barcelona, it's my brain."

"Now, see? *That* does exceptionally well in direct sunlight." With an adorable scowl, she thumped his chest with her fist. In direct sunlight her eyes were sapphire blue, as translucent as the waters off Fernando de Noronha. "We can't lie here all day, much as I'd like to. We have things to do and places to go. Give me the recap, short and sweet."

"First: *What* things? *What* places?"

"We have to make love again—several times. And I

heard mention of a press conference later? I presume you'll want to shower and change and mess with your hair and makeup?"

"I'm the CEO of a billion-dollar cosmetics company and you think I'm 'messing' with my hair and makeup? I'm marketing my brand." She smiled.

"And you do it damn well. But you know you're just gilding the lily, don't you?"

"I'm in the *business* of gilding."

"Times a-wasting, woman," he told her sternly. She shifted her legs and her hips so that his hard dick was centered against the wet, swollen, pink folds of her pussy. His dick was extremely happy, and did a little dance against her. He gave her a warning frown. "That doesn't help speed things up, you know." Mia gave him a wide-eyed, innocent look, spreading her legs a little wider, her knees digging into the sofa cushions on either side of his hips. "Don't taunt me. We're not doing a thing until you finish your story. Keeping in mind it should be as brief— Damn it, Mia!" She wasn't allowing his eagerly reaching dick entry, but she rubbed her wetness against him, making his brain turn to oatmeal, and his intentions float like a balloon filled with helium. "Brief as possible. Just. Hit—holy crap—the high points."

"First, I spoke to Daisy yesterday." Mia dropped a kiss on his nipple, absently running light fingers through the hair on his chest, which made his cock harder and his balls tighten in anticipation. "She's still in a lot of pain, but promised she's doing much better. When I offered her my house on Lake

Como, she told me when she's well enough, you're sending her to the South of France?"

"I have an old farmhouse in Montauban. Took Charlie to see her last night," he told her, cupping the flexing mounds of her ass to keep her still. "She was worrying about—life. I gave her options."

He captured Mia's roaming fingers. Not because he didn't enjoy being petted by her, but because the sooner she gave him the recap, the sooner he could get back to what he'd come here for. "Now give me the abbreviated version of current events so we can get back to what's important without interruption."

"I have a press conference at five."

He glanced at his watch. "Three hours. All the more reason to keep things short. Give me the high points."

"My security guy and my father's third wife conspired to take over Blush before they even heard about my secret buyout. Even with the shares of some of the willing board members, they didn't have enough. They needed sixty percent of shareholders to agree to take over the company. Less than eighteen percent bought into the changeover. So they couldn't do it that way. They had money, but not the stock. So they got together and formed the black pool. The investment company didn't care who bought whom out, just that they'd get their slice of the pie."

"Who was in the pool?" Just as she'd vowed to do back in Bayou Cheniere, he'd make damn sure that every one of them was caught and prosecuted to the fullest extent of the law.

"Basson, Candice, and several board members. They wanted me out when outside auditors started looking into their business and personal expenses when I started the LBO. They found discrepancies, which were red-flagged all over the place. Personal travel, private jets, real estate—they were bleeding Blush dry. And yet they nickel-and-dimed every expenditure I wanted to make for my foundation. Hypocritical bastards.

"Even with Candice's and Miles's shares, they realized that no matter what they did, I'd outbid them and wouldn't go away. They formed the secret black pool and hired hit men to take me out before I could sign the papers in the event they didn't win Blush via that route. They thought they had all the bases covered. They, too, are being prosecuted for conspiracy on various counts."

"You're killing me here, woman." Drawing her knees up beside his hips, she braced her open hands on his chest. Cruz found it damn hard to suck in air. Her small breasts hung over him like mounds of whipped cream with cherries on top. "Were the board members also part of the China deal?"

"No. China was all Miles and Candice. She fooled everyone with that disguise. Including the last guy, whom she apparently hired in a skid row bar and showed my photograph to. Too bad she came to the office pretending to be me so she could do a press conference on the street outside to preempt anything I had planned. Black Raven is still uncovering more—something I'd like you to be doing to me right about now."

When he didn't respond she gave an exasperated sigh and kept her body still, but she was over him, caging him with her arms and legs and hot little snatch that begged to be fucked until neither of them could walk.

"If there's any connection, they'll find it," she told him, her chest indicating that, like him, she was having a hard time not panting like a wolf in heat. "I—I do know that Basson and Candice opened the faux Blush factory in China and were selling knockoff Blush products to Chinese markets. Then they saw an opportunity for Candice to impersonate me so I'd be discredited and vilified in the press, scheming to ensure Blush's stock prices plummeted.

"What brought in Interpol was Basson getting sick and greedy with an Internet kiddie porn ring run out of the factory. They closed in yesterday— a joint task force, intersecting with the police investigation, and also the information from the private security firm I hired."

"I doubt your father left Candice in the poorhouse. What did this woman really want? Was it financial?" People killed for five dollars. It was a case of supply and demand, and it wasn't always the people who worked their asses off who got the big payday. Others stole and/or killed for it.

"Candice had the shares left to her by my father, and a place on the board. But she wanted more. Wanted to be the face of Blush. Knowing her, I speculate that she wanted the fame more than the fortune. She and Basson had been having an affair soon after she married my father. Okay. I have to admit, that was a freaking shocker! I had no idea, no clue that they even knew one another to say more than hi to. For three years she'd been seducing or coercing board members to side with her, claiming I was squandering stockholders' money with my wild schemes and do-good projects."

He'd surmised most of what she was telling him, and while Black Raven Security hadn't breached client confidentiality, Cruz got just enough to add the new info to what he knew, or what he suspected. "Investment company being prosecuted?"

"Hell yes. The people responsible have already been rounded up and taken into custody. You saw Miles being taken out in cuffs. On his way to prison. He'll be tried for conspiracy to commit murder with Candice and several board members as accomplices."

"Class A felony. Solicitation to commit a violent crime. Solicitation to commit murder. Several counts, *and* international child pornography? " He shook his head. "They'll have the book thrown at them." Cruz placed his hands on her narrow back. For a strong woman she felt almost fragile in his arms. Her strength was her will, and her inner capability. But no matter how indomitable she might be, she was no match for a well-placed bullet.

She blinked, and murmured, "Ow."

"Sorry." He'd squeezed her too tightly, and she gave him a questioning look. Cruz relaxed his fingers spanning the small of her back, but didn't drop his hands as he dragged in a shuddering breath, then held it for several beats, and he was shocked at how badly it ripped at his lungs. His chest felt constricted, and that had nothing to do with Mia's weight surrounding him like a warm satin blanket. Cruz shut his eyes for several moments as he gathered himself. "She bled out in my arms. I thought your stepmother was you."

Her soft mouth trembled, and her eyes welled in sympathy. "Oh, Cruz—"

"I died on the sidewalk this afternoon, Mia. I was gutted. It was . . . devastating. Soul-wrenching. I remembered the way your eyes lit up when you looked at me. Blue fire, so pure, so good, it was hard to live up to the person you saw me to be. I remembered the taste of your mouth, and the words you didn't need to say because you showed me how you felt every time we made love. I remembered the silky slide of your hair against my belly as you gave me everything, in every way I never imagined I wanted. I remembered your compassion, your humor, and the dizzying fragrance of your skin. . . . I will never smell a tuberose without my brain and heart being filled to the brim with . . . *you*. And I realized, as I held her, that the woman in my arms wasn't—couldn't be—*you*. She didn't *feel* like you, didn't *smell* like you—I raced through your building like a madman. Your staff was afraid I was a deranged madman come to kill you. An irony of monolithic proportions," he said dryly, using his thumb to wipe away a tear shimmering on her eyelashes. "When I finally made it to the boardroom—when I realized I was being given a second chance—it was as if the sun went supernova and poured into every cell of my body."

"You *are* a romantic."

"I'm not. Never have been. But then I've never met anyone like you."

He relaxed and let her lead, and they came together in a sweet, deep kiss, slow and erotic as hell, as she knelt over him and took him in her small, cool fingers and led him home.

They rose and fell together like the tide. Time stretched as they slowly made love.

When they were both replete, he brushed a kiss to her temple and settled her on top of him, her long legs tangled with his. "Hey," she complained, eyes closed, as he reached out to snag his pants off the floor where he'd dropped them.

"I'm going to frame it in our bedroom." He told her, smoothing out a torn piece of yellow notepaper on his chest.

Mia smiled. "You kept my to-do list? You really are a romantic. . . . Wait, some of these are new." Big blue eyes, rimming with laughter, met his. "FILWEH?"

He closed the few inches between them and kissed her softly, then dropped his head back to the seat cushion. "Fall in love with ex-hitman."

Touching her tongue to a fingertip, she drew an imaginary line in the air. "Cross that one off the list."

Cruz stroked his hand down her back. "There's no way in hell we should ever have met. No way in hell that this should've worked. But it just . . . does. Read number forty-three."

"MEHWLYBR?"

"Marry ex-hitman who loves you beyond reason. Marry me, Mia. I'll give you beautiful babies, and we can live here in San Francisco. Whatever you want."

"I want babies with you, but I'm not the stay-at-home-mom type."

"I think I'd be a damn fine stay-at-home dad. But there's something I think I should tell you before we start making babies. I have a couple more names to add to our mix."

"You mean Phoenix, the world-renowned artist?"

Cruz gave her a startled look. "How could you *possibly* know—"

Mia cupped his face. "Because I was determined and vested. I took every little drop of information—Chicago, construction, your artistic ability—added them together, then gave what I knew to Black Raven. They told me you'd buried it so deep that, without the few crumbs I knew, they would never have put two and two together."

"My God. *Nobody* knows who Phoenix is."

"I know. Not even your New York agent who just mounted your London gallery showing knows who he is. I hate to tell you, but I'd never heard of Phoenix until two days ago. As soon as I knew, I looked you up on the Internet. I was stunned."

"You hate my work?"

"Phoenix is *famous*, for God's sake! That's so bizarre, it boggles my mind. The most closed, secretive man I've ever met has an alter ego that's wildly exciting, flamboyant, and a romantically shadowy public figure of some repute. You must admit, it's a bit surreal. I *love* your work. I don't know how I could not have heard of you. Everything that you are is on those incredible canvases. Larger-than-life. Brilliant, glorious colors. Humor. Passion."

Something inside him broke apart at her insightful words. Yes, he'd heard them from critics. But this was the woman he loved. She didn't just see him, she saw everything he was inside. He'd never had that in his life. It was staggering. "You could tell all that from the images online, could you?"

"Cruz, your work is magnificent, powerful. Quite extraordinary. Which you must know—it's why your canvases sell for a small fortune."

"They're very big canvases with a *lot* of paint on them."

She smiled, extending her hand. "Mia Hayward, Amelia Elizabeth Wellington-Wentworth."

"Oh, boy . . ." He slid his palm against hers. "Cruz Barcelona, Phoenix, Jon Smith, Brian Strong, Pete McCord, Doug Stanford, Dave Bay—" Mia raised a brow at the laundry list of aliases. There were many more, but he cut to the chase, squeezing her hand. "Aiden Cross. Pleased to meet you."

"It's going to be pretty hard to come up with a boy's name, since you've apparently used every one in the baby-naming book," Mia laughed, then sobered, her gaze intent on his face. "I'm going to give more responsibility to Todd; he says he doesn't want it, but I believe he does, and he'd be a magnificent CEO. That will give me more time for my foundation, and those babies. I'm still going to work sixteen hours a day, six and a half days a week. That's who I am. Babies will be a bonus. Eventually. I want us to get to know each other first."

"I might have to become a priest."

Her eyes widened and she gave a choked laugh. "You want to be celibate? Are you even Catholic?"

"No. But I've made God so many promises, I owe Him one."

"I have no doubt you owe Him more than one," Mia told him dryly, combing his hair off his face with gentle fingers. "You can start by stopping killing people. *Any* people. For *any* and all reasons."

An easy promise. "I can do that, unless of course they threaten you or the babies; then all bets are off. You were to be my last job. I was off to Brazil to get ready for my LA showing in six months."

"How convenient, then, that I have loads of space for your studio right here in San Francisco, and we're so close to Los Angeles."

"You seem to have all the answers but one."

She gave him a surprised look. "I think we've covered the Q and A. What else is there?"

"Marry me. We have the rest of our lives to get to know one another better than we do now." She started to speak but he placed his finger on her lips. He didn't want to hear anything she had to say except yes. His heart pounded. His entire life had been on hold until this moment.

"I don't want to wait. I love you, Mia." He replaced his finger with his mouth for a tender, sweet, gentle kiss. He wanted her to know the love he felt for her was more than the hot, grinding sex they shared. It was soft and emotional and real. "I love you more than I've loved anyone in my life." His voice was just above a whisper. "I never knew this kind of love existed. But I don't want to waste a single day anticipating the rest of our lives together." He brushed a tendril of hair from off her cheek and then brushed his lips on the same spot. "I want it all, Mia. I want it *now*. I want it with you."

His throat tightened. He knew that if she rejected him now, he would be shattered just as he'd been when he thought she'd died in his arms. Cruz realized the enormity of how good things were and how in mere seconds they could slip through his fingers from one breath to the next.

"I promise I'll be a good father. I'll be faithful. I'll protect you. I love you. This is my vow to you. I'll be your rock, your sanctuary, your partner." He smiled, but it was fear, not joy, that he felt at this moment as he waited for her to answer him. To say yes to him handing her his heart, to giving her his life so they could have a life together. Yet, looking in her beautiful, intelligent, loving eyes, he had hope she would say she'd be his.

"I can't live without you, Mia. Is that too dramatic?" His heart was beating too fast, his mouth dry. "But without you I'd wither and die. No pressure."

Mia wrapped her arms around his neck. "I love you to the moon and back, Cruz. The answer is yes. Yes, I will marry you, and give you beautiful babies who'll inherit the goodness and integrity of their father, who'll paint wild and exciting paintings. We'll travel the world and, if we have to be apart, rush home to each other as quickly as possible." She brushed his lips with hers. "We have so many names between us; which should we use?"

"How about 'Cruz' and 'Mia' in the bedroom, and 'darling' everywhere else?"